*Dedicated to those people who use their
musical ability to brighten the world
for the people around them.*

CONTENTS

CHAPTER 1

Orphans on A Train

The train started with a lurch, the squeal of steel wheels, a loud whistle and a whoosh of steam coming from the locomotive several train cars ahead. It was both exciting and a bit scary. Katherine who always called herself, Kathy clutched the hand of her younger sister Katy. It was their first train ride and the power and sounds of the train were overwhelming their senses. Kathy was 17 and Katy was only 7 and more like a daughter to Kathy. They were two orphans that were heading west from Boston to a farm in Kansas to meet up with an older sister they had not seen for years.

It was not a good plan but the apartment they shared with their elderly Aunt for the last year was small and the landlord said they would all be evicted if Kathy and her sister didn't leave. Her aunt Karla felt bad for her nieces, but they were barely surviving on the small income they had and didn't know where else they could go. Kathy had tried to help her aunt with the small amount she made working in a garment factory, but it barely covered much more than the food they ate and their share of the rent. Being hungry was something Kathy had gotten used to.

Kathy tried not to be bitter about Thomas, a single neighbor man, who had complained to the landlord about Katy making too much noise. He was usually unkempt and smelled of whisky and tobacco but had tried several times to convince Kathy to move in with him. A more disgusting choice Kathy could not imagine. Lying to the landlord about Katy making too much noise was his revenge for being turned down.

Kathy thought of a verse she had added to "Battle Hymn of the Republic" in her mind.

To the widows and the orphans who were sadly left behind, I ask oh God for mercy and their neighbors to be kind.

Unfortunately, her neighbor had not been kind.

The train headed out into the country, and they were both were glued to the view in the window and amazed at the speed of the train. It was morning in early June in the spring of 1910 and the country was green and beautiful. The clacking sound the cars made on the rails was hypnotic and the scenery outside helped relieve the stress Kathy was feeling.

Kathy also thought about the events that had led to her and Katy leaving Boston. Three years earlier her father had been killed by a bank robber at his job at a bank. Her mother was forced to sell the nice home they lived in, and they moved to an apartment. They also had to sell the piano they both loved. Her mother who had taught piano in the home had gotten a job working long hours in a garment factory. The stress of losing her husband, her home, her piano and working outside took a toll on her health. Two years later she died of pneumonia just days before Kathy graduated from high school. Kathy and Katy moved in with Karla, her elderly aunt. Kathy took a job at the garment factory where her mother had worked doing the same job as a seamstress.

Kathy remembered the love her parents had for each other and for her and her sisters. Every Sunday they went to church where the music enthralled Kathy. Her mother was usually the piano player at church and sometimes Kathy would play. Losing her parents was heartbreaking for her. Kathy's strong faith had not left her, but she now looked at life as a sad journey to Heaven filled with heartbreak and worry about being hungry and homeless. She hoped that somehow, she could give Katy the great childhood she had enjoyed when her parents were alive.

Kathy had written to her older sister Christine about moving in with her. Kathy's older sister had not been encouraging. She had written back that their farmhouse was small, and Katy would have to share a small bedroom with her two daughters. She thought Kathy might be able to get a job as a live-in maid in a nearby town. Kathy had vowed to stay with Katy, but she had saved just enough money to return alone to Boston if necessary. Kathy and Katy had closely bonded after the loss of their parents and being separated would be devastating to both of them. Tears welled in her eyes at the thought. She folded her hands and silently prayed that somehow, they could stay together.

The trip had not started well. They had walked over a mile to the train station and despite packing light they were both exhausted when they arrived. Kathy bought their train tickets and then put the few dollars of change in a small bag carrying their lunch and a jar of water. She handed the bag back to Katy and then heard Katy scream. A small scruffy boy was grabbing the bag. Kathy swung the smaller suitcase she was carrying and hit him as hard as she could. He yelped in pain but managed to run away with the bag. A man came over and asked if she was okay.

"Yes, fortunately he didn't get that much."

"This place is overrun with homeless children," he told her, "they try to steal whatever they can."

Kathy felt bad that they had lost the money and their food and water for the trip. It was hard to feel much anger at the kid who was homeless and desperate. She almost felt guilty about hitting him so hard. What a cruel world this is she thought.

After a couple hours and a couple of stops the scenery was still nice but it started getting a little monotonous and the hard-wooden seats were already uncomfortable. Kathy reached into a bag she had secured tightly to her person and came out with a flute. "Do you think it would be okay if I played a tune on my flute?" she asked the people nearby.

"Go ahead!" a man responded with an encouraging smile.

Kathy played "Yankee Doodle" and was pleased that some people moved closer standing in the aisle to hear her better. She started the tune over, and Katy sang the words in her sweet alto voice. They were rewarded with applause when they finished, and they continued on with other songs. They were finally interrupted when the train stopped at the next station. Several people came over and thanked them. An older couple moved to seats in front of them that had been vacated.

"That was so nice of you girls to sing," the wife told them; "you look awfully young to be traveling alone."

"Actually, I graduated from high school a year ago and worked in a factory last year," Kathy replied. "Our parents are gone and I'm hoping we can move in with my older sister's family on a farm in Kansas."

"You don't sound very confident about that," the woman responded.

"I'm not," Kathy replied, "but hopefully it will turn out okay." Kathy put her face in her hands trying stop her tears. Regaining her composure, she told them, "I'm Kathy White and this is my younger sister Katy."

"I'm Emma Iverson and this is my husband Herman," the lady replied. "You two are so cute and talented, I wish we could help you."

"Could you spare us just a little water?" Both girls got a drink and were offered cookies. Kathy took two and gave them both to Katy.

"We just sold our farm and are retiring to a small house near my daughter's family in Ohio," Emma told her. They were nice people and Kathy felt a little more positive about life. A couple more stops and the four of them were nearly alone in the train car except for a young mother with a baby girl and a small boy.

Kathy corralled the little boy when he started running past her. Herman who was sitting near the aisle then grabbed him and lifted him high in the air. "Gotcha" he told the little boy with a smile. It was clear him and his wife loved children. The mother came over and Emma reached for the baby. Kathy later sang a lullaby for the baby girl as Emma cuddled her.

Emma kidded her that "you are putting us all to sleep." The little boy had fallen asleep in Herman's lap, Katy was sleeping, and a tired grateful mother satisfied that her children were safe was sleeping sitting up. A sleeping baby girl lay in the arms of a smiling Emma. Some grandchildren in Ohio were definitely going to be spoiled.

Since her father died, Kathy had been in survival mode. She had skipped one grade in grade school and then managed to test well enough to skip eleventh grade in high school. She still graduated near the top of her class when she was only 16. Her pretty face attracted the boys in her class, but she ignored them. While other girls were talking about boys and about getting married, Kathy was focused on helping her mother and taking care of Katy. She would have quit school and gotten a job to help her mother, but her mother wanted her to finish high school. Kathy loved babies and children, but she had gotten into the mindset that life was so hard that most people were hungry, most men were nasty and dying young was the norm. Why would you want to get married and bring a child into a world like that? Herman was a reminder that there were nice men like her father. She started reading a well -worn Bible that she carried with her. She knew she should be more trusting in God and be less pessimistic, but it was hard to think positive.

It was late morning when they got to cavernous Grand Central Station in New York City. Kathy and Katy and their luggage were ticketed through to Kansas City, but they had to switch trains. Fortunately, Herman and Emma were going on the same train along with the mother with the two children. They formed a mutually supportive group, and everyone needed a bathroom break. The bathroom on the train was like an outhouse on wheels and smelled really bad. Kathy was hungry and thirsty, but the advantage was not having to go to the bathroom on the train. At Grand Central Station there even flush toilets.

There was a two-hour delay before boarding and Kathy started playing her flute again while Katy sang. A small crowd gathered around them. The crowd enjoyed the sound of the flute, but Katy would steal the show. People could not believe that a cute little girl could sing that well and Katy loved the attention. Kathy's mother had told the girls that God had given them the gift of music and they should use it whenever they could. Kathy put down the flute and sang a love song that had recently became popular. She sang it a little louder than her earlier songs so that her clear soprano voice was carrying a bit further into the huge room and more people started to gather. There was applause when she finished.

"Do you sing on Broadway?" someone asked.

Kathy laughed, "Don't we wish! We are just a couple of poor orphans passing time before heading to a dirt farm in Kansas. Glad you liked the singing." Kathy started playing the flute again for a Christian song that Katy knew, and she sang it beautifully. Boarding was announced and they headed for their train with bystanders wishing them well. A few mothers looked at sweet little Katy and wished they could take her home. A couple young men wished they had Kathy for a girlfriend.

The train made numerous stops while heading across New Jersey before crossing into Pennsylvania. The more rugged terrain of Pennsylvania was more interesting, but it soon became too dark to see much. They went through a couple tunnels coughing on black smoke from the engine that invaded the train car while going through the tunnels. Kathy, and Katy tried to sleep on the hard seats as did Herman and Emma. Kathy braced her shoulder up against the window with Katy's upper body in her lap. By daylight everyone but Katy felt like they had been in a medieval torture chamber.

"I don't think my body will ever be the same!" Emma announced. Kathy got up and stretched and twisted her body until she finally started feeling normal.

"Want a back rub?" Kathy asked. "My mother taught me."

She gave both Emma and then Herman back and shoulder rubs.

"Thank you, thank you!" Emma told her. "Here's our new address. Write when you get settled and we will pray that things go well for you."

The train pulled into the train station in Columbus, Ohio and the conductor announced they would have a 45-minute stop. They all got off the train and Kathy and Katy said goodbye to the Iverson's after meeting their son and daughter in law and their two small children. They were introduced to them and then said their goodbyes. Kathy liked them a lot, but she was a little jealous of the grandchildren who had parents and grandparents. Katy only had her.

The mother with the two children had gotten off too. It was quite warm, and the little boy only had on shorts and a shirt. Kathy babysat him while his mother went off to get some food. She started singing to him a silly ditty she made up when Katy was little. She started playing with his fingers. "1,2,3,4,5 little fingers" then switched to the other hand "6,7,8,9,10 little fingers", she grabbed his toes "10 little toes", she grabbed his ears"2 big ears and 1 little nose" she finished by touching his nose and he giggled back at her.

A smiling middle-aged lady had been watching her and came over. "That song is so cute- is that your boy?"

"No, I'm watching him for his mother, she went to find something to eat. That is how I learned to count. My teachers always wondered why I had to take my shoes off during a math test. Just joking. I'm Kathryn White but I am always called Kathy, and this is my little sister Katy."

"I'm Martha Thompson, what grade are you in?" she asked Katy.

"I just finished 2nd grade, but I will be in 4th grade next year," Katy replied.

RAIL ORDER BRIDE

Alton Knutson

LifeRich PUBLISHING

LifeRich Publishing is a registered trademark of The Reader's Digest Association, Inc.

LifeRich Publishing books may be ordered through booksellers or by contacting:

LifeRich Publishing
1663 Liberty Drive
Bloomington, IN 47403
www.liferichpublishing.com
844-686-9607

Because of the dynamic nature of the Internet, any web addresses or links contained in
this book may have changed since publication and may no longer be valid. The views
expressed in this work are solely those of the author and do not necessarily reflect the
views of the publisher, and the publisher hereby disclaims any responsibility for them.

The photo of the girl on the front cover was taken by jessica@fotofilmstudios.com
and superimposed on a locomotive for illustrative purposes only

ISBN: 978-1-4897-4105-9 (sc)
ISBN: 978-1-4897-4106-6 (e)

Library of Congress Control Number: 2022905700

Printed in the United States of America.

LifeRich Publishing rev. date: 07/21/2022

"Are you smart," Martha teased, "what is 9 times 8?"

"72," Katy answered quickly.

"How about 9 times 13?"

"117," Katy replied after thinking a little longer.

"You are a smarty, I teach school and I wish I had you in my class," Martha told her.

"So where are you going?" Martha asked Kathy.

"We are heading west to live on a farm in Kansas with my sister and her family and you?"

"I'm heading back to southern Illinois after helping my daughter with her new baby," Martha replied.

The mother came back with her baby girl and joined them. They made introductions and Martha asked immediately asked if she could hold the baby. The mother handed her baby to Martha and asked the girls if they would sing again. Kathy got out her flute and they did Yankee Doodle again.

"Should we do our cry song?" Katy asked.

Kathy played the flute and Katy sang.

I love you Jesus, but you make me cry.
Why did Daddy and Mommy have to die?
You took my only brother too!
I love you Jesus, but you make me blue.
Someday take me home to you I pray.
We will all meet in Heaven and sing that day!
Until that day I will sing down here
Please hear my prayers and draw me near."

"Now you have made me want to cry," Martha told the girls.

They did a happier song and boarded the train. Little Katy had completely stolen Martha's heart and she found a seat behind Kathy and Katy. The car was not quite full, and Martha got them to trade seats, so Katy was sitting next to the mother while Martha held the baby girl and sat next to Kathy.

"Tell me about yourself," Martha told Kathy.

"When my mother and father were alive, we used to play a piano at home and at church. Four years ago, my little brother died of a cold, the next year my father who worked in a bank was killed by a bank robber. Last year my mother died of pneumonia just before I finished high school at 16. We moved in with an Aunt and, I went to work at the same garment factory where my mother worked doing the same job. It has been a difficult time for Katy and me. We are going to live with my older sister and her family on a farm in Kansas. She may not have room for both of us, so I might have to leave Katy and go back to Boston. Leaving Katy would break my heart." Kathy had to cover her tears.

Martha knew in her heart that she had no choice. The girls had to come home with her. She knew her husband would approve.

"My husband and I have a daughter who is 25 who lives with us. She lost her husband in an accident and has a boy about the same age as Katy. We also have a son at home who is 20 and will be going back to college this fall. We run a general store and also run a bathhouse where men and women can wash up. I also teach grade school, but I pretty much do that for free. We have a piano at church, but we need a piano player. I want you both to come home and live with us. I can assure you that my husband and children will welcome you and there is plenty of room for you."

Kathy sat there stunned and then replied, "thank you so much, I would love to come; it is an answer to my prayers. We will try to repay you anyway we can. I would love to be your piano player." Kathy bowed her head and said a prayer of thanks and then broke into tears. "There have been times when I thought that Katy and I would be homeless and living on the streets."

The passenger car was only half full and the people were awake but looking bored. Kathy started playing her flute again and this time Martha recognized melody and started singing the tune. An older fellow with a good tenor voice also joined in. Somebody asked if she knew "God Bless America." Kathy put down her flute and sang it from memory. The people in the car applauded.

Martha said, "you are amazing."

They reached the next stop and said goodbye to the mother and the two children. When the mother found out that Kathy and Katy were going to move in with Martha's family, she thought it was wonderful. "I dreaded this trip with my two children, but it turned out to be so great because of you."

Katy was very quiet when they got back on the train trying to understand why they were not going to live with her cousins. Finally, she asked Kathy. Kathy had tried to be positive about them moving in with her cousins. Kathy had hidden her misgivings that she would probably have to leave Katy and return to Boston. Kathy put her arm around Katy.

"I love you so much that I didn't want to tell you that I might have to leave you with your older sister and your cousins and go back to Boston. Martha said we both can live with her. It means we can stay together."

Martha had heard most of the conversation and told Katy. "Please come live with us, we will have such a good time together and I just love little girls. Can I give you a hug?" Katy was a little stiff at first but then she cuddled up to Martha. "Oh, sweetheart I am so happy that you are going to live with us." Martha showed Katy a book she was bringing back for her fifth graders to read.

Katy asked if she could look at it and started reading it.

"Isn't that book a little hard for you?" Martha asked.

"No, this is an easy book to read, Kathy tries to get me to read one chapter of the Bible almost every day and then asks me questions about what I read." It was a book of short stories and Katy was totally absorbed with the book.

Martha looked at the girls again, they both looked younger than their age, but they were obviously very smart.

Kathy was happy but tired, hungry, thirsty, and emotionally drained. She had let Martha buy some food and water for Katy at the last stop but told Martha she was okay. Despite a sore butt from the hard train seat, she found herself falling asleep relieved of the tension that Katy and she might be separated. Martha woke her up to tell her they would soon be getting off.

Kathy had to let the doorman know that she would be leaving the train at an earlier stop. He gave her signed form stating their earlier departure and told her to go to the agent at the depot when she got off. They got off at a small depot station. She was relieved when the porter handed her their luggage.

CHAPTER 2

A New Home

"Hi mother, how was the trip?"

A sturdy good-looking young man called out and came out on the small train station platform in Williamsburg, Illinois giving Martha a big hug. He was followed by a young boy about Katy's age.

"Everything went okay," Martha told him, "Margaret and her baby are fine, I got some new books and lessons for the school. I also have a big surprise for you. I met these two sisters on the train who were going to live with a relative who could only take the younger girl and they don't want to be split up – so I invited them to live with us."

Martha turned to the young man, "this is my son Bobby and my daughter's boy Alex."

She then turned to the girls, "this young lady is Kathy White, and this is her younger sister Katy."

"Wow, this is a surprise!" Bobby said with a big smile. "Glad to meet you." He shook hands with Kathy and then effortlessly lifted Katy by the shoulders and spun around with her. "I'll make sure you have fun at our place."

Kathy smiled as she watched them. When it came to young men, Kathy had pretty much written them all off as problems to be avoided but it was hard not to like Bobby. Alex was friendly too and returned her smile.

Bobby in turn had tried to be formal and polite to Kathy but when she smiled a little thrill jolted his heart. Wow! She is so cute! He looked at Kathy again; she was average in height with big blue eyes in a pretty face surrounded by dark gold shoulder length hair that shined in the sun. Kathy had packed her bonnet in with her luggage while on the train and her hair rippled in a slight breeze.

Kathy gave her signed form and her ticket stubs to the depot agent and was pleased to get back a small refund. She jumped off the station platform and was smiling when she rejoined the others who had walked over to a horse drawn wagon. Bobby had taken her luggage and she could see it on the wagon. Kathy felt so happy, the day was going so well.

Bobby had watched her, Kathy moved so gracefully, and her smile was so pretty.

Bobby had brought a 4-wheel wagon pulled by two horses. A brown and white dog was also on it wagging his tail in welcome. Bobby had some hay bales on it for them to sit on. He helped his mother get up and then lifted Katy sending her skyward before putting her standing up on the wagon. Katy's smile told Kathy that he had made a friend. Kathy tried to climb up by herself, but Bobby grabbed her hand and effortlessly pulled her up.

"Thanks," she told Bobby giving him another smile.

"That was easy," he said, "you girls sure don't weigh much. Don't worry about Shep, he won't bite but he might lick you to death." Shep greeted all of them before getting up on the driver's seat with Bobby. After breathing train smoke for two days, it was nice to get fresh air. Bobby had also brought a couple jars of water and Kathy could not recall water tasting so good.

Kathy listened to Martha as she talked to Bobby about her visit to his older sister. The baby girl was adorable, but she was not pleased with her son in law though she didn't really say what the problem was. She also talked about her grandson with concern. "He is a year older than Alex and way behind him in reading ability." She didn't voice her concern that Katy was younger than Alex and already a year ahead of him.

Martha had spent only a few days with Bobby who was home from college before she left for Ohio. They talked about some of his college courses. He had taken a course on electricity. Kathy asked a couple of questions that led to a friendly discussion between her and Bobby about electrical motors and electrical products. They also started talking about electrons and direct current versus alternating current.

"Are we going to learn more about electricity in school?" Alex asked Martha.

"Not unless Bobby or Kathy teach it; I don't understand it," Martha admitted.

They rode in silence for a while and then Bobby started to hum a song. "I know the melody, but I can't remember the words," he remarked.

Kathy recognized the song and started singing it. Bobby loved music and Kathy was singing with the most beautiful voice he had ever heard.

Martha remarked that "we need to come up with some songs that we can sing together at church on Sunday."

They tried some songs and Bobby could not believe his ears – both girls were great. Bobby was proud of his musical ability, but he knew that he had more than met his match in Kathy. There was another Christian song he did know, and they all joined in. They sang other songs as they rolled along. They arrived in the small town of Springdale where the Thompsons lived late in the afternoon still singing. A few bystanders listened and looked on. They rode past the church and went another block to Thompson's General Store. Martha's house and a bathhouse were connected to the general store. There was a water faucet sticking out from the store and several town's people had lined up to fill their pails from it.

They unloaded the wagon and Bobby helped carry luggage into a small courtyard with a table and some benches under a shade tree. Bobby and Alex then took the wagon with the horses to the town livery.

Martha directed the girls to sit down at the table. "We will eat in a couple of hours but maybe Julia can bring us something now. I hire Julia to help me with cooking and some other chores."

She went into a door on the side of the bathhouse and came back with a smiling black lady who brought them some kind of cake with honey on it. Martha carried a pitcher of milk and some glasses. "This is Julia, one of the nicest people you will ever meet," she told the two girls.

Kathy smiled, got up and shook hands with Julia. "Hi, I'm Kathy White and this is my younger sister Katy."

Katy had rarely seen a black lady but when Julia knelt down to her height, they wound up having a big hug.

"What is this cake?" Kathy asked, "it is so good, thank you for making it – it's wonderful."

"It's just cornbread with honey on it," Julia replied, "we eat a lot of it down here."

"Katy, we have arrived in the promised land where there is milk and honey and cornbread," responded Kathy.

Julia and Martha laughed.

"This is so good," Kathy said again, "I haven't had anything to eat since Sunday night before we left Boston."

Martha was mortified, "sweetheart, why didn't you tell me; I would have bought you something at one of the train stops."

"That's okay, I'm used to being hungry and I don't eat much," Kathy replied.

"Going hungry has got to stop," Martha told her, "I don't ever want you two to go hungry here. We are not rich, but we can afford to feed you."

Martha excused herself to bring her luggage inside the house and then visit her husband inside the store.

They were finishing eating when Martha returned wearing a robe and announced: "Let's go have a bath."

Kathy and Katy carried their luggage through a partially enclosed kitchen where Julia was still working and then through another open door. A beautiful blond lady wearing only a smile and a towel around her waist came running over.

"Hi mother, welcome back!"

Martha made introductions, "this is my daughter Sally, and this is Kathy White and her younger sister Katy. They were kind of on a train trip to nowhere, so I invited them to come home with me."

Kathy tried not to show her shock at seeing Sally half naked.

Sally hung up her towel on a rack with wooden pegs, "there is nobody but me here today so hang your clothes on the pegs and jump in the pool. You both look like you need to cool off."

"I am going to put on a bathing gown; the girls don't need to bother," Martha announced. She walked into one of two small dressing rooms and came out wearing a short sleeveless dark blue gown for bathing.

Katy was more than happy to hang up her clothes and jump in the pool. Kathy quickly undressed too but was visibly shaking.

"You look shocked," Sally told Kathy.

"I admit it, I have never let anyone see me naked since I was a little girl."

"Don't worry," there are no men allowed in here except very small boys and nobody is going to care," Sally assured her.

Kathy relaxed a little, they were alone, and the water felt wonderful.

Sally was in a shallow pool holding a shrieking but happy Katy by her hands and swinging her around in circles over the water before dropping her back in. For Katy, it was probably the most fun she could ever remember.

Kathy joined Martha in a deeper pool that she learned was for adults. It seemed scandalous be outside completely naked, but she was tired, and the day was hot. The water felt wonderful, and it seemed more acceptable as time passed. It had been years since she had had a bath that wasn't just a bucket of water and a wash rag. "I have been a proper Bostonian and I have never let people see me naked before," she told Martha.

Martha laughed. "I think most of the women in Boston would love to have a place where they had the freedom to take their hot sticky clothes off and have a good soak. A lot of women tell me how great it is to come here and relax." Kathy was waist deep in the pool. "You are a beautiful girl, but you are way too thin," Martha told her. "I don't think you have fully grown up physically and your body needs more food to develop properly." Then Martha excused herself, "I need to help Julia get supper started."

Feeling a little braver, Kathy joined Sally and Katy in the shallow child pool. After a short time, Kathy and Sally got out of the water and sat on the edge of the pool and talked while watching Katy splash around.

"Help me again with your names and ages?"

"I am Kathy and I just turned 17. My little sister is Katy, and she is 7. Remember that the smaller name goes with the smaller girl. We were living in Boston and became orphans last year when my mother died just before I graduated from high school. We moved into an apartment with my elderly aunt. I went to work as a seamstress at a garment factory which just barely gave us enough income to get by. Katy and I got evicted because a neighbor man falsely accused Katy of making too much noise. I was going to take Katy to live with an older sister and her family in Kansas. They didn't have room for both of us so I figured I would have to return to Boston. Your mother heard my story and took pity on us and invited us to live here. I am so grateful since Katy, and I are very close."

"I became widow just after Alex turned five three years ago when my husband was struck by a large dead branch from a tree he was cutting down. I am so glad mother brought you home. It is going to be so fun having the two of you here."

"Thank you, this is so great," Kathy told her. "I don't think I have been this clean before in my life."

"Let's get your hair washed too," Sally suggested. She brought over a bucket of warm water to a table next to the pool and filled two wash basins. After Kathy got her hair wet, Sally gave her a bar of soap. "Rub some into your hair."

Kathy did as she was told and finished washing her hair while Sally helped Katy wash hers.

"Let's walk around while your hair dries," Sally told them.

Sally then took the two girls for a tour. Sally showed them an area with a couple galvanized metal tubs plus several inside small enclosures. "When its hot most people want to stay in the pool but when it is a bit cooler, we sell hot baths and provide a dry towel. Most women want a little more privacy, so they want to be in the tubs in the enclosed rooms. Cooling off in the child pool and the adult pool is free. Children never wear anything and neither do some older girls and ladies. We do provide gowns like mother was wearing for anyone who wants to be more modest. We do charge a little for the use of a gown or towel. Mother would prefer that I wear a gown too and I usually do when I am with women and children, but I was scrubbing out tubs when you came. If it's busy, it is hard to give everyone a hot bath at the same time, so we try to keep some of the baths partially filled with hot water and then add the rest of the water when they show up. Julia is really strong and helps me carry water. If it is cool, we add hot water to the child pool too We really don't make any money on the bathhouse, but mother and I love children and it builds up a lot of good will for the store."

Besides the pools and the baths, there was a small garden area with a couple of shade trees and a bench. The bath area and the garden were all enclosed by a privacy fence made of logs about 8 foot high. "I call this our Garden of Eden where I can walk around completely naked and I am not ashamed," Sally commented.

"No serpents?" Kathy asked with a smile.

"A few snakes have managed to get in here, but we got rid of them, but we have been cursed with the weeds and the thistles so I could use your help weeding. I like to work out here without much on but one time I sunburned my back and butt really bad so be forewarned."

They went back near the kitchen to a partially walled off area. Sally showed them a couple bunk beds that were more like hammocks with sheets on them. "I sleep on this side, and you can have the other side. You both look tired, why don't you both take a nap. I will come get you when it is time for supper."

Kathy took the top bunk and Katy took the bottom bunk. Katy remarked, "this has got to be the nicest place on earth."

Kathy was pleased Katy was so happy and she kind of felt the same way herself. After a night of trying to sleep on a train seat, the bed felt awfully good. Sleep overwhelmed her thoughts and she fell asleep and so did Katy.

It was Martha came in and woke her and Katy. "You told me you didn't have any good clothes for hot weather, so I found an old dress that Sally outgrew."

It was a pretty dress and it fit fine with short sleeves but didn't go much below the knees. It also showed some skin below her neck.

"Thank you so much, it is very nice," she told Martha hiding her concern that the dress was pretty but wasn't very proper by Boston standards.

"Find something for Katy to wear and come join us for supper. Don't bother wearing shoes."

Fortunately, Katy had a nice spring dress and looked lovely in it. Kathy found a comb in her suitcase and tried to knock her hair down. Kathy was thinking it was scandalous. Proper Bostonians didn't go out in public with their hair a mess or showing bare arms, bare legs, and bare feet. Then she found herself almost giggling - at least she no longer had a bare butt.

CHAPTER 3

A Girlfriend for Bobby?

They had put two tables together in the courtyard area which they referred to as a patio. They had also added some more chairs. Martha's husband Clarence came out of the house at about the same time as the girls came in from the bathhouse. He was a pleasant looking man of medium height with graying hair. Kathy later learned Clarence had just recently turned fifty years old and Martha was a couple years younger. Martha introduced them to him.

"Thank you so much for letting us stay here," Kathy told him.

"Well, I am just so thrilled you are here. You are two very pretty girls and Martha tells me you are very smart and talented too."

"I hope we can live up to your expectations," Kathy answered."

They sat down to a table with more food on it than she could remember. Bread and butter, ham, new potatoes, green peas, and the food just kept coming. She was sitting next to Sally who looked very nice in a dress. She was also across from Bobby which she found disconcerting since he seemed to be looking at her a lot. Normally, she tried to ignore young men, but she hoped she was making a favorable impression.

Clarence said grace but Kathy continued to pray silently afterwards and then found herself in tears.

"What's wrong?" Sally asked.

"Absolutely nothing, you people are wonderful. I am just overjoyed to be here; the Lord has been so good to Katy and me."

Martha commented, "I am so glad you are here."

Despite eating the cornbread earlier, Kathy ate more food than she could remember. Kathy had acquired a taste for coffee and asked for a cup. Julia brought out a raisin pie and Kathy took a small piece.

Katy had a piece too and told Julia "you are the best cook ever."

Julia gave her a loving squeeze on her shoulder and told her, "and you are the sweetest little girl I ever met."

Martha thanked Julia and told her could leave and to bring the leftovers home for herself and her husband.

A smiling Kathy added: "Thank you Julia for the good food and making Katy and I feel so welcome."

When they were finishing up eating, Sally started teasing Bobby embarrassing both him and Kathy in the process. "Now that Kathy is here, you have put on a clean shirt and shaved."

"I did it to welcome mother home," Bobby replied but then he wound up blushing.

Sally then commented: "Mother you brought home a granddaughter for father and a girlfriend for Bobby, you need to find a husband for me!"

"You didn't ask me to bring you one," Martha joked.

"Is there a stamp on my forehead?" Kathy asked. "I'm beginning to feel like a mail order bride."

"Since you came by rail, you are actually my rail order bride," Bobby replied with a big grin.

"I'm only 17. I am too young for marriage or to even have a boyfriend," Kathy countered.

"That's old," Bobby joked, "most of the girls around here are married off at 14."

Kathy responded, "so the men marry them before the girls know what they are getting into – get married, have baby and then clean dirty diapers, dirty clothes, dirty dishes, feed hungry children and hungry husband."

Sally then commented, "you have got it about right but most of the girls around here get married after they are expecting a baby. Father has a white shotgun he gives to the girl's father when he walks his daughter down the aisle in her white maternity dress."

Martha scolded Sally, "you are being so bad, and I did not bring Kathy home for Bobby. She needs some time to mature, and Bobby needs another year of college."

Kathy joked, "I am going to be fattening up for the wedding altar like a sacrificial lamb in the Old Testament."

Bobby couldn't resist joking back, "don't worry, by that time I will have married one of those 14 year old girls."

"Don't you dare!" Martha responded. Clarence just sat there taking it all in with a smile.

"Enough of this crazy talk," Martha said. "Bobby get your fiddle and Kathy get your flute and let's have some music."

They both left and returned with their instruments. Bobby started playing his fiddle and Kathy started singing. After a couple of songs that were a little off, they tried a gospel song where they really got it together.

After the song, Clarence spoke up: "you sound really great together. I want you to do that song on Sunday."

Kathy played a song on her flute that Katy knew, and Katy sang it perfectly. "You two need to do that one on Sunday too," Clarence said. "I don't know if I dare preach, people are just going to want to hear you sing."

Bobby suggested a lively Christian song, and everyone joined in while he played his fiddle. "Let's open with that one," Clarence suggested, there won't be anyone sleeping after that."

Katy had noticed a stray yellow kitten and picked it up. Clarence moved over and put his arm around Katy. The kitten snuggled into Katy's lap and Katy snuggled into Clarence' shoulder. The three of them looked very contented. Martha smiled, happy to see her husband and Katy bond so quickly.

It was getting dark. "Let's get to bed before it gets dark and we have to put lights on," Martha suggested. "That way we won't attract mosquitos."

Sally gave Alex a hug and a kiss and then picked up a sleeping Katy and carried her back to her bed. Kathy helped slip her dress off and they put a sheet over her.

"She is so adorable, Sally remarked, and then said, "you and Bobby are such a great team when you sing together."

"Thank you," Kathy told her.

So much had happened to Kathy in one day that her mind was spinning trying to think about it. She enjoyed listening to the fiddle and singing with Bobby. She had once heard a fiddle called the Devil's instrument because of its association with saloons and dance halls but she found nothing sinister about it. "Rail order bride!" Bobby could be quite a tease, she decided. She thanked God for letting her and Katy come to the Thompsons before drifting off to sleep.

Bobby talked briefly to Martha before heading to a bunk next to Alex in the men's side of the bathhouse. "Thank you so much, mother, for bringing those two girls home. Katy is so cute and thank you for my rail order bride. Kathy is the most wonderful girl I have ever met. I was teasing about marrying a fourteen-year-old girl; Kathy is the one I want to marry."

"That wasn't why I brought her home, but she does seem like a perfect match for you. You both are too young now, but I could be very happy if she marries you sometime in the future."

Bobby lay awake thinking about Kathy. She was so smart, so pretty, he loved her smile, and her voice was so beautiful. Bobby liked Julia and it pleased him that Kathy and Katy were nice to her. When they sang together, they were in a whole different world. When she was close to him while they were singing, she had this sweet clean fragrance that was almost irresistible. She was so sweet and loveable! He couldn't keep his eyes off of her at supper. He wanted to hug and kiss her so bad.

He knew it was just puppy love, but he had puppy love for Shep when Shep was a puppy and he still loved Shep many years later. He hoped he could change Kathy's mind about being too young for a boyfriend. Bobby had joked about her being his rail order bride. Now he wished it were true. Before Kathy, Bobby had no plans for getting married but marrying Kathy was such a wonderful thought.

Clarence gave Martha a hug before they went to bed. "I am so glad you brought them home. That little girl is absolutely precious, and Kathy is so talented."

"Katy is such a darling," Martha replied, "but when I invited them home, I never even thought about Kathy and Bobby. He has already fallen in love with her. She seems like a really sweet girl, and when I see them singing together, I realize what a good match they are. I like the idea of them getting married but not until next spring."

"We will have to pray and hope and be thankful for our blessings now," Clarence answered. "Kathy has a beautiful voice. I can't wait to hear her on the piano. She could really improve our music for Sunday morning worship. Bobby is really good too and they are so good together."

CHAPTER 4

First Day Working in the Bathhouse

Sally woke up a sleepy Kathy at daybreak. Kathy started to put her dress back on, but Sally told her to leave it off or you will get it dirty. She had Kathy put on a bathing gown instead. She had Kathy clean out the ashes in the wood stove and then fill it up with kindling and firewood before starting it up again. They filled 4 large kettles full of water but only put two on the stove. The kettles were heavy, and Kathy could barely lift a full kettle with both hands. Sally showed her the amount of coffee grounds needed to make coffee in a big coffee pot.

Martha arrived wearing a robe and started making an omelet in a large skillet to which she added small pieces of ham. "We are going to live it up today but tomorrow it's back to oatmeal for breakfast." The kitchen had a sink and Martha partially filled it from the water on the stove.

"Wash up and get dressed," she told them.

Kathy and Sally both went back where Katy was sleeping. Sally kissed Katy on the cheek, "morning sweetie; it's time to wake up and eat breakfast."

Kathy wore the short sleeve dress she had been given the night before and Katy put her spring dress back on. Kathy had tried hard to be a mother to Katy but was realizing that now Sally, Martha and even Julia were all acting like mothers to Katy. It was a relief that others were now sharing the responsibility, but it kind of bothered her that Katy didn't need her that much anymore. Katy was getting so much love and Kathy was feeling it too.

They had gathered outside in the patio area. Katy found the yellow kitten again and was about as happy as a little girl could get. Normally obedient, she had to be asked twice before she came to the table. Kathy had helped set up the table and went around pouring milk and coffee. They said grace and then Martha told her to sit down and eat. This time Kathy was sitting next to Martha who had filled Kathy's plate with scrambled eggs and a couple of biscuits.

"This is too much," Kathy protested. Kathy could not remember a breakfast this good. There was butter and jelly for the biscuits and before she knew it, she had cleaned her plate. "Between you and Julia, I am going to be so fat I waddle," she told Martha.

"I doubt it," she replied, "I want to get you to the point where your ribs aren't showing."

Kathy realized that Martha had become her mother and Sally was sitting between Alex and Katy and being mother to both of them. The weight of responsibility was definitely slipping off her shoulders.

"Let's all get over to the church after supper and practice singing with Kathy playing the piano," Bobby suggested. That was agreed to, and they planned out work assignments for the day. Kathy and Katy would weed the garden, Martha had clothes to wash, and Bobby and Alex would help Clarence unload a shipment of groceries coming in during the morning. Sally would take care of the bathhouse and help Martha with the wash.

Kathy had helped her father plant and take care of a small garden when they were living in their house in Boston. Kathy knew the difference between weeds and vegetables. It was a cloudy day, so it was a good day to weed. Kathy talked briefly with Sally and Martha who were heating water in the bathhouse kitchen for washing clothes.

Kathy and Katy went over to the bunkbed and took off their dresses. Kathy told Katy it was okay for her not to wear clothes in the bathhouse, but she must be dressed if they went outside the bathhouse. Kathy put the bathing gown back on before they went out to work on the garden.

"It's great not having to wear clothes," Katy told her.

"At least for now it is okay," Kathy replied but she wished Katy had an old dress to wear. She got Katy started weeding a row of peas warning her to be very careful not to pull up any pea plants.

Kathy started working on a row of carrots which were more difficult to weed because the plants were still small and looked similar to grass.

They were alone out there, and Kathy's gown kept sliding down over her knees getting into the dirt she was kneeling on. After working for a while, Kathy took the gown off. It was comfortable not wearing anything, but she felt really improper and insecure. After a few minutes she put the gown back on but found a pin in her suitcase to keep it from sliding down.

It seemed like forever before she finished the first row of carrots and there were two more carrot rows to weed. There was also a row of beets, and she knew that they would take forever too. She got up and brushed the dirt off her. Katy was doing well on the peas but needed a bathroom break. There were two outhouses, and they were modern for that time. There was a bucket of water in each bathroom which you would pour into the toilet after you used it and it would drain into a sewer pipe. They were not smelly, but the one drawback was that most children couldn't lift the bucket, so an adult had to make sure that the toilets were getting flushed.

They returned to the garden and Kathy suggested that they sing while they worked. They started with songs that Katy knew and then they went to songs Katy was unsure of. On these songs, Kathy would sing a phrase and then Katy would sing it back to her.

Julia was in the kitchen with Martha and also helping her wash clothes. "It sounds like angels are singing in the garden," she told Martha.

Martha looked out and just barely saw Kathy' s head. "It's those two girls I brought home yesterday," she told her.

Julia laughed, "well I think that is about as close to hearing angels as I am going to get down here."

Trying to concentrate on singing and weeding at the same slowed down their progress but it made the time pass much faster. Katy was starting the second row of peas when Martha came over. "Julia and I loved your singing but now I need your help hanging up sheets. Julia would help me, but I want her to make bread today. Julia makes the best bread, and I am hungry for fresh bread." Katy proudly showed Martha that she had weeded a row of peas and Kathy showed the two rows of carrots she had finished.

"Great job," Martha told them, it's tedious work but this garden provides a lot of the food we eat during the summer."

"It isn't as tedious as sitting for ten hours in a factory sewing clothes," responded Kathy.

"That sounds awful," Martha replied. There were some clothes lines next to the garden where they hung up the sheets.

They finished hanging clothes and Kathy went back to weeding. She finished the last row of carrots and Katy finished weeding the peas. There were still rows of some other vegetables she was unfamiliar with. It looked like someone had already weeded the tomatoes but there were vine crops to be weeded as well. The sun was coming out from some clouds, and it was getting hot.

She returned to the pool area where Sally met her. "Could you watch the child pool, I have two mothers who want baths and I need to get them ready? Then I am going back to help my mother with laundry."

Kathy saw two women standing by the pool and 4 small boys already in the pool.

"Hi, my name is Kathy and I'm a helper here and I will watch the pool." The mothers walked toward the bathtubs following Sally.

Katy also had come over and jumped in with the boys in the pool. The boys were bare and so was Katy. They briefly stared at each other but quickly satisfied their curiosity. It didn't matter to them after that.

There were some floats that were made out of cork, and they liked to hold them and then kick their feet in the water as they moved across the small pool. Kathy played with two of the smaller boys in the water. The gown was awkward for moving around in the water.

The mothers had their baths and came back fully dressed to collect their children who pleaded to stay longer.

The mothers gave in and sat down on the edge of the pool and talked to Kathy. "Who's the little girl?" one of the mothers asked.

"That is my little sister, Katy but I have also been her mother since our mother died last year. I am so grateful that Clarence and Martha are letting us live with them, we were almost homeless."

"I am so glad they did," the mother replied, "the thought of you and your sister being homeless just makes me shudder."

"Katy is so cute," the other mother responded, "I love my boys, but I would love to have a little girl like her, but our house is already too crowded. How old is she?"

"She is 7 and would be in third grade next year but she is really ready for fourth grade," Kathy replied.

One mother pointed to the biggest boy, "my son Sam is almost 4 and is he is almost as big as her."

Sally had rejoined them, "we have got to fatten up both of them up. They are going to be singing with my brother in church this Sunday and you don't want to miss it. Kathy plays the flute and the piano, and my brother plays the fiddle."

"Katy, sing Yankee Doodle," Sally suggested. Katy did it perfectly.

The Mother said" wow!

She turned to Kathy, "your turn." Kathy sang a Christian song and when she finished both women complimented her and said that they would try to get their husbands to bring them to the church. Sally accompanied them to the door and asked that Julia to give them each a half piece of buttered bread and told them to remember to thank her. The bread disappeared in seconds.

One of the mother's said, "thank you, that bread is so good, and we had so much fun; my children are going to be begging me to come back. All of you people are so nice."

After they left, Sally commented that Kathy was going to fill up the Church.

"Well at least on Sunday we will all have clothes on," she replied. "It just felt kind of improper singing to them in here with so little on."

"Don't worry," Sally replied, "it will be about ten more years before they get excited about girls and by then they will be Katy's problem."

"Why will they be a problem for me?" Katy asked.

"Because by that time you will be a beautiful young lady and all the boys will be madly in love with you," Sally told her.

Katy gave her a skeptical look and made a funny face that caused Kathy to laugh.

"Let's go out to the kitchen and get some fresh bread for lunch, "Sally directed. We can eat it out here." Julia gave them fresh from the oven warm buttered bread and glasses of milk which they ate standing up. It was so yummy. Despite a big breakfast, Kathy ate two slices and then another slice when Julia offered it again.

Julia put her hand on Katy's shoulder, "how is my little angel? I thought I was hearing angels singing the garden this morning and then found out was you girls."

"I know I am getting fatter, but I don't think I'm growing wings yet," Kathy joked.

"I don't think you two will ever get fat or grow feathers but I'm under orders from Martha to make you two eat well," Julia responded.

"You are doing a great job of it, thank you so much," Kathy told her.

"I love you Julia, you are so good to me," Katy told her.

After they left, Julia thanked the Lord for letting her work for the Thompsons. At a time when so many white folks treated colored folks badly, they always treated her considerately and these two new girls were so nice. Katy was about the same age as her granddaughter and seeing Katy made her heart ache for her granddaughter. Her thoughts were interrupted by Katy who had hung back.

"Julia, you look sad, what's wrong?"

"Actually, you make me very happy," Julia told her, "but when I see you, I think about my granddaughter who is about your age, and I wish she were here."

"I will pray that she can come," Katy said, "I would love to play with her."

She gave Julia a big hug. Katy walked back to Kathy and Sally. As Katy walked away, Julia smiled - she had a little angel with no clothes on and no feathers.

Sally was wearing a robe and asked Kathy to put her dress on and help bring in the laundry which was now dry. Katy also dressed and followed them.

"Mother hasn't invited you into the house because it is a total mess, and she is embarrassed by it. She's helping get the new stuff that came in today on the store shelves. Some of our store inventory winds up being stored in the living area and we really don't have any other place to put it. Father wants to add onto the store, but we haven't got it done yet."

The house had a large room that was both living room and kitchen with a stone fireplace in the middle. Numerous windows kept it well-lit, but a large assortment of crates, cans and gunny sacks took up a big portion of the room. There was a large, neat bedroom on the far end where Martha and Clarence slept.

"Mother will put these away," Sally remarked as they put clothes, sheets, and towels on the bed. There were two small bedrooms on the other side that Sally told her were mostly filled up with stuff. There was a closet between them, and Sally pried a large bag of clothes out of it. "These are some old clothes of mine that I outgrew that mother was going to use for rags, but they might fit you."

"Thanks, I really don't have much to wear for hot weather."

Sally led them up a stairway right after the entry way. They went upstairs where there were three more bedrooms including a bedroom with a bathroom. The bathroom also had a door leading to an outside balcony. There was also another bathroom at the other end of the hall.

Kathy was surprised that the bathrooms had running water.

Sally told her that they had a windmill that pumped the water up to the second floor. "We rent these rooms out to people who want to stay here for a few days. We have a couple with two girls coming in next week for several days. We will feed them, provide hot water for baths, and let them use the bathhouse. Bobby and you can provide musical entertainment. They have been here before; they are quite wealthy but very nice people. We will earn more money taking care of them then we make in a week running the store." Sally remarked again about the bathhouse. "It really doesn't make any money, we do it mostly as a community service."

Kathy went back to her bunk and tried on the clothes in the bag. She found several dresses she could wear but one was too big. There was also a dark blue skirt and a blouse that were worn and had spots and the blouse holes in the sleeves, but it fit okay. Kathy decided she could use it in the garden but then she had another idea. Kathy asked Sally if it was it okay to cut it up and Sally went and got Kathy a pair of scissors. Buttons on each side of the skirt tightened it up so it didn't slide down. Sally watched as Kathy cut most of the bottom of the skirt off making it into a short skirt and then cut the sleeves and collar off the blouse.

Sally commented after Kathy tried it on, "You look really cute, but I don't think you dare show it to Bobby unless you are ready to be his rail order bride."

"I am sure Bobby was joking about marrying me, but I won't show it to him. I will just wear it when I am in the water or in the garden. I doubt that Bobby is ready to marry me no matter what I wear."

"Oh, he wants to marry you, but we need to fatten you up first," Sally teased.

Sally suggested that Kathy shorten the blouse too. Kathy did which let several inches of her tummy show. She jumped in the water and came out dripping. Both the skirt and the blouse clung to her like they had been painted on. Sally thought it was okay but why bother wearing anything but the bathing gown in the bathhouse.

Two teenage girls came in with a little girl and another girl about Katy's age. "Where can my ten-year-old brother swim?" one of them asked. Sally said she would go out and take him over to the boy's side.

Kathy showed the girls where they could hang up their clothes. They said they lived on adjoining nearby farms and had ridden in on a buckboard when one of their fathers came into town to get supplies and some welding done on a plow. They got really giggly after they got their clothes off. Like Kathy they found walking around without clothes on a little scary. They all squealed when they hit the cold water. Kathy joined them wearing her home-made bathing suit and started playing with the youngest girl. Katy played with the girl that was her age.

"Wouldn't it be great to be able to jump in every day," the one girl said."

"You just want to go naked," the other girl teased.

"That's true, it seems scandalous which is why it is so fun. My mother said we shouldn't talk about it because some people would be shocked."

Kathy found out both girls were only 14 and she couldn't help but laugh. Kathy told them that she was new, and they had teased her that she was old at 17, and most girls around here married at 14.

"I don't think that is true," the one girl replied, "because even if we wanted to get married, there isn't much to choose from."

"How about Danny, I think he likes you," the other girl teased.

"Well don't be jealous because you can have him."

The talk got a little more serious where the girls admitted that they didn't want to be stuck out on their parent's farm after high school and marriage seemed like the only escape.

28

Kathy mentioned working at a garment factory for sixty hours a week.

"Well, that doesn't sound like fun, and I would be scared to move to a city," the girl replied.

Listening to the girls talk, Kathy realized that the girls were not looking at great options for their future. Getting married at 14 did not seem as funny anymore. For them, marrying a man like Bobby would be the best deal they could hope for and maybe for herself as well. As soon as the thought hit her, she dismissed it as absurd. She was not ready to get married and despite Sally's teasing, she doubted Bobby wanted her for a girlfriend.

Kathy started singing funny songs to the little girl and got her giggling. Her older sister came over and they both played with her for a while.

Finally, they sat on the pool edge and continued talking. Both girls were amazed that she was through high school and that they had come all the way from Boston although they weren't very sure where that was. They told her that Martha had been their grade schoolteacher but now they went to high school in Williamsburg. Julia came over and said that their father was outside, and they had to get dressed and leave. They hated to leave, and Kathy and Katy were sorry to see them go. Kathy was reminded again what a great situation she had gotten into.

It had turned cloudy again so Kathy told Julia she would be out in the garden weeding. Julia told her that she looked cute in her bathing attire. Katy reluctantly agreed to help weed. Kathy gave her a hug. "We have a pretty good deal here, let's do our best to be helpful," she told Katy.

Kathy decided to leave her bathing suit on. She got Katy started on the beans and started herself on the beets. Kathy got lost in her thoughts as she weeded. She hadn't really thought about her own future since her father died; she mostly had concentrated on immediate issues like getting through school and taking care of Katy. Having a boyfriend and getting married was something she rarely thought of. Her normal reaction that a young man was a problem to be avoided wasn't happening with Bobby. She found herself excited about singing with him at church after supper.

She finished the row of beets and went to check on Katy. Katy had got part way down the first of several rows of beans when she spotted the yellow kitten. They were laying cuddled up in a shady spot on the grass and Katy was sound asleep. Kathy smiled and went back to weeding the next row .The sun had come out and It had gotten hot. The trees on the west side of the garden were providing some shade. She decided to work only in the shady areas. Her fingers were getting a little sore and she was glad when Martha told her that they were going to have an early supper.

Kathy talked about her bathing suit to Martha. "This is a little more comfortable to work in and move around in the pool."

"It looks cute," Martha told her, "maybe I will make something like it for myself."

"I'm making progress, but my helper quit," Kathy told her pointing to Katy with the kitten.

"How adorable, "Martha replied. The kitten woke up and ran off. "How is my little darling?" she asked Katy who started to wake up.

Supper featured more bread and a pork roast that Julia had made sweet and spicy. Everyone was making sandwiches out of it. It was so delicious. Kathy ate a second sandwich and then had a piece of pie made out of fresh rhubarb. Martha had left the table early to relieve Clarence at the store. Almost all the food was gone when Clarence sat down and Kathy was feeling bad about being such a glutton until Julia brought out more bread, pork, and pie out for Clarence. She remembered Katy's remark about this being the nicest place on earth. Katy could be right, she decided.

CHAPTER 5

Singing Practice at Church

Kathy started to go over to the church to practice but then realized she had forgot her flute. She ran back to get it and then rejoined them just as they got to the church.

Bobby teased her, "I have never seen a girl run that fast."

"I couldn't wait to get to the piano." she replied smiling.

"I thought you couldn't wait to sing with me," he told her.

"Oh, that too," she replied with an impish smile.

Bobby took a deep breath; her smile had a way of totally messing up his mind.

The piano was a bit of a disappointment for Kathy. It was not a top-of-the-line piano and slightly out of tune but at least it was a piano. It had been a long time since she had played a piano, so she started slowly. She played something simple and then felt comfortable with it. She then played a complicated piece with a fast tempo that she had practiced many times over the years. Music was a scarce commodity in the area and quite a number of people had found out they would be practicing and showed up to listen. Kathy was so focused on the piano that she hadn't noticed. When she finished the piece, she was surprised at the applause. "Okay, I'm ready," she said.

"I didn't think it was possible to get that much music out of that piano or any piano," Clarence told her.

"Let's warm up with a popular song and then do some hymns," Bobby suggested.

Kathy sang while he played the fiddle and then they both would sing while she played the piano. They then tried the song Clarence had suggested to open with. Bobby would play the melody on his fiddle and then he would sing with Kathy as she played the piano.

Bobby suggested Clarence join in with his baritone and Sally sing alto. "I'll play it once on the fiddle, then I will sing it with Father while you play the piano then you and Sally sing it high. It sounded really good, and Kathy was impressed how good Sally and Clarence were.

They then did a song without instruments with Bobby singing tenor and Kathy singing soprano and then singing together on the final chorus. Bobby had a really good voice and Kathy's voice would soar high and sweet but then they would sing together, and their voices would blend. Martha had closed the store and come over and heard them. Martha was thrilled at how beautiful Bobby and Kathy sang together. She was reminded again, what a wonderful match they were.

Clarence told them that he was going to speak on sorrow and loss and trying to understand why God allows it. He spoke to Kathy: "Martha tells me you have what you call your cry song. I might want you to sing it before my sermon." Kathy played her flute and Katy sang it with her sweet young voice.

> **I love you Jesus, but you make me cry.**
> **Why did Daddy and Mommy have to die?**
> **You took my only brother too!**
> **I love you Jesus, but you make me blue.**
> **Someday take me home to you I pray.**
> **We will all meet in Heaven and sing that day!**
> **Until that day I will sing down here**
> **Please hear my prayers and draw me near.**

Katy had a way of penetrating even the coldest heart. Sally had fallen in love with little Katy and the loss of her own husband still scarred her. She could not hold back her tears. and neither could a young mother who had come over with two little children. Clarence wiped his own eyes. "I plan to use it, but we better have some handkerchiefs to pass around."

Sally was holding on to her son Alex who began to tear up as he remembered his father. Alex's buddy James remembered his own mother;

started to tear up and held unto Alex. James older sister Janice was a sad and lonely child who Sally tried her best to comfort. James and Janice's father William was a very successful lumberman but his bitterness at losing the wife he so dearly loved and not finding her killer had left him cold and distant. Little Katy caught William off guard, and he felt emotion he tried so hard to avoid. He was not mean to his children, but he was not giving them the love they needed. William was a strong good-looking man, but his aloofness had repelled Sally. He knew how much Sally loved her husband and her tears made him feel sorry for her.

"It is so hard isn't it," he told her, "you love them so much and then they are gone. I know how you feel losing your husband because I miss my wife so much and it hurts so bad."

Sally put her arm around his shoulder- "Your wife was a beautiful, wonderful person," Sally told him. Sally felt his body shake with the grief he was feeling. If William had told her that he loved her she probably would have had no emotion but seeing how much he cared about the wife, he had lost made her love him as a person. His parting words to Sally stunned her.

"I would like to thank you for being such a friend to my children. Someday would like to talk to you about our children and about us."

"I would like that," Sally replied, and they held each other's hands before William and his children went home.

Martha had given Kathy and Katy a hug after the song. Bobby had a very kind heart and the song had hit home what the girls had been through. He came up behind Martha and told them: "I can't make the pain go away, but I hope we can give you a much happier future."

Clarence looked over at both groups and prayed that they would be comforted. "Dear Lord, may their tears wash away their sorrows."

It was starting to get dark as they walked back to the house and the bathhouse. Bobby walked with Kathy and Katy, and they talked about the singing. Bobby praised both girls.

Kathy told him it was a lot of fun. Kathy and Katy realized they were not hurting alone, and Katy remembered how Julia was hurting to see her granddaughter, Jade.

Bobby had planned to see more of the world after college, maybe go out to California; that had seemed like an exciting idea. Now all he could think about was Kathy; it had taken her less than two days to totally take over his mind. He felt sorry for her for having lost her parents; he loved to hear her sing and when she smiled at him, he knew she had stolen his heart.

He also had observed the parting clasp of hands between Sally and William. He had always admired William, but this was a little unexpected. He was an uncle to Alex but was often more like a father. Bobby tried to be a good role model and liked Alex a lot but sometimes he was spending time with Alex when he wanted to be doing something else.

Martha and Clarence walked back behind them with their arms around each other. "Do you think Sally and William are ready to move on?" Martha asked.

"I'm not sure if William and Sally are through grieving yet but they are a good match for each other." Clarence replied. "There is a lot of sorrow here, but I see some good things happening. Thank you again for bringing those two girls home. I think we may be looking at two weddings coming up. I never thought our little church would be blessed by such good music; I will have to really work on my sermons, so they come for more than the music."

Kathy put Katy to bed and then her and Sally talked for a while sitting on a bench next to the pool. "I think I just fell in love again," Sally told Kathy, " I always thought William was cold, but the poor man is still heartbroken about losing his wife. She played the piano at our church. She was killed about two years ago and the killer was never found. I'm still getting over losing my husband David but we both need to move on and tonight he said he wants to talk about us. I would love to be mother to his children too. In a way mother did bring home a husband for me, I think the song you and Katy sang managed to break through the barrier he had built around his heart."

Kathy responded, "I hope it works out for you. I haven't recovered from losing my mother and father. I know my mother sacrificed her health for us trying to keep her job so we wouldn't be homeless. She went to work when she had a bad cold and got caught in a cold rain while walking home and then caught pneumonia and died. I promised her when she was dying that I would take care of Katy. After she died, I found myself sacrificing for Katy. Katy is so happy here and I feel like I have gotten her to the best possible place thanks to your mother and your family. I am very happy here too, but it doesn't seem real yet."

CHAPTER 6

We All Love You

Kathy managed to wake up early the next morning and had the stove cleaned out and ready to light before Sally joined her. They also filled a large heavy metal barrel full of water that sat on a metal grate over a fire pit. It was closer to the bathtubs and Sally said that on busier days they would fill their buckets from there rather than the stove. She said that Fridays and Saturdays were usually the busiest times of the week for women wanting baths or getting their hair washed. They woke up Katy and dressed for breakfast. Kathy had been wearing the bathing suit she had made and changed to her dress.

"I almost forgot to change," she told Sally.

"I'm sure Bobby wouldn't have minded," Sally replied with a big smile.

It was only Thursday, and Kathy's world was now so different.

Kathy was not a big fan of oatmeal, but Martha brought out some strawberries to add to it and Kathy ate her bowl in no time. It seemed like her appetite was now conspiring with Martha and Julia to fatten her up. Katy had surprised them at breakfast by praying that Julia's granddaughter Jade could come and visit Julia.

"I remember her," Sally replied, "Julia brought her to visit several years ago. She was the cutest sweetest little black girl you could ever imagine. We will have to talk to Julia about her when we see her."

Kathy had been taught by her parents that all people were equal under God, but she would sadly discover that Sally and her family were among the few people who weren't prejudiced in the small community.

Martha asked Kathy if she minded working on the garden some more. "We looked at the letter again that we got from the couple who is renting our upstairs for a week, and they may be arriving Saturday. Sally and I will be working to freshen it up a little more upstairs."

Katy and the kitty had found each other again and were fast becoming best buddies. Sally told Katy "you can stay out in the patio and pet the kitty but to watch the door to the bathhouse. Run and get Kathy if anyone shows up."

Bobby and Alex had already left for town to pick up freight due in at the train station for the store.

Kathy went back to the bathhouse and changed to her bathing suit and started weeding. It was cloudy day, and she didn't have to worry about sunburn. Mosquitos were a problem; they had managed to bite her on the back right through her bathing suit. She now had a number of itchy bites on her body. She wondered if mosquitos were part of Adam and Eve's punishment at the fall along with weeds and thorns. It might be part of God's plan for people to be more modest. Yet if she dressed so she wouldn't be bitten, she would be miserably hot.

Weeding was both tedious and boring. After about an hour she decided to sing. She missed having Katy nearby but decided to sing by herself. She had a Catholic friend in high school and sometimes she would go with her to the Catholic Church. Kathy had taken Latin in school and could understand many of the songs sung in Latin. She especially liked one of them sung in a very high pitch that had an ethereal quality to it.

She had just finished singing it when Katy came up to her. "There are a couple of older ladies here that want a bath."

Two middle aged ladies greeted her and one of them asked her about the song she had sung. "It is a song celebrating Mary giving birth to Christ sung in Latin," Kathy told her.

"It was so beautiful that it seemed unreal," the woman told Kathy.

"Thank you, my name is Kathy and you have met my younger sister Katy and we will help you ladies get a hot bath." Kathy sent Katy after towels and wash basins while she filled two enclosed bathtubs from the heated barrel and then gave them each a washbasin full of warm water. Hang your clothes on the back of the enclosure and take as long as you like."

"Do we get to hear more songs while we soak," one of them asked with a smile.

"If you like, I will get Katy to help me."

Kathy got her flute and played "Yankee Doodle" and a Christian song while Katy sang and then Kathy sent her back to watch the door. Kathy then sang "All Creatures of Our God and King" followed by "Amazing Grace". Both women came out of the stalls fully dressed but Kathy helped one lady get her hair dried and combed. They both thanked her and thought it was wonderful that she would be at church on Sunday.

They also praised Katy for her singing when they left. Kathy added some wood to the fire under the barrel and refilled the barrel with water before going back to the garden. She picked peas into a bucket and then sat down in the patio with Katy to shell them. Bobby and Alex were gone, and Clarence was working in the store, so she felt the bathing suit was covering enough.

They were almost done shelling peas when a young mother who introduced herself as June arrived with a darling baby girl and an adorable little boy. Kathy left Katy to finish shelling peas and went over to the pool with the mother. The mother just wanted to nurse her baby and let her boy get wet. The mother undressed herself and her little boy. Kathy picked the boy up and slowly introduced him to the water. At first, he clung tightly to Kathy but eventually he was splashing happily on his own. Kathy sat down on the pool edge with her feet in the water watching him. The mother finished nursing and asked Kathy if she would hold the baby girl while she jumped into the water with her boy. Kathy cuddled the baby girl against her while singing softly to her and was rewarded with a sweet little smile.

"For someone who talks about not being ready to get married, you are really good with children," Sally remarked. She and Katy were standing behind her. "Martha 's making lunch and we decided to get wet while we wait."

Kathy continued to cuddle the little girl and sing softly to her until the girl fell asleep. Despite her protests to Sally about not being ready for marriage, Kathy loved children. Kathy was very willing to work hard but she was not ready to trust in the future. Sally got a couple of towels and they all dried off and got dressed. June left with her two children.

It was time for lunch out in the patio. She helped Martha by pouring milk and coffee. Martha had made biscuits with creamed peas and ham pieces to go over them. Bobby was back and Kathy realized that she needed to get some letters ready to send out to her aunt and her older sister for the next time he went to town. She would have only taken one biscuit, but Martha insisted she take two.

Martha spoke to Kathy and Katy, "I talked to Clarence this morning and he told me that a couple of ladies were in the store this morning and said that you two were the best singers they had ever heard."

Kathy responded, "we are trying to sing for our supper plus lunch and breakfast– thanks for all the good food."

"So, what about my singing?" Bobby asked pretending to be downcast.

"You will have to wait until church on Sunday to show off your talent. Besides unless they have a 14-year-old granddaughter you probably wouldn't be interested in them." She told Bobby with an impish little smile.

"We might have to put another postage stamp on your forehead and mail you back," Bobby retorted with a frown.

"Please don't, I will be good, I don't want to be homeless," Kathy promised with a sad look on her face that made Bobby feel bad.

"I was just kidding," Bobby told her and put his hand gently on her wrist. "It would break my heart if you and Katy left. We all love you and I need you to be my singing partner." The joke had worn thin for Bobby because he could not imagine marrying anyone but Kathy.

Martha ate quickly and went to relieve Clarence in the store. Kathy served him lunch when he joined them, and he thanked her for pitching in so quickly to help around here.

"It has been so fun for both of us," Kathy told him, "We just love it here."

"We love having you," Clarence responded. "We really count on that garden, so I appreciate you working on it but next week I hope to get you into the store."

Kathy knew that everyone was expected to work hard but Clarence was so pleasant to everyone around him. Bobby was nice too. Was he just being friendly when he said "we all love you" or was it romantic? She tried to dismiss the idea that Bobby had a romantic interest in her as a silly thought, but she kind of hoped it was true.

The rest of the day Kathy alternated between gardening, taking care of some children in the pool, and hanging up sheets and pillowcases for the rooms upstairs.

Kathy put on her dress but lay down on her bed for a quick break but fell asleep. Katy woke her up and announced that it was supper time. It was raining and they were eating in the house.

They were having bacon, pancakes and syrup made from some kind of fruit. They also had coffee which helped Kathy wake up a little, but she was still sleepy. She knew she should be helping Martha, but she was so tired. She reflected that that it was only four days since Katy and her had boarded a train in Boston and headed west. Their life had changed so dramatically that Boston seemed like a distant memory. She smiled when she thought about the letter she needed to write to her aunt and older sister, she would tell him they were having a good time. She would not mention the bathhouse, they would think it was scandalous.

Bobby passed her a plate of pancakes. "Have another pancake, you haven't fattened up enough yet."

She had already had two pancakes but accepted a third one. "Thank you," she told him. She thought about his remark. Fattened up enough for what? Was he suggesting that she needed to get fatter before he would marry her?

Bobby marrying a 14-year-old or anybody else but her was no longer funny to her either. She wasn't ready to marry him now, but she was pretty certain she would be ready by next spring. She didn't even know why she was certain, and she was too tired to figure it out. She ate the pancake and started falling asleep in her chair.

Kathy vaguely remembered Sally leading her back to her bed. Kathy fell asleep instantly and dreamed that Bobby was hugging her. She would wake up with part of her mind happy and the other part warning her not to fall in love.

Over in the men's bathhouse Bobby lay awake remembering how adorable a sleepy Kathy looked. In his mind he was enjoying the fantasy that he was cuddling and kissing Kathy and wishing it were real.

Sally woke up Kathy and Katy in time for breakfast. The rain was gone, and the Friday was sunny, but Kathy sat in silence until after she had finished breakfast. "I think there was something in the pancakes or the syrup that drugged me to sleep," Kathy told Sally as they walked back from the patio.

"You looked so cute last night, I think if I hadn't led you back to your bed Bobby would have would have had you in his lap," Sally told her.

Katy spoke up, "I was holding the kitty in my lap and Bobby told me, "you cuddle the kitty, and I will cuddle Kathy". Then Martha said, "no you don't! but she was laughing."

"Well, it sounds like Bobby is not planning on mailing me back to Boston," Kathy replied."

"Don't worry about that," Sally responded, "he wishes you were his rail order bride. He would marry you tomorrow if my parents would agree to it."

"Yikes!" Kathy responded, "I might need to mail myself back to Boston in order to escape."

"You seem to like Bobby, why don't you want to marry him?" Sally questioned.

"Actually, I do want to marry him next spring but four days after we meet is a little too soon."

"Mother wants Bobby to wait until next spring, so she is on your side, but she really does want the two of you to get married. So, when you two do decide to get married, I would like to be your bridesmaid, Katy can be the flower girl and Alex can be the ring bearer. Also, I need you to be my bridesmaid when I remarry."

"You are making my head spin," Kathy told Sally, "can I just go back to bed and start over."

"No, "Sally told her, "today is going to be a real busy day."

"You wouldn't leave me would you," Katy asked Kathy.

"No, they will probably hold both of us captive until I marry Bobby and you are old enough to marry Alex."

"I love the idea of Katy marrying Alex," Sally responded.

"Do I have to marry Alex?" A shocked Katy asked.

"No, we are just teasing," Sally replied, "and you two are not being held captive. We all love you and we want you to be happy here."

CHAPTER 7

Visitors and a Stolen Kiss

Kathy had been warned that Fridays and Saturdays were usually the busiest day for baths with a lot of children in the pool. Bobby usually took care of the men's bathhouse and pool but If there were no men needing a bath, Sally would sometimes wear a robe and supervise boys too old to be allowed in the women's bathhouse. Today it might be necessary since Bobby was arranging to get horses and a wagon to pick up more wood for heating water and cooking from William's sawmill. Tomorrow he would get a carriage to pick up their guests expected to arrive from St Louis by rail in Williamsburg about 2 pm. Kathy realized she needed to write some letters before tomorrow and send them with Bobby.

"Doesn't it bother you to see older boys without clothes on?" Kathy asked Sally.

"No, I hardly notice. A few of them are embarrassed, but I tell them they are no different than Alex who is usually over there with me and doesn't wear anything. Most of the time if the boys aren't rowdy, I just leave Alex alone with them. He is a big help."

Both the adult pool and the child pool were cold from the rain. Kathy put a pail of hot water in each and then refilled the barrel that was heating over the fire pit. Sally was really strong and carrying a pail of water in each hand was easy for her. For Kathy, even carrying one pail was a challenge and she sometimes carried a half pail in each hand and made two trips. Carrying water along with gardening had really worn her out the previous day. She had Katy check out the water temperature which she did with a

41

big splash. It was still cold she reported and ran off to dry in the sun by the garden.

There were no customers or children early on Friday and Kathy decided to sing. She looked out at the garden looking green and healthy after the rain. She felt good about her gardening efforts. Kathy felt a sense of contentment, peace and belonging that she had not felt since her father died. The fact that the family wanted her to marry Bobby was quite an honor and their love for Katy was shown repeatedly. Despite Sally's teasing, she was the best friend a person could have, and she was a mother to every child she met. Kathy sang "Savior Like a Shepherd Lead Us". She didn't realize she had a small audience until she finished the song.

"I hope we didn't interrupt, I felt like I was walking into a Church service," one of the ladies told her.

"No, I just like to sing but Sunday I will sing in Church," Kathy replied. "My name is Kathy. I am new here. How can I help you?"

There were three women and four small girls. The three women each wanted a bath plus one bath that wasn't enclosed for the girls to share. Kathy showed them where the girls could hang up their clothes and was relieved to see Sally returning. Sally helped her get the baths ready and they had enough hot water to add another pail of hot water to the children's pool.

The pool was still quite cool so they set it up so the children would jump in the pool where Sally would swish them through the water. They would run over to Kathy who would lift them into the tub to warm up before they ran back to the pool again. Two of the smaller children wound up in their mother's bathtub after a couple trips to the pool. Katy came over and helped get the two children who had not joined their mothers in and out of the bathtub. It helped because Kathy was able to refill the hot water barrel. The mothers thanked them, and the children all gave Kathy and Sally a hug before they left. Kathy had been told by Sally they had to keep a small but fairly constant flow of spring water flowing into the pools or the water would get scummy.

After they left, Kathy told Sally how glad she was that she came back and helped.

"There were a couple of older boys who came in - probably part of the group we had but Alex and James were there, and they were all having a good time, so I left," Sally responded. "We don't make any money doing this, but we make a lot of children and mothers happy and that makes me happy."

"I really like the children," Kathy said, "they have all been really nice."

Friday afternoon was as busy as Kathy had been warned about. Fortunately, Sally was there to help with baths for mothers. Kathy spent most of her time helping children in and out of the pool. A couple of young teenage girls were in the pool. They loved little children and helped her, and Katy did too. Even with the help, a tired Kathy had only a vague memory of eating supper and going to bed early.

Saturday morning Kathy took the time after breakfast to write two very similar short letters to both her aunt and her sister telling them where they were. "Everyone here is very nice to us, we eat well, and we are both very happy." Kathy didn't mention the bathhouse. "The couple has an adult daughter who is a widow with a son about the same age as Katy. She has been a wonderful friend to us. They also have a son who just completed his third year of college. He is very nice and plays the fiddle which I enjoy listening to. We also like to sing together. The first night at supper he joked that since I had come by rail, I was his rail order bride. It may actually come true because his sister is convinced that he will marry me. I am not quite ready for that yet, but I like him and his family a lot." She added a few more words of greeting before bringing the letters over to the store. She bought postage from Clarence before she put them in the box of outgoing mail that Bobby would take with him when he went to pick up the guests in Williamsburg.

Kathy changed from her dress into her bathing suit and then walked over to the kitchen with Sally. Julia had been given the previous day off but was now back getting bread dough ready to bake. "Mother has pretty much figured out what ingredients Julia puts in her bread, but nobody knows how to knead it like Julia," Sally remarked.

Julia laughed, "there is no secret, just a lot of hard work. I hear we are getting company, so I am making twice as much of everything today. We are having a big pork roast tonight and maybe we can get some stuff out of the garden. I think I will make a rhubarb dessert too, Julia added."

"Now you are making me drool," Sally responded.

"Katy tells us you would like to bring Jade back here for a while; how can we help you with that? Sally asked.

"Well, I would need a ride to and from Williamsburg, a couple days off and some help paying for the train tickets," Julia answered. "Normally I would never ask for help but I miss her so bad," Julia said with a quiver in her voice."

"I will talk to mother; I know she wants you here this week but maybe you can go next Saturday. I am pretty sure we can help with the train fare too."

"You are going to make me cry and I have my hands full of flour," Julia told them.

"I remember holding Jade when she was little, she was so cute," Sally exclaimed.

Kathy handed Katy a bucket and sent her out to pick peas. When they got out of the kitchen, she also told Sally that she had kept just enough money to return to Boston if she couldn't stay with Katy in Kansas. "Since you people have been so good to me, I can be good to Julia and help her bring Jade here."

"Thanks, if we each contribute a little, we should have enough money," Sally said.

Kathy spent the next hour helping Katy pick peas. Then they started on the beans after finding that quite a few of them were ready too. They stopped for lunch in the patio with Kathy only wearing her bathing suit which Sally said would be okay.

Katy came out wearing nothing and had to be sent back to put on her dress. Kathy decided to try to make something for Katy to wear in the bathhouse when she wasn't in the pool. Lunch was fresh bread, butter, and jelly. Kathy found herself eating about twice what she would have back in Boston and Katy was eating a lot more too.

After lunch, Sally, Kathy, and Katy had a discussion that she needed to wear something outside the bathhouse. Sally also explained to Katy that as boys get older, they get fascinated by girl's bodies. "If a boy is older than five years old, we don't want them to see us without clothes on. Mostly the problem is when they get older, they might talk about seeing you and other children might think you are a bad person. I wouldn't worry if either

Alex or James saw you or if you saw them without clothes on but let's try to avoid it."

Kathy finished picking peas and beans and found a shady spot in the bath area to shell the peas and then borrowed a knife from Julia to get the strings off the string beans. Kathy also used the knife to cut the leaves off the rhubarb and then cut the rhubarb into small chunks. Julia was impressed when she brought the peas, beans, and rhubarb back to her.

"For a little gal, you sure get a lot of work done and that garden looks great," Julia told her.

"I hope someday I can cook as good as you," Kathy replied, "I sure appreciate the good cooking I am getting here."

Julia showed Kathy how she made rhubarb dessert mixing flour, oatmeal and sugar and then pouring that over a layer of rhubarb on a greased pan and then putting it in the oven until it gets browned. "In the fall, I use apples instead of rhubarb," Julia remarked. Katy came running and told Kathy that the guests had arrived. Kathy thanked Julia for the cooking lesson and put her dress over her bathing suit. She then went out to the patio joining Martha, Sally and Katy.

Bobby arrived with Richard and Mary Murdoch were a young good-looking couple with two very blond girls, Patty who was about Katy's age and Bonnie who was about four. The girls remembered Sally from the previous year and gave her a big hug. Kathy and Katy were introduced. Once introductions were over, the couple headed upstairs after they told both girls to follow Sally and Kathy into the bathhouse.

"Could you get the girls into the pool and watch the girls while I bring hot water upstairs for the Murdoches," Sally asked Kathy.

Patty and Katy quickly undressed and jumped in the pool. Kathy hung up her dress but still had her bathing suit on. She helped Bonnie hang up her dress. With her blond hair and bare bottom, Bonnie reminded Kathy of a painting in the Boston Public Library of an angelic little cherub. They both got into the pool. Kathy played with Bonnie while Patty and Katy played together. Sally soon joined her and together they swung girls through the water.

The three girls were having a good time together in the water. The girls finally got out of the pool and lay down on their towels in a shady spot on the grass. Sally asked Kathy to watch the girls. Sally got dressed and went back to help Martha set up for supper.

Kathy left her bathing suit on but wrapped a towel around her waist and grabbed her flute. She sat down next to the girls and started playing her flute. Bonnie crawled over and put her head in her lap. Kathy smiled; she had made a sweet little friend. Kathy was feeling very relaxed and happy as she played her flute.

Martha and Mary came into the bathhouse standing quietly enjoying the sound of the flute. Kathy finished the song and Martha announced it was time for everyone to get dressed for supper.

Mary smiled as she picked up Bonnie who was half asleep. "Looks like you won her over, your music is so pretty," she told Kathy.

As they were leaving, Mary commented to Martha "my girls looked so happy, it was like walking into a magical world."

"Kathy and her younger sister Katy just came here a few days ago and everyone has fallen in love with them," Martha replied.

Kathy got dressed before joining Sally and Martha in setting up for the night's dinner. Sally sat with the three girls and Alex. Kathy and Bobby would sit with the adults when Kathy wasn't helping Julia serve. Kathy went around filling glasses with milk or water and cups with coffee. Julia had outdone herself with fresh bread, a delicious pork roast, green beans with bacon pieces and cooked peas. Kathy made sure the dishes moved around and both tables were served. Kathy finally sat down next to Bobby and barely spoke to him as she feasted on the good food.

Richard surprised her by asking her questions about Boston. Kathy had made a habit of reading newspapers gave him detailed answers which resulted in more questions.

"You amaze me," he finally said, "I have never met anyone your age that is that well informed."

"Thank you," Kathy replied, "I guess it is because I like to read newspapers. I also spent a lot of time at the Boston Public Library before I started working last year."

Kathy then excused herself and started to pass out the rhubarb dessert giving herself a small piece. It was so good she wished she had taken more. Martha had Julia come out from the kitchen and they gave her a round of applause for the good meal.

Martha told Kathy to get her flute and they would start singing. Kathy came back with her flute and some sheet music, and she talked with Bobby on what they would sing. Kathy started out playing Yankee Doodle on her flute with Katy singing. Bobby then played his fiddle on a song they both knew. They had fun with it singing back and forth to each other, then they would harmonize on the chorus. Kathy went solo on a new song she had heard caressing the words with her sweet clear soprano voice. It was not meant to be a lullaby, but it had that effect on Bonnie who had crawled into her mother's lap and was falling asleep.

Bobby followed Kathy with a fast melody on his fiddle. Bobby and Kathy then joined together to sing "Savior Like a Shepherd Lead Us". Again, it acted like a lullaby and Patty wound up in her Father's lap. Clarence scooped up a sleepy Katy and Alex cuddled up to Sally.

There was an Irish love song that had been translated into English and both Bobby and Kathy knew it. They sang the phrases back and forth to each other with their voices betraying some of the love they were feeling for each other. They gave each other a little hug when it was over and then Bobby stole a kiss. Kathy pretended she was going to slap him but stopped short of his face and just smiled.

Mary commented, "that is some of the most beautiful singing I have ever heard and you two looked like you meant every word of that love song."

Kathy gave Bobby an impish smile and said, "most of it."

There was still a little bit of daylight, but everyone said goodnight and three little girls were carried off to bed.

Julia said goodnight to Kathy before leaving and then added "I loved the singing and you and Bobby are quite the match."

Similar comments were made between Martha and Clarence and between Richard and Mary.

Alex had walked back with Bobby to the men's bathhouse where they had their bunks. "Are you and Kathy going to get married?" Alex asked.

"I hope so," Bobby responded, "girls have a way of stealing your heart." Bobby lay awake thinking about Kathy. He wanted her more than anything in the world.

Kathy had never kissed a boy or fallen in love before and tonight she had done both. Kathy had talked about marrying Bobby, but it had seemed like a practical thing to do. She prided herself on keeping control of her emotions, but Bobby was stealing her heart. She prayed that their singing at church would go well and for her and Bobby. She touched her lips with her tongue; she wanted more kisses and hugs from Bobby. This is crazy, she told herself, you don't fall in love in five days.

CHAPTER 8

First Sunday at Church

Martha got up early Sunday morning and started making breakfast. She was surprised when Mary joined her and helped set the table. "You are a guest, you don't need to help," Martha told her.

"But I want to," she responded, "yesterday was so wonderful. The girls just love it here and that little Katy is such a sweetheart. The music Kathy makes with her flute is so pretty and restful. How long has Bobby known Kathy? That love song that they sang together was the most beautiful romantic song I have ever heard."

"It is kind of unreal," Martha told her, "I was coming back from my daughter's family in Ohio this Tuesday on the train and met these two girls who were going to a sister in Kansas who didn't really have room for them. They were so sweet I invited them to come home with me and they did. I did it for them, but Bobby fell in love with Kathy almost immediately and now I think he is winning her over."

"Do you approve?" Mary asked.

"Everything is happening too fast, but I can't imagine Bobby finding anyone I would like more than Kathy," Martha replied. "Life has really been rough for Kathy. When she got here, she was almost starving. I'm trying to fatten her up."

"Well, I hope when my girls grow up, they will find a boy like Bobby," Mary answered, "but if I had a boy, it would be hard to improve on Kathy."

They were interrupted by Bonnie who was wearing a pink night gown and looking adorably cuddly as she crawled into her mother's lap. "Of course, I don't really want them to grow up, I love them just the way they are right now," Mary remarked.

"I know what you mean, "Martha said, "having your girls and Katy around is so fun. My daughter Sally does a great job when she works in the store, but she loves little children so much that she always wants to be in the bathhouse during the summer. Kathy has been helping Sally in the bathhouse and she has also done a lot of work in the garden for us too."

Kathy joined them carrying some sheet music and her flute. "I should be helping you," she told Martha, "but I need to look at the songs we are singing in church this morning. Sally is up and she said she would help you." Kathy started going through the songs softly playing her flute while reading the notes. "I think I have got it, but I would like to play some of them on the piano before church starts." Sally and Katy showed up and Kathy told Katy they needed to recite the 23rd Psalm from memory. "We will alternate, I will say a verse then you say the next verse until we finish." Kathy had to help Katy on only one verse.

Clarence who had just arrived joined in with the final verse "and I will live in the House of the Lord forever."

"Ready to go?" Clarence asked.

"I think so, but I would like to practice on the piano before church starts," Kathy replied.

"Sounds good," Clarence replied, "I will go wake Bobby, so he is ready to practice with you too."

After Clarence left to get Bobby, Mary asked Kathy if she could teach some songs to her girls.

"Oh sure, that would be fun," Kathy replied, "when my mother was alive, we used to teach Sunday school together and teach the children to sing. My mother taught me how to read music and play piano; I need to start teaching that to my sister Katy now that I have access to a piano. Thanks to Martha and Clarence we have gone from homeless orphans to maybe having a future."

Mary had wondered why the girls had traveled alone and hearing they were orphans hit her hard. She held Bonnie a little tighter. Mary had been almost envious of Kathy and Katy's talent but now as a mother thinking of sweet little Katy being an orphan was almost heartbreaking. "How sad but thank goodness you are here," Mary said.

"It has been an answer to prayer," Kathy replied.

Clarence showed up again bringing Alex and Bobby with him. Sally helped Martha bring out some milk and coffee followed by some biscuits with a milk gravy with pieces of ham to go over them. "We will get you started and then feed the rest when they come down," Martha told them.

Mary decided to wait for her husband and her other daughter. They prayed for the food and the church service ahead. Kathy went through breakfast quickly. Her appetite was still demanding more food trying to make up for the many days she had gone hungry.

Bobby got his fiddle, and walked down to the Church with Kathy, Katy, and Alex. The Church was stuffy, and Bobby and Alex started opening windows to air it out. Kathy started practicing on the piano singing a couple songs she was going to sing solo. Bobby and Alex were filling some water barrels for people who would come by carriage and need their horses watered. Since Bobby was still occupied, Kathy practiced the songs she would sing with Katy. They were still busy outside when Kathy and Katy had gone through their songs. Kathy realized she had brought the sheet music for the song she had sung in Latin. She played it on the piano and was singing it as Clarence and Sally arrived and waited quietly outside. Bobby and Alex had stopped work to listen too.

"No wonder Julia thought she was hearing Angel voices," Clarence told them. An older couple that had come early was listening too.

"Who is she?" the woman asked, "her voice is so beautiful."

"Her name is Kathy, and her little sister is Katy. My wife and I have asked them to live with us," Clarence told them.

They all started singing together and did some songs they planned to use next week. Clarence went to a quiet spot to review his sermon notes while the rest of them tried different tunes together. Even Alex was singing along, and Kathy was delighted to hear he had a good singing voice. Kathy and Bobby decided to see if they could get his fiddle and the piano in sync and tried a lively tune, they both knew. They were having fun with it and didn't realize the church had started to fill up with some early arrivals. They got some applause when they finished and told the people they were just warming up.

"Well don't quit now," a lady told them, "we like free entertainment."

Kathy decided to do "All Creatures of our God and King" for the benefit of the early arrivals. Kathy would sing the melody in her soprano voice and Bobby would repeat it singing tenor. Their small audience seemed pleased. Even though it was summer, Kathy decided to play "Away in a Manger" on her flute and have Katy sing. Katy sang it out in her sweet clear voice.

"That was beautiful!" one woman exclaimed when they finished.

It was still some time before church, and they started talking to the early arrivals. They liked Bobby on the fiddle, but they were excited to get a piano player again. A couple women were talking to Katy surprised that someone her age could sing so well. Kathy explained that they were sisters that had come by train from Boston and were staying with Clarence and Martha. Kathy had a good memory for names but could not remember all the people she was introduced to.

Several little children she had helped at the bathhouse came running over and gave her a hug.

The Church continued to fill up with people including the Murdoch family. Clarence opened up the service with a prayer and then introduced Kathy and Katy to the church. "My wife met these two sisters on the train last week and talked them into coming to stay with us. I am so happy they came, and I am sure you will be too." The small group that would sing came up and they did the songs they had planned on.

Then Clarence spoke about his message: "Why does God allow sorrow, hunger, pain, and loss to come into our lives? The following heartfelt song by Kathy and Katy raises this question."

Kathy played her flute and Katy sang:

> **I love you Jesus, but you make me cry.**
> **Why did Daddy and Mommy have to die?**
> **You took my only brother too!**
> **I love you Jesus, but you make me blue.**
> **Someday take me home I pray.**
> **We will all meet in Heaven and sing that day!**
> **Until that day I will sing down here.**
> **Please hear my prayers and draw me near.**

The song caught most of the Congregation off guard. Katy had a puppy dog cuteness that made most people look at her and think "she is adorable." They felt for Kathy too but Katy with her sweet voice made every mother and most of the fathers want to hug their children a little tighter and think "Oh that poor little girl." A lot of people had to blow their nose wipe their eyes on their sleeves. Patty had become instant friends with Katy, and she was completely in tears, and she wasn't alone.

After Clarence finished his sermon, Kathy and Katy recited the 23rd Psalm and repeated the last verse joined by Clarence "and I shall dwell in the House of the Lord Forever." Kathy and Bobby finished with the song "All Creatures of our God and King" before Clarence gave the benediction.

Kathy wound up talking to a small group of people after the sermon. One woman told her that the music was the most wonderful she had ever heard.

"Music was a gift that God gave to me and Katy, and my mother said we needed to use it for God." Kathy told them how her father had been killed several years ago and then about her mother dying of pneumonia. "I was going to bring my little sister to my older sister in Kansas and then go back to Boston and try and find a job and a place to stay but I was afraid I would wind up homeless. I also hated to leave my sister Katy so coming to Clarence and Martha has been answered prayer for me. We love it here, but I miss my mother and father so much."

Kathy had been calm and matter of fact but suddenly she was in tears and had her hands over her face. Kathy had been a loving sister to Katy but had internalized a lot of her grief. Singing in church and feeling secure had finally released a lot of pent-up emotion.

Clarence, Martha, and Bobby were several feet away and Martha quickly came over and hugged and steadied her.

"I'm sorry I lost it," Kathy said, "but sometimes I have nightmares that Katy and I are hungry and homeless, and some creepy man is chasing us. I promised mother when she was dying that I would take care of Katy and thankfully she is happy here."

"My family will take care of you two and I think there is a church here that loves you too," Clarence told her.

"We are so thrilled to have you," a woman told her.

"Thank you all so much," Kathy said managing to regain control of herself.

Bobby felt overwhelmed with love for Kathy and the desire to always be her protector.

Kathy sat down at the piano again. Singing was her refuge from pain and sadness. She played and sang "Oh for a Thousand Tongues to Sing". Bobby joined in singing with her harmonizing perfectly. The church had started to empty out, but a number of people stopped or came back. Good music was a rarity in their world and some people would have listened to them all day long.

One older lady came over and told Martha that she could not imagine anyone that young being that good - "your son is wonderful and the way that young lady sings is like a gift from God and her little sister is so sweet."

"Both girls are a gift from God," Martha replied, "I wanted to help the two girls and they are repaying us back beyond what I could ever hope for."

Katy and Patty had gotten together after Church and Mary had given Katy a big hug. Other people came over and told Katy what a good singer she was.

"Kathy and I sing whenever we can, so I get a lot of practice. We also work on reading and memorizing Bible verses. I try to read one chapter of the Bible every day."

"I need to start doing that with my girls," Mary replied.

Sally and Alex had joined William, James, and Janice after the service. "Mother told me to invite you to lunch after Church. Julia is frying chicken and it should be really good," Sally told them.

"Sounds good," William replied. The sermon was a reminder to William again of the loss of his wife but also his need to move on. His children needed a mother and Sally would be perfect for them. Sally was a beautiful young woman and William realized he probably needed her even more than his children did.

CHAPTER 9

Lovesick

Bobby and Kathy had gotten through several more songs before Clarence and Martha told them it was time to come home and eat. Clarence told the remaining audience that they would be back singing next Sunday and to bring their friends and neighbors. They walked back to the patio where they were engulfed with the wonderful smell of fried chicken. Kathy and Martha helped Julia serve and then finally got a chance to sit down themselves. Sally and Mary also pitched in mothering all the children around them. After dinner Martha surprised Kathy by asking her to take all the girls into the bathhouse so Sally could spend some more time with William.

Once the girls got in the pool area, they all got undressed and everyone jumped into the pool except Kathy. A fully dressed Mary joined them a short time later. "You all look so comfortable; I'm tempted to take my clothes off and join you." She spoke to Kathy, who had taken off her dress and was putting on her swimsuit without bothering to use a changing room. Mary saw how thin Kathy was before she got her swimsuit on and realized how hard life had been for her.

"Your mother taught you how to play the piano but how did you learn to play the flute?"

"I kind of learned the flute by trial and error but my mother had a friend who helped me too."

"You should have a great future ahead of you," Mary replied.

"I hope so, but right now I'm just thankful when Katy and I can sing together and get our next meal," Kathy responded.

"You two are very good and Martha is more than willing to feed you," Mary replied. "Maybe you can teach my girls some songs."

"We will work on it," Kathy told her.

Mary told Patty and Bonnie to stay at the pool until she came back.

The combination of a good dinner and splashing around in cold water finally got everyone drowsy and they came out of the pool. Kathy retrieved her flute and started working with the girls to get them to sing. She would play the melody and get the girls to sing sometimes having Katy stay silent. The Murdoch girls had good voices but needed work while Janice was very good. They sang for quite a while before the girls started getting tired. Little Bonnie found a shady spot on the grass and fell asleep and was soon joined by Patty. Katy lay down on her bed.

Kathy and Janice started talking while sitting on the edge of the pool. Janice was thin and tall for her age, but she had a pretty face, and she was a very sweet girl. Kathy and Janice bonded in their sadness of losing their mothers. Kathy was touched when Janice told her that someday she hoped she could sing like her.

"Someday you may even be better," Kathy assured her.

"I remember a lullaby my mother used to sing," Janice said. Janice started it and Kathy joined her. They sang it beautifully and then wiped tears from their eyes when they finished.

"My mother used to sing it too, but I had kind of forgotten it; I need to remember it the next time I want to help a baby fall asleep," Kathy told her.

Janice and Kathy sat and talked. "Do you think Sally will marry my father?" Janice asked Kathy.

"Sally loved her husband a lot before he died just like your father loved your mother but sadly, they are both gone. Sally would be good for your father, and he would be good for her. Sally is very fond of you and James. Right now, you are trying to replace your mother, but wouldn't it be nice to have Sally doing the cooking, doing the laundry, and cleaning the house. Sally says you are a wonderful helper, but you need to be a child a little longer. Sally would be there to give you a hug when you need it. I think Sally will marry your father if he asks her and I think your father will ask her if he knows both you and James approve."

"It does sound nice," Janice said, "and I really like Sally. What about you and Bobby?"

"In just five days, Bobby and I and everyone around us have decided we are a perfect match which is probably not true, but I am hoping it is," Kathy replied. "I want to fall in love with him but I'm so afraid of having my heart broken. Still my mother told me that it is sad to lose someone you love but it would be sadder if there was nobody that you loved enough to cry for. If I marry Bobby, I could wind up being your aunt."

Janice laughed, "that sounds okay to me – I would love to have you and Bobby as my aunt and uncle."

"You two look like twins," Sally commented as she came up behind them. "You both need to eat more." Sally then jumped into the pool next to them and commented, "I think just about everyone has gotten wet except Julia, I don't know how she stands the heat. The Murdoches went upstairs to take a bath and the rest of the men are all next door getting wet. What have you two been doing?" Sally asked.

"We have been singing together. I have also told her that if you marry her father, you will do all the cooking, all the housework and all the laundry," Kathy teased.

"Laundry is easy," we will just wear the same clothes all the time," Sally joked. "Cooking is the hard part; we need to learn more of Julia's secrets for making everything taste so good." Sally looked at Bonnie sleeping and remarked that "everyone probably needed a nap. I had trouble sleeping last night after you and Bobby sang that love song. I wanted to have a man to hug and kiss so bad!"

"I kind of got carried away by the song," Kathy admitted, "we did sound kind of passionate didn't we?"

"You two were just way too cute last night," Sally replied, "you are driving my poor brother crazy."

Kathy giggled, "so what am I doing wrong?"

"Nothing, just don't break his heart," Sally replied, "I love him so much and he has been such a wonderful uncle to Alex."

Kathy started playing her flute again trying to match the tune of the lullaby she had just sang with Janice. "Janice, you sing; I will play." Janice dutifully sang as Kathy played.

"Janice, that was so pretty, we have got to get you singing!" Sally exclaimed when they finished.

"We need to get Alex and James to sing too, and you have a beautiful alto voice," Kathy told Sally. "My mother and I used to teach Sunday School and teach children to sing hymns; we need to do that here." The whole idea of teaching children came to Kathy as she was speaking.

"Sounds good to me," Sally replied, "but now I am going to take a nap; you got yours yesterday before you tried to seduce my brother."

"I was a sweet innocent little girl, he stole a kiss; I was nice enough not to slap him," Kathy protested.

"Did you really want to slap him?" Sally asked

"No, because I might want another kiss."

"You are too funny," Sally answered, "now that I have had my lullaby, I am going to sleep."

Kathy played a stanza of "Away in a Manger" on her flute and then sang it getting help from Janice. They did a couple more songs together and then talked about their mothers finding many similarities.

"My mother loved music and used to sing around the house," Janice said, "my father always encouraged her."

"We had a piano before my father died and my mother would play almost every night and we would all sing; it was so wonderful," Kathy told Janice. "Now I realize what a wonderful childhood I had and need to pass it down but sometimes I felt like my childhood was my Garden of Eden and I have been cast out never to return until death. Now I feel like I have been given a second chance to find happiness here on earth too."

"I feel like that too," Janice replied, "it sometimes feels like I am being punished and I don't understand why but I too am hoping life will become pleasant once more."

"Let's pray that God will give each of us a house full of love and music again," Kathy told her, and they sat there and prayed.

Kathy decided to keep singing doing all three verses of "Come Thou Fount of Every Blessing" from memory but she would sing each verse twice and have Janice join in the second time. "You have such a pretty voice," Kathy told Janice, "you need to carry on your mother's tradition of singing. Could you watch the pool for a few minutes; I am going to get dressed and see if anyone has come back to the patio." Kathy put her dress on and went out to the patio which was empty except for Julia working nearby in the kitchen. Kathy stood there for a few minutes and then Clarence and Martha came outside.

"Everyone at the pool is sleeping except Janice and she is watching the pool in case one of the children wakes up," she told them.

"I want try to sing "Joyful, Joyful We Adore Thee," it's very upbeat but I don't wake anyone," Kathy told them. Kathy wanted to believe that Bobby would marry her, and William would marry Sally. They would all be part of this wonderful community. She sang the song with the same fervor that she had sung the love song with Bobby. Kathy was facing the kitchen and bath area and didn't notice the Murdoches coming in behind her. She sang all four verses from memory and received applause when she finished. "Thank you," she told them, "it is my way of thanking God for letting me be here."

"Well, we are thanking God that you are here," Clarence told her.

Julia came out from the kitchen, "Child, I aint never heard anyone sing like you, it just makes my heart glad."

"Well, I never met anyone who could cook as good as you, you make my tummy glad," Kathy told her. Kathy gave Julia a hug and then got hugs from Martha and Clarence.

"Save a little of your singing energy for tonight after supper," Martha told her.

Bobby had joined them and told Kathy: "You sounded great!"

Bobby shrugged his shoulders and then winced, "I have got a kink in my neck probably from moving firewood yesterday." Kathy went behind him and proceeded to give him a neck and shoulder rub.

When she finished, giving him a rub, Bobby asked with a grin: "are we doing our love song again tonight?".

Kathy gave him a frown which changed to a smile. "No, people might think we are in love!" she told him.

Mary was standing nearby and teased, "we are already convinced of it so you might as well sing the song."

"I am not sure I am convinced yet," Kathy replied, "but he is awfully cute for a man. Okay, I will sing it but only if Sally and William are here."

"Why them?" Bobby asked.

"We might get them to fall in love too, sort of like misery loves company."

"You make love sound like a disease," Martha told her.

"It is, that's why people who have it are called lovesick," Kathy joked.

"You brought it with you from Boston," Bobby told her.

They stared at each other, and Kathy gave him a mischievous smile and then got the giggles.

Everyone laughed. "You two are something else, listening to you two talk is almost as much fun as listening to you sing," Mary told them.

Bobby had to admit to himself that he was lovesick. Kathy was so cute, sang so beautiful, he enjoyed her quick wit and that smile, and that giggle made him want to hug and kiss her so bad. He had never met a girl so fun to be around as her.

Kathy, Martha, and Mary went into the girl's bath area to join the girls and Richard Murdoch had walked down to the men's bath area leaving Bobby and his father alone.

"I thought you were immune to girls until Kathy came along," Clarence told Bobby. "Martha felt sorry for Kathy and Katy when she brought them home, but Sally was right, she brought you home a future wife."

"I admit it," Bobby replied, "I'm crazy about her but she is so smart and talented, it is almost scary. When she was talking to Mr. Murdoch last night, she sounded like one of my college professors."

"Well, your mother might be smarter than me but when you are married, you are a team, and a smart wife can make you seem a whole lot smarter too. The other thing is that you have worked hard physically while she has worked hard to learn stuff. I think you two are a great match, but life has been really hard on her and I think she needs some time to feel secure. Remember what she said in church about her having nightmares about her and her sister being hungry and homeless and threatened. Mary told Martha about talking to Kathy about Kathy having a great future and Kathy said was she was just thankful that she and Katy could sing and get their next meal. My advice to you is to sing with her, be her friend and don't try to rush her into getting married. The other problem for you is that if you get married now, you probably will have to give up on going back to college."

Bobby sighed, "I really would like to get another year of college and graduate but waiting until next spring to get married seems like forever."

Janice was still the only one not sleeping when the women went inside the women's bath area. "I think you also brought sleepy sickness from Boston when you came here," Martha teased Kathy.

"I don't think I brought it," Kathy replied." I think it comes from overeating all that good food that Julia and you are feeding us."

"I'm blaming Kathy," Mary said, "so when are you and Bobby getting married?"

"Sometime after I get fattened up, I will be sacrificed on the wedding altar," Kathy joked with a smile.

"You make it sound like torture, most girls would be excited," Mary exclaimed.

"I am, I can't imagine finding a better man, but I just met him six days ago and it is kind of overwhelming," Kathy answered. "A week ago, my younger sister and I were headed to my older sister who lives on a small dirt farm in Kansas with her husband and her two small daughters. She wrote and told me that Katy could share a small bedroom with her daughters, but I might be able to find a job as a live-in maid in a nearby town. Otherwise, I would have to return to Boston or maybe live in the barn or their pigsty – it didn't sound promising."

"They didn't really tell you might have to live with the animals, did they?" Mary asked.

"No but I was getting desperate enough to do it in order to stay with Katy. So now instead of living in a barn with animals I live in a bathhouse and run around half dressed."

"My girls think it's the neatest thing ever to run around in here without clothes on," Mary added.

"So does Katy, and we love being here. The children are adorable, and their mothers have been very nice. I try to keep myself somewhat covered up because I worry that some man might come in and see us," Kathy responded.

"We have never had that problem," Martha replied, "and Kathy always wears a bathing suit,"

"She looks really cute in it; have you shown it to Bobby," Mary asked.

"No, I am afraid if he saw how skinny I am, he might decide to fall in love with someone else," Kathy joked.

"I'm more worried he would get even more excited about you," Martha told her. "I will be very happy if you two get married but not immediately."

Kathy played her flute and Janice sang the lullaby again.

"Oh, that is so sweet," Mary exclaimed, "no wonder everyone is sleeping out here."

"Janice has a lovely voice," Kathy remarked, "I want to get her and some of the other children singing in church. I would also like to get some of the children together for a few days this summer so I could teach them Bible stories and teach them to sing Christian songs. My mother and I used to do that years ago."

"That is a wonderful thought," Martha told her, "I would love to help."

"It would be great if you practiced on my two girls this week," Mary told her.

"I did and it put them to sleep so I guess I need to make it a little more exciting," Kathy answered.

Mary decided to cool off in the pool and Martha went back to the patio. "Kathy and Janice sang a lullaby and put everyone to sleep," Martha told Clarence and Bobby when she came back. "How was the back rub," Martha asked Bobby with a smile.

"Kathy is right, I am lovesick over her, and that backrub felt so good," Bobby replied.

"I told him I approve of them getting married, but he needs to have some patience," Clarence told Martha. "I would also like him to get another year of college before he gets married."

"I fully agree, I think it is great they are in love but there is a lot to think about," Martha answered. "Kathy does not want to get separated from Katy and she seems to be doing a wonderful job of parenting her. It would be nice if we could all live close to each other, but I do not know if that's practical. Still Kathy and Katy are so wonderful to have around." Martha continued, "Kathy was talking about teaching the children Bible stories and teaching them to sing. Mary wants her to practice on her girls. I want to see how well she does because it would be really nice if she could assist me next fall in the school. I know Katy is smart, but she is at least a year ahead of any of the children her age and Kathy is probably part of the reason."

"Is Katy even ahead of Alex?" Bobby asked with surprise, "Alex is really smart!"

"He is smart, but Kathy has been pushing Katy really hard in math and reading," Martha replied. "Katy was reading a book on the train that I brought back for fifth graders and said it was an easy book to read. She read it nonstop for the next hour and almost finished it. I am going to go back to the bathhouse and watch the girls and see if Kathy can find some vegetables for supper tonight."

Normally Bobby was pretty talkative, but he was a good listener too. His parents had shown him his heart was getting ahead of reality. He needed to do some serious thinking. He needed to find a way to make money for himself and Kathy and probably Katy too. They also needed a place to live. They could move in upstairs where the Murdoches were now staying. Unfortunately, that would eliminate a chance for his folks to make money renting it out to people.

College had given him a lot of ideas about work he could do but he still hadn't decided on a vocation. Before he met Kathy, he had also thought it would be exciting to go out to Colorado or California. Singing with Kathy was so fun and the impact she had on him and everyone around her was crazy. He had never seen so many people hang around to talk after Church before. Kathy complemented his singing so well. With Kathy as his partner, living in this community suddenly seemed a whole lot more promising. He also decided to never make any more comments about dumb girls again since he planned on living with two that were super smart. He wasn't sure if God was giving him a reward or a punishment or a little bit of both.

Julia had made chicken soup with dumplings using leftover chicken and the vegetables Kathy had picked with help from Janice. Fresh bread and rhubarb dessert added to a good supper. William had stayed for supper and was sitting close to Sally. Kathy and Katy's little song had cracked the wall William had put around his heart. Bobby was right, Kathy had brought lovesickness with her from Boston.

Martha thanked Julia and let her go home after a long day. Kathy helped Martha serve and Janice volunteered to help pour coffee and water.

Kathy finally sat down next to Bobby and quickly finished a full bowl of soup plus some bread and dessert.

Mary was sitting next to Kathy and teased, "keep eating, you are not fat enough for the altar yet."

Kathy laughed, "but I can't get there in one night."

After supper Kathy started clearing the dishes again getting unexpected help from Janice. "Thank you, sweetheart," Martha told Janice, "it is so nice to have you around."

Bobby started playing some lively music on his fiddle and Kathy sang with him. Kathy got her flute out and played "Yankee Doodle" and Katy sang along. Kathy then played the lullaby with Janice singing the song. Bonnie curled up with her mother, Patty curled up with her father and Katy curled up with Clarence. William hugged Janice, "you sound just like your mother did."

Bobby and Kathy did a couple more songs before singing the love song again. After singing the last verse William stunned everyone by saying "my turn" and then singing the last verse to Sally in a wonderful baritone voice. Sally and William held each other close and kissed.

Kathy offered no resistance as Bobby held her close and he thrilled to the feel of her warm body next to him while they kissed which seemed to last forever. It was not long enough for either of them. Kathy was shocked at how much she enjoyed being physically close to Bobby.

Clarence watched both couples hug and kiss and told Martha "I think you need to plan for two weddings and a lot more grandchildren."

"That was quite a show," Mary announced with a smile, "I can hardly wait for tomorrow night's show."

"I will admit it, I am in love, but it didn't come from Boston, I think there is something in the water," Kathy joked to Mary.

Richard and Mary said goodnight and started carried their girls upstairs. "I am going to wait until we get upstairs before we do our hugging and kissing," Richard announced.

Katy was partially awake, and Kathy gave her a hug and sent her back to the bathhouse.

"Good night darling," Bobby told Kathy giving her another hug a and a kiss before reluctantly leaving with Alex who had gotten a hug from

Sally. Sally gave hugs to Janice and James before a lingering hug and kiss with William.

Katy was waiting for Kathy when she walked into the bath area. "How soon are you and Bobby getting married?".

"I don't know, I originally wanted to wait until next spring but now I want to get married a lot sooner but don't worry, I won't abandon you."

Sally interrupted them: "You are safe honey; they are going to need you for a babysitter." Sally then asked Kathy, "are you hoping for a baby boy or a baby girl?"

"I will think about that after I marry Bobby. Katy, you need to go to bed," Kathy announced deciding this was not a conversation for a little girl.

After Katy was put to bed, Kathy and Sally sat down near the kitchen and talked. "When you were taking your nap, I kidded Bobby that I would sing that love song again tonight only if you and William were present so we could cause you and William to be lovesick too."

"Well, it worked because we got pretty passionate," Sally replied. "It looked like you and Bobby were getting extra friendly too!"

"We were," Kathy admitted, "until tonight I felt Bobby was this wonderful man that it would be great to marry but for now, I just wanted him for a friend. When he held me close tonight it just felt so wonderful. Now I can hardly wait to get married to him."

Sally laughed, "you think you have a problem; Bobby is probably more ready than you are. I am really starting to like William and I am hoping he wants me as bad as Bobby wants you. Being in love is kind of like a sickness but it is such a sweet misery. Men have this need to have a woman but when I was married, I discovered how badly I needed a man. Now I am feeling that way again. I love the idea of you and Bobby getting married and I hope that William and I will be getting married too."

Kathy tried to go to sleep after praying that she and Bobby would get married. She wasn't sure if she should be thanking God or asking for forgiveness for how she enjoyed it when Bobby held her close. It did not seem possible that it was only a week ago since Katy and she were going to bed in Boston after getting ready to leave. She was now over thousand miles away and she had met her prince charming, and he wanted to marry her. In fairy tales you got married and lived happily ever after. Reality meant she would also get pregnant and have a baby. Remembering the young mother with the cute little boy and the adorable baby girl made that outcome seem a lot more positive.

Sally was right about Bobby; he was almost feverish with desire for Kathy. His mind had told him to curb his passion while he planned a future for the two of them plus Katy. He had been like a father to Alex, and he didn't mind the idea of being a father to Katy. Sally and his mother had told him that Kathy needed to gain weight, but she had felt wonderfully cuddly when he held her tight. He adored her as a person, but he realized his emotions included a lot of selfish desire too.

CHAPTER 10

From a Rainy Morning
to a Fun Afternoon

Kathy woke up Monday morning to the sound of rain. Katy and Sally were still sleeping as Kathy dressed quickly and headed for the kitchen. Martha was frying bacon and making batter for pancakes. Kathy helped by stirring the batter in a large mixing bowl. A tin measuring cup sat on the table that still had flour on it. "Do you measure your ingredients when you cook?" Kathy asked.

"Most of the time if I'm baking," Martha replied, "unlike Julia I am not very good at guessing how much of each ingredient to use."

"I know I would need one," Kathy replied, "I once saw recipe book for sale that showed how much of different ingredients to use to make different breads, cakes, and cookies. Someday I hope to buy one like it so I can keep your son happy if he decides to marry me."

"Bobby is ready, sounds like you are too!" Martha responded.

"I liked Bobby from the first time we met, and it was so great to sing with him, but I wasn't even thinking about getting married. Sally teased me about marrying him and it seemed logical to do so. Then Bobby stole a kiss and stole my heart."

"Well both Clarence and I are glad you two want to marry but I am a little concerned that it is happening too fast," Martha told her.

"My mind agrees with you, but my heart doesn't want to listen," Kathy replied.

"I understand," Martha answered with a smile, "I fell in love with him twenty years ago when I held the most adorable baby boy I had ever seen in my arms." Martha gave Kathy a big hug.

"Clarence is up and dressed, take the butter and syrup in, and put plates on the table from my kitchen cupboard. Then come back out."

Kathy ran through the raindrops and found Clarence already sitting at the table inside. "How is my future daughter in law?" he asked with a smile.

"Very happy," Kathy replied. She put the silverware on the table and then ran back to Martha. Moments later there was a flash of lightning and a crash of thunder that shook the bathhouse.

"That should get everybody up for breakfast," Martha joked.

A sleepy Katy came into the bathhouse kitchen followed by Sally a few minutes later. "That was a really loud wake up call," Sally joked, "is everything still standing?"

Martha started frying pancakes and putting them in a kettle for carrying over to the house. Bonnie came running into the bathhouse kitchen; "mother wants to know if we are eating downstairs."

They told her they were and would be starting in a few minutes. Kathy followed her to the bathhouse door and waved to Mary at the house as Bonnie ran back. Kathy was still at the door when Bobby and Alex came running to the house shortly after. Kathy came back into the bathhouse, told Katy to get dressed and then ran the first batch of pancakes into the house.

Richard and Clarence were talking at one end of the table with Bobby and Alex on the other side. Kathy dished up pancakes and Sally who had come in behind her poured milk and coffee. Sally sat down next to Alex and Kathy ran back to get more pancakes. Martha got more pancakes ready, and Kathy brought them back as Mary and her two girls showed up along with Katy. Martha made a few more pancakes before coming back with Kathy who was making her third trip and had gotten wet in the process.

Kathy was the last to eat and only had one pancake. Martha told her to fry some bacon and have some leftover bread when she went back to the kitchen. They decided to do the dishes in the bathhouse, so Kathy helped clear the table and made several trips to bring the dishes back to the bathhouse. Kathy had started a pail of hot water earlier before she did the dishes. She had some bread and bacon which satisfied her hunger. She also took her dress off which was now soaking wet from running back and forth through the rain. She toweled off and put her bathing suit on. She then washed and dried the dishes and stacked them on the counter in the bathhouse.

Normally the firepit was used to warm water for baths but it was still raining outside so Kathy decided to add more wood to the stove and heat water on top of it. Shortly after Mary came in with both of her girls along with Katy. All three girls hung their dresses up with help from Mary. Kathy still had her bathing suit on. "I am still heating some water so let's sing until we can warm up the pool," Kathy told them.

"We are going to go through the ABCs, and we want to come up with the name of an animal for each letter and imitate what it does or how it sounds. Letter A: name an animal ONE, TWO, THREE, ok how about antelope "The little antelope likes to bounce, bounce, bounce, bounce. Kathy stood on her toes and jumped in the air each time she sang bounce. Let's try that again. The second time they sang and bounced with her. ONE, TWO, THREE, Katy yelled out "bear". ok. The little bear likes to climb, climb, climb, climb. Kathy made climbing motions. The little bear likes to climb, climb, climb. The little cat likes to …., the little dog …" They didn't get very far through the alphabet before they all were getting silly and had the giggles.

It had stopped raining, but the wading pool was really cold. Kathy played her flute and had them sing "Yankee Doodle". She let Katy sing with them the first time and then do it without Katy's help. They were a little rough but got better on their second try. They then worked on "Away in a Manger" until they were able to sing it through.

"I am going to fill up two tubs so you can jump in the pool and then jump in the tub and warm up then go back to the pool." Kathy filled two tubs with a mixture of hot and cold water. The girls would squeal when they hit the cold water of the pool, Mary would help them out of the pool and Kathy would help them in and out of the warm tubs. It didn't take long for all of them to get tired. The sun came out and they went out by the garden to warm up in the sun. Kathy showed the Murdoch girls what the different kinds of vegetables looked like.

Julia had arrived and was working on lunch. "Do you think we could find enough peas for lunch," Julia asked.

"I think so," Kathy replied, "maybe I can get Katy to help." Katy reluctantly volunteered and then Patty decided to help. Patty and Katy started picking into one water bucket and Kathy into another. Their efforts weren't too successful and some of the peapods the girls had picked were small. Kathy put all the pods into one bucket and then shelled peas into the other. Kathy brought the shelled peas to Julia when she finished and was happy Julia said they would be enough. Kathy got a fire started in the firepit and got more water being heated. The day was getting both hot and humid. Kathy had thought of going back to the church where there was chalk and a blackboard plus the piano, but it would be uncomfortably warm.

Kathy was a little frustrated that Sally wasn't in the bathhouse helping her. Mary was sitting with her feet in one of the tubs that had warm water and Bonnie was in the other. "I am heating up more water and hopefully I will soon have the wading pool warm enough so the girls can jump back in," she told Mary.

"Sit down and relax," Mary suggested, "you don't need to provide entertainment for us every minute. Patty and Katy are doing cartwheels and they look like they are having fun."

"Thanks," Kathy replied.

"Well, you are doing fine," Mary replied, "Martha says you have been really busy since you came here."

"I love working here," Kathy answered, "before I came, I was sitting in a factory sewing clothes ten hours a day six days a week and trying to parent Katy."

"That sounds awful," Mary answered.

"It was but now I have it great and Katy loves it here. I also have this wonderful man who loves me and yes I do love him too."

"I am so glad for you two," Mary answered, "you seem perfect for each other."

While they were talking, June, the young mother with the baby girl and the little boy came in. "Can I hold her," Mary asked, and was rewarded with the little girl.

Bonnie had crawled into the tub with Mary using Mary's legs for a backrest. Patty had come over taking the tub Bonnie had just exited. Patty smiled at the little boy, and he came into the tub with her. It was very sweet, but Kathy felt a moment of intense sadness as she remembered taking a bath at about the same age as Patty and her mother putting her adorable baby brother in with her. He died of influenza a year later.

Neither of the pails over the firepit were very hot yet but Kathy was able to combine them and get one more bath ready for June. "I can't afford a bath," she told Kathy.

"Don't worry, it's free today," Kathy told her.

"My cousin has a little boy about the same age as yours and both of my girls want a baby brother to fuss over," Mary told June.

Mary moved over to a chair with the baby girl who went to sleep in her arms. All three girls played with the little boy and Kathy helped them as needed.

June came out of her bath cubicle and announced: "You are spoiling me, that bath felt so good. Taking a real bath in our cabin is almost impossible. My husband does carpentry and cement work and lately has been working in Williamsburg and only gets home a couple times a week. I wish he could get work closer to home."

June talked to Kathy: "I enjoyed the church service, but I was sad to hear you and your sister lost your parents. I loved listening to you and that man you were singing with."

Kathy laughed, "I just met the man who I was singing with 5 days ago when his mother invited me and my sister to stay here."

"And now they are in love," Mary added.

"Wow, that was quick," June responded."

"Sally who was with me last time you were here is also in love," Kathy added.

"By next year, we will probably have three new babies here," Mary responded. "I will have one, Sally will have one and Kathy will have one."

"Well first Sally and I need our future husbands to marry us," Kathy answered, "then a baby is pretty much inevitable."

Mary asked Kathy to sing the love song that she and Bobby had been singing to each other. Kathy hesitated and then sang the song. When she finished, June remarked that it was so beautiful it almost made her cry. Kathy then sang the song she liked that was in Latin.

When she finished Mary commented, "I don't know what you sang but it was unearthly beautiful like an Angel was singing."

"Thank you," Kathy replied, "it is a song about Mary giving birth to Jesus sung in Latin." Kathy sang a couple more hymns in English before June reluctantly decided to leave to do some chores at home. They encouraged her to come back during the week.

"You don't sound too enthused about having a baby," Mary remarked after June had left.

"I love babies and children," Kathy answered, "I would love to have a couple of beautiful children like June, and you have. I just hope my children don't wind up hungry or orphans like Katy and I did. I know I shouldn't think like that because we really have it nice here, so the Lord has been good to us."

"I am sure Bobby will take good care of you and your children, you need to be more trusting of the future," Mary answered.

"Thanks for the encouragement," Kathy told her. Kathy didn't disagree with Mary but between her family, Sally's family, and William's family there were five children missing a parent and four parents who hadn't lived to see their children grow up and a little boy who never got the chance. Mary decided to dress and go back to the house leaving her girls at the bathhouse with Kathy.

The wading pool was still cold, so Kathy added a bucket of hot water to it which helped plus it was getting warmer out. She decided to get all three girls in the water and then have them follow orders. First, she had to get Bonnie oriented to left and right. Right hand up, right hand down, left foot up, left foot down. Both hands up, both hands down etc. They did this for a while getting splashed and wet in the process but finally started doing coordinated movements as a group. She then let each girl in turn take over and call movements. They soon got the hang of mimicking each other's movements. Watching their amateur choreography Kathy wasn't certain whether she had taught them something useful or created a monster.

Sally came in and Kathy led the girls in a choreographed greeting that left Sally shaking her head. Kathy shook her head, and all three girls did too. Sally then made a series of movements which they all mimicked.

Finally, Sally said "quit, you are going to drive me crazy," but she was laughing. "You all need to get dressed so we can eat and then Bobby is taking us for a wagon ride." Kathy changed back to her dress that was now dry.

Kathy expected to stay back after lunch while the others went for a ride, but Martha asked her to bring her flute and help lead some singing while they were riding. James and Janice were also along and so were Richard and Mary. Sally and Alex were on too. Bobby and Richard had played two games of chess during the morning, and each won a game and were bantering who would win the next. Kathy couldn't resist asking, "Can I play the winner?"

"You wouldn't have a chance!" Bobby teased.

"I am not sure I dare play her," Richard said, "she might be pretty good."

"I'm betting on Kathy," Mary commented.

They decided to quit leaving it a draw and neither dared challenge Kathy.

It was the same wagon they had taken when they came from the train with a couple more bales of hay to sit on. They were barely underway when Richard suggested singing "When Johnny Comes Marching Home." The flute was the perfect instrument for this song except when the road got bumpy. Richard surprised her by doing a great job of leading the singing. Kathy was sitting high enough that she could stamp her feet on the floorboards wearing two cowboy boots from Bobby that he joked he outgrew in grade school. Richard picked up on it and did a cadence count left, right, left, right, one, two, three, four. A couple local boys jumped on the wagon and number of people came out of their houses and waved. They went through the song a couple of times adding more sound effects as they progressed. Both the stable man and the town blacksmith also came out to watch them go by.

When the song was finished, Kathy led them in "Onward Christian Soldiers." They then did "Battle hymn of the Republic" with Kathy on the flute, Bobby leading the singing and Richard using a stick to pound out a surprisingly good drumbeat. Martha, Sally, Mary, and Janice did a great job singing together. Kathy sang "America the Beautiful" with Richard and Bobby joining in. Shortly after Bobby led the horses into a shady area overlooking a small lake. It was a beautiful spot that had recently been mowed for hay. They got off the wagon and walked around.

Bobby had brought a bucket and went down to the lake and brought back water for the horses. Bobby also had brought jars of water and Martha had sent cookies. Bobby then sang "Oh Shenandoah" in his sweet tenor voice. Kathy responded by singing:

"Oh Shenandoah, I love you father but please be patient with me. Do not find me a man to marry, my love is across the wide Missouri. He has not left me for another, he will return to marry me. I will wait for him forever until he returns across the wide Missouri."

Bobby commented that he had never heard that refrain before. "I just made it up," Kathy replied.

"You continue to amaze me," Bobby replied.

When they finished singing Mary was cuddled up against Richard dabbing her eyes with her sleeve. "Why are you crying mother?" Bonnie asked.

"I am crying because I am so happy," Mary replied. "I have a wonderful husband; two wonderful daughters and I am listening to beautiful singing in a beautiful place on a beautiful day."

Bobby had brought his fiddle and decided to lighten it up a little bit. Kathy got Katy and the two Murdoch girls skipping to the music. Richard joined in having the girls come to him and then twirling them around and then sending them back toward Kathy. Sally got into the act with Janice, Alex, and James. It lasted just long enough to get all the children breathless and giddy. Even the two boys who had hitched a ride got pulled in. They would go home and tell their mothers about the great singing, the girls that were so pretty they didn't seem real and the best cookies they had ever eaten.

"Richard suggested that he drive the wagon back so Bobby could play his fiddle. It only worked if Richard drove really slowly. They decided to do "When Johnny comes Marching Home" just before they returned to the village. It was repeated numerous times with floorboards used for marching sounds and Kathy playing the melody on her flute. Numerous children started to follow the wagon as they got near their village and more people came out as they came to the village and waved at them. Everyone was a little sorry that their little trip had ended that had been full of so much music, love, and laughter. They closed with one more song and reluctantly got off the wagon before Bobby took it back to the livery stable.

The boys headed for the boy's bathhouse. The three girls all ran for the girl's bathhouse. "Keep my girls until I come for them," Mary asked Kathy and Sally before she went upstairs following Richard. Kathy put her flute away, took her boots and dress off and changed into her bathing suit. She wanted to crawl into bed for a nap. The kitty was sleeping on Katy's bed. Kathy petted it and then buried her face in its soft fur. Kathy was tempted to curl up next to it. The ride had been so great, but now she felt hot and tired.

Kathy jumped into the adult pool which was cold enough to temporarily shock her fully awake. Refreshed she joined Sally and the children in the wading pool. "That ride was so fun, and everyone did their part to make it great so what do we do next?" she asked Sally who was sitting on the edge of the pool watching the girls.

"We sit here and do nothing – actually we need to talk." Sally continued, "thanks for taking care of the children this morning, I needed to spend some time with Alex. Alex and James are buddies and they both like Janice so I think the children will get along great. The problem for Alex is that Bobby has been like a father to him, and he is concerned that William won't be so easy to get along with. I am going to encourage William to try to interact more with his children and I know he cares about them. Bobby has said he expects to be a father for Katy when you get married, and I think Alex is a little jealous of Katy."

"I wouldn't marry Bobby if Katy wasn't included and I was almost afraid to ask," Kathy replied. "I am hoping we can keep our families close together after we are married. I am going to suggest to Bobby that he tell Katy that when he marries me, she comes with. I will also let Alex know that he will be welcome at our house."

"Sounds like Bobby has really won you over, you were still hesitant about getting married a few days ago," Sally commented.

"I am ready, but Bobby needs a job, and we need a place to live, Kathy answered."

"Well at least that is not a problem for William and me, but he hasn't proposed either," Sally responded."

"Neither has Bobby but you and your mother, have made it pretty clear he is ready," Kathy replied. "It all started when you began teasing us that first night I was here," Kathy joked.

"It was going to happen no matter what I did," Sally replied, "I talked to Bobby before supper that first night and he was so excited about you, kind of like when he got Shep as a puppy."

"So, I am his new puppy," Kathy joked, "hopefully Shep won't get jealous and bite me."

"That cry song you had Katy sing got William out of his shell, but I don't think he is ready to admit he needs me as bad as Bobby needs you. You have caused so much to happen in six days here, what are you going to do on day seven.?"

"Do I get a day of rest?" Kathy asked.

"No," Sally replied, "you talked yourself into something. Martha wants all the children at the church tomorrow morning to hear a Bible story and practice singing. I will be there for adult supervision, but you are in charge."

"Is the adult supervision for me or the children?" Kathy asked with a smile.

Sally laughed and replied "both."

"If we had stayed here in the bathhouse, we could be naked and talk about the Garden of Eden," Kathy joked.

"That won't work, James and Alex are going to be there too, and I might recruit the boys that tagged along earlier today and a couple children near town," Sally answered.

"I was just kidding," Kathy responded, "I will start with some simple songs like "Away in a Manger" and "Tell me the Stories of Jesus". Then I will probably cover the Ten Commandments and the Lord's Prayer." Kathy's head was spinning but she was actually looking forward to the challenge. "How come Martha won't be there?" Kathy asked.

"The men are all going fishing including my father and William, so mother is going to run the store. Richard is interested in talking to William about him making oak furniture to sell at his department store in St Louis. Alex and James want to go too but I think this is more about business than fishing, so they don't want to be bothered with children."

CHAPTER 11

Bible School

Bobby opened up the church windows before heading off with the men on the fishing trip. All the children that were on the previous days ride were there plus four new children bringing the total to twelve. Mary had come with Sally and a mother that Kathy didn't recognize. Kathy introduced herself, telling the children she had taught singing and Sunday School with her mother and was looking forward to teaching them. Introductions were made and a few rules were given, and they got started.

Kathy played the piano and started singing with "Away in a Manger" and then "Tell Me the Stories of Jesus". She would sing a line and then have the children repeat it. Kathy then talked about the Bible and how it started with God's creation of everything and then the first man and the first women. She talked about how "God created us in his image which means God has given everyone the ability to think, to remember, to be creative and to love one another and to love Him." Kathy talked about the greatest commandment "which is to love God and to love our neighbor as we love our self."

She then sang "Onward Christian Soldiers." The point of this song is that we are to win the war against evil with love, God's Word, and prayer rather swords and bullets. Kathy then led them in the song "Take my Life and Let It Be." Kathy then went back to prayer and talked them through the Lord's Prayer and what each part of it meant. She then had them all fold their hands and recite the Lord's Prayer. Kathy then gave them a short break.

Martha had sent some cookies along with Sally which were a big hit with the children.

"Great job," Mary told her at the break.

Pam, a young mother came up to Kathy. "I need this class as much as my little boy."

"I am so glad you came," Kathy told her.

After the break, Kathy went back to the Old Testament and the Ten Commandments given by God to Moses. Kathy wrote the Ten Commandments on the blackboard and then went over what each one meant. She also explained how we break the commandments by what we think as well as what we do and that is why we need to ask God to forgive us our sins every day. One boy asked about soldiers killing other soldiers in a war. Kathy told them that God was with the Israelites when they battled and killed their enemies, but we need leaders who try to avoid war without giving up our freedoms. We can be proud of our country she told them and then sang "America the Beautiful." She then prayed over the class urging them to bring other children the next day.

Kathy played and sang a few more songs. She got out her flute and played 'When Johnny Comes Marching Home". Katy led off the singing but when Kathy repeated the line Sally, Mary, Janice, and Alex joined in adding the marching sounds as well. Kathy did a couple more Christian songs before they were invited to come over by the bathhouse for lunch. Pam and all the children came.

Lunch was buttered bread with either jam or pieces of ham. Some of the children put both together and pretty soon most of the children were doing it. Kathy tried it too and it tasted wonderful. Pam's little boy had just turned four and Pam admitted she hadn't been in church since she was a little girl. Billy, her little boy had wanted to come. Pam said she never liked Church as a little girl but today it was so happy and cheerful.

"God loves us, forgives us and cares for us and has a place for us in Heaven," Kathy told her. "Things on earth can be pretty hard but in the end; Christians will all be in Heaven."

Katy came over to tell her that all the girls were going swimming. Kathy held Katy up long enough to introduce her to Pam as her little sister. After Katy left, Kathy added that since both of their parents had died, she had become her mother too. "Sally and her parents have taken us in here and we just love them and love being here." Sally had gone into the store to relieve Martha and she came outside.

"Hi Pam, I am so glad you came with Billy," Martha told Pam as she joined them.

"Based on what Sally told me, I will want you to assist me in teaching school next winter," Martha said turning to Kathy.

"I would love to help," Kathy replied, "the children were great, and I really enjoyed doing it."

"You were so good, I am so glad I sat in on the class," Pam told Kathy. "We will be back tomorrow, but I need to go now. Thanks for the wonderful lunch."

"Clarence will be back tomorrow so I can take in your class," Martha told Kathy after Pam and Billy left.

"Hopefully, it will go as good as it did today," Kathy replied. "I want to review some of what I covered today but I need to add new stuff to make it interesting. I wish we had song books because the children have trouble remembering the words to the songs."

"It would help in church on Sundays also but the donations we get aren't enough to afford them," Martha replied. "I better get back in and run the store so Sally can help out at the pool."

Kathy changed quickly into her bathing suit and found Annie, one of the girls who had come to the class standing next to the pool with her dress on looking very uncertain. Kathy convinced her it was okay to take her dress off. She grabbed tightly to Kathy's hand, and they slowly moved into the wading pool. Annie was soon splashing happily in the water but always made sure Kathy was close by. Annie was so sweet and reminded Kathy why Sally loved being with the children at the pool. Bonnie came over and the two girls played together.

Mary came in with her dress on but sat on the edge of the pool with her feet in the water. "All the children are so cute; I just love it here," she told Kathy.

"They are all so precious," Kathy replied. "Katy thinks this is the nicest place on earth and so far, it has been."

Ellen, Annie's mother had dropped off her daughter at the church and was told by Sally they might have come over by the store for lunch. She was relieved to have tracked down her daughter but surprised to see her in the water. "Hi honey, having fun?" Annie waved at her mother and gave her a big smile. "How did you get her in?" she asked Kathy. "She has always been afraid of water."

"I just took her hand and she walked in with me," Kathy replied.

Ellen sat down next to Mary and put her feet in the pool. "Who's the little girl with my daughter? she asked.

"That is my younger daughter, Bonnie," Mary answered.

"Oh, this water feels so good," Ellen exclaimed, "I feel like jumping in myself."

"Go ahead and I will join you," Mary told her, "it is really getting hot today."

Both of them went to the dressing rooms and put-on bathing gowns before going over to the adult pool. They left Kathy to look after Bonnie and Annie though other children were not far away.

Kathy got out of the pool and quickly retrieved her flute. She started playing tunes on her flute while keeping a close eye on the children in the pool.

Ellen turned to Mary, "this feels wonderful, and the music sounds so pretty. I feel like I have stepped into another world."

"You have," Mary replied, "because Kathy is one of the nicest and most talented young ladies you will ever meet. "

Janice and Katy came over and asked Kathy if they could practice the lullaby song. Kathy played it and the girls sang it beautifully. Mary asked Kathy to do her song in Latin.

When Kathy finished, Ellen turned to Mary, "I am just in awe, I have never heard anything as beautiful as those last two songs."

They watched as Kathy got back in the pool and gave a hug to Bonnie and Annie. She then got them moving in a circle with Katy and Janice making identical movements while singing a song. Patty joined the circle and Sally joined Ellen and Mary in the adult pool. Kathy had made up a funny song "touch your nose, touch your toes, touch your lips, touch your hips" until they were giggling too hard to continue.

"I don't want to leave but I need to go home," Ellen said reluctantly. "We will be back tomorrow; it has been great for both of us."

Sally got Ellen and her daughter a towels to dry off before they got dressed. Kathy got a goodbye hug from Annie and a thank you from Ellen.

"I am so glad you brought her," Kathy told Ellen, "she is so sweet."

The men had returned with a good catch of fish and Clarence had relieved Martha in the store. Martha met Ellen and Annie just as they came out of the bathhouse. "Did you have a good time?" Martha asked.

"I had the best day ever!" Annie declared.

"We will be back tomorrow," Ellen added with a smile.

Martha went into the bathhouse and encouraged Kathy to take a nap. "You will be teaching and singing tomorrow, and I want you to sing tonight too." Kathy didn't feel tired, but she was asleep shortly after laying down.

Sally woke Kathy up in time to help serve. Julia had worked her magic on the fish, and it was crispy breaded perfection with spice that enhanced its flavor. It smelled wonderful and Kathy hoped she would get some. She was surprised that June was there with her husband Ned and their two children. Kathy discovered that Ned had been hired to start building samples of oak furniture. Bobby surprised her by telling her to sit down and eat and he would pour coffee which he did very well. Kathy was used to good seafood in Boston, but the fish was just about the best she had ever eaten. Served with new potatoes, it was a feast. William and Richard were both excited about the furniture venture. For June and Ned, the job was like a dream come true. Bobby was involved too, and Kathy wasn't sure how.

Bobby and Kathy were asked to sing after supper. After a couple of songs, Mary asked Bobby to sing "Shenandoah" with Kathy doing her refrain. After they had finished Mary said she liked Kathy's refrain but said it sounded so sad. They did the lullaby with Kathy playing the flute and Janice singing it which made everybody sleepy. A couple songs later Bobby and Kathy ended with their love song.

June and her husband picked up their sleeping children. "Goodnight, thanks for the job and thanks for one of the best meals and the best singing we have ever heard."

William and Sally had sat next to each other and cuddled up while Kathy and Bobby were singing. Both couples had a long kiss and embrace before heading off separately and reluctantly for bed.

Day 2 of Kathy's little school started with Martha waking them up. Sally was going to be there again but so was Bobby and Martha. During and after breakfast, Kathy worked out with them what she planned to do. Two more children joined the class bringing the total to fourteen. Kathy started by playing the piano and Bobby joined her singing "Holy, Holy, Holy, Lord God Almighty early in the morning our songs shall rise to you..." with Martha and Sally also joining in. Bobby then did a really fast tune on his fiddle.

"Okay, I think everybody is awake now including me, so we are going to get started," Kathy announced. She repeated the rules and prayed for the class. "I will be playing the piano and singing a line of a song and then I will play it again on the piano and you will sing it." She did the songs "Away in a Manger" and "Tell me the Stories of Jesus" again with the children. They then reviewed the Ten Commandments and the Lord's Prayer.

Richard Murdoch was sitting in on the session with Mary and Kathy had him read the part where God tells Adam and Eve not to eat of the tree of good and evil. Kathy played Eve and convinced Bobby playing Adam that it is okay to eat the fruit (a large strawberry). Kathy took a bite and told Bobby it was delicious. Bobby takes a bite. They then threw a blanket over themselves yelling "God is going to see us - let's hide." Richard pulls the blanket off and demands to know why they have eaten the fruit they have been forbidden to eat.

Bobby playing Adam tells Richard playing God "it is the fault of the wife you gave me" blaming Eve.

Kathy playing Eve who replies that "well you should have stopped me, and you didn't."

Richard playing God announces they will be cast out of the garden, and they will have to earn their food by hard work.

Martha then stepped in front of the class and said that this was an illustration of what happened a long time ago where the first man and woman sinned by disobeying God and were cast out of their perfect garden. Men and women have had to live in a sinful imperfect world ever since, but God has given all of us a chance to rejoin him in a perfect world which is Heaven. Kathy is now going to play herself instead of Eve and tell you about it.

"I am glad that I am Kathy and not Eve, so I am not the wife who talked her husband into disobeying God and plunging the world into sin. Think about what happened to Adam and Eve the next time you are tempted to take a cookie after your mother tells you not to. Your mothers love you and wouldn't be that hard on you. Fortunately, God loves us too and sent down his son, the little Lord Jesus who started out as a baby and grew to be a perfect man who allowed himself to be killed by sinful men as a sacrifice for our sins. It says in the Bible in John 3:16 that whosoever believes in Jesus shall not perish but have everlasting life. When we believe in Jesus, when we die, we will go to Heaven and live there with Jesus forever."

"Now I am going to have you all stand up and form a long line and start marching around the room when we start singing. I will be playing my flute, so I need some help on the singing "When Johnny Comes Marching Home." Kathy then designated one end of the room as home. She started the song with the children all marching. Then she had the name of each kid called out and they would march down the aisle. "When Alex comes marching home, when Bonnie comes marching home, etc." With a cheer when each kid reached home. Then Kathy read the passage in Luke about how Angels in Heaven cheer when sinners turn to Jesus. Okay time for recess and a cookie break.

Kathy thanked Richard and Bobby for their help in the program. They announced they were leaving to meet up with Ned to look at some lumber that William was having specially cut to be used in furniture. Mary teased Kathy that Richard had a big enough ego without him playing God. Martha told Kathy she was doing a great job.

"I am going to grab Sally and head back to help Julia. I think it would be easier to serve lunch here then to try to squeeze everyone into our patio," Martha announced.

It took a little bit to get the children settled down for the next session. Kathy decided to sing "Amazing Grace" from memory while walking around the classroom. Martha and Sally had started to leave but stopped to listen. Martha turned to Sally when Kathy finished and quietly said "wow."

"Her singing is unreal," Sally responded.

Kathy then sat down at the piano and led the class in singing "I Love to Tell the Story of Jesus and His Love." Afterwards Kathy talked about how sometimes when we are disobedient, we are punished by our parents. "It doesn't mean they no longer love us, but they need to make us behave for our own good. I grew up in Boston which is a big city with a lot of horses and carriages. I liked to run and jump while my mother liked to walk nice and proper and hold my hand, so I didn't get hit by a horse and carriage. Well one day just before Christmas I got free, and I ran and jumped not watching where I was going. A horse knocked me down and I got a bad bruise on my knee. Well, my mother would go downtown at Christmas and play a piano and sing Christmas Carols at a large fancy store. I loved to go there with her and sometimes she would play the piano and I would get to sing a song. My mother punished me by making me stay home the next two days with my older sister who wasn't too happy about staying home with me either. I learned to hang onto my mother's hand and watch where I was going after that."

"If we are doing things that are wrong God may allow bad things to happen to us as punishment for our sins. Then if we stop doing the bad things and ask God to forgive us, he will forgive us."

"Sometimes God allows bad things to happen to people who are not being punished but even if bad things happen on earth, you will be rewarded in Heaven. We spend only a short time on earth, but Heaven is forever. My mother was very sad after my father and my little brother both died. Without my father's income we were very poor despite mother working very hard, so she sold her piano which she loved to play. A year ago, my mother got very sick, and I prayed very hard for God to let her live. The last thing she told me before she died was that she was going to Heaven to be with my father and my little brother. I promised her I would take care of my little sister. I was glad my mother was in Heaven, but I felt like God had failed me and my little sister and we were both very sad. Last year after my mother died, I had trouble praying because it didn't seem like my prayers were being answered. That was a mistake."

"We need to keep praying to God and asking for help. It is just over a week ago that my sister and I were homeless orphans riding a train across the country hoping my older sister would take us in even though she had written that she barely had room for one of us. I was desperate. I kept praying to God that my younger sister and I could stay together. God answered my prayers. We met Martha on the train who told us we could both live with her family. Living with her family and being here talking and singing with you about my Lord and Savior is so much more than anything I could ever have hoped for."

"We are going to do another song – "Savior Like a Shepherd Lead Us." When they finished the song, Martha and Sally were back with lunch for the children and it was also offered to several mothers who had stayed. Kathy led the class in singing "Be Present at Our Table Lord."

Kathy picked up little Annie who hugged her tight and carried her over to her mother. "Are you coming over to the bathhouse again?" Kathy asked Annie's mother.

"I should be home working," she replied, "but that is too nice to pass up."

Mary joined them greeting her warmly. Kathy admitted she was afraid she would dissolve into tears when she talked about losing her mother.

"That sounded so sad," Ellen told her.

"I will admit it, last year there were a lot of times when I really wanted to die and go to Heaven too, but I felt I had to be strong for the sake of my sister Katy," Kathy replied.

"It is not just Katy who needs you, your ability to sing touches so many people," Mary told her.

"You have really ministered to me," Pam told Kathy. Kathy picked up Billy who also gave her a big hug.

After lunch they headed back to the bathhouse. Alex took Billy over to the boy's side. Annie and Bonnie played while all three mothers talked in the adult pool. Kathy had put on her bathing suit to help with children and Janice was also helping.

Martha came in and said she would watch children if Kathy would try to pick some peas, string beans and rhubarb for supper. Kathy didn't get a lot of peas and string beans, but she was able to get a lot of rhubarb. She got a knife from Julia and worked on getting the vegetables ready for cooking and the rhubarb ready to make rhubarb crisp. She noticed that the garden needed weeding but that would have to wait until the end of the week.

Kathy remembered that they had promised Julia help to bring back her granddaughter. She hoped maybe Julia could ride with the Murdoches so she would not have to travel alone. Kathy realized while talking to the children what a precious gift she had inherited in Katy. She loved Katy so much. Kathy also realized that decisions she had made because of Katy had resulted in her coming with Martha. She loved Martha, Clarence, Sally, and Bobby and now she was teaching these wonderful children. The words to "Lord Jesus, I Love Thee" came into her mind and soon her singing was floating through the whole bathhouse.

Pam listened to the song and had to wipe away tears. "I am so happy I'm crying," she said.

"I feel the same way," Mary told her.

During supper, William, Richard, and Bobby were all talking about their plan for making and selling oak furniture. They were confident it could be done but they were concerned about solving several problems including getting wide enough boards and consistently making the furniture the same.

Kathy mentioned working in the garment factory and having a pattern glued to a board and then one hundred pieces of material would be cut exactly the same and then every seam would be sewed exactly the same. "It was so boring, but you never had to measure or think. You just did one right after another."

William responded, "somehow we have to build furniture the same way."

"You mean sew it together," Richard said with a laugh.

"No, we have a pattern and cut a hundred boards to be exactly the same and then fasten them together exactly the same," William replied.

They then got talking about whether they should ship them finished or assemble them in St Louis. Kathy wanted to hear more of the discussion but dutifully helped with clearing the dishes and washing them since Julia was allowed to leave after a very busy day.

Singing was cut short because everyone was tired, and Bobby and Kathy did not do their love song. At the request of Mary, Kathy did sing "Amazing Grace" one more time. Clarence asked her to do it again on Sunday morning. They finished with Kathy playing her flute and Janice singing the lullaby. Bobby kissed Kathy and said, "goodnight Eve" you led me astray," he said teasingly.

"You didn't stop me," Kathy replied.

Kathy managed to wake up early and sat in the sun out in the garden trying to collect her thoughts for the day. She needed to review the songs again and she wanted the children to do at least one song by themselves on Sunday morning. The sun was already hot, so she got out of the sun and started working on getting the stove ready for cooking breakfast. She was joined by Martha and paid close attention as Martha put together the ingredients for pancakes. Kathy stirred the batter and then helped Martha set the table. "Ready for today?" Martha asked.

"Not really, "Kathy replied, "first couple hours we will do review, but I am a little uncertain what I will do next."

"You might do the 23rd Psalm or the love chapter in Corinthians," Martha suggested.

"Good suggestions, I will also remind children that Jesus loved the little children," Kathy replied. "Do you want to cover some stuff with the children?" Kathy asked.

"No, you are doing great, I might just make a few announcements," Martha replied, "but take some time right now with your Bible."

By the time they sat down and ate breakfast, Kathy was ready. The day went really well, and Martha was so excited about Kathy helping her teach school. Kathy loved the children, and she was excited about teaching too.

CHAPTER 12

Good News Bad News

Martha talked to Mary about allowing Julia to accompany them back to St Louis and she said there would be no problem. "We have an extra room she can stay in too." Mary conferred with Richard who agreed but joked he might hire her away to be their new cook.

Bobby sat down next to Kathy and asked her if she had any more apples to give him. "No apples, no strawberries, no kisses under a blanket," Kathy replied.

"What kisses?" Bobby asked. "That's right, you didn't get any. You missed your chance," Kathy teased and then got the giggles.

"I was a little worried about what might be going on under the blanket. I didn't know if I dared pull it off in front of all those innocent children," Richard joked.

Kathy had turned away from Bobby to look toward the kitchen when he tapped her on the shoulder, she turned to face him, and he kissed her on the lips. "I didn't miss this chance," he announced with a grin. Kathy gave him a frown and motioned like she was going to slap before smiling back at him.

Kathy then joked that she might never eat another strawberry without feeling guilty. Mary responded that Kathy had made a whole room full of children worry about eating another cookie.

Sally joined in: "Bobby wouldn't steal a cookie, he would just wait for mother to go inside and plead with Julia which usually worked for both of us."

The Saturday departure of Richard and Mary came too soon for almost everyone. Patty and Bonnie didn't want to leave, and Katy and Patty were both tearful when they hugged each other goodbye. Mary said how much she wished she could stay and enjoy the singing. She also told Sally and Kathy that she would be waiting for two wedding invitations. Over the years Martha and Mary had forged a deep bond of friendship both being passionate in their love for their own children and other children they came in contact with.

The only person who was excited was Julia who was leaving with them hoping she could have her granddaughter come back with her for the summer. Kathy had given Julia money that had been saved for a return ticket to Boston if she would have had to leave Katy at her older sister. For Kathy, having to go back to Boston was no longer a concern.

The travelers had left midmorning to catch the train. Alex and Katy were playing checkers in the patio with friendly but intense rivalry. Kathy decided to start catching up on weeding the garden since nobody had arrived yet for baths or cooling off in the pool. She told Katy to come in and let her know if anybody came. Kathy had decided to always wear her bathing suit while working in the bath area or garden. This morning it felt a little tight. Kathy patted her hip. She was starting to fatten up from eating well but the wedding altar no longer felt like a place where she would be sacrificed. She worked hard at weeding and was ready for a break when Katy told her lunch was ready. Katy also bragged about beating Alex in checkers.

She spent the afternoon taking care of mothers and children. Sally joined her later in the afternoon after helping Martha tidy up the upstairs after the Murdoches left. Martha had decided to wait until Monday to wash the bedding. Martha also mentioned that they would have a young couple on their honeymoon coming in Monday.

Kathy was tired but did her best to entertain the sweet little girl in her arms finally passing her off to Sally who kept her smiling and giggling. Kathy went and got her flute and started playing the lullaby song and Katy came over and sang it.

"That was so sweet," the mother said when they finished the song. When the mother left with her little girl, she thanked all three of them for a wonderful time.

"Well, we don't get rich, but we make a lot of children and mothers happy," Sally remarked.

"I am exhausted," Kathy replied, "but let's see if we can make your mother happy by helping her with supper."

Martha put Sally to work mixing up batter for pancakes while Kathy cut up and fried small pieces of ham. "I appreciate what you girls are doing for Julia, but I think we are going to realize how much work she does when we have to do all the cooking next week," Martha remarked.

Kathy and Sally helped serve before sitting down to eat themselves. Pancakes again and Kathy remembered how Bobby wanted to hold her in his lap the first time she ate them. It was not a proper thing to do but cuddling up to Bobby seemed awfully tempting to Kathy as tired as she felt. She drank some more coffee, and it helped a little.

They agreed on the music for the Sunday service including having the children sing the one song. Kathy helped clear the table before Martha sent her to bed. She fought sleep long enough to pray for the Sunday service and for Julia bringing Jade back.

The service went really well, and the children did great, they got a round of applause when they finished. Kathy and Bobby sang "Amazing Grace" together and received many compliments after the church service. One elderly lady told Kathy that she had been waiting all week to hear her again and that song you two did was the most beautiful I have ever heard. Kathy thanked her and gave her a hug while telling her how much she loved singing at the church. Annie came running over and Kathy picked her up.

Lunch was a little quieter than usual. Sally had gone over to make lunch for William and his family taking Alex with her. It was great to see Sally and William starting to get closer together, but they all realized how much they would miss her if she married William and moved out. Kathy had grown to love the bathhouse where they could make mothers and little children happy. She would help keep the bathhouse going if Sally left but where would she live with Bobby after they also got married.

Martha had praised the Bible School Kathy had done with the children and was excited about Kathy helping to teach grade school in the fall.

Kathy was excited about it too, but she also wanted to get a sewing machine and start making clothes and what about Bobby? Maybe if I she married him this summer, could they live upstairs where the Murdoches had stayed. Her daydreams for the future were about as fragile as a soap bubble and burst just as quickly.

Bobby started talking about Richard's plan for building the oak furniture. "He wants to build a factory in St Louis and do most of the assembly and finishing work there. He has asked me if I would be willing to go there and help run the factory."

Kathy's heart sank. It was good news that was also bad news. She could not imagine anyone as young as Bobby being trusted to run a factory and she did not want to go with him to St Louis.

Kathy decided to sing a slightly altered version of her "Shenandoah" refrain. "The man I love is across the wide Missouri. He has not left me for another, he will return to marry me. I will wait for him forever until he returns across the wide Missouri."

"Actually, St Louis is across the wide Mississippi, and I was really hoping you would go with me," Bobby said as he looked at Kathy. Kathy was glad Katy had gone back into the bathhouse with her kitty.

"Katy is so happy here that I hate to drag her away to St Louis and I love it here too," Kathy answered. "However, I will go after we get married if you can find a place for all three of us to live."

Bobby admitted that it could take a while since Richard said that he would be busy for a long time after they started.

They both sat there quietly for a while realizing reality was not giving them what they had hoped for. Kathy was thinking that her fairytale romance was facing some serious challenges before they even got to the part where they married and lived happily ever after.

Martha excused herself and went back into the house. Clarence followed her into the bedroom and found her in tears. "I like the idea of Sally and William getting married. I just adore Kathy, so I want Bobby to marry her but if everyone leaves, I am going to be so lonesome," Martha lamented.

"Maybe we could at least have Katy stay here until Bobby and Kathy get more settled," Clarence suggested.

"Katy is such a dear child that I would love to keep her, but I was so excited about Kathy helping me teach this year," Martha replied. Martha got herself composed and went back out to the patio.

They had finished eating lunch and Martha started picking up the plates. Kathy volunteered to help but Martha suggested that Kathy and Bobby needed to talk.

"She is right about that," Bobby commented, "my life was pretty predictable until you and Richard came along and now it's crazy. I will turn down the job in St Louis if you want me to, but it is quite an opportunity."

"I don't want you to turn it down for your sake and mine," Kathy replied. "I don't expect you or us to live off your parents and I know how hard it is to make enough money to live on. My mother struggled after my father died and I struggled last year. I had hoped to go to my sister, but they are struggling to make a living off their farm in Kansas."

"I might be struggling too," Bobby replied, "we haven't discussed pay and I don't know how soon we will get started in St Louis. William is kind of struggling too. He needs to diversify because there are not enough hardwoods close by to keep cutting them up for flooring. He can get a lot more value out of one oak tree cutting it up for furniture rather making planks for floors. Ned is a good carpenter, but he has always made furniture one piece at a time using fairly labor- intensive methods. Making large quantities of furniture on a production line is kind of hard for him to accept but he desperately needs the job. William can only do so much with his sawmill. Ned may have to cut fifty smaller pieces exactly the same using a hand saw. Then they load them all up and send them to St Louis where we screw, glue, or nail them together making lots of furniture that looks the same and goes for about half the price of furniture made out East. Some improvements may be necessary because I am not sure we could have sold the first one we built for even a third of the price."

Kathy shared her thoughts with Bobby. "Two weeks ago, Katy and I were packing up stuff up in Boston. The landlord had been falsely told that Katy and I were making too much noise and all of us including my aunt would be evicted if Katy and I didn't leave. I was pretty desperate when we got on that train. The only thing I was hoping for was to find a safe place where Katy and I could stay together and get enough to eat. I thought it was hilarious when Sally said I had been brought back by your mother for you. I had absolutely no interest in getting married and I wasn't expecting you to be interested in me. Now I love you and I do want to get married, but I would like to have your job situation more settled before we set a date."

"So, you think tomorrow is a little too soon?" Bobby questioned with a grin.

"I think tomorrow is a little too soon," Kathy replied, "I don't have a ring, I don't have a wedding dress, we don't have any money and we don't have a place to live."

"Just minor details," Bobby responded, "but maybe we will have to postpone it until next Saturday." Kathy had this really sad look and Bobby apologized for teasing her.

"No, it is not your fault," Kathy told him. "I just remembered how my mother had to sell her wedding ring after my father died to pay some bills and how she cried afterward."

"When do you think you will leave for St Louis?" Kathy asked.

"It will be a while," Bobby answered, "Richard is going to try to buy an old warehouse that had been used to store cotton. He is going to send me a letter to come there when he gets that building or another building. When I go to Williamsburg tomorrow, I plan to buy some hardware, screws, nails and glue for Ned and me to work with. I will bring our best pieces of furniture that we make with me when Richard tells me to come to St Louis. Then I will return after Richard decides which ones to make. I will spend some more time here helping William and Ned and possibly some other employees get boards ready for shipment to St Louis. Then I will go back to St louis to set up the assembly line, hire workers and start producing furniture."

"Why don't you come with me when I go to Williamsburg tomorrow, we can sing on the way. We are also bringing back a newlywed couple to stay upstairs next week, you can help me entertain them."

"I would love to if Martha can spare me, she is pretty busy with Julia gone," Kathy replied. Kathy went into the kitchen and asked if she could go with Bobby to Williamsburg and Martha said okay.

"Are you ready to leave for St Louis," Martha asked her.

"No, I love it here, Katy loves it here and I want so bad to teach school with you next fall. I also want to marry Bobby and go where he goes, and I want Bobby to be successful."

"I want Bobby to be successful too," Martha replied, "but I hate to see you leave. Do you think Katy could stay with Clarence and I next winter until you and Bobby get more settled?"

"The two of you would be wonderful parents but we don't want to leave each other," Kathy replied. "The problem for Katy is she won't want to leave here either." Kathy continued, "Bobby said it will be some time before they start assembling furniture in St Louis. I told him I wanted him settled into the job before we got married which could be quite a while. Let's not say anything to Katy yet."

"Good idea," Martha answered.

When Kathy got back to the patio, she joined Bobby and Clarence walking up to guest area to look at a dresser. It was worn but well made from maple wood. Bobby showed where they would run into challenges. "If you look closer at the top, you can see that three pieces of wood have been placed side by side and glued together to look like one board. It is also perfectly smooth when you run your hand across the seams. That is going to be hard to perfect. They have also rounded the edges on the top and did some engraving on the wooden drawers. We cannot do all that or it will be too expensive for the people Richard wants to sell to. Richard said the goal is to make something that people will buy for the money they have when wish they could buy something nicer that is too expensive for them."

Clarence went down to the store and came back with a ruler, and they carefully measured every part of the dresser and wrote down the dimensions.

Kathy observed that even though the exterior of the dresser was all of maple, the inside of the drawers was made of other woods such as pine.

Clarence wondered how they would hold the boards together that were being glued. Bobby answered that he thought they could buy a couple of iron clamps to hold the boards together. Then it would take at least a day for the glue to dry.

"At that rate you could only make one dresser a day," Kathy opinioned.

"That is not what I wanted to hear," Bobby responded, "but unfortunately you are right unless we get more clamps or a really fast drying glue. I am beginning to realize that William can make boards a whole lot faster than we can make dressers."

"I am going to go cool off before I give you something else to worry about," Kathy replied. After Kathy left, Bobby observed to Clarence that "I don't like to hear about more problems, but I can't solve them if I don't know about them."

Katy was taking a nap with the kitty, but Martha was in the adult pool. Kathy quickly changed to her swimsuit and joined Martha commenting that they had succeeded in fattening her up a little bit since she came.

"You look a lot better," Martha commented, "but you still need to add some more weight. Mary really hated to leave here, she said summers in St Louis are horribly hot and uncomfortable with no water to jump into."

"I don't want to go there now either, I am hoping I can at least wait until fall before I marry Bobby and join him in St Louis," Kathy replied. "I don't want Bobby being miserable but my being miserable won't help him. I told him I need a ring; a wedding dress and we need some money and a place to live. His response was, how about next Saturday?"

Martha laughed, "he knows better, but men just want elope and live in a tent."

They were interrupted by the return of Sally and Janice. They filled a bucket with a couple of roses they dug up from a small flower garden next to the vegetable garden. "William, Janice and I are going to plant these in the cemetery," Sally announced before leaving with Janice."

Sally and Janice joined William outside, and they walked together to the small cemetery behind the church. Alex and James had already gone swimming in the men's bathhouse.

They planted a rose at the grave of each of their departed spouses and said some prayers before Janice left to return to the women's bathhouse.

Sally and William were standing quietly together before Sally broke the silence. "It has been three years since Cindy was killed. I lost my best friend; you lost a wonderful wife, and your children lost a great mother. It has been three years since Gary died, my wonderful husband and Alex's father. I wish we still had Cindy and I wish I still had Gary. Unfortunately, we can't bring them back just like Kathy can't bring her mother back who died a year ago. She is still hurting but she is ready to move on and marry Bobby. I love Bobby and Kathy, but I am jealous too. I kidded my mother the night she brought home Kathy and Katy that she had brought home a wife for Bobby; how come she didn't bring home a husband for me."

"Maybe because I was available," William replied.

"Are you?" Sally asked. "When Cindy's mother stayed after the funeral to keep house for you and look after the children, I did not feel welcome there. Your mother-in-law left six months ago so that is no longer an issue. I spend almost as much time with your children as you do because I love them, so you do not owe me anything for that. Despite your mother-in-law being gone, you never paid much attention to me until a couple weeks ago. So, have things changed or do we go back to greeting each other only on Sundays."

"What is hard for me," William replied, "is that I have never found her killer and I feel like I need to bring him to justice before I move on."

"Move on to what?" Sally asked.

"I would be interested in marrying you if I could find her killer," William replied."

"It will be great for both of us when that happens so I guess until then we can just greet each other on Sunday mornings," Sally answered before starting to walk back

Martha had gone back to the house; Kathy was sitting with her feet in children's pool playing her flute and Katy and Janice were playing catch with a knotted piece of rope.

Sally held her emotions in check until she lay down on her cot. She tried to cry into her pillow to muffle the sound. It had been such a silly dream to believe that William was ready to marry her, but Sally had wanted so badly to believe it. Kathy didn't hear Sally crying until she paused between songs. Whatever had happened wasn't good. Kathy went in and talked to Sally and then they both cried.

William was a little shocked at Sally's departure. Obviously, the idea of him waiting to find his wife's killer was the end of the line for her. Cindy had been everything a man could ever hope for but if he wanted to remarry, Sally would be perfect. William had made a vow that we would find Cindy's killer before he ever remarried but now, he was faced with the futility of that vow. He didn't know where or who the killer might be. All William knew is that his wife had fought with the killer because there was evidence, she had scratched him before he had stabbed her to death and cut off her ring finger to get her wedding ring. It was more than a robbery because her clothes had been partially ripped off. What had happened then was horrible, but he realized that now it was also destroying his future as well as his children's future. He needed a wife; they needed a mother.

Cindy's widowed mother, Irma, had tried to do a good job trying to mother and feed her grandchildren but she constantly brought up her daughter's death as if William should be doing more about it. Irma also did a good job of making William feel guilty about even thinking about another woman while his wife's killer was still on the loose. William had retreated to his job spending as little time at home as possible. Irma was also paranoid about her grandchildren going anywhere and James rebelled about her restrictions. William had pretty much let her manage the children but finally sided with James. He told Irma to let James be a boy and spend more time with Alex if he wanted to. Irma did not agree. Irma then let William know how hard she was working to take care of his children when she could be living comfortably with her brother and his wife. Irma had been stunned when William suggested that he thought his children were self-sufficient so that if she would be happier moving in with her brother, maybe she should do that. Irma had left reluctantly realizing how much she would miss Janice and even James.

Janice had mixed feelings about Irma leaving. Most of the time they got along really well but she too was frustrated by Irma's restrictions. At first Janice wasn't happy about doing more housework and cooking after Irma left. William started spending more time at home and would help Janice in the kitchen praising her work and patting her on the back. William started doing more activities with James. The three of them started to really bond together.

Back at the patio, supper was chicken gravy and leftover chicken pieces served over biscuits. It tasted really good but most of them at the table were too glum to enjoy it. Alex had found out that Bobby was soon leaving for St Louis and was really sad about it. Katy was sensitive enough to know something else was wrong but wasn't sure what it was it. Martha and Clarence were crushed at the news they got from Sally that William would not consider marriage again until his wife's killer was found. They did not want her to leave but wanted her happy and they knew how much she was hoping William would marry her. They all went to bed early that night and there were a lot of prayers that Cindy's killer would be found. Sally told Kathy that she would pray that Cindy's killer would be found, or she would find someone else to marry. Those prayers would soon be answered but not in the way they wanted.

Kathy did not sleep well but was up in time to help Martha make breakfast. Bobby wanted an early start so that he could shop for the tools and supplies Ned and him would need to make dressers. Kathy said she would go with him and shop for some things to buy if she ever had any money which didn't seem likely in the near future. Bobby gave her a small amount she could spend. Martha made sure they had some rolls and cookies to eat along with fresh water.

CHAPTER 13

That Bathhouse Girl

They left the village singing 'Holy, Holy, Lord God Almighty early in the morning our song shall rise to thee'.

The older couple that lived near the church heard them as they were leaving. "That was so pretty," the woman remarked after they were gone. "Dear Lord, bless their travel," she prayed, and her husband said "Amen."

It was a good morning as they sang and talked on their way to town except that they were disappointed for Sally. Kathy sat up front with Bobby and teased him about how she was replacing Shep.

"Yeah, Shep wanted to come with, "Bobby remarked.

"So did Katy," Kathy responded.

"Sounds like things aren't going well between my sister and William. I had heard before that William was obsessed with finding Cindy's killer, but I don't think Cindy would have wanted that," Bobby reflected. "Isn't there a passage in scripture that says vengeance is mine saith the Lord?"

"Romans 12:19," Kathy replied.

"How do you know your scripture so well?" Bobby asked.

"My father studied to be a minister but switched to banking to better support his younger sister and widowed mother. He made learning the Bible a priority for me. We used to have a lot of discussions about the Bible."

Williamsburg had a general store similar to the one Clarence had except it was much larger with more variety to handle the town's larger population. Bobby was able to find some of the hardware he wanted and a

99

couple different cans of glue to test. Kathy found a sewing machine with a foot treadle and sat down on a chair in front of it. The store was almost empty, and the store owner came over and told her "we just got that in, but we don't know how to work it yet. I think we accidently threw the instructions away with the crate it came in."

"I have spent a lot of time using one of these," Kathy told him. "If you have a spool of thread, I will be glad to show you how to work it." Several women came in and Kathy thought the owner would leave but when women saw the sewing machine, they were curious about it. Kathy carefully showed all three women and the owner how to set up the machine. Kathy had a rag in her purse to wipe off dirt from the trip but had not needed it. Using the sewing machine, she showed how she could quickly make it into a miniature pillowcase.

"My goodness," one woman exclaimed, "that would have taken me an hour to sew by hand." Kathy showed them a few more tricks and one women stated that she was going to come back with her husband and buy the machine. Kathy had the lady take her place and coached her through the process. The woman was so excited about it and the others wanted to try it too. Bobby waved at her and said he would come back later. A couple other ladies came in and wanted to see how the sewing machine worked.

Kathy talked to the ladies while helping them learn how to sew. Other women came in to shop and Kathy would show them how to use the machine and answer questions. Finally, everyone left and the owner profusely thanked Kathy for her help. When he found out she was living with Clarence and Martha he joked about them being competitors but then said he really liked them. "They are great people."

Kathy decided to buy a scissor and some crayons, and he told her there would be no charge. "Thanks to you, I think I am going to be selling a lot of sewing machines," he told her.

Kathy wished she had the money to buy one too. The money she had given Julia would have helped but she felt bad for even thinking it; with all the generosity she had received, she needed to be generous to others.

There was a long bench in the shade outside the store and she sat down and waited for Bobby who came back a few minutes later. Bobby had put his earlier purchases in the wagon and had found some clamps at a carriage shop, but they were not for sale. "I think I can make my own clamps if I can get some big nuts and bolts," he told her and went back in to look. He found what he hoped would work and they walked back to put the wagon to stash their purchases. "We still have over an hour to kill, so I will treat you lunch at the café and maybe you can play their piano" Bobby told her.

Bobby was greeted by Doug, a young man who Kathy learned was a former high school classmate.

"Bobby, what are you doing here?" a young waitress yelled out. Bobby introduced Kathy as his future wife to her.

"I am so jealous," the waitress exclaimed with a smile. "He was the one all of the girls in my class wanted."

"What about me?" Doug protested.

"Maybe if you get a job and one of us gets really desperate, "she teased.

"Is it okay if she plays the piano?" Bobby asked.

"Only if you sing for us," she replied. "Actually, you need to ask Joe, my boss;" she pointed to a grumpy looking older man seated at a table.

Kathy walked over to him. "Sir, my name is Kathy, and I would like to play the piano and sing a few songs with my friend. I have been playing piano since I was seven."

"You don't look much older than that now. Play a short piece and I will decide if you can continue," he told her with a skeptical look.

She returned his grumpy look with a smile and a thank you. Kathy warmed up playing the same complicated piece as she had practiced at the church and was happy with the sound. So were the people who were in the restaurant who clapped when she finished.

"That was great - go ahead," a now smiling Joe told her.

She noticed the three ladies who had come into the store were sitting in the back corner of the restaurant and they waved to her, and she waved back.

"Can I get you to do the love song with me?" Bobby asked.

Kathy made a face but then said okay. "Let me play the melody once before we sing. Kathy played the piano and Bobby sang and then she sang back to him. There was a lot of applause.

Joe came over. "Young man you are really good, but this little doll is great. I haven't heard a soprano that good since I went to a Catholic school in Chicago and there was this one nun who had an amazing voice."

Kathy started playing and singing the song she sang in Latin.

After she finished Joe commented, "I think you are actually better, you can sing here all day."

One of the ladies she had helped with the sewing machine came over. "I don't know what you just sang but it was so beautiful. Do you know "Rock of Ages", and could you sing it for me?"

"I will try to get through it," Kathy told her. Kathy played it and sang it to perfection, but they saw her eyes were closed through parts of it. Kathy was wiping the tears from her eyes when it was over. The lady had stayed close by and noticed the tears.

"I have never heard it sung that well but why are you crying?"

"This is the first time I have sung it since I sang it at my mother's funeral last year," Kathy told her. "I needed to sing it again."

"Oh, you poor darling," the lady replied.

"Let's liven things up," Kathy announced. Kathy got out her flute and Bobby joined her singing "When Johnny Comes Marching Home." Bobby would sing when she played her flute then she would switch to the piano, and they would both sing. Kathy got off the piano bench and the people in the café stood up and applauded them.

Joe was disappointed when he found out they didn't live nearby. "I could fill this place every night with you two singing. Well thanks for coming in and if you are hungry, you can eat lunch for free."

Kathy thanked Joe and patted him on the shoulder.

Joe turned to Bobby, "You take good care of her, I have been around a lot of singers, and she is one of the best ever." Bobby promised he would.

The waitress came over and told Kathy "you are incredible, I can't remember Joe giving anyone free anything."

They each had a ham sandwich, a cup of coffee and a donut. The waitress parting words to Bobby were "you are the luckiest man alive."

The three ladies she had met at the general store warmly thanked them on the way out. "Well, I guess we sang for our lunch rather than our supper," Kathy joked.

"You will be the number one topic of conversation around here for several days," Bobby replied. "They might even put you in the local newspaper."

"I hope you are joking," Kathy replied," I told the ladies that I was helping women and children at your parent's bathhouse."

"You will probably always be remembered here as that bathhouse girl," Bobby told her.

"You didn't leave me on my pedestal very long, did you?" Kathy replied.

"I am not sure I want you on a pedestal, but I will accept that mother bringing you home made me the luckiest man alive," Bobby told her.

CHAPTER 14

The Newlyweds

The train arrived from St Louis at 2 pm and they met the young newlywed couple Peter and Penny. They were quiet and shy at first but very appreciative of the food and water Martha had sent along which Bobby and Kathy hadn't needed. Peter was about Bobby's height while Penny was shorter and a little heavier than Kathy but not overweight. Bobby stepped away from the carriage to pick up some packages that had arrived at the train depot for the store and Peter volunteered to help.

Penny told Kathy, "my father died, and Peter was hired to take care of the family farm for her mother and me. Peter and I went to school together and got along really well so we decided to get married. We went to a Justice of the Peace this morning and then caught the train."

Kathy joked to Penny, "Bobby calls me his rail order bride shipped by rail from Boston two weeks ago. We still have a few details to resolve before he can take delivery. Actually, my younger sister and I came here after Bobby's mother offered us a place to stay and the joke was that I was Bobby's rail order bride. It was a big joke except that we fell in love, and he wants to marry me."

"We were told to provide musical entertainment for your ride and will try to do our best," Bobby told them after they returned with some packages. They started out with "When Johnny Comes Marching Home" with Kathy playing the flute and Bobby singing the song but she would join him on the chorus. They then did the name switch "when Peter comes marching home, when Penny comes marching home." Kathy looked back and saw a big smile on Penny's face. They then did "Shenandoah" with Kathy singing her refrain. Kathy then did "Amazing Grace'" with help from Bobby.

"That was so beautiful," Penny said when they finished, "You two are so good."

"Okay, now we are going to sing the love song we have been singing to each other," Bobby told them "so get ready to hug and kiss."

Penny giggled when Bobby said that. "Peter, are you ready?" Bobby teased.

Kathy and Bobby sang the song with their usual passion and Kathy gave Bobby a hug and a kiss.

Penny teased them. "What is going on up there? I thought we were the newlyweds."

"Kathy replied," we are just practicing for when it is our turn to get married. I thought you two would be too busy to notice."

"We are saving all our energy for tonight," Peter joked.

"You are going to need it tonight," Bobby replied, "you are on the second floor so in order to carry her across the threshold; you have to carry her up a flight of stairs."

Penny laughed, "Is that mandatory, I think I would be safer if I walked. Now I am going to have to eat a light supper, so I won't be so hard to carry."

"No second helpings for you," Peter joked.

"My mother would be disappointed if anyone didn't enjoy supper, so we won't expect you to do any more than carry Penny into the room."

Martha had asked Sally and Katy to be ready to meet them and they had found some pretty flowers and made them into a bouquet. Katy presented them to Penny when she got out of the carriage. Penny was delighted with the flowers and with Katy. "The flowers are so pretty and so are you," she told Katy.

Kathy introduced the couple to Katy, Sally, Martha, and Alex. Martha asked how their trip went and they said it was great. They had enjoyed the singing and the carriage ride.

Martha asked Kathy to go into the kitchen and bring out some milk and cookies for them. Sally and Katy went with her. Penny told Martha That Bobby and Kathy sound like they are ready to get married too.

Martha laughed and replied "they are, and my family loves her and little Katy so much that we couldn't be happier. The problem is that Bobby may be leaving for a job in St Louis and Kathy isn't ready to move."

"Not yet," Kathy remarked after overhearing the end of the conversation as they served cookies, milk, and coffee.

When Martha heard that the couple had been married by a Justice of the Peace, she suggested that her husband could conduct a short marriage ceremony in the church. Peter wasn't too keen on it, but Penny loved the idea, so he agreed.

Martha was always pleased when people praised Julia's cooking and regularly praised Julia herself. Martha was actually very good at cooking and the pork chop supper she served the newlyweds along with the rest of them was delicious. They joked about how Bobby had told Peter that carrying Penny over the threshold included carrying her up the stairs."

"Since Peter is not doing that, I am having a small second helping,"

After supper, Martha announced that she wanted to temporarily split the couple up with Bobby taking Peter to the men's bathhouse.

Sally took Penny to the women's bathhouse where she had a bath in one of the enclosed compartments. "That felt so wonderful," she announced. after she got out, dried off and put on a bathing gown, Sally helped Penny get her hair washed, dried, and combed. Then Sally shocked Penny by bringing out her old wedding dress and having her try it on. It was a little long for Penny, but it fit fine on top and didn't touch the ground. Penny was so thrilled and grateful she kept saying "thank you."

Kathy and Katy had dressed and went ahead of Sally and Penny to the church. Clarence was at the pulpit and Peter and Bobby were there too. Alex had been busy and had invited a number of the neighbors to witness the occasion and quite a number had shown up.

Bobby had his fiddle along with a box camera. Penny and Sally waited just outside the church door as Bobby led off with some fast- moving fiddle music that had some of the little children bouncing in their seats. Kathy then played and sang "Joyful, Joyful We Adore Thee" as Penny walked to the front of the church where Peter stood next to the pulpit waiting for her. Clarence introduced the bride and groom and thanked the people for coming to witness this wonderful event. "Bobby and Kathy will now sing "Savior Like a Shepherd Lead Us." Clarence gave a short sermon urging them to look to God and to love each other. Afterwards Bobby and Kathy did their love song and Peter kissed his bride.

Bobby took the picture of the bride and groom with the camera. Bobby took some pictures of others there too. Martha had made a simple wedding cake and brought coffee. Penny was so thrilled with everything and even Peter was pleased. Penny gave Martha a hug and told her that they all had made this the most wonderful wedding she could ever have hoped for.

Kathy walked back to the house with Bobby carrying his fiddle for him while he carried the camera. "I didn't know you were a photographer," Kathy told him.

"Well, you keep surprising me with things you do but I have a few talents too," Bobby replied.

"We can do a lot together," Kathy assured him. They set the fiddle and the camera down on the patio table before they kissed and hugged and said goodnight. Bobby reluctantly let go of Kathy; holding her close felt so wonderful and he loved her so much. Kathy was also finding her attraction to Bobby getting stronger each time.

"I think your kiss lasted longer than one our newlyweds did," Sally told her as she entered the bathhouse.

"If I could marry Bobby and we both could live here, I would love to be a newlywed," Kathy responded.

Kathy woke up early the next morning but didn't want to get out of bed. Reluctantly she got moving knowing that Martha was probably exhausted from getting food ready for the wedding. Kathy arrived in the kitchen first and got the fire started in the stove. Martha arrived after the fire was going and Kathy started making pancakes while Martha was cutting strips of bacon from a slab. Once the pancake batter was ready, Kathy started setting the table.

"I heard from Bobby that you got a free meal at the hotel restaurant," Martha remarked.

"I asked Joe if I could play the piano and he let me and then Bobby and I sang and he really liked us," Kathy replied. "He told us he could fill his restaurant every night if we would sing there."

"Would you want to do that?" Martha asked.

"No, I would sooner fill our church here," Kathy replied

"You and Bobby are doing a great job on that. Now that you are here, Bobby is more willing to sing."

Katy joined them and they both gave her a hug. Martha thanked Katy, "you were such a good little helper yesterday. She picked peas and beans for me and helped set the table," Martha remarked to Kathy.

Sally joined them announcing that she overslept, and they should have woken her.

"We are doing okay," Martha replied, "yesterday was a lot of work but I think we really made their wedding day special for them. They were met out at the patio by a sleepy looking Penny wearing a robe.

"Oh good, you survived!" Sally teased her.

"Barely," she replied but then smiled. "Could I carry our breakfast upstairs?" she asked."

"You go back upstairs, and we will bring it up for you and leave it in the hallway," Sally told her.

"Oh, thank you," Penny responded. "we are so happy we came here." A few minutes later, Sally and Kathy brought up pancakes, bacon, jelly, syrup, and coffee.

They had just come back down when Bobby arrived, and they talked about some of the pictures he had previously taken. There were so few pictures from the past, and it was exciting to think of capturing future memories with a camera.

Kathy complimented Bobby about his photography again. "Now it is my turn to get off my pedestal and see if Ned and I can build a dresser," Bobby remarked to Kathy as he got up to leave the table.

"What was that about?" Sally asked.

"Yesterday Kathy was the star of Williamsburg showing several ladies at the store how to use a new sewing machine before entertaining people at the hotel restaurant where Joe called her best the singer he had ever heard. Kathy told me I had knocked her off her pedestal when I told her they would remember her as that bathhouse girl."

"Would you use a sewing machine if we got you one?" Martha asked Kathy.

"I would love to have one," Kathy answered. "I am pretty sure that I could make stuff to sell in the store that would pay for it within a few weeks."

"I just got an advertisement for one," Clarence remarked, "follow me into the store and let's check it out." It was a Singer sewing machine, the same make and model that Kathy had demonstrated the previous day so Clarence said he would order her one.

"I am so excited," Kathy told him. Clarence also handed her two letters – one from her aunt and one from her sister. Kathy looked around the store before leaving, it was clean and orderly, but Kathy could see changes she would like to make. She took the letters to the bathhouse and left the letters on her bunk. She left them unopened not certain what kind of a reply she would have gotten back from the letters she had sent. She would share them with Katy later.

Sally had left with Bobby and Alex to go over to William's house.

Kathy had helped Martha wash dishes and was carrying the dirty dishwater to dump it outside when she stumbled spilling much of it on her dress.

"Are you okay?" Martha asked.

"Just soaking wet. Katy and I are going to work in the garden unless you have something else for us to do."

"I might need help later but the garden needs weeding and watering so that would be great. Take your wet dress off and let's go look at the garden," Martha replied.

Kathy hung up her wet dress on the clothesline. Katy joined them and they walked over to the garden. She talked to Martha what they would work on before commenting; "I suppose we should put something on."

"You don't need to bother; both look cute the way you are," Martha replied with a smile. "I am used to Sally not wearing anything out here. You are alone out here today, and you are going to get wet watering the garden. Katy is young enough, so it doesn't matter if she doesn't wear anything as long as she stays inside the bathhouse. But Kathy, I do want you to continue to wear something like your bath outfit when we have customers in here. You have been really good about that. I wish Sally was a little more careful. We also don't want either of you to talk about women without clothes on in here. Unfortunately some man might hear about it and sneak in for a look and do something really bad." Martha went back to the kitchen .

"Let's get you started weeding the peas again," Kathy told Katy. She got Katy started on weeding and remembered Penny wanting a couple pails of hot water for baths later in the morning. She decided to work on that before watering the garden. She went over to the firepit and got a fire going and put a couple pails of water on.

Kathy used the child's pool for watering the tomatoes and vine crops. She concentrated on her task and was making good progress. She had not bothered to put anything on. Being bare was not on her mind until she was startled and a little embarrassed by Penny who had come into the bathhouse.

"Hi, you two look really comfortable. It would be fun to work with nothing on in my garden at home. I don't think Peter would mind but my mother would be pretty shocked. I also would worry that someone else might see me."

"I usually wear something in here, but I spilled water on my dress this morning, so I hung it up to dry. It is just Katy and me out here, so I didn't feel the need to put anything else on."

Penny took her robe off. "I might as well be comfortable too. I hate to bother you. but we would a like a couple pails of hot water for a hot bath."

"I am heating the water, but I don't think it's hot yet," Kathy replied.

Penny followed Kathy over to the firepit carrying her robe.

The water was hot enough. Penny put her robe back on and Kathy put her dress back on which was almost dry. Then they each carried a bucket of hot water from the fire pit to take the bottom of the stairs for the guest rooms. Kathy set hers down and returned to the patio. Penny said she would carry both pails upstairs.

The gate to the patio was open and Martha had temporarily gone back to the house. There was nothing to prevent someone from walking into the women's bathhouse. Martha had said it was okay and Penny had taken her own robe off. Still Kathy still kind of felt like she had been caught being improper.

Kathy went in and hung up her dress. She no longer felt safe. She reluctantly put her bathing suit on and wondered if that was adequate. She glanced at Katy and felt a little jealous of her looking cute and innocent in her bare skin. Kathy had given Katy something to wear in the bathhouse when she wasn't in the pool, but Katy usually left it off. She decided that was okay for Katy but not for her.

Kathy started weeding carrots. They had grown considerably since she had first weeded them, and it was now easier to distinguish the carrots from the weeds Kathy was working on a row of carrots when Martha came in and told her: "Could you pull some carrots and pick some peas. I also need your help making lunch. I see you put something on."

"Penny surprised me by coming into the garden and wanting hot water for baths. I put my dress back on and carried a pail of hot water to the stairway. I noticed the gate was open and you were out of the kitchen. There was nothing to prevent someone from walking in on me."

"Sorry about that, I should have closed the kitchen door when I left. I wish we could lock the bathhouse without locking the kitchen."

Kathy pulled carrots which were still rather small and washed them. She picked some peas and string beans before putting on her dress over her bathing suit. She then shelled the peas, pulled the strings off the string beans, and cut up the carrots before joining Martha in the kitchen.

One of their neighbors had brought in some small new potatoes which added to the vegetables, pieces of fried bacon and milk made a tasty chowder. Clarence had a talent for offering a fair price for meat and produce but then reselling it or trading it for just enough to make a profit. A lot of his customers paid with food, and some of it wound up feeding his own household.

Martha rang the dinner bell and then had Kathy go partially up the steps to call Peter and Penny.

"What's up?" Penny called out from above.

"Come down for lunch."

They came down dressed and ready to eat.

"This soup is great, all the food here is great," Peter enthused.

"Penny, are you taking notes," Peter asked?"

"A few," Penny replied, but it might be a while before we can enjoy this kind of luxury again, but we will still have love."

"True," Peter replied, "but it would be nice if love also came with a hot bath and a good meal."

"I agree," Penny replied, "but just getting enough water to drink out of our well is a challenge and it doesn't taste this good either. Remember when we vowed last night for better or worse. Well, worse is going to include our drinking water."

Kathy reminded herself again how fortunate she was where she and Katy were staying with good water, good food and baths almost daily.

"I will see you tonight at supper," Martha told them, "I am going to relieve Clarence in the store."

Clarence came out and Kathy served him soup before taking a small bowl herself. Both Penny and Peter told Clarence what a great job his family had done taking care of them.

"Work hard, pray hard and love each other and good things will continue to happen for you," Clarence told them.

Peter and Penny decided to return to their room and take a nap. Clarence went back to the store and Martha came back with a couple of butchered chickens for the evening meal. "I was wondering what to fix tonight when one of the local farmers came in selling butchered chickens – perfect timing." Martha then coached Kathy on how to make a raisin pie and decided they needed to make two. Kathy had helped her mother cook but was always happy to learn something new from someone else.

They had just got the pies ready to bake later when Sally and Alex came back. Sally had helped Janice make lunch for William, Ned, and Bobby as well as herself and the children. Sally said it went okay but William didn't have much food around to work with. "How are the newlyweds doing?" Sally asked.

"They seem pretty happy here, but they are not looking forward to returning home," Kathy replied. "Penny was pretty negative about their food, drinking water and getting a bath at home which makes me feel very appreciative about Katy and I being here."

"I can't believe you have only been here two weeks," Martha replied, "it has been so much fun and so many good things are happening. I am looking forward to both of you and Sally getting married, but I am going to be so lonesome without you around."

The day was still cloudy, so Kathy decided that Katy and she should go back to weeding but this time Kathy wore an old dress that Martha had given her. She had shortened the dress to knee length, it fit loosely over her which was comfortable. She decided Penny seeing her with nothing on didn't matter but being seen by someone else could be serious. Katy was weeding and Sally was cleaning bathtubs. Neither was wearing anything, but Kathy left her dress on. Normally Kathy would have started singing but too many thoughts were going through her head. Moving again bothered her. She did not want to move but she did want to marry Bobby. What would be better for Katy? Staying here with Clarence and Martha or coming with her and Bobby to St Louis.

It started to sprinkle which felt good at first, but it rained harder. Both Katy and she ran for the bathhouse building with Kathy ducking under the clothesline to get there. Kathy made a mental note that the clothesline could be dangerous if you didn't see it and ran into it.

Kathy started reading the reply from her older sister which was very friendly in saying: "Please write as often as you can. As much as my daughters and I want to see you and Katy, I am happy you found a good home. Although things are looking up for the future, right now we are barely getting by. We also don't have a boyfriend for you to sing with either!"

Her aunt wrote with candid irony that "the peace and quiet that I now have without you two here is driving me crazy, life is so boring. The neighbor man lied when he complained to the landlady that Katy was bothering him and Elva, the elderly lady down the hall. The landlady admitted that Elva cried when she found out that Katy was gone and kept saying "oh no, not my little angel." Now the landlady says she would welcome both of you back, but it sounds like you are much happier where you are."

Both letters confirmed that moving in with Clarence and Martha had been a good decision for her and Katy. Kathy was glad she had not told Katy that Elva was cited as one of the reasons they had to leave since she knew how much Katy loved her. She let Katy read both letters and Katy cried when she read about Elva and Kathy found herself crying with her.

The next day Peter and Penny were taken back to Williamsburg to catch the train back to St Louis by Bobby. Kathy and Katy got to ride along. Bobby had shown Peter the windmill they used for pumping water and Peter hoped he could put one in at their farm. Kathy was jealous of Peter and Penny being married but their living conditions sounded pretty bleak.

Julia had returned from St Louis with Jade and rode back with them. They sang on the way back with Katy and Jade sitting together becoming friends almost instantly. Kathy and Katy had welcomed Julia and Jade with a smile and a hug for each. Bobby had lifted Jade high in the air and greeted her with a smile. Jade had been apprehensive about coming. Jade had heard from her mother that white people weren't nice to black people, but Julia had assured her that she would be welcome. They all had fun on the way back laughing and singing songs. Kathy managed to get Julia and Jade to sing and discovered they both had great voices.

Katy, and Jade jumped in the pool as soon as they got to the bathhouse. Like Katy, Jade felt this was the nicest place ever. Julia had stepped back into her kitchen overcome by emotion. The Thompson's had been so nice to her and now her granddaughter was being shown so much love and friendship.

The sewing machine they had ordered arrived just before the Fourth of July. Kathy was allowed to take much of the store's inventory of thread and material and soon was busy sewing. Women who came into the bathhouse were fascinated by the machine. Kathy took time to demonstrate how the sewing machine worked though many felt it was too complicated for them. She had some lavender material and made a dress for herself. She also started on identical dresses for Katy and Jade. Kathy didn't have that much material to work with, so she ordered material and thread from a catalogue. Kathy also had been given quite a few dresses from Martha and Sally that needed alterations and repairs and she was happy to do them.

They celebrated the Fourth of July with a church picnic. Everyone brought food but Clarence and Martha contributed more than their share. They celebrated with a few firecrackers but mostly listened to music provided by Bobby and Kathy. Bobby did a really good job of playing his fiddle to accompany Kathy's singing. Everyone was enjoying themselves.

Clarence and Martha were very happy that so many people came. They heard many comments that Bobby and Kathy had made this the best celebration ever. Clarence ruefully commented to Martha: "Now if I could just get the people to come to church every Sunday."

CHAPTER 15

Bad Visitors in the Night

There was a tavern on the edge of town that Martha sometimes referred to disparagingly as a den of evil. Clarence was a little more charitable in saying that he knew some good men who drank beer and alcohol, but he also felt that their little town did not need a tavern.

Velma who occasionally attended the church was a notorious gossip finding satisfaction in exposing the faults in other people both real and imagined which helped her feel better about herself. Steve, her beer drinking husband was one of her listeners and would repeat her gossip at the tavern enjoying the opportunity to slam people in the church who he claimed were all hypocrites. Velma was very self-conscious about her body even though she was only a little overweight. She could not imagine letting another woman see her naked. To her, the idea of a bathhouse for women and children seemed immoral. She embellished that thought to her husband by suggesting that prostitution might also be taking place at the bathhouse. Steve agreed with her that was terrible, but he was actually hoping that it was true. He started to have an obsession about going there.

It was Saturday the week after the Fourth that the obsession really got into Steve's mind. He found himself drinking heavily at the tavern with a rough looking stranger and Benny, a young man who said he was ready to ask his girlfriend to marry him. Neither Steve nor the rough looking stranger thought marriage was a great idea and told him so. Benny insisted he was ready and just needed to buy a ring so he could propose.

"How much can you afford?" the stranger asked. When he heard the amount, the stranger reached into the stuff he was carrying and came out with a small package which he unwrapped to reveal a gold ring with a diamond. "It is worth a lot more than you can offer me, but I need some money now, so I am willing to make a deal."

The stranger called the tavern owner over who said the ring looked expensive and that it was a great price. Steve was asked his opinion and he agreed it was a good deal. Benny gave the stranger the money and got the ring. They decided to have one more round of drinks to celebrate although they were already quite drunk. For Benny it was his first time drinking and his head was really messed up. It was getting late, and the tavern owner said he would like to close.

It was a moonlit night and Steve started talking about how it was too early to quit partying. "I know a place in town where we can get some girls," he told them.

Benny wasn't even sure what "getting some girls" meant and his instinct was to take the ring and go home. Unfortunately, they were able to convince Benny to go with them and they all staggered over to the bathhouse. Once there they found the gate that was locked with a bolt that was only accessible from inside the patio. They could see an open door from the patio into the bathhouse. The patio was accessible by climbing over an eight-foot-high fence.

Benny suggested they knock on the door but the other two said "let's make it a surprise."

They told Benny that they would boost him up and he could open the gate from the inside. The beer was starting to make Benny feel sick and he wanted to go home. The stranger than showed a mean side that even scared Steve. The stranger showed a knife and said, "Don't mess with me kid, I was nice enough to sell you that ring cheap now get up and over the fence and open the gate."

They boosted Benny up and he went over the top and falling hard into the patio. Benny was hurting but managed to open the gate before throwing up and laying down in a corner of the patio. He heard some of the commotion but was in a stupor from the fall and too much beer.

Both Steve and the stranger were now consumed by lust and too drunk to be rational. Kathy, Katy, and Sally were all sleeping. Steve was in the lead carrying a small lamp which he set on a bench. He tried to climb on top of Sally who was laying on her back. She woke up in time to get him with her knee while pushing up hard with her hands causing him to hit his head on the crossbeam for the bunk above. He was temporarily dazed.

The stranger found Katy and put his hand on her body, and she screamed. Kathy was on the top bunk and woke up with her screams. On hearing Katy scream she rolled forward into a kneeling position and launched herself at the stranger's head. He fell backward and they both crashed hard onto the brick floor. The stranger let loose a string of obscenities while threatening to kill her with his foul whiskey breath close to her face. He put his hand on her breast and she bit his hand. "I cut the throat of the last bitch who messed with me," he told her. He now had his hand on her throat and was choking her. Kathy had gotten her hand on a pail handle and swung the pail hard into his head. Kathy broke free but was unable to breathe as she ran toward the clothesline. She stumbled and fell but got up continued running with her head low. She then felt terrible pain in her back as he stabbed her with his knife.

Bobby had heard the screams next door and came to the patio carrying an axe and a lantern. He sent Alex to the house to wake up his parents. Benny had heard the screams and started to stumble away knowing something terrible had happened. "Lay down and don't move or I will kill you," Bobby told him.

Bobby was met by Sally and Katy. "Where is Kathy?" he asked.

"I don't know, I think it is really bad," Sally replied.

Sally carried the lantern and Bobby carried the axe followed by a sobbing Katy. They walked into the garden area and found the stranger dead, his neck broken by the clothesline. A few feet away Kathy lay motionless with a knife in her back, her eyes closed and blood coming out of her mouth.

They had just practiced the song "Rock of Ages" for Sunday worship and somehow when Kathy sang the verse: 'when my eyes are closed in death' it had made Bobby shudder. Seeing her now with her eyes closed the verse hit him again. It appeared that his darling Kathy was gone.

Both Katy and Sally had screamed in horror when they saw Kathy. A crying Katy got down next to Kathy's face and begged "please don't leave me."

Kathy had fainted but regained enough consciousness to hear Katy. Katy had put her small hand in Kathy's hand. Kathy was completely disoriented but she gave Katy's hand a gentle squeeze before trying to spit out some blood she was choking on. Kathy then lay silent. Martha and Clarence had arrived and were also stunned by the horrific scene.

Martha had done some work as a nurse, and she tried to calm herself and act professionally. Clarence and Bobby dragged the dead man out of the building followed by a now conscious but moaning Steve holding his head obviously in pain which they found grimly satisfying. Sally was put to work heating water. Katy was told to continue to hold her hand and rub her arm gently like you would a kitten.

Martha had Sally pull the knife out which fortunately was not in very deep. Pulling it out caused very little additional bleeding which was a relief to Martha. Martha used a sewing needle and some thread to close the wound with some stitches and put a makeshift bandage over it. Kathy had stopped bleeding from her mouth, but she was very unresponsive. Martha found a clean nighty to replace the blood soaked one Kathy was wearing. Sally and Martha then carried her to the sofa in the living room.

"She is having trouble breathing," Martha told them.

Bobby said he wanted to question the two men and find out what their story was.

Benny had fallen asleep, and they had to wake him. They had reheated some coffee and gave him a cup to drink to help him wake up. He was shocked to discover that the man who had sold him the ring was dead. He had always thought Bobby was a nice fellow, but he did not sound very friendly tonight. Bobby went over to Steve who was crying out in pain and told him if he didn't shut up, he was going to get a hot poker and really make him scream.

"Why is he so mad?" Benny asked Clarence.

"I am mad too," Clarence told him. "Steve nearly raped my daughter and the other man nearly killed Kathy, our church piano player."

"Oh God, not her!" Benny responded.

Benny then explained that he was at the tavern and wound-up drinking with Steve and a stranger. "When I said that I needed to get a ring so I could propose to my girlfriend, the stranger showed me a ring that I bought. Then we left the tavern and Steve said we could get some girls over at the bathhouse. When we found the locked gate, I decided to go home but the stranger threatened me with a knife. They had me climb over the fence and open the gate. I hurt my leg, so I just stayed here."

"So, you opened the gate and let two men come in to attack my daughter and my future daughter in law," Clarence told him.

"He threatened me with a knife," Benny repeated.

"You were safe once you got inside, you didn't have to open the gate for them," Clarence responded. "If Kathy dies, it will be because of you."

Benny sat there totally demoralized. He doubted that his girlfriend would ever forgive him or that he could ever forgive himself.

Clarence and Bobby then listened to Steve babble about how his wife had told him there were prostitutes at the bathhouse and they were just going to surprise them.

"There has never been anything immoral going on at the bathhouse, Clarence told him. Women and children have a place to get a bath and get clean. Men and older boys are not allowed in the women's bath area."

Bobby had gotten some rope and they tied Steve's hands behind his back and his ankles together.

"Why are you tying me up?" Steve whimpered.

"For attempted rape and we have a young lady clinging to life because the man with you tried to kill her. If she dies, you are an accomplice to a murder," Clarence told him.

Kathy was in a lot of pain; every breath she strained for hurt, her neck hurt, the knife wound hurt, and she was sore from when she tackled the man and they hit the brick floor. Sally and Martha rolled up a towel and tied it around her head to try keep her neck from moving. Katy was snuggled tight against her side which was both comforting to Kathy and an incentive to stay alive. Kathy's vision was blurry, so she kept her eyes closed. She could feel one of her teeth was loose from the blow she got to her head. She tried to say something and realized she couldn't talk. Kathy kept hearing prayers for God to save her. She felt she had to try to live for their sake otherwise she was ready to give up trying to breathe and join her parents and brother in Heaven.

She overheard Bobby talking about the ring Benny had bought and Sally had gone out and looked at it and was certain it was Cindy's wedding ring. Kathy hoped William would now be ready to marry Sally since her would be killer and Cindy's killer were the same. Little Katy was still up against her and even though Katy was sleeping her body was rigid with tension. Kathy summoned up enough energy to rub Katy's shoulder and she could feel Katy relaxing a little. She thought the night would never end but toward morning she slept a little.

She woke up and wanted to walk to the bathroom but wasn't certain she had the strength to make it. She tried to stand up but fell backward bumping into Katy waking her. The sun had started to rise so there was some daylight. She hung onto Katy and made it to the bathroom. Martha had slept a little bit but woke up and helped get her back to the sofa.

CHAPTER 16

The Aftermath

Clarence had not slept much, and even if he had, he knew his mind was not where it should be for preaching a sermon. He was angry and he was not ready to forgive.

He asked Janice to bring the children forward and sing their song. Janice kept the song going and it went pretty well.

"We do not have Kathy to sing and play the piano this morning," he told the congregation. "Last night three men broke into the women's bathhouse where my daughter Sally and Kathy and little Katy were sleeping. Two of the men assaulted my daughter and Kathy and they fought back with incredible courage. Sally won her battle, and her assailant is now tied up. Kathy fought with her assailant, and he wound up chasing her. Kathy ran out into a little garden we have behind the bathhouse. The man wound up breaking his neck on a clothesline and dying. We found Kathy motionless nearby with a knife in her back and blood coming out of her mouth. She is badly hurt, and we all need to pray for her."

There were gasps of horror from the congregation and many started crying including almost all of the children. Clarence tried to start the prayer but then lost it himself. Finally, he was able to pray.

"Lord you know how much we love her, and she has made herself such a wonderful part of our ministry. We ask that you heal her body and help her to breathe and speak. In Jesus name, Amen."

Clarence continued speaking. "We think the man was strangling Kathy before she broke away and ducked under the clothesline. She is having a hard time breathing and she is unable to talk. Sally heard the man tell Kathy that if she messed with him "I will cut your throat like I did when another women messed with me. William's wife Cindy was killed, and her throat was cut a few years ago. This man sold a ring to a young man at the tavern earlier in the evening and we are fairly certain it was the ring that William's wife Cindy was wearing when she was killed. Normally I would like to see all sinners have another chance for redemption but quite frankly I am glad this man is dead."

William spoke up saying that he had been praying for his wife's killer to be found but not at such a terrible price. William was trying to comfort Janice who was overwhelmed with grief, but it brought the searing pain of the loss of Cindy back to William too.

Clarence began speaking. "My whole family is in shock. My son fell in love with Kathy from the first day he met her and managed to win her heart. My wife and I are absolutely thrilled with the idea of Kathy marrying our son. Poor little Katy has lost her father, her mother, her brother and now is terrified like we are that she may be losing her sister Kathy. Kathy has been her mother for the last year. When we first saw Kathy laying there motionless, we all feared the worst that she was gone. The sight was so horrific and heartbreaking for all of us. I mentioned that Kathy is struggling to breathe but she also can't swallow or talk which is also a serious concern. I certainly see Satan's hand in what happened. Besides her talent for singing and playing piano, Kathy had both the desire and the talent for teaching children about Jesus."

"My wife and my daughter Sally both love children and Kathy showed that love too. We charge a little for women and children to use the bathhouse, but it barely pays for the wood we burn and the towels we wear out and we don't get anything for taking care of children and mothers. My wife and my daughter Sally and now Kathy have done it because they love mothers and children. No men are allowed in there except very little boys. Mothers get to relax with a hot bath and children can cool off on a hot day in a cool pool of water. Our family has a wonderful resource of good clean cold water that we have tried to share with the people around us. Unfortunately, some people feel that women and girls should never see each other partially undressed and feel our bathhouse is improper. We don't force you to come but my wife, my daughter and Kathy are not immoral even though they spend time in the bathhouse. Kathy liked to sing Christian hymns in there. When Katy came here, she thought it was the nicest place on earth."

"So why did the attack on Sally and Kathy happen. Well, we had three men who were very drunk. Two of those men had evil intentions and the third man really didn't know why he was there but followed bad companions. Still this disaster would not have happened if a woman had not been breaking the commandment of 'Thou shalt not bear false witness against thy neighbor. This woman thought the bathhouse was wrong and let her husband know it and went a step further by telling him that it was probably a house of ill repute as well. Well, he liked that idea and came over with two other men and broke in based on her lie. One man is dead, her husband will go to jail for breaking in, a young lady is fighting for her life and a little girl will carry this nightmare with her for the rest of her life. I probably will too. Paul lists a lot of bad behavior in Romans 1:29 and gossips are included and based on what has happened, it definitely belongs."

"I truly believe that we were making the lives of a lot of women and children happier with our bathhouse but as of now, it is closed. I cannot allow members of my household to be slandered and their lives be put in jeopardy because of the evil minds of people among us." Clarence said a few more words before dismissing the congregation and asking them to pray.

Velma had not realized that Kathy lived in the bathhouse, and she had enjoyed Kathy's singing. It sounded really bad and then it started to hit her that Steve had not come home but sometimes he would hide out until he sobered up after drinking. If it were Steve, could he have said she told them that there were prostitutes at the bathhouse. She slunk away from the church ignoring a couple of women she liked to share her gossip with. It was almost a half mile to her house, and it was a long walk. She did recall hinting at prostitution at the bathhouse, but Steve had said that was really bad. She had gone only a block when she decided to return to the church.

Clarence was still at the church talking to William. They had found the money in the dead man's pocket that Benny had paid for the ring. Clarence told Benny the ring was stolen, and Benny had given the ring to Clarence in exchange for the money. William examined the ring and showed a special mark on it that convinced him that it was the ring he had given Cindy. William wondered if the ring was evil. Clarence told him that Sally had looked at it and said it reminded her of what a wonderful person Cindy was.

William left with his two children and Clarence confronted Velma. "Yes, it was your husband who brought the other two men over to our bathhouse. The Sheriff has been sent for and will be out this afternoon to take him to jail."

"You told the congregation it was my fault," Velma said, "I had nothing to do with it."

"You planted the evil seed in his mind," Clarence replied.

"People will shun me, that is so unfair," Velma replied.

"So, do you think it was fair to call members of my household prostitutes, all of whom are innocent?" Clarence replied.

"I am going to kill my husband when I see him," Velma responded and ignored the question.

"I won't stop you, but the Sheriff will then arrest you for murder," Clarence replied.

Sally met them as they came walking up to the patio. "Kathy is still alive, but she can't talk, drink or swallow food. Poor little Katy has vowed not to eat or drink until Kathy does. Katy said that if Kathy dies, she wants to die too. Bobby hasn't eaten either and little Jade has been sitting there praying and crying all morning."

Sally then vented her anger on Velma, "are you satisfied with what you accomplished with your lies about us? My one regret from last night is that I didn't succeed in killing your husband when he tried to rape me. I have never slept with any man except my late husband and no amount of money would induce me to sleep with the creep you married but he is exactly what you deserve."

Velma wanted to slap Sally but wisely restrained herself.

Clarence pulled Sally inside and locked the gate. "Come in and see your husband," Clarence told Velma.

"How can I?", Velma asked, "the gate is locked."

"It didn't stop them last night," Clarence replied, "they got Benny to climb over the fence and unlock the gate from the inside. They didn't knock, and they didn't just walk in."

Clarence opened the gate and let Velma in. Velma shuddered as she saw the body of the stranger and next to him was her husband tied up and looking miserable. Benny was a few feet away with his head down crying. He had heard what Sally said and was so filled with remorse that he would have gladly died if it would make Kathy okay. Velma had planned to yell at her husband but the body of the man next to him and Benny crying gave her a sense of despair as bad as anything she had ever felt before.

"How could you?" Velma finally asked Steve in a quiet voice.

"Well, you said the women here were prostitutes and you never want to make love, so I thought I would come here," he replied.

"Why did you break in," Velma asked.

"We were drunk, and we thought we would surprise them."

"I guess we are both guilty," Velma finally replied, "I should never have suggested there were prostitutes, and you should have never come here and broke in."

The Sheriff showed up an hour later. They told him what had happened and that they were certain that the dead man was Cindy's killer.

The Sheriff went through the meager belongings of the stranger. "That isn't the only one he has killed, there is an award out for killing or capturing him," he commented. "He was a really nasty man. I will see that the little lady gets the award. I am going to give Benny a week to get his stuff together and leave town. If I see him after that, I will have him arrested. I am going let Steve and his wife go home now and then bring him to trial after I find out if the young lady recovers."

The Sheriff walked through the bathhouse with Sally explaining what happened. Velma walked behind them and realized it was hardly the setup for a den of iniquity. Sally was a little sad to hear Clarence tell the Sheriff he was going to shut the bathhouse down.

"There are going to be a lot of disappointed children and mothers," Sally said. "but I guess it is time."

When they came back out, the Sheriff gave a warning to Benny and Steve and then turned them loose. The Sheriff also took the dead stranger with him who he had identified as a wanted criminal with a history of robbery and murder.

Clarence and Sally came back in the living room where Kathy was laying asleep on the couch holding Katy's hand. Katy and Jade were both huddled up against the couch. Bobby had been up all night and finally fallen asleep nearby on the floor. Martha had fallen asleep in the bedroom but woke up when Clarence came in.

They came up with a plan for Katy and got everybody including Bobby out to the patio leaving Kathy sleeping on the couch. Clarence sat down with Katy in his lap, and they all crowded around her including Julia who had come out from the kitchen. "Katy, we are all heartbroken that Kathy is hurt; we all love her so much and we are praying for her recovery. Kathy loves you so much and showed it by attacking that evil man. She cares so much about you, and she would be so sad if she knew you were not eating and drinking water. We all love you so much too and you are making us sad when you do not eat or drink. We all need to take care of ourselves, so we can be there for her. Please honey, eat, and drink for me and Martha and all your friends here." Katy cried, and Clarence almost did too.

Finally, Katy said "okay."

"Okay, Julia has lunch ready, let's all eat," Martha spoke up.

They sat down at the table with Sally sitting between Katy and Jade with her arms around both of them. Clarence prayed a blessing for the food, thanking God for sparing Kathy and asking God to completely heal her. They all ate including Katy, but it was hard for them to fully enjoy the good lunch knowing Kathy couldn't eat.

Bobby was totally spent; they had finally built a good- looking dresser that Richard had approved for production. It should have been a time to celebrate but he was totally demoralized. His brain kept replaying the horrific scene of his precious Kathy lying motionless with a knife in her back and blood coming out of her mouth. Bobby realized what William had gone through when he lost Cindy, but Bobby still had hope that Kathy would recover.

Martha came out and said that Kathy was awake and sitting up. Martha and Julia had given her some cold water and some honey, and she had been able to get a little of both down before she choked a little and they had to stop. Bobby then went in and gently hugged Kathy and gave her a quick kiss on the cheek and told her how much he loved her. Kathy smiled at him and then lay down and went back to sleep. Bobby held it together until he got outside and then he went off by himself and cried and prayed for her.

There were no guests in the guest rooms upstairs and there wouldn't be for several weeks, so Sally moved herself and Katy upstairs to the guest rooms with Alex in the room next to theirs. Sally was exhausted and was glad she was able to talk Katy into taking a nap. She locked the door behind her feeling a kind of paranoia she had never felt before. Sally hated to see the bathhouse close, but she knew she would never feel safe there again. She had always felt like it was a safe sanctuary for women. Now she would always have this worry about men coming in. Despite a troubled mind, Sally drifted off to sleep.

Kathy didn't show much improvement on Monday although she was able to sip a little water and swallow a little bit of honey. Kathy had some bad bruises from when she tackled the man and they crashed down to the brick floor and her left hand was slightly sprained. She also had slightly blurred vision from hitting her head sometime during their fight.

Tuesday, she found it a little easier to breathe, her vision cleared up and she was able to drink liquids and eat a little soup. Being able to see helped her morale and she started writing notes to people. Kathy still couldn't talk, and she worried that she would never talk or sing again.

Seeing that Kathy was recovering, Bobby reluctantly made plans to leave for St Louis on Wednesday to look at the building where the dressers would be assembled and plan an assembly line. Bobby also needed to find a place to live. William was starting to stockpile boards cut to size to be shipped to St Louis.

Wednesday morning Kathy put on a dress and slowly walked out to the patio and sat down at the table. She carefully sipped on a small cup of coffee with a lot of cream. Bobby gave her a hug and a good-bye kiss. "I hate having to leave you right now," he told her.

"Love you, I will be fine." She scribbled to him on a piece of paper.

Kathy started putting her experience into a song writing it down on paper and wishing she had a voice, so she could sing it.

A man tried to kill me, and I nearly died.
My friends around me they all cried
I waited for the Lord to take me away

I thought I would be in Heaven by the end of the day
But then all my friends decided to pray
When the Lord heard them He let me stay
So now I am here. and I am so glad
Because I hated to see my friends so sad

Kathy showed it to Katy and Jade who were now practically inseparable. Katy tried to sing it, but it sounded stilted. Jade sang it in an upbeat bouncy beat you could almost dance to. Kathy got a big smile on her face and signaled success. Katy then sang it with Jade the same way Jade did just as Sally and Alex came down from upstairs.

Sally clapped her hands and exclaimed, "I love it."

The girls did it again for the benefit of Martha, Julia, and Clarence. Bobby had started to leave but realized he had forgotten something and came back in time to hear the song. He waved good-bye again this time with a big smile. Smiles replaced sad faces and the gloom went away.

CHAPTER 17

Sewing and Recovering

Kathy's back was healing fine and by Friday she was starting to get enough nourishment to have a little energy, but she also had to be careful because she got short of breath if she tried to do too much. She walked with Sally into the women's bathhouse. She really didn't find it frightening during the day, but she doubted she could go back to her bunk and fall asleep. Katy and Jade joined them and quickly undressed and jumped in the water. Kathy was a little jealous of them but reminded herself to be thankful she was alive.

Kathy went over to her sewing machine and sat down. After a few minutes she started on the dresses she was working on for Katy and Jade. Kathy worked at a fraction of her normal speed, and everything seemed more tedious. She had almost finished them before she was hurt but was happy that she was able to finish them now. The girls were out of the water and just toweling off. They tried the dresses on and were so excited that they matched and ran off to show them to Julia and Martha. Sally helped Kathy get back to the living room. Kathy lay down on the couch and fell asleep for the rest of the afternoon.

Kathy had worn a home-made neck brace for several days after the attack but finally took it off. Her neck was still stiff on Sunday, but she was breathing a lot better. She put on the lavender dress she had made for herself and slowly walked over to the church accompanied by Sally, Katy, and Jade. Jade had slept overnight with Katy, so she could go to church with them.

Kathy's left wrist was still a little sore but not enough to stop her from playing the piano. It took her several attempts to duplicate the rhythm and pitch on the piano the way Jade had sung the song Kathy had wrote. Finally, Kathy got it right and so did Katy and Jade. Clarence, Sally, and Martha practiced "Rock of Ages" while Kathy played it on the piano. A smaller crowd than normal came into the church, but they were so excited to see Kathy back. People would come over to talk to Kathy, and Katy would explain to them that she had not got her voice back yet.

Clarence had opened the service with prayer including thanking God for sparing Kathy and asking that her voice be restored. Then Clarence announced that "Kathy can't sing yet, but she wrote a song about her ordeal and her little friend Jade came up with the melody for it. We are so happy to have Jade with us this morning; her grandmother is a fantastic cook who has kept my family eating well for years. Katy and Jade will now sing the song Kathy wrote wearing the dresses Kathy finished sewing this week. Kathy still keeps amazing us."

Katy and Jade sang the song perfectly and with enthusiasm and Kathy added a little flourish on the piano at the end. "I think all three of them and our merciful God deserve a round of applause," Clarence announced after they finished the song. The congregation clapped with enthusiasm including a few that had been a little unsettled about seeing a black girl in church.

Clarence then led the congregation in singing "The Old Rugged Cross". After they finished, Clarence announced that "we were going to do this song last Sunday. The night before, when we practiced it, Bobby said he shuddered when he heard Kathy sing 'When my eyes are closed in death'. When he saw her body lying there motionless with her eyes closed, he was convinced she was gone and that he had been forewarned. I think it would have been true if it weren't for all of our prayers."

"Bobby left for St Louis on Wednesday to help set up a factory assembly line for oak dressers that will be built using wood that will be shipped from William's sawmill. Pray for Bobby's safety and the success of this venture which could result in some more jobs here in our community. It could be a real boost for some of our people looking for steady work. Despite her ordeal, my daughter Sally wants to keep the bathhouse going but only have it open on Thursday, Friday, and Saturday."

"Now I want Janice to come up here and lead all the children in singing, "Tell Me the Stories of Jesus'." When the children had finished, Clarence prayed a blessing on the children. "Thank you Lord for entrusting these beautiful children to us and help us to lead them in the path of righteousness and service to you."

After the service, most of the congregation came by to tell Kathy how happy they were to see her back and to tell her they would pray for her voice to return. Several women told her how much they loved the dresses she made for Katy and Jade. One of the women asked her if she planned to be a composer like Beethoven.

Kathy played a short, complicated piece on the piano to the women's surprise. Kathy then wrote her a note: "that was Beethoven, I will stick to simpler stuff."

Kathy was tired when she got back from the church but stayed awake through lunch. She ate some leftover soup that Julia had made for her the previous night. It was chicken soup that was thick but had no big pieces and was easy to swallow but Kathy still had to eat very slowly.

Sally told Kathy that she had managed to get Katy and Jade to change out of their new dresses after they showed them to Julia one more time. "When you get healthy again, could you make me a dress like the one you are wearing? I would like to see Janice in a pretty new dress too."

Kathy signaled she would. Kathy wanted to make new dresses for all the people around her.

Sally said, "I talked to Benny's sister, and she said Benny was glad you were recovering. He was really sorry about his part in opening the gate and he really didn't understand what they were coming over here for. His engagement is off with Tina. Even if Tina forgives him, her parents will never approve of him. He left on the train Wednesday; he was going to try to find work as a miner in the Black Hills. The Sheriff told him he wouldn't arrest him if he would leave town."

Kathy felt a little sorry for Benny and Tina, she was not the only one paying the price for that night. Kathy hadn't known about Benny's participation in opening the gate until Clarence had told her.

Kathy went to the bathhouse after lunch to change to an older dress. Sally, Katy, and Jade were already in the pool. Kathy wanted to go in the pool too, but she didn't dare get her back wet.

Sally came over and talked to her, "I wonder if you could make bathing suits for Katy, Jade, and Janice. Alex has shorts with a rope belt and maybe we can get something like that for James. Janice is getting old enough to need a top, but shorts should be okay for Katy and Jade. I would like to get the boys and the girls together in the same pool. The boys are still young enough that I think the two of us could still get by with just the bathing suits you made."

Kathy gave a thumbs up to Sally.

The issue was more serious than what can we do to allow older children to swim together. Kathy thought of how Satan had come to their little garden of Eden. They needed to worry more about covering up their bodies now and she would never feel really safe in there again. Katy had thought it was the nicest place on earth. Unfortunately, this place like others had snakes and they walked on two feet instead of crawling. This crazy desire men had for women. It was wonderful when it came with a nice man like Bobby who wanted to marry her. It was horrible when it was nothing but lust that they tried to satisfy in a few moments and leave behind problems lasting a lifetime sometimes for both the attacker and the victim. Kathy went back to the house and laid down on the couch; her mind bouncing between the good things at church and her bad memories and finally slept through the afternoon.

Kathy had finished off the soup at lunch and was swallowing better. She had handed a note to Katy to tell Julia she would try eating regular food for supper.

She tried talking before she went out to the patio for supper and only got a faint squawk. For a moment she almost wished she had died. "Please Lord give me my voice back," she begged in prayer. She was able to eat supper by carefully chewing each bite. She ate in silence. She had no choice. It was so frustrating to be unable to join in the conversation.

After supper she went back out to the bathhouse and started sewing again. She tried on her bathing suit and found it fit fine again after her unplanned diet. She modified her bathing suit, so she could still wear it if she gained weight. She also modified the short dress to be a pair of shorts and added panels inside the front top and bottom so that it didn't fit like a coat of paint. She took Katy's dress and started cutting bright red material to make a bathing suit for her. Katy came in and she was able size up the material on her. It was getting dark, and she decided to finish it the next day.

Kathy started sewing again the next morning. Julia had the day off, so Jade didn't come. Kathy had trouble getting Katy's bathing suit to fit securely at first but finally got it right. Kathy had put on her modified bathing suit and Sally put on the bathing suit Kathy had made for her.

Sally went over to the boy's side and brought Alex back wearing his shorts with a belt. Kathy and Alex played catch in the water with a ball of rags tied together. "This is so great having them together," Sally enthused, "and Katy's outfit is so cute."

Kathy wrote a note to Sally to pick out a dress that fit well. Kathy showed Sally some bright colored fabric and got thumbs up. Kathy started measuring and cutting fabric. Kathy's boss at the garment factory did her no favors but he took advantage of her ability to learn quickly and used her to cover absent workers or add extra help to any area that was causing a bottleneck. Now Kathy was using the expertise she had gained to work efficiently. Kathy had Sally try on her new dress in the afternoon and after another hour of work it was done. Sally loved it.

Kathy had moved upstairs in the house and now shared a double bed with Katy, Sally slept in a single bed nearby and Alex was in the next room. Even though Bobby had made it possible to lock the women's bathhouse entry door from the patio, they were still too traumatized to want to sleep there. Kathy took a nap after finishing Sally's dress. The bed was nice, but it was cooler in the bathhouse. Kathy was getting stronger, and she wasn't short of breath except when she climbed the stairs. Martha had removed the stitches from her back, and she was back to normal except she couldn't speak or sing.

Kathy sat at the table and tried to play her flute after supper. She did not have enough breath to get much sound and quickly ran out of breath trying. Kathy put the flute on the table.

Martha came behind her and tried to comfort her as the tears ran down Kathy's face. "Sweetheart it's going to take some time before everything comes back to you, I can't believe all the sewing you did today. When we prayed, God saved you. We need to keep praying that he will give you back your voice and your singing."

Kathy agreed with Martha in her mind, but patience was not one of her virtues. Kathy had a strong work ethic even before her mother died, and ever since then, she felt compelled to always push herself to the limit.

On Tuesday, Sally helped Martha with laundry and Kathy worked on a bathing suit for Jade while wearing her own bathing suit. Alex and Katy played checkers out in the patio and Katy wore a dress since Kathy had borrowed her bathing suit as a guide for doing Jade's. She was able to make Jade's outfit fairly quickly and soon a happy Jade was showing it off to Julia and Katy. The checker game was close, but Katy finally lost a game.

They came into the bath area and Alex jumped into the pool wearing his shorts and then Jade jumped in. Katy took her dress off, hung it up and jumped in after them. Katy remembered she was supposed to wear a bathing suit and got out of the pool when she saw Kathy come walking over to the pool with it. "Why do I have to wear it?" Katy asked before reluctantly putting it on. Kathy couldn't talk and just smiled. To Katy, Alex was no different than any of the other little boys who had seen her naked and it was no big deal. To Alex it was no big deal either since he had often saw Janice not wearing anything. He would have preferred not wearing anything too. It didn't bother Kathy, but she felt that since Jade had her outfit on, Katy should too. Kathy also knew that children talked just as adults did. Like Velma, they could make something innocent sound very scandalous.

Kathy went back to work. She took Sally's bathing suit and modified it similar to what she had done with her own. Sally tried it on and decided to wear it while doing the laundry. Katy, Jade, and Alex played keep away in the water. Martha had decided she wanted a swim outfit too and Kathy already had been given a dress to modify for her and started working on it. Kathy had barely got started when it was time for lunch. Everyone but Martha sat down for lunch wearing their bathing suits. Martha noted she was the only one without a bathing suit.

"I saw Kathy working on it," Sally told her, "what do you think of mine now?"

"Don't wear it to Church," Martha replied, "but it would be proper enough for showing to William but maybe not to Velma" Martha said it with a bit of sarcasm.

In the afternoon Janice and James came over and Sally sent Alex and James back to the boy's side. Janice was fascinated with the sewing machine and liked the idea of getting a bathing suit. Kathy measured her for an outfit and Janice picked out a dark blue shade from the remaining fabrics.

Kathy had written another song and wrote a note asking the girls to come up with a tune. After a few attempts, it sounded good. Martha and Sally were talking to Julia, so the three girls came over and sang it for them. Jade got a hug from Julia; Janice got a hug from Sally and Martha gave Katy a hug.

"It is so wonderful to hear you girls sing, I hope Kathy can write more songs for you," Martha told them.

> **Our righteousness is a total mess.**
> **but Jesus loves us none the less.**
> **Ask for forgiveness when you pray.**
> **Ask for guidance through the day.**
> **Jesus sees us from above.**
> **Ask for him to show his love.**
> **Get your Bible, read God's word.**
> **When you do His voice is heard.**

The girls came back after singing and Janice took off her dress and jumped in the pool. Kathy wasn't sure if she was making progress toward modesty since Katy and Jade had taken their bathing suits off before they also jumped in the water. Kathy decided why not, they really weren't needed if the boys weren't there. It was a hot day; she almost took her own suit off but then left it on and joined them in the water for a few minutes until she cooled off.

Kathy decided to work on a bathing suit for Janice and try to get back to Martha's bathing suit later. Kathy took her wet bathing suit off and dried herself with a towel. She sat on her towel, and almost went back to work on her sewing machine. She reluctantly put on her dress. Kathy didn't care if the girls saw her undressed except that a remark by any of them that Kathy didn't wear anything in the bathhouse could be passed on and embellished by someone like Velma. Even the innocence of the three girls could be made to sound scandalous. Kathy still had a sore neck from the attack which tired her each day and right now she wanted a nap. The tooth that had been loose from the blow to her head seemed firm again; that was encouraging. She tried singing and could barely hear her voice but some of the words were almost legible. Kathy rubbed her neck, and it made a funny sound, but her neck felt better.

Kathy finished the bathing suit for Janice and waved for her to try it on. She handed Janice a towel first which was good since it was a little loose on top. Kathy made a few adjustments on the sewing machine and had Janice try it again. This time it fit fine. Janice was happy with the bathing suit and said she would like a new dress too. Kathy measured the dress that Janice took off and wrote down the measurements on a piece of paper.

Kathy started on Martha's bathing suit. She finally got Martha's outfit ready to try on. Kathy went looking for Martha. Kathy found Martha upstairs talking to Sally.

Martha tried on the bathing suit, and it fit.

"This is really great," Martha said, "now I can feel more proper in the pool area even when little boys are around." Kathy got a hug from Martha, laid down on her bed and was sound asleep after saying a faint goodnight.

"Let's try our suits out," Martha suggested to Sally.

"Kathy also made a bathing suit for Janice today and she wrote another song for Sunday," Sally remarked.

"I know the Bible says we are supposed to forgive our enemies, but It hurts so bad that Kathy can't sing anymore," Martha commented.

"I made Steve pay pretty dearly for what he tried to do to me, but Kathy is such a sweetheart, and she has had so much heartbreak and now this," Sally replied in agreement. They entered the bathhouse and went in the pool. Martha was impressed that even after they got wet, they looked proper in their outfits.

The three girls were laying on their towels on a shady spot on the grass. Janice and Katy were half asleep, but Jade was reading a book. Martha looked at them and commented, "I need to get some more books for Katy to read, I have even handed her high school books and she goes through them in a couple of days."

"Does she understand them?", Sally asked.

"I have asked her questions and she knows the answers," Martha replied.

"So, I need to start pushing Alex a little harder," Sally replied.

"If you want him to keep up with Katy," Martha responded. "Jade has been reading a lot too, she is a very smart little girl. Julia wants her to stay here and go to our school next year. I would love to have her but there are probably going to be some unhappy white parents when their children can't keep up with a little black girl."

"Nobody is paying you so if they are unhappy, their children can ride for over an hour on the school wagon to Williamsburg," Sally replied.

"I was hoping Kathy could help me teach this fall, but I don't know if she will get her voice back," Martha wondered out loud. "Just now when she laid down, she said a faint goodnight so maybe there is hope. Bobby wants her to marry him and move to St Louis, but Kathy says she wants a ring, a wedding dress and a two -bedroom apartment to move into. Kathy did seem somewhat willing to leave Katy with Clarence and me through next winter."

Sally had trouble getting Kathy awake for supper but finally succeeded.

"Are you okay?" Sally asked.

"Just tired," Kathy replied in a weak, but distinct voice which surprised both herself and Sally.

"Hey, you are talking," Sally exclaimed.

Kathy followed Sally down to the patio wondering if she dared to try more words. Everybody was seated when Kathy got to the table. "Sorry I am late," Kathy said as she sat down. Again, her voice was soft, but it was distinct.

"Kathy, would you like to say grace?" Clarence asked.

"I will try, Dear Lord, thank you for this food, thank you for my friends that have been praying for me. Thank you for giving me back my voice; strengthen it so I may serve you better. Amen."

They had ham and corn on the cob for supper. Kathy didn't have any trouble chewing. Kathy still had a little trouble swallowing but the buttered corn was good, and she worked her way through a couple cobs of corn.

"Keep eating, you need to build your strength back up for all the women who I am going to send into the bathhouse who want new dresses for themselves and their daughters," Clarence told her.

"I will have to come into the store tomorrow and order more material and thread," Kathy replied. Kathy would have been more excited about the news if she wasn't so tired, but a cup of hot coffee helped.

"If Bobby were here, I would be tempted to curl up in his lap," she told Sally who was sitting next to her.

"I thought the plan was for him to return Saturday morning, so you will have to wait until then," Sally replied.

Jade would stay through supper before leaving with Julia and got hugs from everyone, but Alex, before she left. Alex wasn't ready to hug a girl, but Alex, Katy and Jade enjoyed playing together. Kathy smiled, there was so much love here.

Kathy went to bed right after supper. She finally had no neck pain and enjoyed her best night of sleep since the break in. She woke up early leaving Sally and Katy still sleeping and went down to help Martha in the kitchen. "Good morning," Kathy announced with a voice just loud enough to be heard.

"It is so wonderful to hear your voice again," Martha told her, "and I keep praying that someday soon you will be singing again."

"Me too," Kathy replied.

Martha let Kathy make the pancake batter. Kathy tried to be good at everything she did, and Martha had complimented her skill one day by saying "my son will be marrying a good cook."

Kathy knew that Bobby loved her singing, would he still want to marry her if she couldn't sing anymore. The thought bothered her, casting a shadow on a sunny morning. Kathy started setting the table after getting the pancake batter ready. Kathy tried singing the song "Softly and Tenderly Jesus is Calling" which did not sound great to her but at least she was singing.

After breakfast, Kathy went over to the store and bought the remaining stock of thread and material that was on the store shelves which wasn't a lot and then ordered more from a catalogue. Clarence told her that there was a peddler that comes through here with yard goods every other week and he thought he might be here tomorrow.

Kathy had returned to her sewing machine when a lady walked in asking about a dress. Kathy did not have much material to choose from, but the lady really liked one pattern. Kathy asked Alex if he would mind playing next door and Jade and Katy went with him.

"Those outfits the girls are wearing are so cute," the lady remarked. She changed to a bathing gown so Kathy could use her dress for a pattern. Kathy said she was welcome to jump in the pool while she waited. It was a warm morning and after hesitating for a while she jumped in. Kathy finished cutting out the dress and told her she could come back in a couple hours or wait. Kathy threw her a towel which she used to dry off in the dressing room and changed back to the dress she had given Kathy. She was fascinated by the sewing machine and how fast Kathy worked.

The girls had decided to come back, and Kathy suggested they sing a song for the lady. They did a great job and the lady thanked them. Kathy had her try it on, made some adjustments, hand sewed on some buttons, and she was ready to go. She was happy with the dress and happy with the price. Kathy was pleased that she finally had a paying customer, but she also felt good about making things for Sally, Martha, and the girls.

Kathy had leftover scraps of material from the dresses she had made and started piecing them together to make a colorful apron. She had just finished it when Martha walked in and Kathy gave it to her.

"Thank you, it is almost too pretty to wear," Martha told her. "You need to make more of these, and we can sell them in the store. That is if you ever have time, I was in the store when the lady came in and paid for her dress, she was so happy with it."

They were interrupted by Sally walking in with Velma. Velma was crying and looking very distraught. "I want to beg for forgiveness for myself and my husband," she told them.

Velma's husband Steve made a good living making cheese and if he went to prison, they could be facing financial ruin. Velma also said that Steve was very depressed and was still suffering headaches.

"As Christians we are supposed to forgive but that doesn't mean that crimes should not be punished," Martha told her. "Benny and his girlfriend are not getting married because of that night. Kathy can barely talk, and right now her beautiful singing voice is gone, possibly forever."

They told Velma to sit outside in the patio while they talked. Sally spoke up, "I am willing to drop the charges but only if she humbles herself.

I want her to spend three days working at the bathhouse and go half naked. It doesn't bother me but to her that is the ultimate disgrace."

"I think she is crying tears of self-pity," Kathy replied, "I don't think she really cares what happened to me or Benny and his girlfriend. My mother, myself and Katy all faced financial ruin after a bank robber killed my father. We learned what it is like to go hungry, she can too. Another tenant lied to my landlord forcing Katy and me to leave and we almost became homeless. I will go along with Sally's plan, but I really don't care if her husband goes to jail."

Martha then spoke up, "I will agree with Sally, but I think she needs to come here for six days so she remembers the next time she decides to gossip."

Sally went out to talk to Velma. "We don't think you care about the fact that Kathy can no longer sing or that Benny and his girlfriend aren't getting married. Kathy and her sister came here broke, homeless, and hungry so now it is your turn."

"Isn't there anything I can do to make it right," Velma asked. "You can't make it right," Sally replied, "but I will drop the charges if you agree to come here Thursday, Friday, and Saturday this week and next and work in the women's bath area with almost no clothes on."

"I would never do anything that scandalous," Velma said.

"I do it all the time and women and children thank me because they get clean and can cool off on a hot day," Sally replied. "I will see your husband in court two weeks from next Monday unless you are here tomorrow morning by nine. You have a long hot walk home, I am going to cool off in the pool, you might want to do that too." Sally took her dress off in the bathhouse doorway and waved to Velma. "Goodbye."

Sally then went and put her bathing suit on and went and got Alex before joining the girls in the pool who had their bathing suits on.

Kathy was able to make a couple more aprons before she ran out of material. She brought them into the store and told Clarence how much to charge for them. She then went back to the bathhouse and changed from her dress into her bathing suit. She had forgotten that Alex was in the pool but fortunately it looked like he been facing the other direction. It was nice to have the children play together but she would have to be more careful about what day it was.

Kathy went out to work in the garden for the first time since the break in. She shuddered a little at seeing the clothesline that killed her attacker and saved her life. Poor Julia found it really spooky that a man had died out there. The garden had two weeks of neglect and showed it. It was a very warm but cloudy day. She started on the peas but realized they were about done for the season. She switched to the string beans and realized they needed to be picked. She got a bucket and started picking them and then got a small knife from Julia to pull the strings off.

"My favorite helper is back," Julia told her, "you should grab Jade and put her to work."

"Children grow up too fast, I want them to have some happy memories that will help them remember that God loves them when they grow up," Kathy replied.

"Well, you and Katy have made Jade a very happy little girl," Julia responded.

"We all love her, she is a very sweet, very smart little girl," Kathy replied. Kathy got the strings off the beans and went back to weeding. Kathy thought she was done sewing for the day but wound up working on a dress in the afternoon for a lady who had brought her own material for her dress.

CHAPTER 18

Redemption

Thursday arrived and to the surprise of Sally, Kathy, and Martha, so did Velma. She told them she did not get much sleep and she looked it. Martha left to help Clarence in the store. Katy was playing checkers with Alex out in the patio.

Sally filled up one of the tubs that was not enclosed with hot water and told Velma to undress and take a bath. Velma did as instructed but was very distraught and started crying.

"This is so hard for me," Velma told Sally. "When I was fifteen, I was living on a farm and one hot day I got really dirty. Rather than take a sponge bath inside the house, I went to a secluded spot behind the barn with a pail of water and cleaned up outside. It was convenient since it wasn't far from the pump. I did it several times then one day when I washed up outside, a teenage neighbor boy was hunting and saw me. He snuck up on me and raped me. I wound up getting pregnant and my father said it was my fault because I was outside without clothes on."

"I was sent to live with an aunt until the baby was born to save my reputation, but the story got out anyway. I gave my baby boy up for adoption and never saw him again. I never wanted to see my father again, so I stayed with my aunt and got a job at a cheese factory which is where I met Steve. He was a widower with a beautiful little girl who I adored. Sadly, she died of the flu a year later. I guess I am too bitter to be much of a wife for Steve and I don't really love him, but we work well together. I guess I like him well enough to come here since he said he would commit suicide if he had to go to prison. I don't know why I go to church because to me the idea of a loving God is a joke."

"You are safe in here," Sally told her, "I am going to get you a bathing gown to wear when you get out of your bath. Your father should have stuck up for you, going naked behind the barn might have been unwise but it was not immoral, and it did not justify you being raped."

Sally talked to Kathy out at the patio. "Velma has had a very sad life and her fear of being naked is justified even if what she said about us was not. Let's be nice to her and try to get her playing with a child."

Soon after a mother came in with a young girl and a baby boy. "Would you mind letting these two play in the water while I go to the store."

Sally handed the little boy to Velma who was now wearing a bathing gown. "We haven't changed your bathwater, why don't you sit down in there with him."

Velma gave the baby boy a smile and he gave her a smile back. For the next twenty minutes she played and cuddled and cooed to the little boy while Sally was entertaining the little girl.

The mother came back and thanked them. "Both of my children looked so happy when I came in here, you people are so wonderful."

Velma started crying after they left. "What's wrong?" Sally asked.

"I felt so bad after our little girl died that I decided not to have children but now I realize how badly I want a child."

Sally replied, "I suffered a lot of heartache after I lost my husband, but you need to love people in order to be happy."

Kathy was surprised when Sally asked her if she could take Velma's dress for a pattern and create a bathing suit. Kathy had a grey piece of material that looked kind of drab for dress but might be okay for a bathing suit. Kathy started working on it and soon had Velma trying it on.

"I don't know why you bother for an ugly old lady like me," Velma told her.

"The Bible says to love your enemies and you are not ugly or old, but you look a lot better when you smile," Kathy replied. Kathy made some adjustments and added some black trim that made the outfit more attractive. She had Velma try it on and it fit well and looked good.

Three ladies and a bunch of children came in and Kathy, Sally and Velma were all kept busy. Katy and Jade came back in and played with the other children too. Velma soon realized helping the children in and out of water could be tiring but everyone was happy. Velma enjoyed playing with the children. Just in time for lunch, the mothers and children finally left. Velma had expected one of the worst days of her life but found herself in really good spirits.

They all sat out in the patio wearing bathing suits except for Martha who was getting ready to relieve Clarence in the store. Martha prayed a blessing on the food and thanked him that Velma had come today. "We pray for Kathy to get her singing voice back and we pray that Velma will see your love." Velma didn't think that would happen but appreciated the prayer.

Almost on cue, Katy and Jade sang the song Kathy had written: "When our righteousness is a total mess, Jesus loves us none the less". Velma knew the song fit her perfectly, but she was reluctant do what it said. Velma had some prejudice against blacks, but Jade was both so cute and talented that she found herself really liking her. Both girls came over to Kathy who gave them a big hug and then they got a hug from Martha.

They ate a lunch of buttered bread, sliced ham, and apple jelly. Coffee, water, and milk were offered with cookies for dessert. Velma was trying to be polite and not take too much food, but Sally told her to eat more. "you are going to need it for energy this afternoon."

"Thanks for a really good lunch, that bread was so good," Velma told them.

Sally, Velma, and Kathy went back into the bathhouse. Martha came back in and told Kathy to change to a dress.

Kathy changed and went out to the patio where Clarence introduced her to Alfonzo, a traveling peddler of yard goods. "I am going to treat him to lunch and then he will show you some of his material."

"Clarence tells me you have been doing some amazing work on a sewing machine," Alfonzo commented.

"Last year I was sewing dresses ten hours a day six days a week at a garment factory, so I have had a little practice," Kathy replied.

Alfonzo had a sample case like a small suitcase full of thread and needles, and some small metal buckles. He started eating his sandwich and showing her what he had in the case. "Clarence, I am jealous - you have wonderful food here and pretty girls here, I need to stop here more often," Alfonzo teased.

"Well, we do have good food and this young lady is my future daughter in law," Clarence replied.

"Your son is a lucky man,' Alfonzo replied.

Kathy found his prices to be higher than what she would pay if she ordered out of a catalogue but having the stuff now would allow her make dresses and sales now.

"How much can we afford to buy right now?" Kathy asked Clarence when Alfonzo stepped away to bring back some more stuff.

Kathy ran back into the bathhouse and came back out with a paper and a pencil. Kathy quickly made out her order based on the amount Clarence said she could spend. Clarence paid for Kathy's selections and Kathy started carrying them into the bathhouse which required several trips.

Alfonzo's parting comment to Clarence before leaving: "that was one of the smartest, most decisive buyers I have ever had and definitely the prettiest."

Most of the women and children were curious about Kathy's machine and what she was doing. A lot of the women said that if they got a little extra money, they would come back and buy a dress. Both Sally and Velma were busy with mothers and children, but they were doing okay.

Kathy wanted to see what she could make with the little belt buckles she had purchased. She cut a piece of material several feet long and a couple inches wide and then folded it so it was a half inch wide and had four thicknesses of material which she sewed together and then sewed on the belt buckle. She had made a belt, but she realized the prong of the belt buckle would rip through the cloth material when buckled. She wondered if she could reinforce the material where the prong was coming through with a little piece of leather. The blacksmith in town also worked on harnesses. She would have to visit him and see if she could buy some strips of leather.

Sally had let Kathy display the dress she had made for her. Kathy also displayed the dress she had made for herself. A few minutes after Kathy stopped work on the belt, an older lady who introduced herself as Barb Nelson came in and wanted a dress like Sally's and was excited about one of the fabrics Kathy had just bought. Kathy quickly took some measurements of her using a fabric tape measure she had made.

Barb was going to leave and come back, but she spotted Velma and went over to talk to her. "Velma what are you doing here, that outfit you are wearing looks so cute," the lady enthused.

"Kathy made me this outfit this morning and I have been playing with some adorable children," Velma replied.

"An outfit like that would be great for playing with my grandchildren on a hot day," Barb remarked. Barb pulled her dress up, put her feet in the pool and started talking about her grandchildren. Barb thought the bathhouse was really fun and she decided she would bring her granddaughters over. They kept talking and Velma never had to explain why she was there.

Kathy finished the dress which Barb loved and then Barb picked out fabric for a bathing suit to be like Velma's. Barb said she would pick it up when she brought her granddaughters back the next day.

It was getting late in the afternoon and the place had emptied out. Sally told Velma she could leave early.

"Thank you, I am exhausted, but I loved being with the children. I am truly grateful for the kindness you have shown me after the evil I caused. I thought this would be one of the worst days of my life, but it was one of the best." Velma had tired feet but a lighter heart. The words of the song the girls had sung kept coming back to her about asking for forgiveness and asking for God to show his love. Velma had talked about having nothing to feed her husband when she got home, and Sally gave her some bread and ham to take with. Velma resolved to bring some cheese back the next day.

Kathy was still sewing when Velma left and wondering how she survived ten- hour days six days a week at the garment factory. I am getting lazy she decided. Finally, she finished the bathing suit for Barb. Clarence had told her the aprons had sold right away so with more material she started working on more aprons. Martha went to get her for supper and found her asleep with her head on the sewing machine.

"Time for supper, honey," Martha told her while gently rubbing her shoulder to wake her. "You need to take it a little easier on yourself, your body hasn't recovered from what you went through," Martha told her. "I am amazed with what you are doing with that machine, but you don't have to try to take care of everybody at once."

"You don't want your future daughter in law to get lazy do you," Kathy replied.

"I have no worries about that, but I am worried about keeping you healthy," Martha replied.

Kathy went to bed not too long after supper. She woke up Friday morning with more energy than usual and went down to help Martha make breakfast. "Good morning," Kathy called out and was happily surprised that her voice had a more normal sound to it.

"Want to make pancakes?" Martha asked.

"Sure," Kathy responded and started to measure out the ingredients for the batter. Kathy loved working and being with Martha. Kathy prided herself on her self- reliance but emotionally she still needed a mother. Martha had taken over that role in her life in such a wonderful way. Kathy finished making the batter and started setting the table.

Forgetting her voice problem, Kathy started singing "Tell me the Stories of Jesus." Her vocal range was limited but it was a big improvement over the last time she had tried to sing. Katy had come down and joined in and together they finished the song.

Martha came out of the kitchen and said: "That was really good."

"It was mostly Katy," Kathy replied, "but I am getting better."

After breakfast dishes were cleared, Kathy brought the aprons she had made to Clarence in the store to be sold. "You are one busy little lady, I am soon going to be selling more clothing than goods," Clarence said with a smile.

"I doubt it, but I do hope to keep them coming," Kathy replied before returning to the patio just as Velma arrived.

"Good morning, Velma, how are you doing?" Martha asked.

"I am doing good, and I brought you some cheese to thank you for being so nice to me," Velma replied and handed her a small pail full of cheese.

"Thank you, Martha replied, "I can't wait to make something out of it."

Velma walked into the bath area and was greeted by Kathy, Sally, and Katy. Sally and Katy were in bathing suits, but Kathy left her dress on.

Velma hung up her dress and changed into her bathing suit. Katy left the bathhouse to play checkers with Alex. In Katy's absence, Velma talked to Sally, Kathy and Martha who had joined them about how remorseful her husband was about what had happened. "Steve admits that your family would have been justified in killing him for what he tried to do and is grateful to you for agreeing to drop the charges against him. Both Steve and I need to ask God for forgiveness and His love like the song the girls were singing."

"We need to pray," Martha announced, "Lord we ask that you comfort Velma who feels like her family has abandoned her and also feels abandoned by you. Lord, I ask you to help her to reestablish ties with her family and to see fit to forgive them. I ask that Steve would turn to you for forgiveness and redirection for his life. I also ask that you help us to forgive the harm that was caused on that night, and I thank you that Kathy is getting more of her voice back." They all were in tears afterward.

Barb came in with her two granddaughters who were about five and seven years of age, and very excited. Barb changed to the bathing suit Kathy had completed for her and absolutely loved it. Barb joined her granddaughters in the water for a short while before getting out. Sally then jumped into the water and started swinging the girls around to their delight. Jade and Katy joined the two girls and they started playing catch with a ball made of rags. June came in with her little boy and baby girl. Velma was soon in the water with the little boy and Barb got to hold the baby girl.

Kathy had switched to her bathing suit and got a bath ready for June. June told her that Ned had been working hard but it was nice to have him home every night. With Ned having a steady job they could afford to eat better and had plans to expand their cabin. She also had heard that Bobby was coming in for the weekend but wasn't sure if he was arriving today or Saturday.

"Well at least my voice is back enough so I can talk to him," Kathy commented.

"I had forgotten you had lost it, you sound pretty normal," June replied.

Kathy went and got her flute and this time she was able to play it. The notes floated across the bathhouse like a fragrant breeze. Barb felt the little girl in her arms snuggle in a little tighter and fall asleep. She watched her granddaughters playing with the other two girls all smiling and happy. Velma had taken the little boy out of the water and wrapped a towel around him, and they were all cuddled up. Katy had come out of the water and when Kathy played a hymn she knew, Katy sang it beautifully.

When Katy finished the song, Barb whispered to Velma: "this is so wonderful."

"Little children are such a joy," Velma replied.

All the girls had come out of the water and Sally had brought them towels. Kathy then led Katy and Jade in singing "Tell Me the Stories of Jesus" and everyone was singing by the end of the song. Kathy was surprised to see Janice had showed up.

She played the lullaby on her flute and Janice sang it. "You realize that song works on adults too," Sally joked to Janice and Kathy. "We are all going to take a nap so if anyone comes in, you two have to take care of them."

Barb's two granddaughters had laid down on their towels and only Katy and Jade showed a little movement. Kathy decided to try singing "Savior Like a Shepherd Lead Us" with help from Janice, Katy, and Jade. Kathy still did not have her soprano voice, but the lower pitch made the song very much a lullaby too.

After they finished the song, Janice told Kathy that William said she could buy a dress from Kathy. Kathy had one beautiful cream-colored fabric and that is the material Janice wanted. Kathy had almost made herself sleepy but was happy to get started on the dress. She measured Janice again and then started cutting out the fabric. The physical work wasn't that much different than working in the factory, but it was so rewarding to know the person who would be wearing the dress. Kathy had it finished by lunch time and Janice proudly showed it off before changing back into her bathing suit.

Martha had helped Julia make a lunch of cheesy potatoes with ham and invited everyone in the bathhouse out to the patio to eat. Kathy and Velma put their dresses on over their bathing suits, and everyone was proper. They were joined by Alex and James who were wearing shorts still wet from being in the water. Almost nobody but Martha and Velma had eaten cheesy anything. After a few cautious bites it got very quiet at the table as everyone discovered how good it was. Martha told everyone that they Velma had brought the cheese that tasted so good.

"I am so glad you enjoyed it and I had a wonderful morning here," Velma replied.

Kathy helped serve and got help from Velma which allowed Martha a chance to hold the baby for a few minutes. Sally wound up holding the little boy and helping him eat.

Barb was pleased when her granddaughters told her: "gramma this is the best place ever." Barb thanked them and departed with her granddaughters after eating.

Julia had kept back enough food for Clarence, Velma, and Kathy. Clarence also thanked Velma for bringing the cheese and remarked "this is so delicious."

"It is a small gift after all the harm I caused," Velma replied. "I feel so ashamed about what I said about this place, you people are so nice, and children and mothers love it here. Coming here has shown me how much I love children and I think my husband does too. I married Steve who was a widower with a little girl who we dearly loved. When she got sick and died, we both felt so bad that we didn't want to have another baby for fear we would go through the sorrow again."

"I understand how you feel, Kathy responded, "I lost my mother, father, and baby brother. My sister and I were almost homeless when we arrived here. I love children too, but it almost seemed like it was cruel to bring a baby into this world. I think I am finally ready to trust God that when I marry Bobby and we have a baby; it will go well for us."

Clarence suggested that they pray: "Lord I ask that you be with both Velma and Kathy helping them trust you to take care of the children that you give them. Be with Velma's husband Steve and have him turn his heart to you. Lord, I see you making something good come out of something that was bad."

CHAPTER 19

Future Promises

It was late afternoon when Martha came in and said Bobby was home and was out in the patio. Kathy ran out in her bathing suit and said: "welcome home." They held each other tight and enjoyed a passionate kiss. "I can't sing yet, but I can tell you that I love you," Kathy told him.

"I missed you so much," Bobby told her.

"How is the factory coming?" Kathy asked.

"Well, the building is hot, dusty and has too few windows, so lighting is terrible. Richard gave me one man to help me clean the place. We are going to load up a boxcar in Williamsburg on Monday and start production the following week. I would love to have you join me in St Louis but realistically it could be months before I have a normal life. Right now, the factory is my home. I hate to admit it but the best thing I can do to show you I love you is to let you stay here. Father says you are working non-stop on your sewing machine."

"Not quite but I am really busy," Kathy replied. Kathy excused herself to finish the dress and Bobby went to get his first bath in days.

Bobby smelled and looked a whole lot better at supper after his bath, but he was exhausted and showed it. "I haven't had a decent drink of water or a decent meal since I left here," he said at supper. "Now I can understand why Richard and Mary want to spend time here. It is a great opportunity I have in St Louis but living here is so much nicer."

Bobby retired shortly after supper joined by Alex and Shep. Bobby fell asleep with his hand on Shep's back and his mind replaying how adorably cute Kathy was in her bathing suit. Kathy was tired too but helped Martha clear the table and wash dishes. She went upstairs with her mind replaying how wonderful it felt to be back in Bobby's arms before falling asleep.

Poor Sally, she loved her brother and Kathy, but she felt jealous and sad. She had hoped that by now William would have said something to her. It was almost three weeks since he had learned that his wife's killer was dead. Sally thanked God that her brother was home safe, and Kathy was talking again. She asked God to show her if William were to be part of her future, or if not, that another man would come into her life. Like Kathy and Velma, Sally found it easier to talk about trusting in the Lord than to actually do it. Sally was physically tired and fell into a troubled sleep.

Kathy was up early and had the fire in the stove and the coffee started before Martha joined her. Martha announced they were going to have pancakes and Kathy started mixing the batter while Martha set the table. Clarence was the next to show up and Martha sent him over to wake Bobby and Alex while Kathy went up to get Katy and Sally. Bobby still looked beat at breakfast and Kathy gave him a quick shoulder and neck rub.

"That felt so good," Bobby told her with a smile.

Bobby had not said much at supper but confided more at the breakfast table. Talking to them, Bobby said that getting the factory ready to go was a big challenge for both him and Richard. We need to make some changes to the building, but Richard can't really afford to do it until we sell some furniture. I might need to bring Ned back with me, so we can get some furniture built and sold before we commit to much hiring. The job is important to me, but I am more concerned that neither William nor Richard lose any money on this deal.

"Listening to Bobby, Sally realized that William was probably too busy with his part of the furniture endeavor to find time for her. Bobby left after breakfast to meet up with William and Ned.

Velma arrived early and got the firepit ready to go for heating bath water. Kathy had bought some cheap white cotton material and cut a square piece into two triangles and then sewn the corners of the triangle together to create an underpants. She tried it on, and it was a little bit loose. She took it off and put a button on the top left side of the triangle and added a strap with two buttonholes, so it could be tightened. She tried it on again and it fit fine. She showed her creation to Sally and Velma while wearing the top of her swimsuit.

Sally couldn't resist teasing her. "It looks great, I'm sure Bobby will love it. It works for your skinny bottom, but do you think you could make them for people like us who have normal butts." Despite the teasing, they both wanted a couple pair. Kathy showed it to Martha in the kitchen and she also wanted a couple pair.

Kathy started working on them. She made one and had Sally try it on. It fit fine, so she cut out five more pair and ran out of material.

The lady who had ordered the dress came in and tried it on and bought it. She wanted an underpants too, but she wanted a fancy one. Kathy had a piece of material that she liked, and she waited until Kathy finished it. Her comment before leaving was: "This is so neat.""

Kathy spent the morning sewing underwear. Barb came in again with her two granddaughters; she also wanted underpants like Kathy was wearing. Kathy said she couldn't make them until next week unless she wanted them out of nicer material. She said she would wait but suggested that Kathy could make underpants like that for her granddaughters to wear while in the water. They agreed on some dark blue material. They dried the girls off and measured them before letting them go back in the water. Kathy finished them and they worked fine in the water.

Sally admired her work: "the girls look really cute, almost as cute as when they go naked. God gives children these beautiful bodies that we have to cover up to keep them safe."

After Sally left, Kathy decided to put her bathing suit on and kept sewing. What Velma had said about them was wrong, but the incident had exposed their danger. All of them including Sally were concerned about what people might say about the bathhouse and their illusion of being safe in there was gone.

Just before noon a lady came in with material for a dress and wondered if she could have it done that day. Kathy measured her and measured the material and there was just enough material to do it. Kathy told her she would need at least three hours to do the dress.

Kathy worked very carefully knowing she had only a little margin for error. She was almost sorry she had agreed to do the dress, but she made good progress on it. Lunch was great, but she ate quickly and got back to work on the dress. She made one minor mistake on the dress, but she was able to fix it. The lady came back two hours after lunch and the dress was done. Kathy had decided to charge twice as much per hour as she made at the garment factory. The lady was happy with the dress and happy with the price.

Kathy had not asked Velma for money, but Velma paid for both her bathing suit and her underwear. Velma said she had dreaded coming, but she had really enjoyed being there and would be back next Thursday. They told her that Bobby was going into town Tuesday and would tell the Sheriff that all the charges against Steve could be dropped. They encouraged her to come to church the next morning. Kathy had been so busy that she almost forgot it was late Saturday afternoon. Kathy changed to a dress and brought the money she had made into Clarence.

"You have really been busy, you have almost paid for the material you bought," he told her.

Kathy had kept her own tally, so she knew she was doing well even after not charging Martha and Sally. She loved them both so much and felt so happy making clothes for them.

Saturday night both Kathy and Bobby were tired and went to bed shortly after supper too tired to sing. They enjoyed a goodnight hug and kiss before turning in.

Sunday Kathy joined in with Janice and Katy doing "Savior like a Shepherd Lead Us." Kathy had Katy and Janice do the song she had written about when our 'righteousness is a total mess.' Katy and Janice both did great, and Janice looked so lovely in the white dress Kathy had made for her. Kathy noticed Velma arrive and sit in back just as the service started. Clarence did a good job on the service, but it was the end of the service that everyone talked about.

William came up front all dressed up along with Janice and James. William said he had something important to announce. "Three weeks ago, I found out that the person who killed my wife was dead. He died after he nearly killed Kathy and I am so grateful that Kathy is recovering. I had made a vow not to remarry until I found the killer of Cindy, my wonderful wife. I cannot bring Cindy back so now I have a question to ask a wonderful lady with a wonderful son who sadly lost her wonderful husband. Sally will you marry me?" Sally said yes while trying to stop her tears. Almost everyone in church was either cheering or crying or both. Kathy was doing both.

Clarence spoke from the pulpit. "As a father I could not imagine a better man to be my future son in law than William. Several weeks ago, something bad happened but God is taking what was bad and making good things happen. Kathy is getting back to normal and still using her talent for our benefit and my daughter will soon have a wonderful new husband. God is good. Go in peace."

William had alerted Bobby and he had his camera ready to take pictures. Sally was so glad she had worn the new dress Kathy had made for her. Two other ladies in the church were also wearing dresses that Kathy had made. Kathy was proud of her work but mostly she felt happiness for Sally knowing how much she loved William and his children.

Bobby came over and put Kathy's hand between his. "I will publicly announce our engagement when I can afford to put a ring on your finger. Right now, I think you are making more money making clothes than I am making dressers."

"I am trying to create a need for your dressers," Kathy joked.

"You would have a bigger market in St Louis," Bobby told her.

"I can make them here in the bathhouse and ship them to Richard's department store in St Louis," Kathy replied with an impish smile.

Bobby started taking pictures and Kathy started talking to people who were so glad she had her voice back. Kathy told them that she couldn't sing yet but at least she was talking again. Kathy was standing with a group of ladies when someone asked her when Bobby and she were going to get married. "We won't announce our engagement for a while because Bobby is too busy setting up a furniture factory in St Louis and he hasn't found a place for us to live yet. I plan to marry him but despite the attack on me, I really love living here and hate to leave."

"We don't want either of you to leave," one of them responded and the rest of them agreed.

Bobby had promised to take two pictures of Kathy and Katy, so Kathy could send one picture to her sister in Kansas and the other to her aunt. Bobby then took a picture of Kathy standing alone. "I want one to take back to St Louis to look at before I fall asleep, so I can dream about you,"

Bobby told her. Kathy had William take a picture of Kathy and Bobby standing together so she could send it to her sister in Kansas.

They all headed back to the patio for lunch including William, James, and Janice. Dinner was fried chicken and corn on the cob. Dinner was good enough that for a few minutes, food became the focus of their attention. Sally had recently tried on the wedding dress she had lent to Penny, and it was tight, but it looked like it could be let out a little. "I have gotten too cuddly," Sally remarked to Kathy.

They planned to invite the whole church for the wedding and Martha felt they needed at least three weeks to get ready. "I know Mary and the girls will want to come and I don't think Richard would let them come alone" Martha opinioned. "I know your sister Margaret would like to come but they really can't afford it."

"What is the deal with Gerald, I thought he and Margaret were going to inherit the family business from his mother," Sally asked.

"His father was going to have him inherit it, but he died and left the business to Gerald's mother. Gerald and his mother don't get along, so she changed the will so her daughter and her younger son will inherit it."

"Gerald's mother sounds mean," Sally said.

"No, I won't tell you why, but Gerald deserves what happened; unfortunately, Margaret and her children will pay the penalty with him," Martha replied.

They determined that everyone had a bathing suit or shorts to wear if they jumped in the pool. Kathy started helping with the dishes, but Martha told her to join the others.

Kathy came down from upstairs wearing her bathing suit just as Bobby emerged from the house wearing shorts. They walked into what was normally the girl's bathhouse past the little sewing nook Kathy had created. Kathy had modified her bathing suit, so it was rather proper, but Bobby loved what he was seeing. He absolutely adored her.

Jade had come with Julia and was playing with James, Alex, and Janice. Martha finished the dishes and joined them in the pool. Bobby was amazed that Kathy had made all the bathing suits for the girls plus her mother and his sister. Martha expressed what Bobby was thinking. "Kathy has made these really neat outfits that women and girls can wear in the pool even when men and boys are around. James and Alex just love being able to play with Katy, Jade, and Janice."

"We are being chaperoned," Bobby kidded Kathy.

"That's good, I need your mother to protect me from you," Kathy replied with a smile. They started throwing a rag ball around with the children and even Martha joined in.

Clarence came in wearing a pants and a shirt, but he put his bare feet in the pool. Martha, Bobby, and Kathy joined him on the edge of the pool and Martha talked about Velma and how she was remorseful about what happened. "Some bad things have happened to her, and we actually feel sorry for her. We have agreed to drop the charges against her husband, so we need you to talk to the Sheriff next week. Velma loves children and she says she likes coming here and she has fit in here really well. "

Bobby started talking about getting the factory ready to go. "It seemed like a pretty straight forward idea but once we got started it was like getting lost in a swamp. There were several windows that were gone so we had to get them boarded up, but we need to replace them. We need to secure the building before we can bring in tools and building material. There is no water, no lamps, no furnaces, no stoves, and no furniture. I have got to create one reasonably secure room where I can secure tools and papers. There are no stores nearby or places to eat so it is almost like camping out except there are a lot of people around. There are signs some people have been camping out in the building. I will probably need to roust them out of there when I get back."

"Sounds kind of dangerous," Martha said.

"Well Richard is going to lend me his security man for when I return, and he knows the police for the area, so we will meet with them," Bobby replied.

Kathy did not like the sound of it; Bobby's job sounded both unpleasant and dangerous as well.

William, Clarence, and Bobby talked about loading up wagons with the wood that had been cut and then bringing it to Williamsburg to be loaded in a railroad box car. They figured it would take two days to get it all loaded. Bobby briefed William about the lack of internal structure at the plant and he said he would send lumber for building some of it. He also would send Ned back to do some of the internal structure. Clarence said he would help load and have Martha and Sally run the store.

Sally, Martha, and Kathy started planning the wedding. The first priority they decided was to try and get Sally's dress altered so it wasn't so tight. They decided that Bobby would be the best man and Kathy would be the maid of honor. They also decided that Janice could be the junior bridesmaid and wear the dress Kathy had just made. Katy can be the flower girl and ether James, or Alex can be the ring bearer.

"I wish we could have both boys in the wedding," Sally lamented. "Maybe they could walk up together with the ring. Have you ever made boy's clothes?" Sally asked Kathy.

"Only a few times but it shouldn't be that hard," Kathy replied.

"It will probably be pretty warm so I wouldn't try making the boys wear any more than dark pants with a white shirt and a tie," Martha suggested.

Kathy thought there was enough of the white material left that she had used to make the dress for Janice to make one for Katy.

"Don't make her too cute," Sally joked, "I am supposed to be the center of attention."

They then talked about trying to feed everybody at the reception after the wedding. "I am going to talk to Julia about having her brother do a hog roast and just have sandwiches and something to drink," Martha suggested. "I suppose we need to make a cake too and we will have to borrow dishes from everyone we know. Hopefully, it will be a nice day and we can have most people spread blankets on the ground and have a picnic behind the church."

"Kathy, I was really hoping you could sing at my wedding, but I need you to play the piano and maybe Bobby, Janice and Katy can do the singing," Sally remarked. "I also need some suggestions for songs."

Kathy really felt bad that she couldn't sing for Sally's wedding, but she would try to work with Katy and Janice. Sally wanted the Murdoches to come to her wedding but that meant that Kathy, Katy, and she would have to move out of the upstairs before they arrived.

"I don't think we can go anywhere after the wedding because William is so, busy but I think we need to have a few days alone before we rejoin our children. I think we will move a double bed into the bathhouse and shove Alex and Bobby out until after our honeymoon. Bobby and Alex can go over to William's house."

"Why don't you just send James and Janice over here," Martha suggested.

Kathy played her flute and was happy that she was now able to play it as good as ever. She tried singing "Savior Like a Shepherd Lead Us" and was pleased that she was now singing some of the higher notes.

She had been composing a song in her head that she finally put on paper. Bobby had sat down next to her. "I have a song to sing to you:"

When I see you, it is like the sparkle of the dew in the morning.
It brings a flash of joy that hits me with no warning.
When the sun shines, it warms me from high above
But when you hold me, I am warmed inside by love.
Thoughts of you are like pretty flowers I see along my way.
Thoughts of you make me happy through the entire day.
Knowing you love me gives me courage to face the days ahead.
Knowing you helps me face the things that I used to dread.
When I thought that I was dying I saw you cry for fear that I might go
I hoped that you would find another one to love because I loved you so.
I knew that God in Heaven would provide me with unending delight.
But I still wanted to stay here for you to hold and kiss me every night.
So now that God has spared me, I look forward to becoming your loving spouse.
I will be there to love you darling when you become the master of the house.

"I am flattered by what you sang," Bobby responded. "I wish I had a house for you, so we could move in. I love you so much but right now I need to get established with a job and make some money. I don't see myself becoming your master; I see myself as your partner. You have this gift of making life better for people around you and I want to be your partner in doing that."

Clarence and Martha had overheard the singing and the conversation. They held each other close. "This is such a wonderful day," Martha whispered to Clarence. "I am going to be getting a wonderful son in law and adding two wonderful grandchildren. "Kathy will be the most wonderful daughter-in-law I could ever hope for."

"We are blessed," Clarence replied.

It was Bobby playing his fiddle that provided most of the entertainment Sunday night. Kathy did join him singing a couple songs together. Kathy also played her flute while Katy and Janice sang the lullaby song. It had been a wonderful day, but everyone was ready to turn in early. Bobby held Kathy close for a long goodnight kiss.

Kathy barely got a chance to say good morning to Bobby before he left to meet William and Ned at the sawmill. She started working on Sally's wedding dress and happily discovered that whoever sewed it had let material overlap the seam inside of both sides of the dress by almost an inch. Kathy carefully ripped apart the seams and then resewed them with no overlap. Sally tried it on; it fit fine making them both happy.

Katy and Alex were both working on watering the garden and pulling weeds. Kathy had them pull some carrots that were now big enough to eat. It was nearing lunch time when Kathy finished redoing Sally's dress.

Julia had the day off and Sally and Kathy had told Martha they would make lunch while she minded the store. There were some left over corncobs that had not been eaten from the previous day. Kathy cut the kernels off the cobs and added them to a large kettle of boiling water along with cutup carrots, potatoes,and a hambone with some meat on it. Sally came into the kitchen and was surprised that Kathy already had soup cooking on the stove. Kathy told Sally what she had put in the kettle to make corn chowder.

"I am the one who needs to practice cooking. That is the one thing about getting married again that I am not looking forward to. I don't mind housework, but cooking is a problem. I hope I can talk Janice into helping me cook."

Kathy tasted the soup when the vegetables were cooked. It needed the addition of salt, pepper, and milk to make a good corn chowder.

Kathy had made more chowder than they needed for themselves, but the loading crew surprised them by showing up with a fully loaded wagon of furniture pieces. Janice and James had come along with Ned so now there was eleven people to feed. Sally started putting out bowls of soup on the tabled. Kathy cut up bread they could use to dip in the soup to make it go further. Everyone liked the chowder and Kathy said that she and Sally had made it even though Sally had done little more than stir it.

William told Bobby "It looks like we are going to eat well after we get married."

Sally laughed when Kathy and they were together in the kitchen. "I think Bobby is getting the better cook."

Sally relieved Martha in the store who came out and ate with Kathy. The men were really hungry, and they got just enough as they cleaned out the kettle. "This was good," Martha said, "I wasn't expecting them to come back for lunch, soup was a great idea."

Alex and James were allowed to ride into town on the wagon. Janice stayed back at the bathhouse. Janice hadn't brought her bathing suit but with the boys gone it didn't matter. Kathy borrowed Katy's bathing suit for a pattern and started working on a flower girl dress for her to match the white dress she had made for Janice. She had just enough material to do it. Kathy spent most of the afternoon on it and finally had it done. Katy showed it off to Sally and then ran into the store to show it off to Martha.

"She is way too cute in that dress," a smiling Sally told Kathy, "everybody is going to be looking at her."

Kathy celebrated getting Katy's dress completed by taking her own dress off and jumping into the pool. She was feeling sleepy, and the cold water temporarily shocked her awake. She got out of the pool, toweled off and put her dress on. She went into the kitchen and drank some cold coffee. It didn't help. She lay down on the lower bunk that Katy had used and fell asleep.

Kathy was awakened by Sally and then got a kiss by Bobby who had been let in by Sally after she made sure that Katy and Janice had clothes on. "I need some help making supper," Sally informed her.

Kathy tried to wake up. "Let me up or we will be eating breadcrumbs," Kathy informed Bobby as she gently and reluctantly pushed him away.

Bobby said he was going to the men's bathhouse to clean up for supper. Bobby was hopelessly, happily, deliriously in love with Kathy convinced that she was the most beautiful girl imaginable.

Kathy followed Sally into the kitchen and found a gunny sack of corn that needed to be husked. They got the fire going in the stove and got a large kettle of water heating. They then started husking corn throwing the husks in a pile of weeds in the garden. Martha closed the store and joined them in the kitchen. She had traded with one of the farmers for some fresh pork sausage that they could fry up.

Kathy had seen Julia make biscuits and figured she could come close to the right mix of ingredients. She mixed up the ingredients into a pan and put them in the oven. "If it doesn't turn out, I will eat it," she told Sally. Except for Ned who had gone home, everyone was back who had lunch.

The biscuits got slightly burned but they put them out with corn, butter, and fried sausage. Janice helped Sally and Kathy serve. The men were exhausted. Alex and James had helped and were almost falling asleep in their chairs. Everything including biscuits was disappearing fast from the table. Kathy and Sally had kept a little back in the kitchen for themselves and they made sure Janice sat down and ate. After feeding everyone, Kathy and Sally finished off some corn, sausage, and a couple of burned biscuits.

Martha came back to the kitchen and thanked them. "You did a great job of feeding us today and Katy looks like a little angel in that dress you made for the wedding."

They went back out to the patio and Kathy gave Bobby a shoulder rub. She could feel from his knotted muscles that he needed it.

"Where's my rub," William asked.

Kathy asked Sally to come over and showed her how to give William a good back rub.

Sally got the idea and William told her "that feels so good."

After finishing with Bobby, Kathy went over and gave Clarence a rub and his muscles were pretty knotted too.

Kathy got her flute and Janice sang the lullaby. They were already tired, and backrubs and the lullaby had almost everyone ready for bed. William thanked them for the food and headed home with James and Janice. Katy still had some energy, but she reluctantly came upstairs with Sally and Kathy. They said their prayers and went to bed. It had been another good but tiring day.

Tuesday was like a repeat of Monday. Kathy came down and would have helped Martha make pancakes, but Martha wanted Sally to do it. "Sally has done a lot of cooking, but she has started to depend on Julia and me and needs to relearn a few things," Martha commented to Kathy.

"It always tastes better if someone else makes it," Sally responded as she walked in on the conversation. "So how much flour how many eggs and whatever else goes into the pancakes?" Sally asked Martha. Kathy had made them a couple times, but she listened carefully to Martha's instructions even though Sally was going to make them. Kathy got a pot of coffee going and then set the table.

Bobby, Clarence were still stiff from loading boards the day before and not looking forward to handling another load of it. They both wanted their coffee and a tired Alex wanted it with a little cream in it. Alex was trying to get sympathy from Katy for how hard he had worked. Kathy went over to Bobby and Clarence and gave shoulder rubs again. Martha had told Sally to prepare an extra-large batch of pancakes which was good because William, Janice and James showed up for breakfast.

Janice had brought her bathing suit and Sally suggested everyone should be wearing them even if the boys aren't here. Then you can go out to the patio, and you don't have to change. Julia and Jade came later in the morning and Sally told Julia she might have a full crew coming in for lunch."

"What happened to all the food we had," Julia asked.

"We ate it yesterday," Sally replied. Julia decided she would bake bread and they could eat ham sandwiches for lunch. Kathy reflected that Sally and she had done okay without Julia, but it was nice to have her back.

Kathy was running out of material for sewing. She got her flute out and got the three girls singing hymns. Kathy was pleased that she could now sing all but the high notes when she put her flute down and sang with them. They had just finished a song when Kathy saw they had visitors and welcomed them. Barb had come back with an attractive younger lady and her granddaughters. Barb introduced the younger lady as her daughter Beverly who was the mother of the two girls. Beverly spoke up: "my girls thought this was the greatest place ever and I can understand why. Those three girls who were singing are so good." The two granddaughters put on their bath shorts and all five girls played in the water.

Sally came back from helping her mother at the store and all four women talked. Sally explained that "normally children just take all their clothes off and jump in the water to cool off. Sometimes I haven't bothered wearing anything either. The only people we allow in here are women, girls, and very young boys. I have never felt I was doing anything wrong by letting them see me without clothes on. Unfortunately, some people think that is wrong and then assume we commit adultery too. We never had a problem until several weeks ago when several men got drunk and had the idea that we were prostitutes and broke in. I managed to clobber the man who came after me and left him moaning in pain. Kathy managed to kill the man who came after her, but Kathy almost died in the struggle."

"Oh, my goodness, how terrible," Barb remarked.

Kathy told them "the man was threatening to cut my throat, but I got away and he broke his neck running into that clothesline over there."

Sally continued: "now that Kathy is making these bathing suits, those of us who are here a lot are wearing them most of the time. We are trying to avoid having some women tell her husband about naked women here and then he tells another man and pretty soon some drunken man heads over here looking for a girlie show."

Sally told them how her husband had built most of the bathhouse with help from her younger brother Bobby. "Women and children love it because for many it is the only place where they can cool off or get a hot bath. My wonderful first husband died in an accident and this place is kind of like a memorial to him. I would like it to keep going but I am getting remarried to a wonderful widower in just three weeks. My younger brother Bobby just got a job in St Louis. He and Kathy will get married as soon as he can get settled with a place to live. My mother is amazing, but I don't think she can keep the bathhouse open after we leave. I am excited that I am getting married again and so happy for Kathy and my brother, but I am sad that the bathhouse will need to close."

Realizing that Sally's first husband was responsible for building the bathhouse helped Kathy better understand Sally's attachment to it. Kathy had wondered about the future of the bathhouse; it didn't make any money and took a lot of work.

Barb and her daughter Beverly decided to have a hot bath. "We better enjoy it while we can." The girls came out of the water to warm up.

Kathy played her flute and Janice sang the lullaby. Barb and Beverly were sitting in their hot tubs listening to the music. "It will be sad when this ends," Barb said, "this is about as perfect as life gets."

"That flute music is so pretty, and that girl has such a beautiful voice. I am falling asleep," Beverly commented.

Sally had left and come back. "Don't do that, you always put everyone to sleep." she said with a smile. Play "When Johnny Comes Marching Home." Sally formed up all five girls and they started marching as Kathy played the flute. Sally did a good job of leading the singing and then did a pretty good cadence count. Kathy quit playing the flute and added a new verse.

We will be in heaven some day and the angels will sing and the saints will shout, and we will all feel gay when "Janice comes marching in, when Katy comes marching in, when Jade comes marching in, when Betty comes marching in, when Connie comes marching in, when Sally comes marching in, when Barb comes marching in, when Beverly comes marching in.

Kathy went back to playing her flute and Sally led them through the song again.

They all sat down, and Kathy sang "Savior Like a Shepherd Lead Us", with Janice Katy and Sally joining in. Kathy was the only one who knew all the words, so she would sing each stanza twice. Kathy was pleased that she was reaching some of the higher notes. Kathy would point to a different girl to sing solo on the refrain. Janice, Katy, and Jade each did it perfectly and then Kathy had Betty try it and she did really well. Beverly found herself almost in tears listening to the song. The words touched her and hearing her oldest daughter sing was so sweet. Kathy then sang a new song.

The love of friends flows from above.
It shows to me that our God is love.
The love of friends is my secret treasure.
It fills my heart with so much pleasure.
I do not seek riches or search for gold.
For love is warm and money is cold.
So, thank you God for friends to love.
It gives me a glimpse of heaven above.

All the girls sang it afterward and Sally said she liked it, but it was the first time she had ever heard it.

"I just wrote it in my head," Kathy answered, "God just kind of drops it into my brain."

"I would think your head would hurt with all the stuff you have crammed in there," Sally replied with a laugh.

Barb and Beverly dried off and got dressed and came out of their bath cubicles. Barb told them that she and her husband were taking their daughter and granddaughters back to their home in Springfield, Illinois the next day. Beverly thanked Kathy and Sally. "I can understand why my daughters love it here and I enjoyed it so much too. I hope they can find a way to keep this place open."

After they left, Sally admitted that talking to them made her feel kind of sad. "Hopefully, I can come back here with the children and join you a couple days each week this summer after I get married. I want you and Bobby to get married too. I just hate to see you and Katy and Bobby all moving away. Mother loves having all of us around and doesn't want any of us to leave."

Kathy was sad about it too. "This has really become home for me and Katy so leaving is going to be so hard. I love being with the people here so much. and you have been such a wonderful friend."

The men had gotten the second and final load on the wagon a little a little earlier than the first. Julia said they had to wait a while until the bread was ready. Clarence looked tired and Sally volunteered to take his place. Clarence reluctantly agreed knowing that Sally was a strong young woman.

They didn't have to wait long before they were enjoying fresh bread out of the oven with butter and ham. Kathy and Janice helped Julia serve and afterwards ate with Martha. Clarence covered for Martha while she ate. Bobby showed up and told them he was going to catch the train back to St Louis when they got to town.

He hugged his mother and kissed Kathy goodbye. They both had expected him to stay another night and were sorry to see him leave. Ned was going to leave the next day, so he would be there when their boxcar of lumber arrived.

CHAPTER 20

Back to Sewing

They all felt a letdown after Bobby left for St Louis with the second load of lumber. Martha went back to run the store after she ate, and Clarence sat down in the patio and worked on his Sunday sermon. Like Martha, Clarence wanted Sally to marry William and Bobby to marry Kathy, but he was also sad about the thought of everyone moving away. He also worried about Bobby, and he hadn't been sleeping well.

Kathy went back to her sewing machine after lunch. She didn't have a good selection of material left but she thought she could at least make a couple of nice aprons. Working on the aprons helped Kathy take her mind off Bobby leaving. Katy, Jade, and Janice had found a shady spot and were reading books.

Kathy finished the aprons and brought them into the store for Martha to sell. Martha told her: "The men had come back with packages besides groceries from the rail depot yesterday. I think this package is material you ordered."

It was a fairly large package that Kathy lugged back to the bathhouse. Kathy opened the package by her sewing machine and was a little disappointed at the color selection but at least she had more material to work with. She started cutting up some of the cheaper plain white cotton material to make more underwear. She worked like she was back in the factory making a pattern and then doing all the cutting at once. She cut up enough material to make eight pair and then started sewing. She was still sewing when the crew came back from loading the box car.

A hot and tired Sally came in to take a bath. "We should have brought you along too," Sally commented, "Bobby had to catch the train as soon as we got there. We needed a little more help, but we all worked hard including the boys and we got it done."

"I think I would rather stick to sewing," Kathy replied.

Kathy kept working until supper and had finished everything except buttons and buttonholes which were the most tedious part of the job.

Supper was hamburger and gravy with potatoes and carrots. Julia's brother had butchered a cow and it was the first beef they had eaten for a while. Everyone filled their plate and most had seconds. Martha let Julia leave right after supper and Kathy volunteered to clean up and do the dishes. Kathy got help from Katy which made the task more pleasant.

Kathy went back to her sewing after finishing in the kitchen. Kathy had Katy read from the Book of Proverbs. It started to get dark, and they discovered they were locked out of the house.

Kathy thought about pounding on the door, but she knew everyone was tired and probably sleeping. "Let's just sleep where we used to," she told Katy. Kathy put the heavy bar down that had been added to the kitchen door where the men had gotten in. They said their prayers together and laid down where they used to before the break in. Kathy laid there and prayed for Bobby's safety and the success of the furniture making endeavor. Hymns started running through her mind and she fell asleep.

Kathy woke up early and took the bar down on the kitchen door. Pancakes had become a breakfast favorite and she started making the batter. She had gotten the fire going in the stove and the batter ready when a surprised Martha came into the kitchen. "The door to the house was locked when I got up, how did you get here?"

"It was locked last night when we were going to bed, so we slept in here like we used to."

"I am so sorry the kitchen was empty, and it was quiet, so I thought you were upstairs in bed."

"Katy was reading, and I was probably sewing on buttons, but we slept fine down here. I didn't have any problem with it so if we need the upstairs for guests, we can move back down here."

"We didn't want to ask you, but we do have people coming in at the end of next week for a few days, so it would really help," Martha replied.

"Barb and her daughter and the two girls stopped in the store before they left and told me how much they loved your singing."

"I loved having them, I wished the girls lived near here," Kathy replied.

Kathy had to wake a sleepy Katy who was cuddled up to the yellow kitty. Kathy then went up and woke a tired Sally who said she would wake Alex. She went back down to the kitchen and set the table in the patio. Kathy poured coffee for herself and Clarence. They were joined by Martha, and they sat and talked about all the things that were going on. Clarence told Kathy how much they loved having her and Katy around. "We are thrilled that you and Bobby are planning to get married, but we are sad about the thought of you leaving us. I think Martha has already told you that we would love to have Katy stay with us when you marry Bobby and move to St Louis."

"I promised my mother when she was dying that I would take care of Katy, but I know she loves you both and she loves being here just like I do. I will let Katy make that decision after I see what our home in St Louis is going to be like."

Sally and Alex came down and Katy came out and Martha started frying pancakes for breakfast.

Kathy had hung up the dress she had made for herself in the store saying that a similar dress could be purchased in the women's bathhouse. Two women came in and picked out material they liked while a third said she would wait until Kathy had more material to select from. Kathy said she would have the dresses ready the next day and spent the rest of the day and part of the evening on them. Katy wanted to move back because the kitty wasn't allowed upstairs. Kathy didn't feel as safe in the bathhouse, but she realized that with the door locked at night she was probably safer than when she was alone in the bathhouse during the day.

Sally tried to talk Kathy into staying upstairs at first but then decided that it would give her more time to spend alone with Alex in the next three weeks. Alex felt a little threatened by Sally marrying William. Alex liked James and Janice, but he loved Clarence and Martha and he knew he was going to miss Julia, Jade, Kathy and especially Katy.

A smiling Velma showed up Thursday morning bringing cookies that she had made. Velma almost seemed like a different person and talked about how happy she was that Sally was engaged. "Steve and I have agreed to really try hard to make our marriage work," Velma said. We are also planning to take a trip next week to go back and reconnect with my family and also visit Steve's relatives

Kathy was busy sewing almost the entire day. There were a lot of children and Kathy was glad Velma was helping Sally because even though she loved the children, she could bring in more money sewing. She really wasn't concerned about getting any money for herself, but she wanted to prove she could make money for the store by sewing. She knew that she would be more profitable if she had gotten money for all the stuff that she had made for the people around her. They were very thankful and that was payment enough.

Despite that one horrible night, Katy and she were so much happier than when she was working at the garment factory in Boston. She wondered how Bobby was doing and said a silent prayer for him.

CHAPTER 21

Bobby Sets Up the Factory in St Louis

The first night back Bobby had stayed with the Murdoches so that had been okay. He went in with Richard to the store where he was introduced to Butch, who handled security for the store. Bobby was also given a pistol.

"It is kind of a rough neighborhood," Butch told him.

They had a horse available for Bobby and they rode over to the neighborhood stopping at a local police station where they met the deputy in charge of the area where the factory was located.

"Your biggest problem is vagrants looking for a place to hang out. Most of them will leave when confronted but some can get belligerent," the deputy told Bobby. "Try to have someone else with you so they are less willing to take you on."

They then went over to the factory where they met up with Clyde who Richard had assigned to work with Bobby. Clyde met them outside and said that a group of tramps had broken through one of the boarded-up windows and were living inside. They unlocked the main door and the three of them walked in. There were five bearded scruffy looking men in there. "Grab your stuff and get out of here and don't come back," Butch ordered them.

Seeing both Butch and Bobby armed with pistols, they grabbed their stuff and left. Bobby discovered that a hammer and saw he had left at the factory were missing. Fortunately, they had brought another hammer and the nails were in a separate location and were still there. They nailed the window back in, but the place was no more secure than it was before the break in. Several plans Bobby had drawn up for setting up the factory had been used to start the tramp's cooking fire and only a partially burned scrap of paper was left. Bobby didn't need the plans for himself, but he wanted Clyde and Ned to use as a guide. They locked the building and left. Butch went back to the department store.

Clyde knew the way to the train depot, so they doubled up on the one horse and rode there. They had just a little time to spare so they found a café on the route and ate lunch. Bobby was extremely frustrated but tried to stay calm. Ned was relieved to see Bobby when he got off the train and Bobby relaxed a little too. They hailed a horse drawn buggy for hire and talked on the way over to where the freight car would be unloaded while Clyde followed on the horse. Bobby paid for the carriage ride which was higher than he expected. Richard had sent two wagons and four men and Clyde recognized them and headed right over to them.

Hanson was an older man who oversaw the group Richard had sent.

Bobby got good advice from him after explaining what the lumber was going to be used for. Bobby put him in charge of loading. It was a good crew and they loaded up fairly quickly.

Clyde knew the shortest way back to the factory, so Bobby had Clyde ride the horse and lead. Bobby and Ned hitched a ride on the wagons loaded with lumber. Bobby sat behind Hanson on the lumber and learned about the city from Hanson. Hanson was a little unsure of the factory's exact location, but he was familiar with the route they were taking. "There's a general store where you can buy more tools and there is a bakery around the corner from it," Hanson pointed out to Bobby.

It was only a few blocks further when they came to the factory site. They managed to get a couple of large doors open at the freight dock that were almost falling off their rusty hinges and unloaded their wagon. Afterwards they toured the building including walking out on a small roof deck off the second floor.

The wagons left, taking the horse Bobby had ridden with them. Clyde was going to walk home.

Bobby left Ned and the pistol at the factory and walked back to where the general store and bakery were. They needed a couple screwdrivers and some more nails. He went to the general store and found what he needed but he could see that his cash was disappearing fast. The bakery had fresh bread and cookies, but not much else. He asked about a café and was told there was one a couple blocks further up the street. Bobby returned to the factory with a water pail and bread from the bakery. Bobby still had a small jug of water he had brought with him.

Supper for Ned and Bobby was unbuttered bread and a few cookies, and they drank most of the water. Bobby had not expected the break in by the tramps. He had hoped the building could be left unguarded so he could return to the Murdoches and spend the night.

He now wished he had brought supplies to camp out in the factory. It looked like he needed to live at the factory and figure out where to get food, water, and supplies. Julia and his mother had spoiled him.

Bobby let Ned sleep on the roof but decided to stay downstairs where he could guard against break ins. Bobby had a troubled sleep but at least there were no break in attempts.

Bobby wrote down his expenses for tools and the ride from the train depot to the train freight yard. Ned joined Bobby and they made a list of what they needed including lamps, a storage chest, a stove, and a load of firewood. They needed to have an outhouse and Ned said it should only be accessible from inside the building. They needed a spot where we could tether and water horses outside. Bobby also realized he needed an advance of money from Richard, so he could buy some food for living at the factory. They needed to either drill a well or find someone to buy water from. They ate some more of the bread and finished off their water. Bobby was both frustrated with his situation and his failure to plan for it. He said a silent prayer that he could get some help and find some solutions.

Clyde showed up and said he was unfamiliar with the neighborhood but had heard that most of the people were colored. Bobby left the pistol with Ned. He then put Clyde and Ned to work repairing the loading dock doors. The factory site was on the edge of town and there was a well-traveled road and a railroad line between it and the nearest buildings.

Bobby walked across the road and over the railroad line carrying an empty pail. It was definitely a poor neighborhood that he was walking into. He hailed a young black man who looked like he was going to run away. "Hey man, I need some help," Bobby told him.

"I don't know nothing," the young man said.

"Well, you probably know a lot more about this neighborhood than I do," Bobby replied. "I need to know where I can get drinking water and where I can buy groceries. See that building back there across the railroad track. There are several of us working there and we need food and water. We are setting up a factory to make furniture and I might be able to get you a job there. My name is Bobby Thompson, what is your name?"

"Mr. Charles Johnson,"

"Glad to meet you, Mr. Johnson." Bobby reached out to shake his hand.

"Okay I will try to help you," he said and shook hands.

Charles led him to a community water pump several blocks away. There was a young woman with two small children.

"Here, let me help," Bobby told her and pumped water for her.

"Thank you," she said.

Bobby then pumped a pail of water for an elderly lady.

"So where would I find a store," Bobby asked Charles after she left.

"Why did you help those two people?" Charles asked.

"Because Jesus loves black people just as much as white people," Bobby replied. "Lead me to the store and I will get my pail of water on the way back."

It was another three blocks to the store which looked like a fortress with windows covered with metal grillwork. Charles wanted to stay outside, and Bobby left the pail with him hoping the pail, and Charles would be there when he came back out. Bobby bought some beef jerky, and a small bag of rice, and some pieces of candy. He was frustrated that he couldn't afford to buy much more. The owner was a grumpy looking older white fellow who made a comment that: "You must be new to the area."

"Yes, I'm part of a crew trying to set up a furniture factory in that old cotton warehouse on the other side of the tracks."

"Well, be careful, there's a lot of poor people in this neighborhood that are pretty desperate," the man told him.

Bobby didn't see Charles when he came out and figured both him and the water pail were gone. "Did you get what you wanted?" Charles asked, as he seemingly appeared out of nowhere.

"No, I got what little I could afford," Bobby told him, "here, have a piece of candy. How old are you, Mr. Johnson?" Bobby asked.

"I am seventeen and you can call me Charles. I really need a job to help out my mother, we lost my father last year. I was working building a house, but we finished that job last week and I haven't found another job yet."

"I am sorry to hear that," Bobby told him, "I am twenty and I would be very sad if I didn't have my father. Do you have a church around here?"

"They let us use the school over there, but I haven't been going for a while. My mother goes every Sunday."

"My father runs a store and preaches on Sunday and then my mother teaches grade school at the church during the school year," Bobby replied. They got back to the well and Bobby filled the water pail. Bobby handed Charles a silver dollar. "This is all I can afford right now but if you want to work, follow me back to the factory and I promise to pay you by Saturday night."

"Okay, but I would like to go by my house and tell my mother," Charles asked.

"Sure."

The house Charles lived in was neater and better constructed than most of the other houses around. Charles introduced his mother, Alma Johnson, a sturdy middle-aged woman who looked at Bobby with a bit of suspicion.

"Hello, Mrs. Johnson, my name is Bobby Thompson, and your son has been very helpful to me this morning. We are starting a factory to assemble oak furniture in that old cotton warehouse. I would like to hire him to work there. I would like to have him go with me and start now but if you want to think about it and pray about it, he can start tomorrow morning."

"Do you pray about stuff?" she asked.

"I prayed this morning because there are three of us working there and we didn't have food and water. The first person I met was Charles and he helped me find both." Bobby told her about how much Charles would make.

"Okay, Charles, go with him but put on your father's old work shoes first." After they left, she sat on the porch steps feeling stunned. Most of her dealings with white folk had been unpleasant. Bobby had seemed so different and polite. She had been praying a long time for Charles, afraid he would get in trouble. It would be so wonderful if he had a job. "Dear Lord, thank you," she finally prayed.

Charles carried the pail of water as they walked to the factory and Bobby carried his small bag of groceries. They arrived at the factory door just as Mr. Murdoch showed up with a horse drawn cart and spoke to Bobby. "Mr. Hanson told me you didn't have food and water and some of the tools you left here were gone. So, Mary sent along some food and a pail of water, and I brought you some more tools."

Charles grabbed the other pail of water and Bobby grabbed the bag of food from Mary. Bobby had Charles set the water down on the stone floor and he put the food down on some of the lumber. Bobby introduced Charles to Clyde, Ned, and Richard.

"I didn't know when you were coming with food and water, so I went looking. I met Charles. He showed me where I can get food and water."

They took a tour of the building and Bobby showed Richard the boarded-up windows. We need to put glass windows in, but we need to cover them with metal grillwork, so people can't break in. They looked at the dock doors that were now wide open letting in both light and fresh air. "Clyde and I got them fixed this morning," Ned said with a touch of pride.

"I like your idea about metal grillwork over the windows, but I want to hold up on glass windows until after we get the metal grillwork. For now, use the boards that are on them to make shutters that can be shut at night.," Richard told Bobby. "Let's go up on the roof and talk."

"Okay, let me get the men working first," Bobby replied. "Ned, I want you to get Clyde working on the larger drawers and Charles nailing and gluing boards for the smaller drawers."

Richard and Bobby then went up on the roof and talked. Bobby showed him his list of things he wanted. They then talked about paying Charles.

"You can go ahead and hire him," Richard told Bobby, "but I have had problems with white workers not willing to work with black workers. You might wind up being the only white man out here with an all-black work force. I hate to see you marooned out here but having you live out here is a bonus to me. I will try to bring you out a coffee pot, a fry pan and a couple of chairs. I don't know where we could put a stove, so you will have to cook on a campfire for now."

Ned joined them as Bobby was walking with Richard to the door. Charles had several drawers complete except for the hardware. "Nice work," Richard commented. Clyde was sorting through some of the lumber." I would like to keep you here until next Wednesday," Richard told Ned. "I want at least a couple dressers ready for sale before you leave."

After Richard left, Ned made a statement that surprised Bobby: "Charles is really good, but I don't know if Clyde can do the work. Clyde is a nice man, and he is a willing worker, but he doesn't seem to have the knack for what we are doing."

Bobby went back and talked to Charles and inspected a couple of the drawers he had made. "You are doing really good work; you must have done this kind of work before."

"When my father was alive, he ran a repair shop, he repaired all kinds of things even a stagecoach; I used to be his helper," Charles answered.

"He taught you well," Bobby replied.

Bobby looked at the clock that he had brought with him. It was only eleven in the morning and already things were getting done. Everything looked so much brighter than they did this morning. The one bad thing was hearing that Clyde was not working out. The top, back and sides of the dresser were glued together but also held in place by wood screws. Bobby decided to see if Clyde would do better working on that. Bobby started moving some wood around to set up a workspace for doing that. Bobby quickly realized that making the outside frame of the dresser would probably be a two-man job. Charles had volunteered to help but Bobby told him that he needed him to keep making dresser drawers.

Bobby went outside by the loading dock and created a grill out of some bricks. He used some wood scraps that had been thrown out when they had cleaned the building to make a fire. He had a banged-up kettle that he started heating water in before adding rice and some of the beef jerky he bought. Mary had sent along some sandwiches and cookies with Richard and a few eating utensils. The beef jerky and rice mixture wasn't great, but it was edible, and they were all hungry.

Ned couldn't resist teasing Bobby. "I will never complain about my wife's cooking again, are you sure the beef jerky didn't come from a horse."

"No, but I thought you might be hungry enough to eat a horse, this could be your chance," Bobby retorted. Bobby had saved the sandwiches for supper for him and Ned but handed out the cookies. "Our boss's wife made the cookies, so you better not complain about them."

"So why is she so nice to you," Ned asked. "My mother and her are best friends and her two girls love my sister," Bobby replied. "My girlfriend and I were singing for them, and she also appreciated that." Bobby thought of Kathy and sang part of the song. "Okay, I have fed you and sung for you, back to work," Bobby told them.

"You sing better than you cook but thanks for both," Ned told him.

The three of them started working on putting a dresser together. Glue came in a jar and was put on with a brush. Clyde was a little sloppy at that, but he had strong hands and was good at getting the screws tight. A couple hours later the first dresser frame was done. They used it to create a contraption to help hold the boards for the next dresser in place. Building the contraption took longer than making the first dresser and they had to modify the contraption when they tried to use it. Using the contraption made the assembly of the next dresser faster and Clyde was doing a better job gluing. Bobby was happy that Clyde was getting good at this job.

Bobby had Charles bring over a couple of the first drawers he had made and try them on the dresser. The dresser was still on its side, but the drawers went in smoothly.

"Wow, at the rate we are going, I should be able to go home after tomorrow," Ned exclaimed.

Bobby was excited too because they were doing much better than he ever expected.

They took a water break and Ned asked if he was going to sing for them. Bobby sang "Oh Shenandoah". "Now if we could just get you to cook as good as you sing, I might want to stay here," Ned teased.

"You have to go back and help my future brother-in-law get rich making boards for our dressers," Bobby replied.

"When is the wedding?"

"Two weeks from this Sunday," Bobby answered.

They went back to work . Finally quitting with four dresser frames put together and sixteen small dresser drawers finished. Bobby handed Charles an emptied water bucket and asked him to bring it back full in the morning. He also paid Charles for his first day's work. You get to keep the dollar I gave you plus you did eight hours of work. We start at eight in the morning so if you here by eight you will get ten hours pay tomorrow. "You are doing a great job, I am so glad I hired you," Bobby told him.

Charles hadn't said much during the day, but he was a good listener. Charles came home and proudly handed his first day's pay to his mother. "Mr. Thompson told me I did a great job, and I even got a compliment from the man who owns that big department store downtown."

"You are making really good money," his mother said. "You were a boy this morning, you came home a man."

"I spent all day making dresser drawers, they really look nice, "Charles told his mother. "The owner of the department store's wife sent Mr. Thompson cookies and he shared them with us. Mr. Thompson also made lunch for us and sang for us."

"I am glad he fed you because there is no food in the house," his mother said. "I am going to try to run to the store before it closes." She managed to get to the store and get some groceries before it closed. As she walked home, she kept repeating "thank you Lord" to herself.

Richard had given Bobby money to pay Charles and for his expenses. Bobby decided to use some of it to go the hardware store again and get hinges for the shutters for over a window. He also needed more glue. He got there just in time for the hardware store, but the bakery was closed. He came back and shared the food Mary had sent with Ned for supper. They were both tired, but Ned wanted to get another dresser frame done before dark.

"If Richard brings us varnish and the dresser handles, we can have at least four of them ready for sale by tomorrow," Ned told Bobby. They got another one done and were starting a second one when it got too dark to see. "I don't care about the food, and it is great seeing the dressers coming together but I hate leaving my wife and children alone."

After making sure things were secure, Bobby decided to also sleep on the roof using a rolled-up towel for a pillow. Bobby had originally thought they needed a much bigger workforce but Charles, Clyde and himself could do the work.

Hanson rather than Richard came out with the varnish and the dresser handles in the morning. He also brought a couple lamps, a can of oil, a frying pan, and a coffee pot. He was really surprised at all the progress they had made. William had predrilled all the holes for the dresser handles but they discovered the hardware needed a larger hole. Bobby had Hanson take him back to the general store with one of the pieces of hardware. They were able to find a hand drill that was the right size. He was also able to buy coffee grounds and groceries including salt and pepper. Bobby bought more bread and cookies at the bakery.

Hanson expressed concern about Bobby hiring Charles. "Ned says he is actually a better worker than Clyde, but Clyde is working out okay," Bobby told him. "Charles has put together all the dresser drawers by himself."

"That is surprising," Hanson replied, "Richard had Clyde come work here because he has always been reliable. So, Ned is going back and there is just going to be three of you. I thought you would need at least twice as many people."

"So, did I," Bobby replied.

"Richard really wanted to have a dresser in the store by tomorrow morning, but he didn't think it could happen," Hanson stated. "If you can get those holes drilled so the handles fit, I will be back with a wagon tomorrow and pick up some finished dressers. There is a big new hotel going in downtown and Richard thinks he can sell them dressers for all thirty rooms."

The drill worked, and Charles was finishing the larger bottom dresser drawers almost as fast as the smaller ones on top. Clyde and Ned were working on a dresser frame. Hanson left saying: "I am going to promise the boss that I will bring in two dressers ready for sale by tomorrow morning."

As soon as he left, Bobby started varnishing two of the dresser frames and then started varnishing the front of completed dresser drawers after drilling bigger holes for the handles.

Bobby was able to make coffee and a better tasting lunch, but Ned still teased him about his cooking. "I didn't hear you volunteer to take over," Bobby replied with a smile. Charles tried drinking coffee but decided to stay with water.

Bobby handed out cookies again that he got at the bakery. Ned asked Bobby to sing, and he sang "Rock of Ages." Okay, Preacher man, we got the message; we will get back to work before you call down judgement upon us," Ned said as he got up."

Don't worry," Bobby told them, "I like all of you."

Charles was still sitting there looking sad as the other men walked away. "Thinking about your father up there in Heaven?" Bobby asked.

Charles answered, "he was a great father."

"My fiancé nearly died a few weeks ago and she said she was torn between staying here or joining her parents in Heaven. Sometimes she still cries when she thinks about them. I am so fortunate I still have my parents and my fiancé."

Saturday morning Hanson showed up with a wagon and they loaded up four completed dressers. Ned jumped on board with the few possessions he had brought happy to be returning home. Bobby hated to see him go. They could get the job done without him, but it was reassuring to have his experience on the team. They went back to work with Charles putting together dresser drawers and Bobby and Clyde putting together the frames.

Charles' mother Alma Johnson showed up at noon carrying a kettle of food for them. Bobby greeted her warmly and told Charles to show her the dressers and show her around the building. "I hope Charles warned you that we cook on a campfire," Bobby told her. "Hopefully, we will get a little more civilized when we get settled in."

Charles proudly showed her the dressers they were making and the dresser drawers that he made.

"They really look nice," she said with enthusiasm. Alma declined Bobby's invitation to eat with them saying she had eaten but she did accept a cup of coffee. "Charles said you sang "Rock of Ages" yesterday, I would appreciate it if you would sing it sometime when I am here.

Bobby looked at Clyde, "sure go ahead," he responded. The food was a big improvement over Bobby's cooking. Bobby sang "Rock of Ages".

"The Lord blessed me when you hired my son and now, I am blessed with your singing," Alma told Bobby.

"Well, the Lord blessed me by bringing me a good worker and now a good cook."

Charles walked his mother to the door when she had finished washing the dishes. Clyde spoke up to Bobby after Charles and his mother were out of earshot. "I respect you for being a Christian but I kind of fell away after my wife and baby died when she was giving birth to our first child. It was five years ago, and I still hurt whenever I think about it. At first, I wasn't happy about you hiring a black man, but Charles is a good worker. I also have a widowed mother to take care of plus a younger brother and sister. I had been helping to take care of them before I got married; otherwise, I would have put a gun to my head and pulled the trigger."

Bobby folded his hands and prayed. "Dear Lord, Clyde's wife and baby are in Heaven, but he does not feel your love down here. Bring him comfort and peace and restore his faith in you." Bobby continued speaking: "My sister is a widow marrying a widower and they both lost someone they loved a lot; it took both of them a long time to heal," Bobby told Clyde. "My future wife almost died three weeks ago. I believe in God, but it would have almost destroyed me if I had lost her."

Clyde was silent for a moment but then told Bobby that he appreciated his concern for him.

It was Saturday night and Bobby was alone. He heated some of his water in the old kettle and walked up on the roof to a secluded spot, took his clothes off, and washed himself with a rag. He then made a pathetic attempt to wash his clothes and only succeeded in getting them wet. He now had food and water, but he needed to figure out how to get himself cleaner and get his clothes clean. It was a cloudy evening with a nice breeze up on the roof so was comfortable on his bare skin. He was on the backside of the building not visible to anyone.

Only a few small windows high up on the wall provided light in the factory when they closed the one shuttered window and the loading dock doors. Bobby carefully walked through the gloom to get a camp stool Ned had hammered together and bring it up to the roof. He was king of his castle that felt like a fortress after the break in by the tramps. Bobby did not feel safe going outside the gates and he felt lonely and confined inside.

Bobby ate some bread and a cookie and then lay down on some warm boards on the roof and fell asleep. He was awakened by rain on his back. He put his shoes into the office like room on top of the roof. He then walked back out in the cold rain using it like a shower before getting inside and toweling off. He lay down on the floor of the room and could not get back to sleep. He daydreamed about Kathy. Their plan was working for making dressers, but he could not see how he could bring Kathy here and bringing Katy would make it even harder. A litany developed in Bobby's head.

"I am daydreaming about loving you at night when I should be asleep. Then when I finally fall asleep, I keep dreaming that I am still loving you. Then I have nightmares when I wake because the dreams, they all were fake. You are nowhere around and my heart hits the ground. You are far, far away and my heart cries out for you each day. Oh Lord, this makes me blue, what am I supposed to do?"

It was still raining Sunday morning when Bobby got up. His room leaked near the door, but it wasn't a big problem. He went downstairs into the factory and found one of the freshly varnished dressers was getting dripped on. He moved it out of the way and wiped it dry. It was dripping in several places in the factory but except for the dresser, none of their wood needed to make dressers was getting wet. Bobby put the clothes on that he had worn on the train that were still clean and dry. For breakfast, he had bread and a cookie washed down with a cold cup of coffee left over from the day before. Maybe someday he could have a small stove in the room for heating coffee, making breakfast, supper and to keep warm when winter came. He also wanted a hammock or bed for sleeping.

CHAPTER 22

Wedding

Hanson picked up Bobby the following Saturday morning on the weekend of Sally and William's wedding and took him to the train depot. There he met Richard and Mary with their two girls, and they all boarded together.

They were hardly on the train when Mary asked Bobby when he was getting married to Kathy. "I wish I knew," Bobby replied, "there is no suitable housing within walking distance of the factory. We are really busy right now, so it would be hard to find time with Kathy even if I could find a place. Besides Kathy has started her own little factory making dresses, bathing suits and underwear."

Richard spoke up: "Maybe I could start selling her stuff at my store."

"Richard, you are not helping; I want to get them married and you are keeping them too busy," Mary complained.

"I wasn't the one who ordered three dresses from Kathy and wanted two of the oak dressers," Richard responded. "I just want to make sure they get rich enough to afford all the children they are going to have," Richard teased. "I hope William and your sister don't take too long of a honeymoon, those dressers are selling as fast as they arrive at the store and people asking 'when we are going to offer oak nightstands'. Ned is coming to the wedding, and I hope he brings me one to look at."

"I might need to hire another worker if we start assembling nightstands," Bobby replied. "Besides cooking for us, I now have Alma do all the varnishing and she also puts the handles on the drawers. Clyde and I make the frames and Charles makes the dresser drawers. I hope William has another shipment ready to go because we are going to run out of stuff next week."

They had sent the school wagon to pick them up at the station. Mary talked about the wedding, "Sally has this crazy plan to get all the children in the wedding. Bobby, you walk up first with Kathy. Janice is going to be a junior bridesmaid and William is going to walk up with her. James will walk up with Patty; Alex will walk up with Katy and Bonnie will be the flower girl."

There was a group waiting for them when they arrived in Springdale including William, James, and Janice. Bobby and Kathy drew aside out of view and held each other close as they kissed.

Kathy wiped tears from her eyes and said, "I missed you."

"I had daydreams about you every night about kissing you and holding you tight," Bobby told her. "I wish we were getting married too but the factory is not in a good location for finding a place to live and I am working almost 60 hours a week." Bobby told her.

"I admit I don't want to move but I do want to be with you," Kathy replied." I am also busy sewing about 60 hours a week. Right now, I need to find Mary and her two girls and have them try on their dresses."

Moments later, Mary and her girls found Kathy and they headed to the bathhouse to try on dresses. Kathy had to make some minor adjustments, but all three dresses fit fine. Both girls looked almost too cute to be real with their gold hair and white dresses.

Sally came in and looked at them and laughed. "You girls are way too cute; you have to hide behind something when I walk down the aisle, or nobody is going to look at me. I am just kidding; I am so happy you came."

Mary patted a slight bulge on her stomach, "I think it's a boy so if you have a girl, we can marry them off in about eighteen years.

"Before that I want one of my boys to marry Katy and the other to marry Patty," Sally said only partly in jest. Katy showed up and got hugs from Mary and both of her girls.

Mary walked over to where Kathy was sewing another pair of underwear. "I like making pretty dresses, but I can make more money sewing women's underwear," Kathy commented. Kathy pointed to a big roll of white cotton material. "I have Janice cut them out using patterns for different sizes and then I start sewing them together. William is going to get Janice a sewing machine and I am going to show her how to sew. Sally and Martha want to learn too. Katy doesn't want to learn because she says she will never get to play."

Mary laughed, "I don't want to learn for the same reason. You and Bobby are so talented. I thought Bobby was too young to oversee that furniture factory, but Richard says he has succeeded way beyond what he expected." Mary tried on a pair of underwear in a dressing stall in a size that Kathy thought would fit. They did, and Mary bought all four that Kathy had for sale in that size.

Martha walked in. "Hey girls, almost time for rehearsal."

They all walked down to the church. Clarence was standing up front giving directions. "When I give the signal, Kathy and Bobby walk up together. Bobby stand to my right and Kathy, go to the piano, and start playing. As soon as Kathy starts playing, William walks up front with Janice, followed by Katy and Alex, Patty, and James and then Bonnie will walk down with the flowers and turn and wait for Sally. Bonnie will hand the flowers to Sally and then sit down. Sally will turn around and face the audience and William will step forward to join her. Kathy will then sing and play "Jesus like a Shepherd Lead Us". Kathy, do one stanza. I will then do a short sermon. Bobby and Kathy will step forward and do the love song and then William will take over and sing at the end. Let's try it."

Bobby started it and then it was Kathy's turn and she surprised Bobby as her sweet soprano voice hit the high notes. Then William sang to Sally, and she sang back to him.

"Then they will exchange their vows and be presented to the church. Kathy and Bobby will close by singing "Joyful, Joyful We Adore Thee". Go ahead and sing," Clarence instructed.

Bobby and Kathy sang together as Kathy played the piano. Mary turned to Martha afterwards, "when they sing, it is so beautiful, it gives me goosebumps."

Martha replied, "so many prayers are being answered. Sally is getting married, and Kathy is alive and has regained her beautiful voice."

Sunday morning Clarence opened the combination church service and wedding with a prayer. He repeated much of what Martha had said to Mary thanking God for this wonderful day with so many prayers being answered.

Bobby and Kathy walked into the church together going up front where she played the piano, and he played the fiddle. William walked Janice up to the front as Bobby played his fiddle and then Kathy would play the same tune on the piano. Katy and Alex, then James and Patty came down the aisle looking adorably cute with the girls wearing beautiful white dresses. Just when people thought nothing could be cuter, sweet smiling little Bonnie came next. She carried the bouquet of flowers looking like a little angel with her blond hair and beautiful white dress. Bonnie turned and faced the back door.

Sally walked down the aisle looking very beautiful and smiling all the way. Sally took the flowers from Bonnie and put the bouquet in her left hand and then bent down to give Bonnie a hug and a kiss.

"When do I get a kiss?" William teased.

"Not until I finish marrying the two of you," Clarence answered with a smile. Everyone laughed. Richard was taking pictures as they were walking forward.

Clarence talked about the heartbreak they both endured when they lost their first spouse. "Sometimes when we have heartbreak, we want to give up and decide we never want that pain of loss again. Sometimes we feel we need to show how much we loved the one we lost by deciding to never marry again. The person that is gone is now enjoying Heaven and you being miserable is of no value to them. Neither of you need to forget the good times you had with the partner you lost. You remember how wonderful it was and that gives you confidence on how wonderful your new marriage can be. Be good to each other, overlook the faults of each other, appreciate the things they do well. Avoid making comparisons with your previous spouse. My wife are thrilled at getting a new son-in-law and two wonderful new grandchildren. After you get married, I want you to think of the children as our children not yours and mine. James and Janice need a loving mother. Alex needs the guidance of a loving father." Clarence reinforced his message with some scripture.

Kathy and Bobby did the love song with William and Sally completing it. They said their vows and William and Sally kissed holding each other tight. Clarence then presented them to the Congregation as husband and wife.

"Now we are going to bring Bonnie back up front with the other children forming in behind her so Richard can take some more pictures," Clarence informed them. Richard took several pictures.

"Okay Bobby and Kathy will sing "Joyful, Joyful We Adore Thee" as the wedding party files out." Instead of walking out the back door they stopped and waited for Bobby and Kathy.

Kathy and Bobby finished the last notes and came together. Bobby got down on one knee with a ring in his hand and asked Kathy to marry him in front of the whole congregation. Kathy said yes, and they exchanged a hug and a kiss.

"It will be a while, but we will be inviting you all back someday for our wedding," Bobby announced before walking out with Kathy. Bobby had left no doubt that he wanted to marry Kathy, but his formal request and the ring still caused her to be in tears even as she smiled while walking out. Bobby explained to Kathy that Sally had given him the ring. "Sally told me that she wanted the two of us to share in the excitement of this day by announcing our engagement at the end of her wedding ceremony."

Through her tears Kathy told Bobby: " I just love you and your family so much."

Bobby and Kathy's engagement was a happy surprise to many in the Church, and they were both very well liked. Sally and Kathy were both favorites of the girls in the church and all of the girls were so excited for them. Martha and Mary were both overjoyed. Martha received a lot of comments about how beautiful the wedding was, how darling the girls looked in their beautiful white dresses, and they absolutely loved the singing. One lady asked Martha about her future daughter-in-law.

"She sings, she made my dress, she made Mary's dress and all the dresses for the girls in the wedding," Martha replied. "I absolutely adore her and her little sister. I am so blessed; this is one of the happiest days of my life." Janice came over and Martha introduced her as "my adorable new granddaughter" before giving Janice a big hug.

Richard was lining up everybody for pictures. The camera was a new toy for Richard, and he was as excited about it as Kathy was when she got her sewing machine.

Kathy and Bobby were talking to people when Doug and Sandy, the waitress from town came over and congratulated them. Doug had gotten a job with William working on dressers. It was apparent that Doug had won over Sandy after getting a job. "Everything about this wedding was so perfect, it seemed unreal," Sandy enthused. "Those little girls looked so darling in their white dresses. Where did they get them?"

"I made them," Kathy told her.

"She does everything," Bobby joked, "I would be afraid to hand her a hammer for fear that she might take over my job."

"When are you two getting married?" Sandy asked.

"I am camping out at the factory in St Louis right now and there is no nearby housing, so we are going to have to wait awhile plus Kathy is probably making more money making dresses than I am making furniture," Bobby replied.

Julia was busy serving food but came over and gave both Bobby and Kathy a hug. "God made you two special for each other," Julia told them before moving on. Julia was getting help serving from Velma and Jade. Jade was looking cute in the dress Kathy had made for her.

Bobby had his fiddle and started to play, and Kathy joined in singing. It was a beautiful Sunday afternoon. For the people there, it would be remembered as the best day of the whole summer with the beautiful wedding, good food and wonderful music. Bobby and Kathy did "Shenandoah" and Kathy sang the refrain she had composed. Although the words did not exactly match their situation, it was close enough that they both sang it with a lot of emotion.

"You are almost making me cry," Sandy told them when they finished.

Kathy had her flute and played "Yankee Doodle" and Katy who had come over sang it.

"Are you sure I can't hire you two to sing at my place and I will pay extra for the little gal who just sang."

"Hi Joe, welcome, that was my little sister Katy," Kathy responded to the hotel owner from Williamsburg.

"We could do your place tomorrow morning but then I am leaving for my job in St Louis," Bobby told him. "If you feed us lunch, we will do it for free."

"That's a deal," Joe told him, "if she will sing that song in Latin. Also tell your boss to make a few of those dressers for my hotel too. Hey this my friend Henry who writes and publishes the Williamsburg Journal."

Henry was an older gentleman, tall and slim with an easy smile. They spent some time talking to him and answering questions before he moved on. Katy was all excited when she found out she could go with them to Williamsburg the next day.

Bobby played his fiddle some more and then they sang "Amazing Grace". Joe was with Henry when they sang.

"That gal Kathy has the best soprano voice I have ever heard," Joe remarked.

Bobby started playing the Shaker hymn "Come Thou Fount of Every Blessing" on his fiddle and then Kathy would sing the verse.

"That young man with her is awfully good too," Henry remarked.

Most of the children from church were still there and Kathy had them sing "Tell Me the Stories of Jesus" while she played her flute. Most of the people had brought blankets so they could sit or lay on the ground.

Kathy had Janice and Katy sing the lullaby song while she played the flute and put a few people and small children to sleep. Kathy then had the children sing "Away in a Manger", while she played her flute.

Sally and William came by and thanked them for the musical entertainment and Sally told them how everyone told her much they loved the little girls in their white dresses. "We are going to sneak away and go back to my new house. Janice, James, and Alex will be staying with you tonight."

Kathy was fighting fatigue. It had been a very emotional day and a lot of work leading up to it making dresses and helping plan the wedding. Kathy got dressed in an old dress and went into the kitchen. Julia had gone home for the day, and Kathy knew Martha was exhausted.

Kathy went out in the kitchen and discovered that there were no leftovers from the wedding. She found a gunny sack full of corn and started husking the corn. Kathy was relieved when both Katy and Janice came in and started helping. Kathy started heating up a large kettle of water and found a ham that she could start cutting up. When she finished cutting up the ham, she started making the dough for some biscuits. Most of the corn was husked and the biscuits were ready for the oven when Martha came into the kitchen apologizing for having fallen asleep.

"We have corn ready to be cooked and I have some biscuits ready for the oven," Kathy told her."

"Oh wow, thank you," Martha replied, "I was thinking of making pancakes, but we can do them for breakfast. Velma and Julia got all the dishes clean before they left."

Katy and Janice started setting the table in the patio.

Martha told Kathy that she would serve, "you need to sit with Bobby. I was so thrilled with Sally marrying William today with such a wonderful wedding, but I am equally thrilled about Bobby formally proposing to you although I think he was ready the day he met you. This has been one of the most wonderful days of my life."

"For me too," Kathy replied, "Sally has been such a wonderful friend and I am so happy for her, and I am thrilled to be engaged to Bobby."

Kathy put on a nicer dress before she went out to the patio and joined Bobby at the table. Bobby was sitting next to Ned and had Ned's little boy in his lap. Once the boy saw Kathy he wriggled into her lap. "Practicing your parenting skills," Mary teased from across the table.

"I have been practicing on Katy and Bobby has practicing on Alex," Kathy replied. "Speaking of children, here they are."

Fortunately, the children had all changed into play clothes because they were rather smudged from playing tag and running around. By now everyone was hungry, and food disappeared fast. Kathy was glad she had made an extra-large batch of biscuits because everyone liked them with the ham. Ned left right after supper to take his wife and children home. William had put him in charge of getting all the lumber ready to go.

Bobby had a chance to talk to Kathy about the factory in St Louis after Ned left. He talked about hiring Charles, a black man and then getting Charles's mother to do the cooking for them. "I am going to bring my fiddle with me and possibly play at their church; I think I will be the only white man there."

"I also have a Clyde, a white man who is a good worker that has been working for Richard. He supports his mother and a younger brother and sister. He lives about a mile away and walks to work. Clyde lost his wife and the baby during childbirth five years ago. He said he wanted to kill himself, but he felt obligated to take care of his mother and the younger children."

"Poor man," Kathy responded. Kathy remembered the night she almost died. She would have given up fighting for breath, but she felt she had to live for the sake of Bobby and Katy. "I will pray for you and your crew and your new church," she told Bobby. "When I accepted your proposal today, it was because I love you and I expect I will start having babies after we get married. I am sure Clyde's wife expected to have a baby when she married him, so he should not feel guilty about her death," Kathy told Bobby.

Bobby told her he understood how hard it was for her to leave and go to St Louis because he was homesick too. Everyone was tired and after a long hug and kiss, Bobby and Kathy reluctantly went to bed early.

Bobby, Ned, Richard, and the boys were all leaving early the next morning to haul cabinet lumber into Williamsburg where Doug would meet them to help load it on the train. Martha would man the store while Clarence drove Mary, Kathy and all the girls to town. Everyone would meet at noon at the hotel.

Kathy and Martha arrived at the kitchen at the same time early in the morning to get breakfast started. Mary came down a little later and started setting the table. "I wish we could stay longer," Mary lamented, "this has been so much fun, and the girls and I love being here so much."

"It was so great to have you," Martha replied, "your girls are so darling. I would like to have Bobby working around here and have Kathy and Katy close by, but this furniture venture has been wonderful for people around here needing jobs like Ned and Doug. I think William may be hiring another man too. Kathy is so busy she might have to hire somebody too."

"Not yet but I am thinking about it," Kathy commented, "so far Janice is helping in return for getting some new dresses. Lately I have been working almost as many hours as I did when I was in the clothing factory, but I enjoy it now." They would have talked more but the men had shown up and were ready for breakfast.

They sang and talked on their way into Williamsburg with Clarence occasionally joining in on the singing while driving the horses. Mary told Kathy that "sometime, I want to have you and Martha along with Katy and Janice come down and visit us in St Louis."

They got there a little early and headed over to the general store. The owner greeted them by teasing "oh no, here comes my competition."

Clarence and the owner shook hands and engaged in friendly banter. Clarence introduced the group to the owner. Kathy was introduced as his future daughter-in -law.

"We have met, your son is a lucky man, she helped me sell four sewing machines the last time she was in here," the owner replied. He was really impressed when he found out that Mary was the wife of the owner of one of the big department stores in St Louis. "I have been in there, that place is huge," he replied. "Henry, the newspaper man, told me about the wedding. He said it was beautiful and the music was wonderful."

Kathy looked at some of the clothing on sale which was more expensive than what she was selling but similar in quality. She was glad she didn't have to cut her prices to compete. Some of the dresses had some features she liked, and she thought maybe she could incorporate some of them in the dresses she was making. Kathy bought some ribbons and some buttons and a small cookbook. Kathy also bought some candy and treated the girls. Kathy had made enough money to pay for the material she had used for the clothing she had made. She would soon be able to pay for the sewing machine. She was starting to make more money than she had ever made at the clothing factory.

They headed down to the hotel where a sizable crowd of women and children along with a few men were waiting. They had been told by Joe that a good singer was coming. This time she didn't need Joe's permission to play the piano. Kathy started out by singing Beethoven's arrangement of "Joyful, Joyful We Adore Thee". She then did her own song, "A Man Tried to Kill Me" with help from Katy and Janice. She talked briefly about losing her voice and getting it back. She then sang "America the Beautiful". "This next song is for Joe from the days he attended a Catholic Church in Chicago. It is sung in Latin about Mary giving birth to the baby Jesus." Kathy sang the song slowly in her high sweet soprano voice that had an ethereal quality that made her listeners feel like they were getting a glimpse of Heaven. Joe had to wipe a tear from his eyes when Kathy finished. Mary was seated a few feet away from her and simply said "wow." Kathy then played a song on her flute she had written, and Katy and Janice sang it.

Last night when I was sleeping, I dreamed I was in Heaven above.
Multitudes of people were singing, all redeemed by Jesus' love.

> There were no problems in Heaven, there was nothing
> to annoy.
> We were all like happy children, full of love and full
> of joy.
> Jesus help me serve you and bring many souls to thee.
> Then we can all rejoice in Heaven for all eternity.

Bobby came in carrying his fiddle joined by the rest of the loading crew just before they did the song. They did "When Johnny Comes Marching Home Again" and got everything into play, the flute, the fiddle, the piano, and Richard counting cadence. They had the room rocking. Bobby then did some fast music on his fiddle.

Kathy then sang another song she had just wrote while holding onto Bobby's hand.

> I came here hoping for food and a roof above.
> I never had any hope of finding love.
> I had left home a thousand miles away.
> You smiled at me and wanted me to stay.
> We sang together, and I felt love to my surprise.
> I tried to tell my heart that love was very unwise.
> Then I let you kiss me and hold me tight.
> I had never felt anything that felt so right.
> Then I thought of spending my life with you.
> I realized that was the best thing I could do.
> My spirits have gone from darkness into day.
> And I said yes, I will marry you yesterday.

Kathy held up her hand showing the ring on her finger. Bobby and Kathy kissed after that song to cheers from the crowd which had filled up the entire room.

Kathy and Bobby then did "Shenandoah" with Kathy singing her response back to him. "I am actually going across the wide Mississippi not the Missouri, but we are parting for a while," Bobby announced. "I hope you are enjoying the singing; we are going to take a quick lunch break. Thank you."

ALTON KNUTSON

Kathy walked over to Mary who was sitting with all the children at one table. "I loved the songs you wrote. I wish you two could get married now," Mary told her. They talked for short time and then Kathy sat with Bobby and the men at the other table.

Joe came over and thanked Bobby and Kathy for their singing. Joe also congratulated Bobby on his engagement to Kathy. They started eating lunch but were repeatedly interrupted by well-wishers who also congratulated them on their engagement and told them how much they enjoyed their singing. "Singing is fun, but I think we can make more money making dresses and dressers," Kathy commented.

"It would be nice if we could do both near each other," Bobby responded.

After lunch, Kathy played the piano while singing with Bobby. They did "Amazing Grace", and then did their love song with more passion than usual. Only a few people had left, and they got another big round of applause. They waved goodbye. It was time to leave.

CHAPTER 23

Fall Arrives

Alex and James rode with them on the ride back home. Kathy played her flute, and they sang along the way. It was nice day and the singing kept Kathy's spirits up temporarily blocking out the sadness of Bobby going away again. They all dressed in their bathing suits after they returned, and all four children jumped into the pool. Kathy had changed into her bathing suit too but then decided to start sewing. Martha came into the bathhouse having been relieved by Clarence at the store.

"Clarence tells me that you and Bobby did an amazing performance in town, I wish I could have been there."

"It was fun," Kathy answered, "so many good things have happened for me since you brought Katy and me home with you."

"Well, you have made some wonderful things happen too," Martha answered, "and I am so excited about you helping me teach this fall. It is only three weeks away now."

"I better get caught up on my sewing before we start," Kathy replied.

"I hate to ask but Sally and William are coming over tonight for supper and I gave Julia the day off, so I need some help," Martha told her.

Kathy joined Martha in the kitchen after picking some green beans. Martha peeled potatoes while Kathy got the beans ready. They then made some milk gravy flavored with bacon. They also added some bits of bacon to the green beans. They got the potatoes boiling and some ham cooking. Martha thanked Kathy for helping. "I need the practice, so I can feed your son after we get married," Kathy replied with a smile.

Kathy liked cooking and she had learned a lot from her mother and now was learning from Julia and Martha. There was a cookie recipe she found in the cookbook that she had bought that sounded awfully good and she couldn't wait to try making them.

Everyone enjoyed supper, but everyone was tired too including the newlyweds who sat very close together looking very contented. Martha had managed to get the sheets changed on the bed upstairs, so the newlyweds could spend the night up there. Kathy, Katy, and Janice were in the girl's bathhouse and Alex and James were in the boy's bathhouse. Night came early and so did sleep. Kathy prayed with Katy and Janice before saying a silent prayer for Bobby. She missed Bobby, but she reminded herself how great life was compared to what she expected when she left Boston. Her only problem now was she had way more things to do then she had time for. She also knew she needed to spend more time with Katy.

Bobby arrived early afternoon in St Louis where he was met by Hanson who ran him over to the freight yard to join the rest of the crew unloading lumber including Clyde and Charles. Bobby was already tired from loading the lumber in the morning but did his best to do his share of the work. It was late afternoon when they had it unloaded at the factory.

Clyde now rode a bike to work and was glad he could pedal home while it was still daylight. It made Bobby think about the possibility of living a couple miles away where there was nicer housing and have Kathy and Katy join him. Bobby really liked Katy, but it would be easier if he only had to worry about finding a place for him and Kathy.

Bobby was so tired he didn't even bother trying to make supper; he locked the building and went upstairs. He had some more things with him including his fiddle and was glad it had survived the trip okay. Bobby now had a cot to sleep on which he usually used outside on the roof, but he would bring it into the small room on the roof if it were rainy or cooler.

Sally spent most of her time at her new home and came over only a couple days a week bringing Janice, James, and Alex with her. She would help at the pool, and they would eat lunch there. Kathy and Katy both missed having Sally and Alex around. Katy would spend more time playing with Jade, but Mondays Katy wanted more of Kathy's time since she had nobody to play with.

Kathy made a couple different batches of cookies from the cookbook, and they were a big hit. Kathy taught Julia how to make them and they were selling out at the store almost as fast as Julia could make them. The cookies were priced just high enough to pay for the ingredients and Julia's time. With Bobby, Sally and Alex gone keeping Julia as a cook was a bit of a luxury. The cookies helped justify keeping Julia around along with selling loaves of bread that she made.

They also started offering coffee and cookies either out in the patio or at a little table by the swimming pool. Jade and Katy were adorable little waitresses for that. Kathy took some of Julia's bread dough and made it into cinnamon rolls. The results were very good. They all had a cinnamon roll for breakfast and Clarence commented, "we are not selling these, we are keeping them for ourselves," as he helped himself to a second roll. They actually did start selling them after they doubled the recipe.

When school started, Kathy would lead the students in singing and then work with the younger children on reading. They would switch roles and Martha would work with the younger children on math while Kathy would teach multiplication and long division to the older children. Kathy would sometimes teach history and geography and Martha would find herself being the student. She marveled at the depth of Kathy's knowledge of geography and history. One day Martha watched as Kathy sketched out a map of the world on the blackboard from memory and started showing students where their ancestors came from. They also taught lessons from out of the Bible. Martha would often call on Kathy to teach these lessons. Martha got feedback from parents how excited their children were about school.

Katy and Jade were having an impact too. Jade was younger than Katy and only in the second grade. Jade loved school and reading. Kathy and Martha had tried to keep Katy, Jade, Alex, James, and Janice supplied with books all summer and it showed. Several white parents who had complained about having a black child in the school were now mortified to discover their children were not doing as well as Jade. Martha and Kathy laughed about that. Alex and James were competing with Katy, they did not want a younger girl to be ahead of them in school. What was even worse was that both Katy and Janice could outrun them. Kathy would wear loose fitting skirts and could outrun even the older boys when she joined them on the playground.

Kathy usually would leave school early on Thursdays and Fridays to try to keep up with her sewing and take care of bathhouse customers. Kathy would also sew after school other days until it was time for supper. Clarence occasionally had to go into town to pick a shipment at the freight office if payment had to be made when delivered. Then Kathy would run the store while Martha taught. The one constant for Kathy was that she never ran out of work, but she didn't mind being busy. Kathy was proud of the progress the students were making.

CHAPTER 24

Bobby Attends a Black Church

Bobby was just as busy as Kathy. They now were assembling night stands as well as dressers. Alma, Charles's mother was still doing the cooking but now she was coming in with Charles and working the entire day. Bobby hired Claude, a friend of Charles as a helper for Charles to keep up with the growing workload. At first Bobby doubted that the new man would work out. He did not have either the skills or the work ethic that Charles had.

The third day after Claude was hired, Charles talked to Bobby after Claude left. "I told Claude to either work like a man or stay home and we will get someone else. I think Claude is capable if he keeps his mind on what he is doing. If not, there are other men I know that need a job."

Before Charles talked to Bobby, Claude had exchanged words with Charles telling Charles that he wasn't a very good friend. "Look man, "Charles told Claude, "I gave you an opportunity to have a job so that you can marry a girl and be a success. Sure, the work is hard, but you don't see those two white men standing around either."

Claude showed improvement the next day and got his first paycheck at the end of the week. "You start collecting a paycheck every week and you start to see the world a lot different," Charles told him.

Claude wasn't convinced at first but when someone told him they hadn't him around, Claude proudly announced that he was assembling furniture. "I am working with some white men; they even have a cook that feeds us lunch." What touched Claude most was how happy his parents were for him, and his younger brother and sister were very impressed.

Sometimes pride prevents a fall when you try harder, so you don't let your friends and family down. Claude would never be as good as Charles, but he became a valued member of the team. Claude also liked to sing with Bobby.

Alma invited Bobby to come to Sunday dinner at her home along with Claude. Much to Claude's delight, Alma also invited her Pastor, Ralph Ferguson, his wife Opal, his daughter Sapphire, and Sapphire's friend Helen. Claude had a real crush on Sapphire.

They had a great time and Opal knew Julia and Jade. "Kathy, my future wife has a little sister who plays with Jade all the time. They are so cute together; Kathy made them matching dresses for when they sing in church." Bobby showed a picture that Richard had taken of Kathy with Katy and Jade. It was one of the first photos they had ever seen, and they were so excited about it. "Both of those sweet little girls prayed all day for Kathy after she was nearly killed, and God answered our prayers," Bobby told them.

"Your girlfriend is beautiful, and those little girls look so precious," Opal replied.

Alma had put pork roast in the oven along with potatoes, squash and carrots and it was all very good. Charles was sitting with Helen, a friend of Sapphire. Helen was a sweet quiet girl and was very attentive to Charles as he talked about the work they were doing. They had been casual friends for a long time. Charles hoped to impress her, and he was succeeding. From Helen's perspective, Charles was a good-looking man who had a good job and attended church. She couldn't do much better than that but was he ready to think about marrying her.

After lunch, Sapphire then did to Charles and Helen what Sally had done to Bobby and Kathy. "Now that Charles's got a job, you two can get married and we can have a wedding at our Church."

"Sapphire!" her mother said with disapproval at her for making such a presumptive statement.

Charles responded, "I can't afford the ring yet, so I am not ready to ask anybody yet. Then if Helen turns me down, I will have to see who else is available. I am open to suggestions."

Claude started to name off some girls and Helen responded by saying, "Claude, I don't think he needs your help, you better keep those names for yourself." They all laughed at that.

Charles reached for Helen's right hand and compared his little finger to her ring finger. Charles then teased Helen that it would take about a year for him to save up enough money to buy the ring.

"Don't believe him," Alma told Helen, "he's fibbing, he will have the money long before then."

"Mother, you are supposed to be on my side," Charles protested.

"I am but want you to marry someone who will bring you and my grandchildren to church on Sunday morning," Alma replied.

"I will let you have a week off of work for the honeymoon," Bobby teased Charles who had the look of a trapped animal.

They went outside in the shade where it was cooler, and Bobby started playing his fiddle again and Sapphire started singing. It wasn't long before children started coming over attracted by the music and their parents followed. Charles knew a song that Bobby was playing on his fiddle and started singing it with a very good voice.

When they finished the song. Sapphire whispered something to Helen who whispered something back and then they both were laughing. When questioned, Sapphire said she told Helen that the ring would look really nice on her finger.

Bobby then did a song on his fiddle that Claude knew, and Claude sang it very well too. It was a good afternoon, and they were blessed by Bobby, and he was blessed by them. Despite appearing hesitant, Charles was liking the idea of getting married to Helen. They quit singing for a while, and just talked. Bobby and Pastor Ferguson got into a friendly discussion about the Bible and Bobby complimented him on his knowledge. Pastor Ferguson invited Bobby to come to his church the next Sunday.

Alma gave Bobby some leftovers to take home when he left late in the afternoon. Bobby walked around on the roof after he got back to his home at the factory. It had been a good day.

Bobby with his fiddle became a regular at the black church that Charles and Alma attended. Bobby was viewed with some distrust at first by the members on his first Sunday there. His acceptance came immediately when a little black toddler got free of his mother and came over to Bobby.

Bobby picked him up and put him on his lap and smiled at him. Bobby handed him back to his mother but now there were a lot of smiles around him. Bobby did not play during the first service, but he played some songs afterwards and quite a few people stayed and listened. Alma was happy because Charles came because Bobby came. Claude started coming too because he liked Sapphire. Bobby was soon singing with a couple of the black men. He also used his fiddle to accompany Sapphire. She had a great voice, and everyone was pleased.

Work was not easy, but it was satisfying. Everyone was making good money and Claude was working really hard with the hope that he could win over Sapphire. Bobby did his share of the physical work, but he also had to make sure that they had all the materials to get the job done. He was both tired and lonely at night. He missed Kathy and his family. He wished that he at least had Shep with him.

CHAPTER 25

Clyde

Clyde had not been happy about Claude being hired feeling like he was the only white worker despite Bobby being his work partner most of the day. Bobby was always easy to work with but as time passed Claude saw the camaraderie that had developed between Bobby, Charles, Claude, and Alma. One day Clyde delayed leaving until the others were gone.

"How come you hang out with black people on Sunday," he asked Bobby.

"Because they have welcomed me into their Church, and I enjoy singing with them. I would join you at your Church, but you told me you don't go to Church."

"I stopped going after my wife and baby boy died during childbirth," Clyde responded. "I figure if God loved me, he wouldn't have allowed that to happen." Clyde had listened earlier to Bobby, but he hadn't changed his mind.

"My sister went through that when her husband was killed by a falling tree branch, but she knows he is in Heaven and someday she and their son will rejoin him in Heaven," Bobby replied. "She recently got remarried to a widower with two children whose wife was murdered by the man who nearly killed Kathy, my future wife. Fortunately, Kathy survived, and the man died. Kathy was an orphan with a younger sister when my mother brought them home with her. Kathy sang a song in which she sings 'I love you Jesus, but you made me cry, why did Daddy and Mommy have to die.'

Someday Kathy will rejoin her parents in Heaven. Someday you can rejoin your wife and baby boy in Heaven, but you need to go back to church."

Bobby then prayed for Clyde again. They talked some more, and Clyde found his heart a little lighter as he pedaled home that night.

Clyde's mother Ava was shocked when Clyde put on a suit and joined her and his brother and sister at their church the following Sunday. His sister Anna was now seventeen and had a boyfriend who attended the church. Clyde was introduced to him and found him to be a very likeable young man.

Ava sometimes baby sat for money and sometimes did house cleaning. There was a little girl about three years old that she sometimes babysat for free because the mother was a young widow and very poor. The little girl was with her mother at church, and they came running over to Ava and Anna. The mother asked if they could watch the little girl until later in the day and then excused herself saying she had a job serving lunch at a home that day. The little girl's name was Maria and she sat between Clyde and Ava at church. Maria was pitifully thin, but she was very cute with blond curls and big blue eyes that looked sad. Clyde put his arm around Maria to steady her and she fell asleep against him. Clyde picked Maria up and carried her home with him after the church service.

Anna had gone with her boyfriend to his parent's house for lunch and Clyde's brother had also gone home with a friend. Ava made lunch and Maria cuddled in Clyde's lap. Maria gave Clyde a sweet little smile and went back to sleep. Clyde took good care of his mother and his brother and sister but like William his heart had grown cold with grief.

"She is so precious," Clyde thought and found himself feeling very protective of little Maria. They managed to get Maria to wake up for lunch and she ate well which pleased them. They had a rope swing outside, and Clyde pushed her on it, and she enjoyed it. Ava was surprised, Clyde had shut out the world ever since his wife had died but he was clearly enjoying being with little Maria.

Clyde learned from Ava that the little girl and her mother were living in a shed behind someone's home. Maria had fallen asleep again and Ava told him that the mother was hoping she could find someone to adopt Maria, so the little girl could be better taken care of.

"What would the mother do then?" Clyde asked.

"She told me that she loves Maria so much that without her she would just want to lay down and die but she thought she could get a job as a live-in maid if she didn't have a child."

"They could have my room and I could live at the factory," Clyde suggested.

"That wouldn't be fair to you," Ava told him.

"Bobby is doing it and he seems to be doing okay" Clyde replied. "It wouldn't cost that much more to feed them, would it?"

"I didn't want to suggest it because you are already taking care of us, but the little girl is really sweet, and the mother is nice," Ava replied.

They talked about the situation some more and decided that Clyde would sleep on the couch for the next two nights before moving in with Bobby. Anna came back from her boyfriend's house and scooped up Maria with a big smile. Amber arrived late in the day clearly exhausted. Amber was of average height but very thin. Amber was blond like her daughter, but stress and lack of food had taken a toll on a once pretty face. Amber ate supper with them mentioning that she hadn't eaten all day. Amber had briefly met Clyde when she dropped off Maria at Church and was favorably impressed with him.

They were almost through eating when Amber found out that she and Maria could live there. Amber said thank you and then started to cry. Maria wondered why she was crying, and Amber tried to explain that she was crying because she was happy.

Bobby had no problem with Clyde moving in with him and Clyde's personality changed. He started to sing with them at lunch and would complement Alma on her cooking and joke around with Charles and Clyde.

Maria had stolen everyone's heart at Clyde's house. Clyde adored little Maria, and now she was eating well and was full of energy. Amber had gotten a job as a waitress at a restaurant and would leave Maria in the care of Anna and Ava. Clyde would ride home for supper but then ride back to spend the night at the factory. Maria would come running to him when he came home, and he would pick her up and give her a big hug. Charles had helped Clyde build a carrier on the back of his bike for carrying groceries, but it also worked for carrying Maria and she loved her rides with Clyde.

Amber was getting lunch at the restaurant and now she was eating breakfast and supper in her new home with Alma. Amber's job as a waitress wasn't easy but she was gaining weight. She was now smiling and more attractive. Clyde found himself drawn to Amber as well as Maria.

Clyde loved his bicycle and his enthusiasm had rubbed off on Bobby and Charles who also bought bicycles. Charles built carriers on the back for them. Bobby got invited to come Clyde's home for supper one night and brought his fiddle on the bike carrier. Anna's boyfriend Jerry was also there, and it was a fun evening. Bobby started playing his fiddle and little Maria started to dance to the music. Clyde sang along with the fiddle on one of the tunes and Amber joined in with him. Amber had been sitting near Clyde and afterwards they were sitting with Maria in Clyde's lap. Amber put her arm around Clyde's shoulder.

"I am going to pretend Kathy, my fiancée is here and sing a love song for her and you can pretend that the person you love is singing it to you," Bobby told the room. Bobby closed his eyes and sang it with the same fervor as if Kathy were there. Anna and Jerry kissed after the song.

It was getting dark, and Clyde and Bobby needed to leave. Clyde got a hug and kiss from Maria when he was ready to leave. "Don't I get one too?" Amber asked.

"I was afraid to ask," Clyde replied. Clyde and Amber then hugged and kissed goodbye both reluctantly letting go. Bobby thanked Ava for supper, and she thanked him for a wonderful evening.

"When Clyde said he was bringing his boss here I expected an older man," Ava remarked after the men had left, "but he is such a nice young man and so talented."

"I love my boyfriend, but that Bobby is quite the prize," Anna replied. "If Bobby were my boyfriend, I wouldn't let him out of my sight."

"It was one of the nicest evenings I can ever remember," Amber said, "Clyde is such a great man, and everyone here has been so wonderful to me and Maria."

It was almost dark when Bobby and Clyde returned to the castle as they jokingly called the factory. "That little Maria is so cute, and her mother seems really nice," Bobby told Clyde.

"I wasn't looking for a wife and child, but they were hungry and homeless, and I just wanted to help them," Clyde responded. "Now I am getting awfully attached to both of them."

"My mother brought home these two orphan girls and that was the most wonderful surprise of my life," Bobby replied. "I think that they were a gift to me from God. I think when you went back to church, Amber and Maria were God's gifts waiting you."

"Stop it," Clyde responded, "you have almost talked me into getting married again."

It was a beautiful Sunday afternoon in the second week of October when Anna and Jerry decided to have a double wedding along with Clyde and Amber. Kathy and Katy had come by train and stayed with the Murdoches overnight. They both went with the Murdoches to their church in the morning and then they all went over to Clyde's church in the afternoon where Kathy met Bobby for the first time in weeks.

It was nice being asked to sing at a wedding, but Kathy wished it were her wedding she was going to. Kathy and Katy found immediate acceptance by the wedding party. Clyde proudly introduced the Murdoch family to his family. Richard was very gracious, and Mary loved everyone without any thought of their status. Mary congratulated Ava on marrying off two of her children at once. Maria was an excited little girl about all the goings on. They got Maria stopped long enough so Richard could get an adorable picture of her and Bonnie together. They had just a little time before the wedding started for Kathy to practice on the piano and practice singing with Bobby again.

The wedding ceremony went really well, and the married couples exited to "'Joyful, Joyful We Adore Thee" sung by Kathy and Bobby with Kathy on the piano. The congregation was told that there would be cake, cookies and beverages served outside the church, but Bobby and Kathy would be singing inside the church for a while if you wish to listen.

Bobby and Kathy sang "Amazing Grace" and many of the people who had started to exit found a seat and sat down. They then did "Shenandoah" and then sang their love song back and forth to each other before joining the others outside.

Little Maria was sitting near them, and Kathy couldn't resist singing "Ava Maria". Amber came over after and told Kathy that it sounded like an Angel was calling her daughter.

"Bobby talked to me about Clyde weeks ago and I have been praying for him. You and Maria were the answer to those prayers," Kathy told her.

"Well Clyde is the answer to my prayers for myself and my daughter."

Richard took lots of pictures, but they managed to leave while most of the people were still there. They went by the factory and Bobby gave them a quick tour. Kathy liked the view from the roof and Bobby's area was okay, but the rest of the building seemed forbidding. Mary whispered to her that the place looked like a prison. Kathy had entertained thoughts about marrying Bobby and living with him at the factory while Katy stayed with Martha. Seeing the reality of the place kind of killed that thought for the moment. Still, it was hard to leave him alone at the building and go back to the Murdoches. Richard was driving the horses and only Mary noticed Kathy crying into the sleeve of her dress as they left.

Richard suggested they do 'When Johnny Comes Marching Home" and Kathy dutifully got out her flute and played it and Katy led the singing.

The following morning Kathy and Katy were brought to the train station. Katy was enjoying the trip but the heartache of leaving Bobby was still with Kathy.

They went over to the hotel in Williamsburg to wait for a ride and Kathy was warmly greeted by Joe. Sandy came by and showed off the engagement ring she had been given by Doug. Kathy played "Joyful, Joyful We Adore Thee" trying to do it with enthusiasm that she was having trouble feeling. They waited for the school wagon and returned to Springdale.

Kathy's head was still spinning from her trip to St Louis, but she joined Martha in the kitchen and got a hug. Martha told her that Julia had left fresh bread along with a pork roast and squash ready to go into the oven. Julia had also left an apple pie ready to be baked. Kathy set the table in the patio and felt a little chill in the air. She was glad to be back and warmed by the good food but wishing she had Bobby. Kathy was told that this fall had been warmer than usual but a few times lately the weather had reminded her that fall, and winter came to Illinois as well as Boston. She wondered how long she and Katy could stay in the bathhouse before cold weather would force them indoors. Clarence had gotten a shed built that got a lot of stuff out of the house. Kathy and Katy could now move into one of the bedrooms if they needed to.

The weather turned colder the next week. Kathy and Katy moved into one of the bedrooms in the house.

CHAPTER 26

Relatives Move In

Martha, Kathy, and Katy walked back to the house after another day of school on a sunny day in mid-November unaware that their lives were about to change. They arrived at the house to discover they had visitors in the living room surrounded by their luggage. Martha's daughter Margaret, son-in-law Gerald, grandson Bruce and baby granddaughter Elizabeth had arrived from Ohio unexpectedly. Margaret said they were so busy packing that she forgot to send a letter announcing they were coming.

"We were hoping that with Sally and Alex gone, you might have space for us to move back here. Gerald's mother has made life really difficult for us, so we decided to leave."

"You can move in upstairs," Martha replied. Martha made introductions introducing Kathy as Bobby's fiancée and Katy as her younger sister. "Kathy and Katy are staying with us, and Kathy helps me teach school."

Gerald was taller than Clarence and was somewhat overweight. Margaret was taller and not as pretty as Sally and looked tired. Bruce was chubby and a foot taller than Katy but only a year older. Martha reached for the baby who was sleeping and cuddled her in her arms. "We just cleaned the upstairs so make yourself at home up there," Martha told them.

"Could you see if we have some ham and bread that we can have for supper and maybe we can have cinnamon rolls for dessert?" Martha asked Kathy.

Katy came with Kathy as they walked back to the bathhouse kitchen and helped her carry back a ham, bread, rolls, carrots, and potatoes to the kitchen in the house. Kathy made several trips outside to bring in more wood for the stove. Kathy peeled and cut up the potatoes and washed the carrots and cut them into smaller pieces. Kathy partially cut up the ham roast so there would be some ham slices to put on bread. She then sprinkled brown sugar on the ham and the carrots before putting everything in a big metal pot for baking.

She was interrupted by Bruce who wanted to know where he could get wood for the stove upstairs. Kathy asked Katy to help him. Kathy added to the fire in the downstairs stove, it would be a while before it was hot enough for baking. Kathy also added wood to the stove that heated the house.

Martha confessed to Kathy that she was happy to see her granddaughter, but she was concerned how well it was going to work out with her daughter and son in law moving in. "To be honest I love having you and Katy around, but Gerald can get on my nerves really quick. Hopefully, it will go okay."

Kathy said nothing but put a blanket over Martha and the baby and went to work setting the table. Kathy looked at the time and put the food in to bake. Kathy almost forgot to make coffee but got that started too.

Kathy began singing a hymn softly so not to wake the baby. Margaret came down as Kathy was singing and quietly listened, but they were interrupted by Bruce who asked in a loud voice, "Where's supper, I'm hungry!"

"It's in the oven," Kathy replied, "it will be ready in a half hour."

The baby woke up and started crying and Margaret went over and picked her up. Martha got up and gave Bruce one of the cinnamon rolls. Kathy went back to the bathhouse kitchen and came back with some jelly and more bread.

Bruce was already on his fourth cinnamon roll when Kathy grabbed the last two saying "we want to save these for your mother and father."

Clarence came in after closing the store. Gerald did not sit near Clarence and neither of them said much. It was rather clear to Kathy that Clarence was not happy to see Gerald. Kathy dished out food and Katy poured coffee and water. Kathy put out a small plate of food for Katy, but Bruce grabbed it while Katy was pouring drinks. Katy started to protest but Kathy sat her down at the kitchen counter and gave her some food there.

Food had disappeared quickly from Gerald's plate and Bruce's plate. Kathy had served up a generous second portions and had already given the last two cinnamon rolls to Gerald and Margaret. Margaret let Gerald have her roll. Kathy handed out some buttered bread with jelly which also went. "Kathy, you need to sit down and eat something," Martha told her.

"There is some ham left on the bone," I will eat that with some bread."

"That's the best part of the ham," Gerald spoke up. Kathy handed the ham bone and a knife to Gerald and said, "have at it.""

"I am going to go out to the other kitchen and get some more food from out there," Kathy said.

Kathy took a lighted candle with her and went out to the bathhouse kitchen and Katy followed. It was still warm by the stove. Kathy found a couple crusts of bread that were slightly burned and started eating them. The door opened, and Martha walked in as Kathy was chewing on the burned bread.

"Honey, you shouldn't have to eat that," Martha said with concern.

"It's the only thing left," Kathy responded, "I should have baked more potatoes, but I thought I had enough food."

"I thought you did a great job. They don't need to eat that much," Martha replied.

"Okay, I am going back in," Martha told her, "but see if you can't find something else to eat."

"They eat like pigs," Katy commented after Martha left. Kathy stirred up the batter for a double batch of pancakes, so it would be ready for breakfast.

Martha returned to the house and started to pick up dirty dishes. Gerald spoke up in a rather irritated voice, "What's wrong with that servant girl, I thought she was going to bring us back some more food, she probably kept all the good stuff for herself."

"Sorry but we our completely out of food until we do some more cooking or baking, and we are not going to do that tonight," Martha replied. "The good stuff she kept for herself were two burned crusts of bread. There is nothing wrong with that girl, but I will be happy to let Margaret take over the cooking."

Clarence also spoke up, "I thought Kathy did a great job of making supper and she was the only one who didn't get enough to eat. Kathy is a very talented young lady and Martha and I love her and her Katy very much. They are part of my family, and they will not be treated like servants, and neither will my wife."

"I was just joking," Gerald replied.

"I wasn't," Clarence responded. "Good night."

Margaret knew her father. He didn't yell or scream but she knew they had been given a very serious warning.

Gerald and Bruce headed upstairs. Margaret stayed behind with the baby, clearly demoralized by the sour note that the evening had ended on. She would try to salvage the situation as she had so many times when Gerald's words had alienated the people around them. She had shuddered when she realized that Bruce had taken Katy's food. He would do things like that and then wonder why nobody liked him. "I am so sorry mother; I realize how rude and inconsiderate Gerald sounded but I am sure he didn't mean it."

"So, does either Gerald or Bruce ever say anything nice to you when you work hard to make them a good meal?" Martha asked.

Margaret didn't answer. Finally, Margaret replied, "I will help cook but I don't want to take it over. I am not going to pretend I can do better than you or Kathy."

Martha put her arm around her, "I will try to make things work out but like Clarence, I am also very protective of Kathy and Katy. Bobby absolutely adores Kathy and Sally considers Kathy to be her best friend. Kathy and Katy are both wonderful with children."

"I better rejoin Gerald," Margaret said and went upstairs with the baby.

Margaret was exhausted, but she wasn't sleepy. In some ways talking to her mother was more troubling than what her father had said. Kathy and Katy were rivals for her parent's affection and Gerald and Bruce were not helping her. She had listened to Kathy serenading her mother and baby with the most angelic sound she had ever heard only to be rudely interrupted by her son. Sweet little baby Elizabeth, Margaret hoped that maybe she would grow up to show the love and compassion that her husband and son were lacking in. It seemed like all Gerald and Bruce cared about was food.

Bobby had been such an adorable little brother and Kathy was going to be so fortunate marry him. Kathy was so lucky, Margaret tried not to cry. If Gerald woke up, he probably tell her to "shut up or I will slap you and give you something to really cry about." Sometimes it was worse than a slap. She had miscarried a few weeks after Gerald had punched her in the stomach and she still wondered if that had been the cause.

Kathy got up early, dressed in the dark, and lit a candle in the kitchen. She put a coat on and went back to the bathhouse kitchen and came back with the pancake batter. She made a second trip to get a slab of bacon, syrup and butter and then had a third trip to bring back cold milk. She got the stove warming up for frying pancakes and added wood to the one heating the house. She looked at the time and woke up Katy and told her to get dressed. Kathy started brewing coffee on the stovetop. Martha joined them, and Kathy fried three pieces of bacon and then made one pancake each.

Martha asked Kathy to go back out and get some eggs. They each had a pancake with bacon and a fried egg. They sat there and ate breakfast eating quietly. Katy finished breakfast and went back to the bedroom.

Kathy broke the silence by telling Martha that maybe she and Katy should return to Boston so there would be more room for her daughter's family.

"Please don't leave, it would break my heart," Martha replied, "I need you now more than ever. Get school started and I will bring Bruce over later in the morning"

Clarence was finishing up breakfast when they came down from upstairs. He would have left but Margaret handed him Elizabeth. "Where's Kathy and Katy," Margaret asked.

"They already ate and are over at the school. Kathy will keep the children busy until we bring Bruce over later in the morning. What grade level is Bruce at?"

"He was in third grade back in Ohio," Margaret replied. "What grade is Katy in?"

"Right now, we have her with the fifth graders, but she already knows most of what we are covering," Martha replied.

Margaret grimaced at the news because she was thinking: "Katy is so smart it makes my kid look stupid.

"Isn't Kathy too young to be teaching school?" Gerald asked.

"She is only seventeen, but she graduated from high school at sixteen with honors," Martha replied. "Most of the children and their parents are very happy with her."

"Some aren't?" Gerald questioned.

"A few children don't want to learn, and they don't like me either," Martha answered. "I tell their parents that their children can catch the school wagon at seven in the morning and get an hour ride into the school at Williamsburg."

Margaret started serving up breakfast and Clarence kissed the baby, handed her to Martha and headed to the store. Gerald loved the pancakes and Martha decided not to tell him that Kathy had made the pancake batter. Gerald was going to help Clarence move some stuff from the shed into the store.

Martha, Margaret, Bruce, and the baby headed for the school with a light mist falling. Bruce had the demeanor of a prisoner sentenced to the gallows. They entered quietly in the back of the school while Kathy presented a lesson on the geography of the United States sketched out on the blackboard. She showed the original states that started as the thirteen colonies and then started adding other states drawing them mostly from memory occasionally looking at a small map. Kathy was making comments about the various states and showing major cities. She kept asking the children questions forcing them to pay attention. Kathy continued until she reached a good stopping point.

Bruce was introduced to the class. Martha made the comment that Bruce was younger than he looked so he would be with the younger students. She introduced Margaret to the class. "Margaret is my daughter and Sally's sister, so she has a niece and two nephews in this class."

They took a break and Kathy played "When Johnny Comes Marching Again" on her flute while Katy and Janice led the singing. Marching wasn't mandatory but most of the students enjoyed doing it. The marching didn't last long, and the children milled around afterward. Janice came over after the marching to admire the baby. Janice was allowed to hold the baby while sitting on a chair and she started singing her lullaby song and Elizabeth smiled back at her. Martha told her to let Sally know that they should all come over for supper that night. Kathy brought the class to order by singing while playing the piano and then having the class join in.

The hard work of a busy little bee makes something sweet it's called honey.
If I work like that busy little bee, I can make life sweeter for the people near me.
Or I can buzz around like a fly and make a lot of noise.
The fly does nothing, but it really annoys.
So, do you want to be like a bee and make life great.
Or be a noisy pest like that fly that people will hate.

Kathy then went back to teaching the geography lesson. Martha and Margaret walked back to the house with baby Elizabeth.

"Janice seems really nice, and I have never heard school children sing like that before," Margaret remarked. "That was a cute song they did."

"Kathy has done wonders with getting the children to sing," Martha remarked, "she wrote that song for the children to sing last week. She has sung some songs she has written at church too."

Rather than be happy about Kathy's ability, Margaret was feeling jealous.

"You have a little black girl in the class, how does she do?" Margaret asked.

"That's Jade," Martha replied," she should be in second grade, but she has worked her way up to third grade math and she can handle fifth grade reading assignments. She is the granddaughter of Julia, our cook who helps me. Jade and Katy are best buddies and they both love to sing and to read. I love having her around."

"Gerald doesn't like black people," Margaret commented.

"Clarence and I love Julia and Jade and we are not going to change so Gerald will have to accept that," Martha replied.

"It doesn't sound like we are going to fit in here very well" Margaret confessed.

"We will have to work at it," Martha replied. "You have moved back under our roof, and we will provide for you, but Gerald will not dictate how we run this household. I love Kathy and she is my future daughter-in-law not a servant."

"I told you that Gerald didn't mean it," Margaret replied.

Martha did not reply but she remembered Gerald telling her to do things when she visited them in Ohio when Elizabeth was born. Gerald never thanked her, and Bruce didn't listen to her.

Julia was already in the bathhouse kitchen and Margaret was introduced to her. "Margaret and her husband have moved back here from Ohio, and they have a boy a year older than Katy, but he eats twice as much so we will more than double the amount of food we cook for lunch," Martha told Julia. Julia said she was making beef stew for lunch, and she would add more vegetables.

At lunch time Kathy told Bruce to head back to the house for lunch and be back in an hour. Bruce took off at a run followed by Katy and Jade. Martha seated Bruce at the table when he arrived but suggested to Katy and Jade that they eat with Julia. Gerald and Bruce were too intent on eating stew and fresh baked bread to care that Kathy and Katy were not at the table, but Margaret took notice. "Where's Katy," she asked Martha.

"She and Jade are eating with Julia in the bathhouse kitchen. The girls sing songs to her, and she calls them her little Angels. Okay, I am going to run over to the school so Kathy can come back and eat lunch. There is more stew on the stove, but I left one bowl for Kathy."

Clarence had gone back to the store and Margaret emptied the kettle giving a third helping to Gerald and Bruce.

Elizabeth needed her diaper changed and when Margaret came back to the kitchen, Gerald was gone but Bruce was still eating. Kathy came in and walked into the kitchen.

"Hi Margaret, Martha said she left me a bowl of stew."

Margaret turned her head and saw Bruce eating out of a second bowl. "I am so sorry," Margaret said.

"I will live, "Kathy replied, "there are two crusts of bread left which is more than I used to get to eat some days." Kathy buttered them, ate them, and drank a cup of coffee.

"Bruce needs to head back to school after he finishes eating my lunch," Kathy said as she left. She stopped off at the bathhouse and walked back with Katy and Jade.

"Was your stew still warm?" Martha asked.

"Bruce was eating it when I got there," Kathy replied, "but at least the two crusts of bread that were left weren't burnt. I am going to start the children out with some singing, then we will do some reading, and then we will work on some math problems."

"Sounds good, I will make sure you get fed tonight," Martha replied. Martha left Kathy in charge at the school and went back to help Julia.

Even though they had beef stew for lunch, Martha decided to have a beef roast for supper. There were still apples left from the fall harvest and Julia planned on making a couple of apple pies. Martha helped her by peeling and cutting up the apples. Working in the kitchen helped calm Martha down. Clarence really didn't have a need for Gerald in the store and Bruce was making himself a serious annoyance. Martha took a deep breath and went back to the house.

Martha could have used Margaret's help, but it was almost better not having to talk to her. Martha moved a small table away from the wall and set up five chairs around it for the children. Then decided to have the women and girls at that table. Martha set the tables and realized she didn't have enough silverware. She went back to the bathhouse kitchen and was able to find enough forks to get by. She sat down and prayed for the evening and for peace of mind.

Kathy gave the same math test at the end of the day on the blackboard for all the children with the intent of finding out what they knew. It had problems for all grade levels. Janice and Katy had all of them correct, Alex and James missed only 1 problem. Jade still had trouble with division. Bruce was able to get all the problems right through the third-grade level, but earlier he appeared to be struggling reading a book for second graders. She reminded Janice, Alex, and James that their family was invited over for supper.

Sally came over early with Janice. James and Alex were going to come with William after he finished work. Sally and her sister had got along really well when they were younger, and Sally was so excited to hold Elizabeth.

Kathy had retreated to the bathhouse where she still had her sewing machine and Katy had come with her. Kathy liked teaching school, but it was hard to teach and get much sewing done. It was even worse now that the days were shorter, trying to stay warm and trying to work by lamp light. Kathy had come up with an idea for mittens. She would sew a piece of leather onto the palm of a mitten that she made of heavy cotton fabric. A buckle the wrist would allow the user to tighten it around their wrist. Besides being useful for working outside they were great for protecting hands from hot iron stoves. Kathy had just started making them and so far, only Martha, Clarence, Julia, and herself had one plus she had a few more to give away to Sally and William. Katy was carefully cutting out material following a pattern Kathy had laid out while Kathy sewed.

They had been working for a while when Janice joined them. Janice wanted to help so Kathy had her cutting fabric for aprons. The three of them got a lot of work done before Sally came out and told them supper was ready. The men and boys sit at the main table with the women and girls sitting at the smaller table with Martha doing the serving. Kathy mostly listened as Margaret and Sally tried to fill in the gaps of what had happened since they were last together. Kathy had a full plate, and it was delicious She then carried her plate to the sink and had Martha take her place. She soon got help from Janice and they kept plates and coffee cups filled. Kathy ate a small piece of apple pie before serving it to the others.

Bruce was sitting on the end of the big table and ate his piece of pie quickly. He then asked for another. "Let me see if we have enough," Kathy told him since she hadn't brought pie to the women's table. Kathy brought pie to Margaret, Martha, Katy and Janice and there was none left.

Bruce impatiently reached for James's piece of pie who was still cleaning his plate. "Hey, stop," James told him. Bruce ignored him.

A loud yelp from Bruce was heard around the room as James whacked Bruce hard on his wrist sending the piece of pie careening across the table. Kathy retrieved the pie and handed it back to James.

"Hey, what are you doing, hitting my kid," Gerald yelled at James."

"Well, he took my pie," James responded.

"Let him have the pie and let's go before we have another food fight," William announced.

A stunned Margaret watched them leave, she picked up Elizabeth and went upstairs. Martha went into her bedroom followed by Clarence. Gerald turned on Kathy, "If you had given Bruce his piece of pie when he asked for it, this wouldn't have happened."

"Sorry, we each got a piece of pie, I didn't have a second piece for Bruce," Kathy replied. She joined Katy in their bedroom and made sure the door was locked.

Gerald was fuming when he got upstairs. "If that damn girl had given Bruce a second piece of pie, this never would have happened, and I let her know it," he told Margaret.

"So where do you plan for us to go after we leave here?" Margaret asked.

"Why, what do you mean?" Gerald asked.

"Well Bruce grabbed Katy's plate of food last night, he ate Kathy's bowl of soup at lunch and he grabbed the piece of pie away from my sister's boy at supper."

"He is a growing boy, and he isn't getting enough food here," Gerald argued.

"Okay, I will try eating less so he gets more food," Margaret replied.

"Those two girls should be eating less, not you," Gerald countered.

Margaret knew what Gerald was saying was idiotic since Bruce had been stuffing himself since they arrived. Bruce had probably eaten far more food than Kathy and Katy combined.

Margaret continued talking, "when I was talking to my sister Sally, she made the comment that 'Kathy is so amazing, she is the best thing that ever happened to this town'. You seem determined to make my parents choose between those two girls and us and I don't think we are going to win. We are not making friends here. Elizabeth is the only one of us they care about."

"Your right about that," Gerald replied, "I wish we hadn't come here." Elizabeth was fussing, and Margaret picked her up and gave up on the argument.

Gerald sided with Bruce on eating because he was sensitive about being overweight himself, rather than because he was protective of Bruce. Gerald's resentment of his mother was often taken out on Margaret. Like Bruce, Gerald saw the world with a focus on his wants and needs that blinded him to the needs and concerns of others. Unfortunately for his family, this focus caused both him and Bruce to make statements and decisions that had worked against them. Something had happened between Gerald and his brother-in-law's teen age sister that caused Gerald's widowed mother to order them out of the house that they shared with her. Gerald was no longer part of the family business after he had been caught taking money from the store he ran with his younger brother. Margaret had begged Gerald's mother for enough money to pay for their train tickets to get home to her parents. Gerald would not admit that staying with her parents was the only option they had left but he agreed to come.

Margaret felt that if forced choice, her parents would choose to keep Kathy and Katy over her family.

Gerald had succeeded, however, in making Kathy feel threatened too. Kathy had a bad feeling about Gerald and Sally had been pretty negative about him too. If it were just about her, Kathy would marry Bobby and live with him at the factory which was now looking more attractive than being around Gerald. Martha would be a wonderful mother to Katy, but Gerald made that a bad option. Her aunt had said that they could move back with her. Kathy had saved enough money to move back to Boston and buy another sewing machine there. Kathy had gained enough confidence in her sewing ability that she felt she could support herself and Katy by selling clothes that she made to stores in Boston.

Kathy found a match in her apron pocket and lit a candle in the bedroom. It was still quite early in the evening. Kathy decided to sing "Amazing Grace". Kathy sang it softly and it just barely carried upstairs.

Margaret was enjoying listening to it when she heard Gerald footsteps go downstairs. The next thing she heard was Gerald loudly saying, "will you shut up, we are trying to sleep." Margaret shuddered. What a stupid jerk she had married.

Pancake batter was already on the stove when Martha woke up. The door to the girl's bedroom was ajar but they were gone. Martha felt a sense of panic. She dressed quickly and went out to the bathhouse kitchen. They had made a fire in the stove and apparently eaten. Martha hoped they had gone to the school. Martha walked out far enough so she could see a light in the school and felt relief. Kathy's suggestion that maybe she and Katy should return to Boston had really shaken Martha.

Kathy got a fire going at the school and started singing with Katy. They practiced some songs for church on Sunday. Kathy stopped singing and prayed. Kathy realized she was having trouble forgiving Gerald and

Bruce. Once it warmed up in the school room, Kathy started playing the piano though the keys were still cold on her fingers.

Margaret had bundled up Elizabeth and herself, so she could walk over to the school with Martha and meet up with Sally. "I am so embarrassed by Bruce grabbing food and Gerald's statements," Margaret confessed as they walked over. "Please take pity on me and Elizabeth."

"We are trying to, but Kathy doesn't deserve to be treated so rudely by Gerald and neither did James last night, "Martha replied.

They arrived at the school just as Kathy began playing the piano and singing "'Joyful, Joyful We Adore Thee" with every ounce of strength and energy she had. Another mother had come bringing her two young daughters and about half the students had also arrived. When Kathy finished the song the mother enthused, "Kathy is unbelievable, no wonder my girls are so anxious to get to school."

"Our church attendance just about doubled after Kathy came," Martha remarked.

Rather than being uplifted by the song, Margaret felt demoralized. It confirmed her concern that her husband had chosen to pick a fight with one of the most popular people in town and his inflated ego would not allow him to apologize and back down.

Kathy then played the piano while the students sang "This Is My Father's World". Margaret reluctantly admitted to herself that the students sounded wonderful. Sally had also arrived and was listening with a big smile on her face.

Martha decided to stay and help Kathy teach. Kathy was so good that Martha was now assisting Kathy as much as Kathy was assisting her. There was no competition between them, and they bonded over their desire to get each student to succeed. Despite her talent and ability, Kathy had an emotional need for a mother and father, Martha and Clarence had filled that role. Margaret's perception that her mother and father loved Kathy and Katy more than her family was true but that was neither Margaret's fault nor Kathy's.

CHAPTER 27

Making Adjustments

Margaret and Sally walked to Sally's house which was about a half mile from the school. It was a sunny day. Sally was in a good mood and made no mention of the night before. Margaret's spirits brightened a little.

Sally's house was small, and Sally joked about it. "My husband runs a sawmill, and we have one of the smallest houses in town but at least it is nice and warm. William keeps talking about adding to it, but they can't keep up with the furniture orders coming in from St Louis. Bobby is in charge of the factory that assembles them in St Louis. He says they are selling stuff as fast as they can make them. I guess it's a good problem because it keeps money coming in."

"Unfortunately, being busy isn't Gerald's problem," Margaret said ruefully, "He got on the wrong side of his mother who controls his family business, and she basically threw us out. We came back here because we didn't have any other choice. Unfortunately, Gerald is acting like we came back as a favor to me."

"Well, my son and I hung unto mother and father for a number of years after I lost my first husband," Sally remarked. "They never seemed to mind taking care of us. Marrying William has been good for the two of us. William's first wife was my best friend and I have known his two children since they were little so being their mother is so wonderful for me. My son Alex and William's son James have been buddies for years. Then there is Janice, so much like her mother and such a joy to be around. After I lost my first husband, I prayed that things would get better, and they finally did. I don't see mother and father throwing you out so at least you have food and shelter."

"I almost feel like an intruder," Margaret confessed, "and Gerald and Bruce aren't helping. Gerald isn't a very loving parent to Bruce, but he lets Bruce get away with bad behavior and then sides with Bruce when I try to correct it. Gerald doesn't like going to church and makes it hard for me to go. Bruce has a very poor understanding of right and wrong like when he grabbed your son's pie last night. I was embarrassed by Bruce, and I don't blame your son for hitting him. Gerald should have reprimanded Bruce not your son."

Sally didn't say anything, but William had not taken Gerald's reprimand to James lightly. He had made it pretty clear to Sally that he wanted nothing more to do with Gerald or Bruce. Elizabeth whimpered, and it gave Sally a chance to change the subject. "I have some hot water, let's give Elizabeth a bath and then let's make some cinnamon rolls." They spent most of the day together before they walked back to the school just before closing. Margaret walked back to the house with Martha and Bruce.

Kathy had brought lunch to school and ate there. After school, Katy joined Kathy in the bathhouse and was put to work cutting material. Martha came to get them for supper. Kathy said Julia had left them some bread and ham for sandwiches. They would eat in the bathhouse so they could sing if they wanted to. Kathy also had some sewing projects she wanted to finish.

Supper inside was a baked chicken with rice and some cinnamon rolls that Sally had given to Margaret. Supper was very quiet with nobody talking. Margaret gave a cinnamon roll to Martha and Clarence and then put two rolls on a plate near Bruce and Gerald. Bruce immediately grabbed both rolls. Gerald grabbed his hand hard, and Bruce said "ouch."

"Hey, you only get one," Gerald told him.

Clarence couldn't resist calling out: "Hey, stop hurting my grandson."

"He was taking my roll," Gerald replied.

"So, it is not okay when he takes your food, but it is okay when he takes food away from someone else?" Clarence responded. For once Gerald decided to remain silent.

"Where are the two girls?" Margaret asked. "Katy is helping Kathy with some sewing projects she is trying to get caught up with." Martha replied. "Kathy also wants Katy to practice singing some songs with her."

"I was kind of hoping that Katy and Bruce could play together," Margaret said wistfully.

"Katy loves to read and sing but she will sometimes play checkers, "Martha replied. "Unfortunately, Katy is almost impossible to beat. I will do the dishes if you want to play with Bruce."

Martha had already seen that Bruce was not fitting in at school and she confirmed what Kathy had told her that Bruce struggled with reading. Martha tried to remember where she had put some children's books. Margaret and she would have to start working with Bruce on his reading at home.

Gerald went upstairs after supper and Clarence joined Martha in the kitchen. "So how is school going," he asked.

"It is going really well, but I am starting to rely too much on Kathy. She is way beyond me in her knowledge of history and geography. I have this selfish desire to keep her here, but I hate to see her separated from Bobby."

"Do you think she would let Katy stay behind with us?" Clarence asked.

"I doubt it, Katy loves us, but she idolizes Kathy and Kathy feels Katy is her responsibility," Martha replied. Martha had not told Clarence about Kathy talking about returning to Boston with Katy knowing how much Clarence loved them. Her own heart still ached at the thought.

The next night Martha asked Kathy to rejoin them for supper along with Katy. Kathy didn't serve but helped clean up after supper. Margaret talked Katy into playing a game of checkers with Bruce.

"I will play the winner," Margaret announced.

Katy beat Bruce decisively and then beat Margaret. Gerald wisely decided not to play.

Kathy finished helping Martha with the dishes and went back out to the bathhouse and returned with an armload of aprons and mittens for Clarence to sell. Kathy went over to Elizabeth with her tape measure and took some measurements and played with her fingers. Katy started singing a sweet little song and Kathy stopped her, "remember, no more singing in

227

the house. Let's go back out to the bathhouse, we can sing out there and not bother anyone."

Winter evenings could be so long and boring. Margaret felt so sad that Gerald had made them afraid to sing in the house.

Kathy had ordered two rolls of cotton canvas and had decided to use one to block off her sewing area from the rest of the bathhouse. She had borrowed a hammer from Clarence and bought some nails. She made a flap that allowed passage to the rest of the bathhouse that could be closed using several large buttons. Much of the heat from the bathhouse kitchen was now trapped and it was much cozier in the sewing area. It would be a bit cramped, but Kathy wondered if she could move one of the bunk beds into the sewing area. Gerald had succeeded in making Kathy feel uncomfortable living in the house.

The next day was Saturday and Kathy got some help from Julia moving a set of bunk beds over into her sewing area. She had to undo part of her partition to get the bunks in and then put the partition back together.

Kathy went out to the store late in the morning to have Clarence order more material and thread for her sewing work.

"You need to get more material for making mittens, a logging crew came in this morning and bought all the ones I had for sale. I asked a little more for each one then you told me," Clarence told her.

They talked about what songs she should sing on Sunday, and he wanted the children to sing at least one song. Clarence also talked about the arrival of his daughter's family. "Martha and I are in an awkward position; we love you and Katy as much as anyone of our children and grandchildren. We also feel the need to help my daughter, but we know Gerald and Bruce are making it difficult for you and Katy. We feel bad about that and so does Margaret."

Kathy felt good about Clarence assurances, and she was happy the mittens had sold. Kathy started cutting out material for more mittens and then remembered she was going to make a cold weather outfit for Elizabeth. She had some pink material for the outside and some pink blanket material to line the inside. She decided to make sure it would fit before she finished it. Martha was watching over Elizabeth and Martha was excited about the outfit. It looked like a good fit except for a minor adjustment and Kathy went back to her sewing machine to complete it.

It was midafternoon when Kathy finished it complete with little mittens attached to the sleeves. Martha and Margaret were together when Kathy brought in the finished outfit for Elizabeth who was laying nearby. Margaret put it on Elizabeth, and it fit perfectly.

"Oh, this is so cute, I love it, thank you so much!" Margaret exclaimed.

"Kathy, Gerald is in the store helping Clarence. Why don't you get your flute and have Katy sing that lullaby song, " Martha told Kathy.

Kathy got her flute and Katy put down the book she was reading. Kathy played the flute and Katy sang it in her sweet alto voice. Elizabeth closed her eyes and Margaret nearly did too.

"That was so sweet," Margaret said, "Gerald told you to stop singing but I never would. I love listening to you."

CHAPTER 28

Benny

Unlike Gerald, Benny had a very good conscience and felt overwhelmed with guilt about his part in the bathhouse attack. He also felt very sad that he would not be able to marry Tina. After arriving in the Black Hills, Benny had gotten a job working as a miner in a gold mine. Benny was slightly built, and the work was exhausting for him, but he toughened up to withstand it. He rented a tiny room with just enough room for a bedroll and a place for his few possessions. The lady who owned the building also provided him with a spartan breakfast, lunch, and supper.

Sundays Benny would attend Church; he was one of the few miners that did. Isabel, his older landlady was there with two small children who he learned were her grandchildren that she was taking care of after their parents had died. The little boy was about two and sleepy after church and the landlady accepted Benny's offer to carry him home the first Sunday. The little girl was almost four and like her brother was very cute. Isabel had a low opinion of miners but made a living by running a boarding house for them. She found Benny very different and invited him to join her for a simple lunch after church. Isabel was starting to have trouble reading and Benny was more than willing to read the Bible to her.

After a few weeks of working, Benny started buying treats for the children and would play games with them. Benny never talked about his job as a miner, but she knew it was dangerous. Over the years, a number of her boarders had been killed. One Sunday, several people had come over to commend Benny. He had risked his life to save two miners trapped in a partially collapsed mine tunnel. It bothered Isabel because her grandchildren were getting very fond of Benny, and she was too.

Benny didn't mention to Isabel that he was taking on one of the most dangerous jobs for a miner. He would help drill the hole for the black powder and then he would be the one to set off the charge. Benny had a couple of close calls and came back to the boarding house a couple times pretty banged up. Benny started giving most of his paycheck to Isabel after paying for his room and board.

"Save it for me but if anything happens to me, pay for a simple burial for me and give the money to your grandchildren." Isabel wished Benny would find a safer job, get a wife, and adopt her grandchildren. He was always so nice and so gentle with the children.

Isabel had been proud of Benny for bringing one of his coworkers to church. Several weeks later the man was killed in a mine accident. At his funeral Benny had talked about the man being ready to die. "I know that he will be in Heaven waiting for me when it is my turn to get killed." Benny then sang a song he had written in memory of his friend.

> **Someday I will die. There is no need for my friends to cry.**
> **I know where I stand, I am going home to Jesus' land.**
> **If you love me if you care; come to Jesus and join me there.**
> **I hate to leave the people I love but I have a home in Heaven above.**
> **Tell people where you stand. You have a home in Jesus' land.**
> **Jesus went to prepare a place. We are accepted by God's grace.**

Pastor Johnson talked to Benny after the service in his small office. "That was a very nice song you wrote. It is good to be ready to die but you sound like you want to die?"

"That is alright isn't it as long as I don't commit suicide?" Benny asked.

"Not really," Pastor Johnson replied. "Isabel tells me that her grandchildren both love you and everyone in church is glad you are here. So why did you want to be the one setting off the black powder?"

"Well, I am ready to die, and It would be better for me to die than someone who wasn't?" Benny replied.

"Isabel thinks her grandchildren need a father and you would make a good one," the Pastor answered.

"I am flattered but I don't have a wife and I don't think my former girlfriend would even speak to me," Benny responded. "I have been feeling guilty for being alive and now you tell me I should feel guilty for wanting to die." Benny told Pastor Johnson about the night he had gotten drunk and opened a gate and Kathy had nearly been killed. "She forgave me, but my girlfriend's father said that my girlfriend would never speak to me again."

Pastor Johnson told Benny they needed to pray about it.

Benny prayed that Tina would forgive him, and they could marry and adopt the children. The next day Benny said a morning prayer as usual. "If I should die before I sleep, I pray the Lord my soul to keep." He then went back to work drilling holes and setting off black powder. Later in the week he set off a blast and tripped and fell running away. They found his body nearby and took it to the morgue thinking he was dead.

CHAPTER 29

Thanksgiving

Bobby had come home the evening before Thanksgiving and was warmly greeted by Kathy, Katy, and his parents. Margaret was pleased to see Bobby and he was also introduced to Gerald and Bruce.

After a light supper, they went over to the church to have an evening service before Thanksgiving Day. Margaret had managed to drag Gerald and Bruce along both prepared to be completely bored. Bobby brought his fiddle and Kathy was excited about singing with Bobby again. They did "Joyful, Joyful Adore Thee" with every ounce of energy they had. Bobby led off with his fiddle followed by Kathy playing the piano and singing it. Then Bobby sang it solo while Kathy played the piano and finally Katy and Janice sang it while Kathy played the flute. Kathy then played the piano while the children sang "Savior Like A Shepherd Lead Us".

Clarence spoke after that admitting: "You would probably like to hear more music, but Kathy and Bobby promised to come back Friday afternoon at three o'clock to sing some more."

After the service, Bobby teased Kathy that "you were about two octaves higher than I have ever heard before."

"I think she has been practicing with the Angels again, "Sally joked.

"I just wanted to sing it a little higher for contrast," Kathy said defending herself.

"The only thing you were missing in that song was smoke, and fire, and flashes of lightning," William said with a smile.

A lot of people stayed around talking and were glad to see Bobby back. They thought the singing was great. Janice and Katy had a number of people coming up complimenting them too. Margaret hadn't seen Bobby for a long time and was excited to hear him and was very impressed with his musical ability. Even Gerald had conceded that the music was really good. Elizabeth was in the pink outfit that Kathy made for her and getting lots of attention.

Some of the children from school came running up to give Kathy a hug. Kathy loved the people in the church, and they loved her and Katy. Kathy wanted to be with Bobby, but the small community was now her home. Bobby echoed her thoughts when he said, "I wish my job was closer to home."

They walked back to the house and went inside. Kathy got a long hug and kiss from Bobby before going to the bathhouse to sleep. Bobby slept in the bedroom the girls had vacated a few weeks earlier. Bobby and Kathy were both exhausted, but they lay awake for a while wishing they were married and cuddled up to each other.

Clarence talked with Martha before they went to sleep. "I don't know if anyone will remember what I said in my sermon, everyone was so captivated by the music tonight. I have never heard children sing so perfect before. The Lord has given us so much to be thankful for."

Clarence had replaced Kathy's fabric curtain with a door so keeping warm on their bunk beds wasn't too bad. Kathy and Kathy wore flannel nightgowns and as the nights got colder, they had started to cuddle up on the same bunk.

Kathy woke up early the next morning and left the warmth of the bed and Katy to get up and add wood to the stove. She then started making pancake batter. It had been a great evening, but a new day had started, and firewood needed to be put in stoves and people needed to be fed. A lot of life each day was drudgery that could not be eliminated. Kathy felt that becoming an adult included the realization that work was a reality that could not be avoided, and you did it automatically without complaint.

Kathy heard a knock on the door and let Martha in. "I want you to join us for breakfast now that Bobby is here. Clarence and I feel really bad that you don't feel welcome at the table anymore. Have Katy sit between me and Clarence."

Breakfast actually went pretty well, and Gerald even said "thank you" when Kathy brought him more pancakes.

Bobby talked about finally getting a stove for his upstairs room at the factory and a larger one to try to keep the assembly area warm enough, so the glue would set properly. "Clyde keeps checking for a place I could rent or buy in his neighborhood, but so far he hasn't found me anything I can afford."

Kathy stayed silent as she contemplated her situation. Kathy loved teaching, but it left little time for her to earn money sewing. She was pretty sure she could make enough money if she were sewing full time to help pay rent in St Louis. Living with Bobby in the room above the factory might even be fun but she couldn't leave Katy behind because of Gerald.

After breakfast cleanup, Kathy went back to the bathhouse kitchen to start cooking several dishes that would add to what Martha was cooking for Thanksgiving dinner. Katy joined her and started singing. Singing was still something they hesitated to do in the house for fear of offending Gerald. William and Sally were bringing the children over for Thanksgiving dinner. Kathy had volunteered to sit at the children's table which would not include Bruce. Marriage had been great for William and Sally and their children, but they all had negative feelings toward Gerald and Bruce. This would be their first meal together since that disastrous first encounter.

Gerald had tried to improve his image a little bit since their arrival a couple weeks earlier. Gerald recently had told Margaret that the only jobs to be had were working for Clarence or William. Margaret had the good sense not to tell him that she had known that since they arrived. William had hired another man since Gerald arrived and had no interest in adding Gerald to his work force. Clarence had found some work for Gerald to help offset the cost of feeding Gerald's family. Even with her reduced clothing output while helping at school, Kathy was still paying for herself and Katy with clothing sales.

Sally and Janice came for dinner early and mostly took turns playing with Elizabeth while helping Margaret and Martha in the house kitchen. Gerald, Bruce, and Bobby were busy carrying in firewood. Clarence was keeping the store open until noon for anyone needing something at the last minute.

This time there were no problems when dinner was served. Kathy made sure that Janice, James, Alex, and Katy had enough to eat at her table and ate only a modest amount herself. After lunch, Kathy took Katy and Sally's three children over to the schoolhouse to sing and play games.

William and Bobby talked about the furniture they were making and some possible changes. Bobby came over to the school about an hour later followed by Sally and William. Clarence came over too since he had no desire to sit and talk to Gerald. William took his family home early in the evening and the rest of them returned to the house to eat leftovers for supper. Too much food made them all sleepy, and they retired early.

CHAPTER 30

Benny and Tina

It took Benny a couple weeks to recover enough after the blast to go back to work. Benny wrote his sister Linda about his situation. "I woke up in the morgue several weeks ago after tripping over a rock when I was setting off a black powder charge. When they found my body, they mistakenly thought I was dead. I have started working grinding ore samples because right now I can't run anymore. To be honest, I miss the excitement of having one of the most dangerous jobs at the mine. My landlady takes care of her granddaughter who is four and her grandson who is two because their parents are dead. I spend a lot of time with her, and the two children and I love them a lot. I think Tina would too. If was married, I would want to adopt the children, but I am not ready to think of marrying anyone but Tina. Unfortunately, Tina's father said she never wanted to see me again. I also sent her a letter and never got a reply. Maybe, you could help me find a nice family to adopt the children. I would like to visit you at Thanksgiving and bring the children with me along with their grandmother."

Benny had enclosed a newspaper clipping that mentioned his near fatal mishap.

Thomas, Tina's father did not approve of Benny. Thomas had told Benny that Tina never wanted to see him again without asking her. Poor Tina thought Benny hadn't said goodbye because he didn't care about her. He also did not tell Tina about Benny trying to see her and threw away a letter Benny tried to send her.

Several weeks after Benny left, their neighbors little girl got sick and died. The mother was a good friend of Tina's and Tina adored her little girl. Tina was as heartbroken as the little girl's parents. In the weeks that followed Laura found Tina increasingly withdrawn, dirty and disheveled looking.

It didn't help that Thomas kept encouraging Tina to marry Olaf, an older neighbor that she couldn't stand.

Tina worked hard feeding chickens and milking cows out in the barn, but she did it to satisfy her father not because it gave her any pleasure. She was feeling really tired and discouraged one morning when her father interrupted her thoughts.

"You know Tina we wouldn't have to work so hard if you would marry Olaf. He could help me get a lot more work done on this farm. Look, that sissy Benny is never coming back, it is time you married up with a real man. You should think about it."

Tina did think about it. She was so depressed and felt so isolated. She could not please her father. It had been several weeks since he had taken either Tina or Laura with him to town and it was months since they had last gone to church. For the first time in her life she started thinking about suicide. She knew suicide was wrong, but she would sooner die than marry Olaf.

Laura came into the barn a little later in the morning to gather eggs and found Tina sitting high up on a beam. Laura got her to come down. "You could get killed if you fell from there."

"Who cares? I have nothing to live for. I have no friends. I wish I was dead!" Tina replied. "I would sooner die than marry Olaf. The only thing father cares about is this stupid farm."

Laura tried to comfort Tina who cried for a long time.

Laura made lunch for Thomas and Tina. Tina ate a small amount before going back out to the barn. Laura then spoke to Thomas; "Tina does not want to marry Olaf, please quit talking to her about it."

Thomas said a few words of profanity before telling Laura: "You don't tell me what to do. The Bible says women are subject to their husbands! I ought to smack you!"

"Tina will kill herself before she marries Olaf."

"You are so stupid, you have no idea what you are talking about," Thomas told her before slamming the door as he went outside.

Laura dressed warmly before walking a mile over to Linda's house for a visit. Linda talked to Laura talked about Benny: "My brother bought a ring from the stranger and was going to ask Tina to marry him. He had no idea why they were going over there to the bathhouse that night. He is so sorry about what happened."

"Tina is heartbroken that Benny never said goodbye," Laura replied.

"Your husband wouldn't let him. He told Benny that Tina never wanted to see him again."

Laura read the letter and the newspaper clipping. Laura was willing to give Benny another chance. Laura had always had a good opinion of Benny before the incident at the bathhouse. She also was unhappy that Thomas had kept Benny from saying goodbye to Tina. They talked about getting Tina and Benny back together.

Laura reflected on the situation as she walked home. Her son Jonathan and Tina were opposite in temperament. Her son would openly disagree with Thomas while Tina would comply but internalize her resentment. Laura realized she was more like Tina. Thomas was bitter about Jonathan leaving and took his resentment out on her and Tina. She had to help Tina get away hopefully by marrying Benny. Tina loved children so Laura was fairly certain that Tina would want to adopt the two children Benny was fond of. Laura felt she needed to honor her wedding vows, but it was getting very hard to live with Thomas.

"Where have you been?" Thomas demanded when Laura came home early in the evening.

"I walked over to Linda's place and talked to her."

"Why didn't you ask me, I could have hitched up the horse and buggy and brought you over," Thomas responded.

"You told me the buggy was broken so we couldn't go anywhere for weeks. So if it is working maybe we can go to town and church again."

"Don't tell me what to do and where is my supper?" Thomas demanded.

"Where is Tina?" Laura asked while starting to put together supper.

"She is upstairs in her room, she said she was tired and didn't feel like eating supper." Thomas replied.

Laura peeled potatoes and fried them along with some bacon. She also made coffee remarking: "we are almost out of coffee; we need to go to the store."

Thomas did not reply, and they ate in silence.

"We have to talk. You have got to be honest with Tina," Laura told him after finishing eating.

"Stop telling me what to do. The Bible says women are subject to their husbands! I ought to smack you!"

"It also says "remember the Sabbath Day to keep it Holy and thou shall not lie, and thou shall not steal," Laura replied. "You don't go to church on Sunday, you lied to Benny, and you didn't give Tina the letter Benny sent her. Olaf's first wife left after he started smacking her around. Since you are so ready to smack me, I guess you think it is okay for your daughter to get smacked around by Olaf."

"Shut up. You have no right to talk to me like that. I am trying to protect my daughter. I keep telling her she should forget about a wimp Benny and marry a farmer like Olaf. Olaf could also help me here on my farm too."

"Benny is not a wimp; he has been working hard at a very dangerous job as a miner. Olaf is almost twice Tina's her age, is always dirty and smells like an outhouse. Tina told me she would sooner die than marry Olaf. I keep telling you not to talk to her about marrying Olaf."

"So you want her to marry Benny, he will never be able to take over the farm here."

"Our son didn't want to be a farmer and moved away. We don't even know where he is. It is not your daughter's fault that she is a woman not a man. Your daughter's happiness is more important than keeping this farm in the family."

"Easy for you to say, you don't work hard out in the hot fields all day like I do. Tina doesn't seem to mind helping me out in the barn, so I think she is fine. I talked to her this afternoon, and she told me that she would marry Olaf. Let's talk to her."

Thomas yelled. "TINA, WE NEED TO TALK!"

There was no answer. Laura ran up the stairs. "Oh no she is gone! I hope she didn't kill herself!" she told Thomas before grabbing her coat and rushing out into the darkness of a very cold night. Thomas put on his coat and followed.

Laura found Tina out by the barn sitting on a bale of hay looking up at the stars without a coat on. "The stars are pretty out here, somewhere up there is Heaven," Tina's speech was slurred and barely audible.

"You are going to freeze to death out here," Laura told her.

"I know, love you mom, but I want to go to Heaven. Tell father I am sorry, but I won't marry Olaf. I asked God to forgive me for dying. Bye." Tina whispered and then slumped over.

Thomas had been a few steps behind them, and Tina had not seen him. He picked Tina up and carried her inside. He sat in a chair with her in his lap near the stove trying to warm up her icy hands with his. She felt so cold and unresponsive. He was terrified he was going to lose his daughter. So many wonderful memories of Tina flooded into his memory. "Why didn't you warn me?" he said accusingly to Laura.

"I did. I told you Tina would kill herself before she would marry Olaf. You yelled at me, told me I was stupid and threatened to smack me. I warned you several times to quit trying to get Tina to marry Olaf." Laura put a blanket over Tina and put another blanket in the oven to warm it up. Laura then waited for another angry tirade.

Laura started praying out loud: "Dear Lord, please forgive Tina and let her enter into Heaven. She loves you and believes in you. I pray that Benny will find another girl to marry him so he can adopt the two little orphans that he loves. I know Tina would have loved to be a mother to those two little orphans but that is not to be so take her to Heaven where she will be happy."

"Why don't you pray for her to live?" Thomas asked.

"Not if that means marrying Olaf and being miserable. She will be better off in Heaven. I wish I was going there too since you don't love me anymore."

Thomas sat there in silence holding Tina in his arms, her hands were still icy cold, and her breathing sounded labored. He felt so guilty. If only he had listened to Laura, Tina wouldn't be dying. There also had been strong words between him and his son before his son had left. Thomas sat there with tears in his eyes feeling demoralized realizing he had nearly destroyed the family he loved. He had been a good farmer, but he had put that ahead of his wife, his son and now his daughter. He needed to ask help from God who he had ignored as well. Finally he begged in silent prayer, "Lord please save my daughter and help me be a good husband and father."

"Laura, please forgive me, I was wrong, I am so sorry about what I said. I have never smacked you and I never will."

They moved a couch closer to the stove and laid Tina down on it covering her with warm blankets. They took turns staying with her through the night.

The next morning Tina finally woke up and a very contrite Thomas asked her to forgive him. "Please forgive me, I will never ask you to marry Olaf again. We will also start going back to church on Sunday. Laura has some good news for you."

"I went over to Linda's place yesterday and we talked about Benny. Benny wanted to marry you and had tried to buy you a wedding ring the night of the bathhouse attack. He really didn't know why they were there. He is coming back the day after Thanksgiving and still wants to marry you."

"I will give him permission to marry you," Thomas told her. He also admitted he had kept Benny from saying goodbye to her and threw away a letter that Benny sent her. "Please forgive me."

They all forgave each other and then Thomas prayed that Jonathan would write to them. It took a few days before Tina was fully recovered.

Thomas fixed the problem on their horse drawn buggy made a trip to town for supplies. Laura added extra wood to the stove and heated water. By the time Thomas came back both Tina and Laura had taken a bath in a washtub and gotten their hair washed. They both had fixed their hair and put on nice dresses.

"You both look beautiful," Thomas told them admiring his wife. Tina was so pretty, and she had a happy smile that he had not seen for a long time. He shuddered to think how close he came to losing them. If they had gone to bed that night thinking Tina was sleeping upstairs, they would have lost her. He also realized that if they had lost Tina, Laura probably would have left him.

Tina started walking around the house singing again. Thomas started being very nice to Laura and she started feeling loved again. They went to church the next Sunday. They got there a little early and Kathy came running over to Tina. "Tina, you look so cute, how are you doing?"

"I am doing better now. I think Benny and I may be getting married soon."

"Wonderful! " Kathy exclaimed. "Poor Benny had no idea why they were here, that night, he had just bought a ring and wanted to marry you. I have completely forgiven him. I will pray for both of you .You two will be such a cute couple."

"Thank you for forgiving Benny and thank you for praying for us," Tina replied.

Friday morning after Thanksgiving Laura had Tina wearing a pretty dress. Benny's sister and Laura had talked and came up with a plan. They wanted to make sure Tina would be happy with the children before she met Benny. Benny was sent to Williamsburg to get some supplies.

Thomas brought Tina came over with Laura to help babysit the two children, but she did know where they were from. Tina and the two children were soon cuddled together on a rug on the floor playing together. Laura could not remember seeing Tina so happy and the children were happy with her. Laura fell in love with the children too.

Seeing that Tina was so happy with the children Linda and Laura confided with her. Tina then learned that Benny and Isabel were looking for a family to adopt the two children. "Benny really loves the children, but they need a mother," Linda told Tina. "Benny is hoping you will forgive him, marry him and adopt the children." She also showed Tina the last letter she had received from Benny along with the newspaper clipping.

Tina excused herself and went into another room and cried bittersweet tears. She was upset that Benny had been doing such dangerous work. Tina felt her affection for him flooding back and the two little children had stolen her heart. She loved Benny and the desire to be mother to those two little children was overwhelming. She had met Isabel and she had seemed really nice. Tina dried her tears and put a smile back on her face.

Benny returned from Williamsburg just before noon

"Hi Benny, welcome back, you have been gone a long time; you never said goodbye," Tina said as she came up to Benny.

"Oh Tina, I was so ashamed of myself that I just wanted to go somewhere and die. I wanted you to be my wife so bad and that night killed all my dreams," Benny replied.

"Mine too, but Kathy is okay, and she forgave you. I forgive you too. I am still willing to marry you and I want to be a mother to these two darling children." They held each other close and then they both had to wipe away tears. So did Linda, Isabel and Laura who had overheard the conversation. Laura was so glad realizing that both of them had nearly died of love sickness.

Michael and Mandy couldn't understand why they were crying. Benny and Tina explained that you sometimes cry when you are very happy. They then embraced the children.

"We are going to get married, and Benny is going to be your father and I am going to be your mother," Tina told Mandy and Michael. While hugging and kissing both of them. Michael didn't quite understand but Mandy was thrilled, and Tina was overwhelmed with joy. For the rest of their lives they would remember how God had spared them from killing themselves and giving them each other and two wonderful children to love.

Kathy and Katy were the first ones to leave for the church on Friday afternoon. Bobby came a little late, but he played some really fast music on his fiddle that got the group wide awake. Margaret came over with Sally and William in time to hear Bobby sing "Shenandoah" with Kathy singing her refrain. When they finished Sally confessed that the song always made her want to cry.

They livened it up again with "When Johnny Comes Marching Home" with Kathy playing the flute. Since this was not a church service, the people were applauding after each song. Kathy and Bobby sang their love song back and forth to each other and several couples discretely gave each other a hug. They followed with some gospel music. People found the music mesmerizing as did Margaret.

Benny was there and came over to Kathy and Bobby during a break walking with a limp. "I want to apologize for that horrible night, I was too drunk to understand what we were doing. I haven't touched alcohol since."

"You are forgiven and I'm fine now but what happened to you?" Kathy asked.

Benny laughed, "I almost succeeded in making it to Heaven when I set off some black powder in a mine shaft and tripped on a rock when I was running away. It didn't kill me, but now I can't run anymore so I got a job grinding ore samples. I have been renting from a nice lady whose two grandchildren are orphans and we all kind of adopted each other. Now I want to stay alive for their sake. Best of all Tina has forgiven me and agreed to marry me and we are going to adopt the children" Tina brought the children over and he introduced Michael and Mandy, and their grandmother Isabel.

"I am so happy about marrying Benny and being mother to Mandy and Michael and Isabel is so nice," Tina told Kathy with a big smile on her face.

"The children are absolutely darling," Kathy replied.

Laura observed to Martha who was standing nearby, "I am getting a son-in-law and acquiring a couple of darling grandchildren. I just wish they weren't going to live so far away"

"Well, I got a son-in-law and two new grandchildren, and I am so happy. I think you will be too," Martha replied.

By Sunday morning, they had found a wedding dress for Tina and had a short ceremony after church to marry them off. Bobby and Kathy provided the music and Clarence officiated.

Thomas had given his blessing, but he was sad that Tina was moving away. Laura was also sad about Tina moving away and she would have loved to be close to her new grandchildren. They had come over to Thomas and Laura's house on Saturday and Michael had fallen asleep in Laura's arms. Thomas had held Mandy and she had stolen his heart. What a joy they were. Both Thomas and Laura wished they could be close to Tina and the children she was adopting.

Bobby and Kathy both agreed that Benny had suffered enough for his part in that assault. The downside was watching another happy couple get married while they were postponing their own wedding to some distant date. Bobby and Kathy held unto each other as a carriage took Benny, Tina, Michael, Mandy, and Isabel away from the ceremony to catch a train for their return trip to Rapid City.

The following morning. Bobby left for St Louis and Kathy went back to teaching school. Bobby had spent most of Saturday going over production issues with William, so Bobby and Kathy did not spend much time together.

Margaret felt bad because when she started talking to Bobby they got interrupted by Gerald. Gerald had found out from Margaret that Bobby had three black people working for him.

"Why would you hire some dumb, lazy black people?

"They are neither dumb nor lazy and they are very good workers," Bobby had replied and walked away. He avoided talking to them after that.

CHAPTER 31

Christmas

It was probably easier for Kathy to be apart than it was for Bobby because she loved teaching the children and the children loved being with Kathy and Martha. Kathy kept busy sewing, but she gave away a lot too. Most of the children came from families that didn't have much money. Kathy gave a number of children warm mittens and some of the girls got snow pants to wear under their dresses when they played outside. The classroom wasn't always that warm, so the girls tended to wear their snow pants all the time.

Kathy started to sing Christmas Carols both at school and in church. At church Kathy played one verse of "Oh Come, Oh Come Emmanuel" on her flute before singing it. Kathy had the children sing "Away in a Manger" and they sang it to perfection. One mother told Martha that she wished she could listen to them sing all week long. Bruce was now singing with the rest of the children and was actually quite good. Martha had been tutoring Bruce in his reading and he had improved almost a whole grade level.

Kathy and Katy continued to eat breakfast early and then go over to the school. Katy would eat lunch with Jade over at the bathhouse kitchen. Kathy would bring lunch to school and would eat her lunch quickly. She would then play the piano and sing until class started again. Kathy had reluctantly agreed that she and Katy would join the others for supper. They tried to avoid doing or saying anything that would offend Gerald. Sometimes Martha would try to draw Kathy into the conversation, but Kathy usually kept her silence.

With the colder weather, they were selling more meat in the store and Gerald did a good job butchering meat into easy to cook sizes. Gerald was actually trying to get along after realizing that he had few alternatives. Margaret got along well with both Katy and Kathy, but they usually retreated to the bathhouse after supper.

Kathy found the time before Christmas both rewarding and exhausting. She was working with the children in her school to have them put on a Christmas concert. She was making gifts with her sewing machine as well as making stuff to sell in the store. She was also trying to do what she considered her share of food preparation and housework.

Martha was busy too, but she became concerned that Kathy was pushing herself too hard. "Sweetheart, you can't do everything, you have got to take a break," Martha told her after finding she had fallen asleep in the bathhouse kitchen while trying to make breakfast. Martha insisted Kathy go back to bed and she finished the task Kathy had started. Kathy came into school late that morning.

It was a week before Christmas and the church was full. Clarence smiled at the problem he faced almost every Sunday trying to get people to remember his sermon after Kathy had been singing. Katy and Janice had sung "Away in a Manger" accompanied by Kathy playing the flute. The girls were so good. Clarence now listened as Kathy played the piano and sang "O Come; O Come Emmanuel" with that wonderful voice she had. Clarence squeezed Martha's hand and she smiled; both of them loved the music.

Bobby arrived from St Louis the afternoon of Christmas Eve. He had barely arrived before he joined in with Kathy and Clarence planning the music for a Christmas Eve Service. Clarence made some opening remarks and Alex read the Christmas story from Luke. Bobby played some Christmas music on his fiddle. Then Kathy played the piano and sang "O Come; O Come Emmanuel" with Bobby. Kathy then sang the song about Jesus' birth in Latin. The children came up and did "Oh Little Town of Bethlehem" with Kathy playing her flute. Kathy then played the piano and sang "O Holy Night" with Bobby following it with "Hark The Herald Angels Sing" and finally closing with "Silent Night".

There was a really good turnout for the Christmas Eve program. People were thrilled with the singing and parents were rightfully proud of how well their children sang. Kathy was so happy to be singing with Bobby again and so proud of her students. Several people told Clarence and Martha that it was the most beautiful music they had ever heard. Bobby looked at a radiant smiling Kathy with complete adoration. Little children would run up and give Kathy a hug. People also came over and told Bobby how glad they were to see him.

Margaret had come over with Elizabeth and Bruce. Gerald stayed back and indulged himself in a small bottle of whiskey. Margaret admitted to herself that Kathy was wonderful, and her brother was too though she felt a little jealous of them. She wished Gerald had come with her, but everyone was in good mood. Margaret was talking to several ladies who were admiring a smiling little Elizabeth.

Margaret wanted to talk to Sally but was interrupted by Bruce: "Let's go home, I'm hungry." Margaret tried to ignore him, and he started banging the piano keys.

Kathy said: "stop it" and tried grabbing his hands but he yanked one hand free and banged the piano keys even harder.

Bobby then came over and stopped him.

Margaret carried Elizabeth and led Bruce out of the church feeling humiliated by his actions. Margaret listened to the sound of Bobby playing the fiddle as she retreated back to the house wishing she could have stayed. Margaret was demoralized by what Bruce had done.

Bobby and Kathy decided to do some more singing to the delight of people who had stayed around. Martha and Clarence were still there and so was Sally and William with their children. Bobby started some really fast music that had children bouncing up and down. Kathy knew the words to one of the songs but changed the words slightly to 'I come from Alabama with a fiddle on my knee' and then later to 'I was mailed from Boston Massachusetts just to marry thee'.

The house was dark when they returned home long after Margaret and Bruce left. They lit a candle and then a lamp in the kitchen. Martha was frustrated because a lot of the cookies she had planned to put out on Christmas day were gone.

Kathy and Bobby hugged and kissed goodnight. Kathy headed for the bathhouse with Katy. Kathy locked the door with the wooden bar. She had to add wood to the bathhouse kitchen fire before crawling in with Katy. It had been a good evening. She then drifted off to sleep.

Kathy awoke to a knock on the bathhouse door. It was Martha. Kathy got dressed and helped Martha prepare breakfast. Kathy prepared pancake batter while Martha cut strips of bacon from a slab. "I thought I had enough ham for breakfast, but Gerald must have eaten it last night," Martha announced. "A lot of the cookies I was going to serve for lunch are gone too. I swear Gerald and Bruce eat almost as much food as everyone else combined."

Kathy felt frustrated that they ate so much and were never appreciative of their efforts to make it. "I will make another batch of cookies," Kathy announced.

"You shouldn't have to, but that would be nice," Martha told her.

Kathy started working on the batter for the cookies. She had most of the ingredients, but she needed to add either butter or some grease from the bacon being fried. She woke Katy and told her to come to the house when she was dressed.

Kathy ran across the patio to the house carrying the cookie batter. Several inches of snow had fallen making it more like Christmas back in Boston. The snow had stuck to the branches of the trees, and it looked really pretty.

There was fresh coffee in the house and Bobby and Clarence were already up. Kathy joined them at the table. "That was quite a concert you two put on last night and the children were great too," Clarence told them.

"It was so fun singing with Bobby again and listening to the fiddle," Kathy replied.

"I am trying to be worthy of being your singing partner," Bobby responded.

"You are more than worthy," Kathy smiled.

Margaret felt like she had three babies to take care of when she got up in the morning. Elizabeth was the easiest, she was her sweet cuddly self after getting fed and getting a diaper changed. Bruce had come back to the house and Margaret found the cookies in the downstairs kitchen and gave him one. Margaret had been distracted by Elizabeth and Bruce was able to grab about five more. When Margaret got upstairs, she smelled whisky and Gerald had left a hambone picked clean.

Bruce woke up complaining of a stomachache. Gerald woke up with a hangover and a swollen big toe. Margaret grabbed Elizabeth and headed downstairs.

She arrived and heard the sweet exchange between Kathy and Bobby. Katy came running in and got hugs from Martha, Clarence, Bobby and finally Kathy. Margaret felt so sad because everyone loved Katy, nobody liked Bruce.

Clarence reached out and got to hold Elizabeth. Margaret sat down at the table with her head down crying. Martha came behind and gave her a hug. Martha gave her a cup of hot coffee and Margaret sipped it slowly.

Finally, Margaret spoke: "I loved the music and I wanted to stay. I am so embarrassed by how Bruce acted last night. Both him and Gerald are sick this morning from overeating last night. I promised Bruce one cookie if he behaved himself and came home quietly. I gave him one cookie and then he grabbed a bunch more when I was tending to Elizabeth."

After breakfast they sent Margaret upstairs with coffee for Gerald and suggested that Bruce drink water. Elizabeth was left with a smiling Bobby holding her. Elizabeth took an instant liking to Bobby, and he kept her smiling and happy.

Margaret came down and was pleased that at least one of her children had found favor. Margaret and Bobby got a chance to catch up on each other's lives which they had not done at Thanksgiving. Gerald had tried to belittle the work that Bobby was doing in comments to Margaret, but she was very impressed that he was in charge of a small factory. Elizabeth had cuddled up in Bobby's arms and was drifting to sleep as Bobby softly sang a lullaby to her.

They were interrupted by Bruce who came down in his night shirt and loudly said Gerald wanted breakfast brought up to him. Elizabeth started to wake up, but Bobby was able to get her to go back to sleep. Margaret grabbed a plate of pancakes and bacon to bring up to Gerald wishing he were sweet and gentle like Bobby. Katy was sitting on the couch between Clarence and Bobby. All four of them looked so content all cuddled up together. Kathy wished she could cuddle up too, but she had work to do.

Kathy finished making her cookie dough and put her first batch on a greased pan and ran them back to the oven in the bathhouse kitchen. A large turkey was roasting in the oven in the house. She came back to the house and started peeling potatoes while Martha worked on making raisin pies. Kathy almost forgot about the cookies but ran back just in time to pull them out of the oven before they got burnt.

William and Sally came over late in the morning pulling a sled full of Christmas gifts. Sven who worked for William had made the sled and the children were excited about trying it out on a small hill near the school. Bobby had relinquished Elizabeth to Sally and gone outside. Bobby was working on a sled of his own inspired by one Charles had made. Bobby had brought back a couple of key pieces with him, so it didn't take him too long to finish it.

Gerald and Bruce finally made it downstairs, and they decided to open presents before lunch. Kathy had made dresses for Martha, Margaret, Sally, Janice, and Katy. For the men and the boys, she had made heavy wool button down vests to wear under their jackets. For Elizabeth, she had made a cute two-piece outfit that could be unbuttoned quickly for diaper changes. Everyone was pleased and Martha marveled at how she could get so much work done.

Margaret told Kathy: "I don't know how I can repay you."

"Just let me go sledding with the children and you help with the dishes."

"That's a deal."

Bobby gave Kathy a gold necklace with beautiful gold heart shaped locket which he placed around her neck after showing it to her. Kathy rewarded him with a hug and a kiss. Clarence and Martha gave Kathy a new hymnal and a recipe book. William and Sally gave Kathy a beautiful wooden hope chest. Other gifts were passed around.

Kathy and Bobby ate Christmas dinner with the children. Gerald and Bruce sat at the end of the adult table unable to enjoy the food after overindulging the night before. Everyone else was enjoying a feast of turkey and side dishes along with fresh bread that Julia had made the day before. Kathy did the serving for the table but had help from Janice. Kathy and Janice went over to the adult table to pour coffee, water and milk as needed.

Finally, Kathy sat down next to Bobby who started telling jokes and funny stories until all the children were laughing. Kathy tried not to overeat which wasn't easy because everything was so good. She remembered her father taking her and her little brother snow sledding and how much fun it was.

Kathy and Bobby and all the children except Bruce went sledding. Shep had come too and was chasing after sleds and barking at them. The sled Sven made was a little faster, but the sled Bobby made steered better. Kathy sat behind Bobby, and they went flying down the hill hitting a bump at the very end and flying off into the snow. Kathy was lying face up and Bobby gave her a kiss before helping her to her feet. Kathy was so happy; it was so much fun. Bobby looked at Kathy's pretty smiling face with her cheeks rosy from the cold and felt overwhelmed with love for her. Kathy was so happy to be with Bobby.

Katy and Alex were next to use the sled and came back up the hill all excited. Bobby let them have another run before Kathy went down with him again. They were starting to get tired after numerous trips when they were joined by Richard, Sally, Margaret, and Bruce.

William and Sally went down first on separate sleds. Bruce and Margaret followed also on separate sleds. Bruce enjoyed going down, but he was tired and ready to quit after walking back up while Margaret was ready to go again. Bruce did finally go again, and eventually they all returned to the house tired but happy.

The cookies Kathy had made started to disappear really fast and Sally wanted the recipe.

William talked about the two sleds: "I think if we could combine the best qualities of the two sleds, we could sell a lot of them at Christmas. They are a lot of fun, but they are also handy for moving firewood and other stuff."

Bobby and Kathy were sitting on a couch and Elizabeth crawled over and wanted up. Bobby had his left arm around Kathy, he was petting Shep with his right hand. He started making funny faces at Elizabeth after Kathy picked her up and held her. Then Bobby started singing a children's hymn to Elizabeth softly like a lullaby. Kathy felt Elizabeth's little body relax and snuggle into her. Kathy felt herself getting sleepy too. Kathy felt so cozy, so happy, and so loved. Bobby did too.

Margaret had gone up to check on Gerald and came back down after finding him sleeping. She looked at her daughter blissfully asleep in Kathy's lap with her face turned toward Bobby. Margaret sighed before she sat down next to Clarence and got a badly needed hug from him. Gerald didn't cuddle, neither did Bruce and Margaret so wished they would give her the sweet love she saw between Bobby and Kathy.

They had made more trips down the hill than anyone, but Katy and Alex were still awake enough to be intensely competing in a game of checkers. Despite the intensity of their games, the two of them liked each other a lot. Sally was cuddled up with William and smiled as she watched Alex and Katy. Sally loved the idea of Alex marrying Katy. James liked Katy too and both boys were studying hard not wanting to be beat by a girl. Sally thought of the many good things that had happened since Martha had brought home Kathy and Katy.

Janice was singing the lullaby song as if anyone needed any more incentive to relax. Janice was such a joy to have around. One day when Margaret was frustrated with Bruce she joked to Sally: "You wouldn't be willing to trade Janice for Bruce would you?"

"No, but if we had more room, I would love to keep Janice and get Katy, but mother wants Katy too."

The room got cooler and less cozy. Bobby got up and started adding wood to the stove. Gerald woke up and came downstairs complaining about being cold and limping due to his sore foot. Kathy also got up and carefully carried a sleeping Elizabeth over to Margaret.

Kathy then went to the kitchen to help Martha prepare supper from Christmas Dinner leftovers. Kathy started cutting slices of bread for turkey sandwiches, They also heated leftover gravy, potatoes, and dressing in the oven and some of the turkey too.

After supper, Bobby played his fiddle and Gerald didn't say anything. Kathy and Bobby sang a couple songs together, but everyone was ready to turn in early. William and Sally headed home with their children and Gerald and Margaret went upstairs with theirs.

Katy had fallen asleep on the couch and Clarence and Martha had turned in. It gave Bobby and Kathy some time talk. Kathy was disappointed that Bobby was going back Monday. They would have Friday, Saturday, and Sunday together, but Bobby said he needed to spend most of Friday and Saturday working with Sven and Ned on some minor changes to the dresser and some new furniture ideas. Kathy had a backlog of sewing to get caught up on too, but she had hoped to spend more time with Bobby. It also been so much fun sliding down the hill being a kid again.

Bobby and Kathy enjoyed a hug and goodnight kiss before he helped her get a sleepy Katy out to the bathhouse. After Bobby left, Kathy added wood to the stove and both her and Katy changed to heavy nightgowns.

Friday and Saturday Bobby worked all day with William and Ned. Kathy sewed all day. The children wore off all the snow on the hill with the sleds. Friday night everyone retired early.

Saturday night Clarence, Bobby, Kathy, and Katy got together over at the church to prepare for the first Sunday after Christmas. Many of the songs would be a repeat of their Christmas Eve service on Wednesday night. Bobby and Kathy were both tired, but they were energized by singing together. Kathy felt that she had improved as a singer and on the piano, but she was impressed with Bobby both as a singer and his fiddle playing. Kathy had noticed it Christmas Eve and became aware of it again, as they practiced. She complimented him after he did a great job on a melody.

"I have been doing a lot of fiddling on lonely nights wishing you were with me," Bobby replied.

"I try to stay busy almost every night for the same reason," Kathy responded.

The church was packed on Sunday, and everyone was glad to see Bobby. Clarence remarked after the service to Martha: "The children sounded great, Bobby and Kathy sounded great, and I think a few people even paid attention to what I said in my sermon."

After church, they had a great Sunday dinner with William and Sally's family present. Everyone decided to go back to the church and sing except Gerald and Bruce. Martha and Margaret came with Elizabeth after doing dishes. Bobby had told a few people that they would be coming back to church in the afternoon. People loved to hear Bobby play the fiddle so quite a few showed up.

Kathy sang and played some songs on the piano. Others including Katy and Janice got involved in singing. Martha had brought food over too so there were snacks to munch on. It was also a good time for people to visit and it turned into a really fun party. Kathy had brought the song book she had been given for Christmas and was able to play the tune on the piano and sing one of the songs.

They left the schoolhouse before it got dark, and Bobby said goodbyes to people at the school. Bobby would say goodbye to William and Sally and their children in Williamsburg the next morning. Ned would drive a second wagon bringing in Bobby with Clarence, Kathy and Katy coming to Williamsburg for Bobby's departure back to St Louis. They returned to the house feeling glum about Bobby leaving the next day. Bobby had brought life back into the house and even Gerald did not complain when they sang inside. Bobby talked about the factory closing down midwinter for a couple of weeks and he might come home.

Bobby and Kathy looked at her new songbook after supper. Bobby wrote down the words to a couple songs he liked, and Kathy sang them so he could hear the melody. Bobby was getting better at reading notes, but he still marveled how Kathy could sing a new song by just looking at the notes. Their good night hug and kiss was longer than usual but left both of them wanting more.

It was a cold morning on Monday traveling to Williamsburg that tended to discourage singing as they huddled under a couple blankets for warmth. They spent a short time at the store in Williamsburg and Kathy bought some fabric and buttons. Kathy also picked up some supplies for the school. They then went over to the hotel restaurant. Kathy was disappointed that the place was nearly empty, and Joe wasn't there.

It was still too early for the lunch crowd, but Kathy sat down at the piano and started playing and singing Christmas Carols. Kathy sang a couple songs solo before Bobby joined in with her. Bobby had brought his fiddle and played the melody for several songs. William and Sally showed up with their children and joined them. Kathy played "Away in a Manger" on her flute with Katy and Janice singing it together. Afterwards Sally said it was so pretty it almost made her cry.

Joe showed up at noon and greeted them warmly. Kathy sang the song in Latin that Joe liked, and Bobby was able play background music for the song on his fiddle. They then did "Silent Night" together. They ate lunch and got free cookies from Joe. Kathy hugged and kissed Bobby at the train station and they all waved goodbye. Clarence held Kathy as she wiped away her tears as the train left.

CHAPTER 32

A Tme to Leave

Martha had gotten a letter from Mary asking if she could spend several weeks with her. Mary was expecting to give birth to her third child and wondered if Martha could be there for her. Martha left by train for St Louis the second week in January.

A week later Clarence got an urgent telegram from his sister-in-law in Springfield, Illinois saying that his brother had suffered a heart attack and she needed help running the family store. With Martha absent, Kathy was now fully in charge at school with occasional help from Sally. Clarence had let both Margaret and Gerald run the store for short periods, and they were both competent, but Clarence did not trust Gerald.

Reluctantly, Clarence left Gerald in charge of the store and left for Springfield. Clarence had put Gerald on a pretty tight lease saying he would not tolerate drinking or going to the tavern in town. Gerald had managed to sneak away to the tavern a few times undetected, but he had been pretty well behaved.

That changed soon after Clarence left for Springfield. Gerald then grabbed some money out of the cash box and headed for the tavern Sunday night feeling liberated at last. Gerald came home later that night feeling happy after drinking despite having lost most of the money he had brought with him in a poker game.

Gerald was still sleeping Monday morning when Margaret fed Bruce breakfast and sent him off to school. She then grabbed Elizabeth and opened up the store. It was cold in there and the fire had nearly gone out. She got the fire going and held Elizabeth close waiting for the store to warm up. She had only vague memories of her Aunt and Uncle in Springfield so was mostly concerned that her father was gone.

Things had been going pretty well but now she was worried that Gerald would take advantage of her folks being gone to do something stupid. Margaret counted the cash, and it was short a large amount from Saturday night's tally. Gerald finally came into the store about midmorning and suggested Margaret stay until he got some meat ready for sale. They talked about the extra work of heating the downstairs while Clarence and Martha were gone, and Gerald said they should move downstairs until they came back. Margaret reluctantly agreed.

Kathy was concerned about both Clarence and Martha being gone. Kathy decided that Katy and she would live and cook by themselves until Clarence and Martha came back. Kathy stayed later after school and played the piano and sang with Katy. Kathy was not getting much clothing sewn and ready for sale but not many people were buying clothing during the winter. The biggest problem with Martha gone was that some students and especially Bruce were misbehaving in class.

It was several days after both Martha and Clarence were gone that Kathy and Katy came home a little later from school to see Bruce running out of their bathhouse area. They found papers and clothing scattered around and some money that Kathy had set aside for groceries was missing. Katy said Julia had set aside a couple cinnamon rolls for their supper, and they were missing too. Kathy was furious. Words like fat, stupid, worthless, lazy, stinking lout were running through Kathy's brain, but she managed not to say them. Fortunately, Kathy had kept most of her money and her flute with her, but it destroyed her sense of security.

Kathy had frozen some stew earlier in the week in a kettle and she heated it up on the stove. Kathy had loved teaching the children and loved the community but now she had this dark feeling of wanting to leave. They ate in silence and then Kathy asked Katy if she would mind moving back to Boston and they could live with their aunt Karla again.

"It was so nice here until those pigs moved back, I hate them," Katy fumed. Katy then started to cry. "I don't want to leave my friends," Katy wailed.

"Okay, we will just have to try to keep him out of here," Kathy replied. Kathy wasn't really sure how she could keep him out when they weren't there.

Clarence had left his hammer and a long bolt behind when he replaced Kathy's cloth partition with a door. Kathy used a kitchen knife to enlarge a hole in the door frame that separated her sleeping area from the bathhouse kitchen. She was then able to push the bolt into it until it touched the door. She then made a small hole in the side of the door that she could push the bolt into. She showed Katy how they could push the bolt in, which was hard to see, and their sleeping area would appear to be locked when they weren't there. Kathy hoped it would keep him out when they weren't there. The downside was that their room would get cold in their absence.

William filled in for Clarence on Sunday morning and did a very good job. The children sang really well it and was a very satisfying Sunday morning. Sally invited Kathy and Katy to come over for lunch. Kathy's spirits had lifted, and she felt happy again. It was a fairly long walk back to William and Sally's place on a cold day. They started singing "When Johnny Comes Marching Home" as they walked.

Kathy helped in the kitchen while the children played. The house was warm, and cozy and William and Sally didn't hide their affection for each other and the children. It was a great afternoon. Kathy and Katy left before it got dark. Sally had confided to her that she was expecting a baby by spring which was hardly a secret due to Sally's expanding waistline.

Margaret, Elizabeth, and Bruce had not come to church. Margaret was home trying to get the house and the store heated up as well as making something to eat. Gerald was nursing a hangover from another night at the tavern and suffering remorse after losing more money playing poker. He had covered up some of the money he had lost earlier by not recording sales including some mittens and aprons Kathy had made. After a couple cups of coffee and breakfast, Gerald's head was starting to clear. He looked in his billfold and grimaced at how little money was left.

This was the second time Gerald had lost a significant amount of money to Sven. Sven worked for William cutting wood and would refer to himself disparagingly as "just a dumb Swede" and his heavy accent helped create that impression too. Unfortunately for Gerald, it was all a cover up. Sven was probably one of the shrewdest card players in the county and the locals had learned to be very cautious when Sven was playing. Gerald fancied himself as an expert card player which he wasn't. Gerald's ego along with a few drinks resulted in him taking risks and taking big losses. Gerald was now doing the same thing that caused him to be disinherited back in Ohio, taking money from the store, and losing it playing cards.

Gerald told Margaret that he was going out to the store to see if it was warm enough. The store was warm enough, but his main concern was the cash box. Gerald confirmed what he was already afraid of. Saturday afternoon before closing the store he had looted the store cash box of most of its money. Now he had come back with only a little money to put back in. After a week of Gerald running the store, almost all of the money Clarence had left was gone. There was barely enough money to make change and hardly any money to buy eggs or meat to butcher. Plus, a shipment of groceries was arriving next week, and there was no money to pay for it.

Margaret already knew they were in trouble. Margaret had taken the cash box key when Gerald was sleeping and looked herself. She had also looked in his wallet. Margaret almost wished she had just taken Elizabeth with her when she left Ohio and let Gerald and Bruce fend for themselves. Margaret dared not say anything to Gerald for fear of an angry tirade.

By that evening, Gerald had come up with a coverup story. "We have got a problem," Gerald told Margaret, "your father took most of the money in the cash box to pay for his trip up to Springfield and I don't have any money for a grocery shipment coming in on Tuesday."

Margaret knew what Gerald was saying was a lie, but she replied, "Oh, that's too bad, is there anything we can do about it?"

"Do you think we can borrow some money from your sister?" Gerald asked.

"I doubt it but maybe we can get it from Kathy," Margaret replied, "I think I can talk her into helping."

Kathy and Katy had just returned from William and Sally's place when there was a knock on the door. Kathy opened the door to Margaret who repeated the lie that Clarence had not left enough money for a shipment coming in.

"That surprises me," Kathy replied. The estimated amount needed was a fairly large amount, almost a month's wages. "That's a lot of money,"

Kathy told Margaret, "It used to take me a month working in a factory to make that amount."

"I am sure father will repay you as soon as he gets back,"

"Okay, I will talk to Andy when he is picking up children at the school. I will have him find out the exact amount tomorrow, and I will send a check with him on Tuesday," Kathy replied. "I missed you at church this morning," Kathy told Margaret.

"We overslept and I had to get stoves going in both the house and the store. I better get back to the house, thank you so much for helping us get this shipment in," Margaret said and then left.

Margaret brought the news back to Gerald who was frustrated that Kathy was going to deal directly with Andy. "I wish she would just give us cash; It makes me look incompetent with her dealing directly with Andy," Gerald complained.

"Well at least we will get more groceries to sell," Margaret replied. In her mind she was thinking that Gerald really was incompetent. Her father had left more than enough money to cover the shipment and Gerald's story would unravel as soon as her father came home. She also knew that not many things stayed a secret in a small town very long. In fact, Kathy had already heard from William that Gerald had been playing poker with Sven and some other men and Sven had won quite a bit of money from Gerald.

Kathy had heard from Martha that Gerald and Margaret were almost broke when they arrived from Ohio. Kathy was pretty certain that Gerald's gambling money had come from the store.

Sally came in Monday morning to help at the school. Bruce started talking to another kid and repeatedly ignored Kathy's request to be quiet. Sally got right in his face and told him "either be quiet or I am going to take you home and talk to your mother."

"My father will stick up for me," Bruce asserted.

"Fine," Sally replied, "then he can either teach you himself or you can get up early and you can ride to Williamsburg and go to school there. So, go get your jacket and your parents can decide what to do with you."

"I will be quiet," Bruce replied, not ready to follow through with his bluff. Sally left soon after, but Bruce behaved after that.

Kathy talked with Andy on Tuesday and sent a check with him on Wednesday. Andy's laughed when she told him that the store was short of cash, and she was helping out.

"I think Gerald's been paying for his losses to Sven playing poker with store money," Andy commented "I don't think Clarence is going to be very happy when he gets back."

"I agree, I miss Martha at the school and Clarence running the store," Kathy replied. "It will be the end of next week when Martha gets back, and I don't know when Clarence is returning,"

Gerald headed back to the tavern in the evening of the Sunday after Kathy had paid for the shipment, but Sven declined to play poker with him. "I work for William, and he doesn't want me to take any more of your money," Sven told him.

"That's none of his business," Gerald replied.

"Well Clarence and William pretty much run this little town so it's best not to mess with them or their wives," Sven told him. Gerald didn't gamble that night, but he had too much to drink.

When Gerald left the tavern there was a light on in the schoolhouse and he walked over to it. Kathy had come over with Katy to start a fire in the stove so it would be warm in the morning for school. Kathy had just got the fire started when Gerald walked in startling them since only a small lamp provided light to the mostly dark room.

"Kind of late for school, isn't it?" Gerald asked.

"If I start a fire in the stove tonight, it won't be so hard to warm up the school tomorrow morning," Kathy replied.

"Hey, we could cuddle up to it and get warm.," Gerald exclaimed.

"I am warm," Kathy replied, "now that I have got the fire going, we are going to head back."

"Hey not so fast, I just got here," Gerald responded while grabbing her arm and putting his other hand on her butt. "Bobby's not here so I am sure you could use a little loving. "

Kathy was thoroughly repulsed. "Let go of me!" Kathy yelled. She screamed as loud as she could and tried to pull arm free.

"You're not going anywhere, we are going to have some fun," Gerald told her as she struggled with him to no avail.

"Please let me go, you need to go home to Margaret."

"No, I am going to have you tonight," Gerald said, and used his free hand to start unbuttoning Kathy's coat.

Katy came up behind Gerald and hit him on the head with a piece of firewood. Gerald cursed Katy, grabbed her arm, and sent her flying. Kathy heard a crash and a cry of pain from Katy.

Kathy then butted his jaw with her head and used her foot to kick Gerald's shin bone. "Damn you," Gerald yelled, pulling her arm, and sending her flying as well.

Kathy landed hard hitting her head and shoulder on the floor. Kathy scrambled to her feet despite the pain she felt and ran for the door. Katy was hiding in the darkness and pushed a chair into Gerald's path as he pursued Kathy. Kathy heard a tremendous crash and curses behind her.

They heard Gerald say, "I'll kill you damn girls." Katy followed Kathy through the door. Once outside, they sprinted for the bathhouse. Kathy locked the bathhouse door behind them and added wood to the fire going in the bathhouse kitchen stove.

Kathy trembled thinking about what could have happened to her. She hugged Katy for warmth as she waited for their sleeping area to get warmer but also to calm her nerves. Kathy packed the suitcases that they had brought from Boston, it was time to return. Kathy shuddered every time she thought of what could have happened in the schoolhouse. Kathy slept fitfully, her left hand, wrist, and shoulder all ached, and she had a headache too.

Kathy opened the school door cautiously the next morning on Monday half expecting Gerald to still be there. They put their suitcases behind her desk and waited for the students to show up. Alex, James, and Janice came early, and Kathy explained that they were leaving to go back to Boston to stay with their aunt. She told them to tell the other students that school would resume in a week when Martha came home, and they should all go home. Kathy also put a note on the blackboard. She also gave them written notes to give to Martha, Sally, and Jade.

Kathy confided to Janice what had happened but told her not to tell the other students just Sally and William. Kathy tried to stay unemotional, but Katy was crying, and she was too, after hugging Janice goodbye.

Andy was upset to hear they were leaving but helped them get themselves and their luggage on the school wagon. They rode in silence and darkness to Williamsburg with the older students. The school wagon was covered over for warmth. Their arrival eight months earlier by wagon was so fun, their departure was so sad. Once in town Kathy went to the bank and drew out her remaining money. They went over to the hotel restaurant and Kathy killed time sitting in the lobby. Finally buying a light lunch at the nearly deserted restaurant before walking over to the train depot with their luggage.

The station master was shocked to hear they were returning to Boston. Kathy paid for the tickets, and they boarded the train when it arrived. Kathy felt so depressed; a feeling of defeat swept over her. Unlike the trip down when Kathy and Katy had the urge to sing. Kathy's hand and arm were still sore, and her neck hurt. Katy's right shoulder hurt too. They rode silently and glumly back toward Boston as they listened to the monotonous click of the rails. The skies were gray like their spirits, and trees were leafless sentinels on a white background. This time they had food and water, and Kathy felt she could spend some money on more food and water if she needed to.

Kathy looked forward to meeting her aunt again, but nothing would ever be quite as magical as that first day when Alex and Bobby met them at the railroad station and then meeting Sally, Julia, and Clarence. Kathy hoped she still had her wedding to Bobby to look forward to but nothing in this world could be counted on. Kathy felt bad for Katy. She was taking Katy away from so many people that loved her.

Kathy didn't know what other choice she had. Bobby had told her at Christmas that he had to sleep in the factory to stay warm and her sister Christine had written to Kathy they had no room for them. Kathy had been so proud of the happy life she had found for Katy and herself but now it was gone.

Kathy fell asleep and woke stiff and disoriented in darkness. Katy was cuddled up to her and they were on a train. Her mind reviewed the last two days and realized that some of the stiffness to her shoulder could have come from hitting the floor in her fight with Gerald. They were probably somewhere in Ohio by now. She tried looking out the train window, but there was nothing but a blur of darkness. She had taken a blanket with her which was cumbersome to carry but it helped keep them warm. She prayed for safety for Katy and herself. She also prayed for Martha and

Clarence who would have to deal with the problems Gerald had created. Kathy also prayed that she could make money back in Boston to pay for their food and rent.

Kathy woke up again to the faint light of dawn traveling through a hilly region of Pennsylvania. Her head was clear, but her body was even more stiff. Kathy tried to ease her way from Katy's grasp to get up and go to the bathroom. Katy woke up and they both walked stiffly holding on to seats to steady themselves. When they returned, they each had a cinnamon roll which was the last of their food and nearly finished off their water. It was a sunny day, and the rugged snow-covered landscape was beautiful. It was midafternoon when they reached Grand Central Station in New York. They picked up their bags and Kathy bought a little food for them. They then rechecked their bags and boarded a train for Boston.

A song formed in Kathy's head:

> I left my heart when I boarded the train.
> I think I left it back at baggage claim.
> Is it the smoky ash that makes my eyes sting.
> Or shattered dreams in the baggage that I bring.
> A thousand miles is a long, long way.
> My dreams got lost along the way.
> Everyone said we were a perfect match.
> But getting together is a very big catch.
> We can sing together in Heaven above.
> But I want to sing now with the man I love.

It was early evening and already dark with a light snow falling when they walked out of the train station in Boston. This time Kathy paid for a ride on a streetcar powered by electricity. It took them to within a few blocks of her aunts' apartment, but they were still exhausted when they got there. Her Aunt Karla was startled to see them, and she looked older than Kathy remembered her. The bed they had used before they left was buried in stuff, but Kathy told her that two pillows and the floor would be fine for sleeping. Kathy understated the problem they had faced.

"The couple we were staying with had their daughter's family move back and we had problems with the daughter's husband, so I decided we should leave."

The next morning Kathy woke up feeling stiff but rested. It took a few moments to realize she was back in Boston staying with her Aunt Karla again. She replayed the last few days in her mind wondering if coming back to Boston was the best decision she could have made. Karla was now only renting one room instead of two. Karla had said the other room was now available to be rented again.

Despite paying for the grocery shipment, Kathy had come back to Boston with a lot more money than she had when she left. Despite a sore hand she was able to go to the store and come back with a good supply of groceries. With some help from Katy and her aunt Karla, she started making bread and cinnamon rolls. The neighbor that had caused then so much trouble was gone, and a young couple had moved in with a young daughter and a baby boy. The father was working but they invited the mother and daughter in for coffee and cinnamon rolls. Aunt Karla got to hold the baby boy and Katy was having fun with the little girl. The lady was Italian, and her name was Gina. The children were so cute with dark hair, dark eyes, and happy smiles.

Kathy sang 'Yankee Doodle" and some other songs with Katy singing along.

"You two are so good, this is so fun," Gina exclaimed as her little girl was swaying to the music. Kathy also sang some Christian songs and Katy surprised Kathy by singing them from memory. Gina reluctantly left to start making supper for her husband and retrieved her sleeping baby from Karla.

After she left, Karla told them: "I had forgotten how much fun it was having you two around." Kathy helped make pancakes for supper and fried some bacon she had bought to go with them.

CHAPTER 33

The Reckoning

Gerald had a sprained knee, some bad bruises, and a black eye from hitting the edge of another chair when he fell over the chair Katy had put in front of him. His ankle was painful from where Kathy kicked it and so was his jaw from her head butt. He also had a lump on his head where Katy had hit him. Margaret did not know what happened to him and knew better than to ask. Gerald slept in on Monday and Margaret opened the store and sent Bruce off to school.

Bruce was happy not to have school and ran into the store to tell Margaret. "Children at school said that Kathy and Katy went back to Boston, so we are not having school until next Monday when Martha returns."

Margaret stood at the cash register and was quiet finally saying "Oh no." It was bad enough that Gerald had taken money from the store and lost it gambling but she now worried that Gerald was responsible for the girls leaving. Margaret had really wanted to be friends with the girls, but they tended to avoid her because of Gerald and Bruce.

"Dress warm and play outside and try not to bother your father who is sleeping," Margaret told Bruce.

There really wasn't much to do outside and it was cold. After a short time, Bruce came back into the store. Bruce wanted to buy candy and Margaret was surprised that he had some coins. "Where did you get the money?" Margaret asked.

"I found it on the ground," Bruce lied after some hesitation.

Margaret sold him the candy, but Kathy had talked about someone going through their sleeping area and making a mess and taking a handful of change. Like father, like son, Margaret thought.

She thought again about Kathy leaving without saying goodbye. Something really bad must have happened for them to leave so unexpectedly and it probably involved Gerald. Several customers came in talked about how sad it was that those girls went back to Boston. Margaret closed the store that night, glad they were starting to get a little more money back in the cash box.

Margaret was tired and Elizabeth was fussing and was Gerald fuming that she didn't have dinner ready. "I just closed the store up, I will get started on it," Margaret responded, wishing she were the one that had left for Boston.

"I kept hearing Bruce in the living room, how come he wasn't in school?" Gerald asked.

"Kathy and Katy have moved out and returned to Boston," Margaret replied. "School will be out until next Monday when Martha returns."

"Did they say why the girls left?" Gerald asked.

"No, a couple of people who came to the store talked about them going back to live with an aunt, but I'm surprised they didn't wait for Martha to return."

Even though Gerald was hurting, he was pleased that things were turning out okay for him. "You would think Kathy would have been more considerate of the school children and not walk out on them without warning," Gerald responded. "Last night I tripped on a piece of firewood, and then fell headfirst onto another. I still can't put any weight on my right leg."

Margaret said nothing, still concerned that the two events were connected.

Things were going really well for Mary and her beautiful new baby boy. Martha was no longer needed to help but she hated to leave. It was so pleasant being with Mary, her two children and the precious new baby boy. She also got to spend part of a day out at the furniture factory with Bobby. She had met Alma and they had bonded immediately.

Martha decided to leave a couple days early so she could arrive Friday and catch a ride on the horse drawn school wagon. Once the train started heading back to Williamsburg, Martha's mind kept returning to a nagging worry about Gerald running the store. She could understand Clarence leaving to help his brother, but it was such a bad time. Her other worry was Kathy and Katy.

Gerald was always finding fault with Kathy no matter what she did until both girls avoided him as much as possible. Would Gerald cause trouble while Clarence and she were away?

Her worries increased when she got off the train. She asked the station master if he would watch her suitcase. "I am going to spend some time over at the hotel restaurant while waiting for a ride," she told him.

"No problem," he told her, "welcome back, I think they need your help back at the store. I will explain later," he said and went to help another passenger with her luggage. The wind was cold, so Martha decided to talk to him after she had lunch.

It was pleasant in the hotel restaurant and the waitress came over and poured her coffee. "Aren't you Bobby's mother?"

"I am, I just came back from helping a friend in St Louis and saw him while I was there," Martha replied, "he is doing great."

"When are him and his fiancé getting married?" the waitress asked.

"Probably this spring, Bobby is having a hard time finding a suitable place to rent"

She handed the menu to Martha and left to help another customer.

Martha was about to order a beef sandwich when the waitress said she was surprised that Bobby's fiancé had decided to return to Boston. Martha almost dropped her cup of coffee.

"She and her little sister were in here last Monday morning and left on the train."

Martha said, "Oh no!" and put her hands in her face. The waitress apologized for bringing her bad news.

Martha decided to just order a roll and barely tasted it. Martha decided to go to William and Sally's house first before returning home. Martha caught the school wagon and one of the girl's that attended their church confirmed that Kathy and Katy had left and returned to their aunt in Boston. Andy dropped the children off at the school but took Martha over to William and Sally's.

Sally was surprised to see her, but she was glad she had come to their place first. Sally talked about what happened. "Sven is a fantastic worker in the sawmill, but he likes to go over to the tavern and drink beer and play poker. After Clarence left, Gerald started showing up at the tavern and lost quite a bit of money to Sven while playing poker. When Sven bragged about it to William, William asked Sven to quit playing with Gerald. I am sure Gerald used store money to pay for his gambling losses."

"Last Sunday evening things got really bad. Gerald came into the church drunk where Kathy and Katy were firing up the stove so it wouldn't be so cold on Monday morning. He grabbed Kathy's hand and would not let go. He said something to Kathy like 'I am sure you would like some loving now that Bobby isn't here.' Kathy started screaming when he started unbuttoning her coat. Sally talked about how they had fought and how little Katy had gotten Gerald to fall over a chair. The last words that Kathy and Katy heard when they went out the door is that he would kill them."

Martha just shuddered. She spent the night on Sally's couch unsure what to do next.

Sally and Martha talked more about the situation over breakfast the next morning. "Kathy told everyone how much she loved them and the school children, but she didn't talk about what had happened. If she had said something, women wouldn't feel safe going to the store."

"I don't even feel safe going there now" Martha replied.

"My children know what happened, but I told them to keep quiet about it for now," Sally responded. "Let's wait until Clarence returns and then William and I will go with you and Clarence and confront him."

"Then what?" Martha asked.

"We run him out of town, Margaret would be better off without him," Sally replied. "For now, we will just listen to the lies that Margaret and Gerald tell us. Margaret admitted she lies when he tells her to because otherwise, he beats her."

"She hadn't told me that, but I don't doubt it," Martha replied.

William and Sally took Martha back to her home after lunch on Saturday. They went into the store and found Margaret running the store with Elizabeth sleeping nearby. "I am glad your back, Gerald took a really bad fall last week and he can't put any weight on his right leg, so I have been running the store," Margaret told them. Margaret then repeated Gerald's lie that Clarence hadn't left much money at the store when he left.

"That's too bad," Martha replied, "I imagine he left in a hurry and didn't plan far enough ahead."

"You heard that Kathy and Katy left, didn't you?" Margaret asked.

"That was a sad and unexpected surprise, Clarence and I wanted to adopt Katy and keep her here after Kathy marries Bobby," Martha replied.

"We moved downstairs and kind of need to stay there until Gerald's leg gets better," Margaret commented.

"Okay, I will get a fire going in the bathhouse where the girls were staying and then come back in here until it warms up."

William and Sally helped Martha get a fire going in the bathhouse kitchen and carried in some wood for her. "Sounds like the girls got Gerald pretty good," Sally commented, "too bad it didn't kill him."

William and Sally left, and Martha went in and relieved Margaret at the store. Martha was glad that Gerald hadn't been killed but was grimly pleased that he was banged up. Martha looked at the store records and they confirmed there was very little cash in the box right after Clarence left. There were, however, some smudge marks suggesting that numbers had been altered. Martha opened up a box that contained tins of cocoa to put them on the shelf. The box also contained newspapers as packing material. Martha was surprised the newspapers were quite recent, so the cocoa had arrived after Clarence had left. That was strange because there was no record of payment in the cash box for a grocery shipment. Martha then remembered Andy telling her that Kathy had sent along money with him for a shipment that had come in at the railroad depot and it looked like it was all groceries.

Margaret came back into the store just before Martha closed it and invited Martha to come in for supper. Gerald came to the table moving very stiffly using a chair to help him move. He still had discoloration from bruising around his right eye. Martha pretended to be concerned for him but almost smiled. Supper was pancakes and bacon. The pancakes were okay, but Martha decided to help Margaret improve her recipe in the future.

Martha decided to retire to the bathhouse after supper. A letter from Clarence had just arrived that she wanted to read. She was afraid also she might say something around Gerald that would alert him that she knew what had happened. Clarence had written: "My brother is still not well enough to run his store. Unfortunately, his wife does not seem to grasp that only a small percent of what they sold was income and the rest of the money was needed to replace inventory. My brother's wife treated herself and their two children to a shopping spree until I got her to understand reality. We just barely paid for the last shipment of goods that came in so are eating rather simply now." Unlike Martha, her sister-in-law did not work with her husband at their store.

The area where Kathy and Katy had been staying was now warm enough, but Martha found it pretty cramped. Martha looked at the sewing machine which was pretty much useless without Kathy. Kathy had taught Margaret to do a little work on it, but she did not have the experience or the talent. Martha would also have to rely on Margaret to run the store until Clarence returned.

Martha had successfully taught school for years, but Kathy had gotten the students so excited to achieve that school would not be the same without her. Kathy and Katy were gone. Martha felt so sad, and she wished she had Clarence to comfort her.

It was two weeks before Clarence returned. His brother had gotten well enough to oversee the store and they had hired a smart young fellow to run it. Gerald and Margaret had moved back upstairs but Bruce was now in the downstairs bedroom that Kathy and Katy had once shared. Clarence was met at in Williamsburg on Saturday afternoon by Martha. Sally and William were also there with their children.

Clarence was happy to see everyone, but he sensed something was wrong. "So, did everything go well while I was gone?" Clarence asked.

"No," Martha replied, "Gerald raided the cash box for gambling money that he lost at the tavern. Even worse he tried to assault Kathy at the school. She fought him off with help from Katy but they both returned to Boston."

Clarence sat motionless and said "oh no, oh no" several times.

"Kathy and Katy told Janice what happened and left me a note about it. Janice didn't tell anybody but Sally and William. I don't think even Margaret knows about the attempted assault," Martha continued. "We have not let on to Gerald that we know about the assault or the missing money."

They waited to confront Gerald until Monday morning. They first asked Gerald about the missing money in the till. Gerald tried to claim that Kathy had taken the money and when he confronted her, she agreed to pay for the next grocery shipment out of her checking account. "Isn't that right Margaret," Gerald asked.

"I don't know why she took it," Margaret lied.

"Why didn't you tell Martha that when she returned," Clarence asked.

"We knew Martha was upset that Kathy and Katy were gone so we didn't want to bring it up," Gerald replied. "You should be asking Kathy; I don't want to talk about it." Gerald then started to get up to leave.

"Sit down, we are not done yet," William told Gerald.

"This is none of your business," Gerald replied.

"Yes, it is! Why don't you explain how you got hurt three weeks ago coming home from the tavern on a Sunday night?"

"I tripped over a piece of firewood," Gerald replied. "Are you sure it wasn't a chair in the church that Katy pushed in front of you to when you were chasing Kathy?" William responded.

"I have nothing more to say," Gerald replied, "if you want to believe Kathy's lies, I can't stop you".

"We already know that you lost a lot of money gambling at the tavern to Sven and Margaret told me you were broke when you came here, and she begged to stay. So, where did that gambling money come from?" Clarence asked. "William found a broken chair at the school and neighbors told Sally they heard a girl screaming at the church that Sunday night. I let you have my daughter for your wife but then you try to molest my future daughter in law in the presence of her sister."

"That is a big lie, I never touched her," Gerald protested.

"Kathy and Katy were crying when they left, and you hurt them. They were not making up a story," Sally declared.

"Hey, those damn girls hurt me a lot more than I hurt them, I almost broke my leg," Gerald retorted and then realized he had just confirmed the fight. Margaret started crying in despair.

William then spoke; "We will give you enough money for a train ticket, and some money to live on while you look for a job. Once you have a job and a place to live, you can send for your wife and children."

"You can't make me go," Gerald announced.

"Mother, father, why are you doing this to us," Margaret whimpered. "Can't you forgive us and let Gerald stay?"

"Gerald didn't ask for forgiveness, he never admitted he was lying, and he never said he was sorry," Clarence retorted. "If I let Gerald stay, women are going to be afraid to come to the store."

William left the house for a few minutes and came back with two rough looking men from his logging crew that had been waiting outside. "Gerald, you can have an hour to get packed and say goodbye and then we can be on our way," William announced.

Gerald took one look at the men and decided to leave. Gerald left without saying goodbye to Bruce and never gave a parting hug to Elizabeth or Margaret. Gerald's final words to Margaret hurt the most; "It was your idea to come to this damn place, I never want to see you again."

The four men took a buckboard wagon into Williamsburg in silence.

Sally walked home feeling sorry for Margaret but still sad about Kathy and Katy leaving.

Bruce didn't fully understand what happened. He didn't love Gerald, but he knew his mother was crying. Margaret was hurt by her parents running her husband out of town but equally hurt by what they said Gerald had done. Margaret held Elizabeth close. She knew she wasn't innocent either, her fear of Gerald had made her try to confirm his lie about Kathy stealing money. Now she knew that Gerald had used a chair from the church as a crutch to get home the night he said he fell.

Kathy had sent a poem along with her first letter from Boston to Martha and Clarence. Martha had brought it to school and showed it to Sally and Janice and all three got teary eyed.

Last night when I went to bed, I cried myself to sleep.
I cried for the friends I miss instead of counting sheep.
I think of all the friends I love who are all so far away.
I hope to return to you upon some distant day.

**Until then I will dream of you and dream of coming
back.**
**A thousand miles of riding down a lonely railroad
track.**
**I still love the man who got my first kiss and only ones
since then.**
**My heart is still so hopeful that we can once more kiss
again.**

Margaret had also been sad after Gerald left. During the week, Bruce
and Martha went to the school and Clarence worked in the store. Martha
would leave food for Margaret and often come home to find it uneaten.
Margaret had tried being a loyal wife to Gerald and now felt she had failed.
It had not been a good marriage or even one that she had wanted. At first
Margaret was angry at her parents and Sally. She finally accepted that the
fact that Gerald taking money might be forgivable but Gerald trying to
assault their future daughter in law could not be tolerated.

Margaret had trained to do medical work and became good friends
with a classmate, Gerald's younger sister Pam. Pam had invited Margaret
to come home with her at Christmas where Margaret met Gerald. Gerald
had a younger brother, but it was Gerald who was being groomed to
take over his father's small but very successful department store. Gerald
was a big strong man with an image of success and made a good initial
impression on Margaret. It was a little like the instantaneous attraction
between Bobby and Kathy except Gerald's interest in Margaret wasn't love
it was only lust. Gerald forced himself on Margaret despite her protests
in the large mansion they lived in. Gerald had thought they were alone,
but his mother and sister heard Margaret's screams. Gerald's mother and
sister had also gotten the support of Gerald's father and the three of them
coerced Gerald into marrying Margaret.

Gerald and Margaret had married back at Margaret's church and also
had a reception back in Ohio. Gerald was financially successful at first but
drinking and gambling started to take their toll. Gerald was eventually
caught financing his drinking and gambling with store money. Gerald had
also protested that his brother's young sister-in-law had seduced him, but
she claimed Gerald assaulted her. That is when Gerald's mother evicted

them. Margaret doubted Gerald then and was completely doubtful now. Kathy had made no secret of her dislike of Gerald, so Margaret had no doubt of Kathy's innocence.

Margaret finally made peace with her parents after a couple of weeks. Margaret felt bitter about her situation, but now blamed Gerald and nobody else. Margaret started helping at the school and spending more time with Sally. It was kind of like being a widow except she wasn't sad that Gerald was gone. Gerald had often undermined Margaret in parenting Bruce but now Margaret was able to start holding him accountable. Margaret made it clear to Bruce that lying, stealing, and taking more than his share of food was not acceptable. It was awkward for her going to church at first, but she was surprised that most of the people were nice to her.

When Margaret went to the school with Martha, she tried to be helpful to the students and they showed their appreciation. Bruce became more popular too as Margaret encouraged him to be nicer to other students.

Elizabeth was brought to the school by Margaret and often wound up being cuddled by Janice. Alex and James would sometimes pick Elizabeth up too.

Margaret would sometimes ask Bruce to carry his little sister to the school and he would do it willingly. Positive changes in Bruce were gradual but significant. Clarence started spending more time with Bruce. Margaret began to have hope that her son might grow up to be someone she could be proud of.

CHAPTER 34

Back in Boston

When Kathy had been living with her Aunt the first time, they had two rooms with a door between that could be locked and both rooms had access to the hallway. Her aunt had given up the one room after Kathy left and the landlady had rented the room out to a single man. He had recently moved out and the landlady was willing to let Kathy rent it. Kathy purchased another sewing machine and started making clothes, mittens, and aprons to sell. She also used the room for a bedroom for her and Katy. Kathy worked long hours making items to sell and got help from Katy and her aunt.

On the second week, Kathy took samples to a large department store and talked to a well-dressed middle-aged lady who was the floor manager for the women's department. She liked the samples Kathy showed her, but the manager could only recommend it to the senior buyer. She led Kathy up a flight of stairs and down a hallway. She knocked on the door and was told to enter.

The door opened to a fancy office, and Kathy was introduced to the senior buyer. He was a good-looking well-dressed man in his thirties sitting on a large stuffed chair reading a newspaper. He dismissed the floor manager and told her to shut the door.

The man stared at her in a way that made Kathy feel uncomfortable, she quickly realized he was more interested in her than the clothing she wanted to sell.

"We could have a fun time together," he commented.

"I did not come here to have a fun time; I would like to sell items to this store that the store can resell at a higher price."

"I am interested in having some fun with you, I could care less about the junk you are selling," he replied. "Sit down in my lap and maybe you can change my mind."

Kathy had started to take some of her samples out to show him but quickly put them back in her bag. "I don't plan to change your mind, goodbye," she replied while opening the door.

"Okay, then get out of here you little bitch," he replied but then he jumped up and grabbed her as she started to leave.

"Please let me leave or I will start screaming", Kathy told him. He started to pull her back into the office. Kathy screamed at the top of her lungs and kicked him his shinbone at the same time. He knocked her down and she scrambled to her feet and ran down hall carrying her sample's bag.

He yelled "stop thief!" A large middle-aged man came running to stop her and Kathy shoved her samples bag into him knocking him down hard, but he hung onto her sample's bag.

Kathy yelled "fire! fire!" and ran down the stairs and out the building. She stopped running a half a block away. She watched with grim satisfaction that quite a number of people had emptied out of the store. Four days of tedious work and a lot of material was left behind in the samples bag that the man had hung on to.

A week later Kathy pulled a small wagon she had borrowed full of items she had made and took Katy with her. They went to a much smaller store that was run by a husband and wife. The owners said they would sell them on consignment and wanted to keep 30% of each sale. It was not a good deal for Kathy, but she could still make more money than working at the factory. Kathy and Katy came back a few days later and they had sold most of the items. She restocked them and collected her money.

She was down near the harbor and had walked by a small church where she heard a piano playing. She walked in and an older gentleman said that it was a Christian mission for sailors. Kathy asked if she could sing and play the piano. He introduced her to Gus who was playing the piano.

"I would like to sing along while you play," Kathy told him. Gus played "Amazing Grace" and Kathy sang. Men had started to file in for lunch and listened quietly as Kathy's beautiful voice filled the room.

A few songs later Katy sang "What a Friend We Have in Jesus". One sailor who was far from his wife and children had to wipe a tear listening to a child's voice.

The older man and Gus begged them to come back. Kathy agreed, she was so happy to be singing again.

Money was tight the last week of February just before the rent was due. Kathy needed another five dollars to pay the rent. She cut back on her own eating but made sure Katy and Karla had enough to eat. She went to the store with more items for them to sell and was happy to come home with enough money to cover the rent and some food too. Kathy pushed herself hard to make more items to sell with help from both Katy, Karla, and Gina.

The one pleasure she had was stopping at the mission for sailors and singing while Gus played the piano. She would take time to go there with Katy every day even when she didn't have more items to sell at the store. One day Gus was absent. Kathy played the piano and sang "Joyful, Joyful We Adore Thee". Later after several more songs, she and Katy were starting to leave when a well-dressed man approached them.

"My name is Harold Brown, my church helps to support this mission and I appreciate you coming here to sing," he told her. "I was hoping I could talk you into singing at my church some Sunday."

"Where is it?" Kathy asked. He told her. Kathy declined. "It is too far away. I wouldn't feel safe going that far" Kathy replied.

"I understand." He said but was clearly disappointed.

The small mission church seemed to have more men every time they came. One day a man came up to her and identified himself as a newspaper reporter for the Boston Globe. He asked Kathy and Katy some questions and talked to some of the men attending. A few days later Gus handed her a newspaper that had an article about 'The Harbor Angels'. Kathy and Katy were shocked.

Kathy was able to buy several copies of the paper and mailed clippings of the article one to Martha and one to Bobby. She sent a note with it to Bobby that 'Harbor Angels' sounded better than 'that bathhouse girl'. She also told him about the fight with Gerald which is why she returned to Boston but didn't elaborate.

The article read:

Some of the sweetest music in Boston is found at the Harbor Gospel Mission Church. It is a small mission church in a rundown neighborhood by the harbor. Gus, an aging playing piano player has been joined by two talented young sisters who sing as he plays. Their beautiful voices lift the spirits of the men who come here who in many cases have little else to look forward to. Gus said that when he sits down at the piano, some men ask him if the two little angels are coming today. Kathy, the oldest girl is 17 and her younger sister Katy is only 8. Kathy seems to be able to sing almost any song from memory. Kathy said they are orphans living with their aunt. Kathy said she makes money by selling items she sews. Their singing has an out of this world quality that makes you think you really are hearing angels. The Harbor Angels show up at lunch time at the mission and then disappear.

CHAPTER 35

Winter Blues

Bobby had smiled at Kathy's note, but then he felt so sad thinking about Kathy so far away. Hanson had delivered the mail just before lunch. Kathy had mailed it to Bobby in care of Richard Murdoch. Bobby had quickly opened the package from Kathy.

Charles saw the pained look on Bobby's face. "Are you okay boss?" he asked.

"My fiancé sent a newspaper clipping from Boston about her and her sister singing in a small church," Bobby replied. "She is so far away, and I miss her so much."

"Well maybe by spring you will have enough money to get a place to live," Charles said. Charles then read the article "She must be awfully good to get that kind of a writeup."

Bobby took the letter and the newspaper and put it in his room. He meant to write back to her immediately, but he wanted to write something positive. He couldn't think of anything to say, so the letter did not get written.

Winter had slowed things down at the factory a lot. Bobby had to cut hours for everyone. It took longer to get the glue to set properly even after getting everything that they were gluing closer to the stove. Richard Murdoch had managed to sell some furniture at sale prices that didn't make a profit but helped keep production going. He also had sold quite a few dressers to hotels in the St Louis area.

Besides keeping the factory warm enough, Bobby had tried keeping his own little room on the roof warm but had pretty much given that up. He would sometimes cook on the cookstove in his room, but he would bed down near the stove heating the factory. The weather started warming up in March and Bobby was able to move back upstairs and get away from the smell of glue.

Clyde wasn't the craftsman that Charles was, but he was good with planning and details. Clyde had lost his racial prejudice and now got along great with Charles and Claude. Bobby knew that if he left, Clyde could take over and run the factory.

Bobby thought about going home for a visit but without Kathy it would be too sad. Bobby had gotten a letter from his mother and was glad that Gerald had been run out of town. Yet he still had a feeling of resentment that Kathy felt she had to leave. Martha had written a letter saying how heartbroken Clarence and she were that Kathy and Katy were gone. Martha went on to say that they found Gerald to be difficult but never expected him to attack Kathy. Bobby knew that it was wrong to be angry at his parents or even his sister Margaret for what happened. Yet he kept feeling that somehow this whole problem with Gerald could have been avoided. Bobby wanted to write back to Kathy but had misplaced her letter with her return address.

Martha had the same feeling wondering what she could have done different. Her maternal instinct made her bring Kathy and Katy home and that had been so wonderful. Her maternal instincts were to allow her daughter and grandchildren to move home also along with her son-in-law. That had not gone well. Gerald was not fun to have around but he was starting to pay for his family's living expenses. The meat they had been selling in the store that Gerald was butchering was getting fairly profitable. Gerald could have started a new life for himself and his family in their small town.

Gerald had quickly run out of money after arriving in St Louis. In desperation, he had taken a job with the railroad clearing railroad tracks blocked by snow. He was poorly fed and usually slept in a railcar turned bunkhouse heated by a small stove. His mother had run him out of town and now his in-laws had also. Gerald was not ashamed of what he had done. Like most losers, he blamed all his problems on bad luck and other people. Now he was somewhere in western Kansas and a howling blizzard outside was stealing much of the heat their little stove was trying to provide. He huddled in his bunk trying to stay warm. His leg still hurt where he had fallen on the chair Katy pushed in front of him. He mentally cursed both girls. Kathy, Katy, Margaret, Bruce, and Elizabeth all slept warm and well that night. Gerald did not.

Gerald had a diabolic plan for revenge on Kathy. He had hated her because he couldn't dominate her. The attack at the school was meant to totally humiliate her and show his dominance. It had failed and he was now paying the price. A plan formed in his twisted mind. If he didn't freeze to death, the crew would return to St Louis in a couple of days. Gerald started thinking of getting revenge on Kathy. Warmed by his evil thoughts, Gerald endured the night.

CHAPTER 36

New Admirers

On the third Saturday morning in February, Kathy took over the piano for a few songs before Gus arrived. She sang and played the song about almost being killed. She also sang and played a new song she had written.

> **Without God I would be like a ship adrift at sea.**
> **Where storms and waves would shatter me.**
> **Jesus is an anchor to keep me near the shore.**
> **When in the sea of life, the oceans roar.**
> **The Bible provides a light to guide my way.**
> **And I get more instructions when I pray.**
> **When I come at last to that final shore.**
> **Jesus will be there to open Heaven's door.**
> **Jesus keep my body safe and warm.**
> **Jesus keep my soul from Satan's harm.**

Kathy also sat down and played and sang the song she liked that was in Latin. Gus walked in and listened.

Someone else had come in early too, Harold Brown had come in with his wife who he introduced as Maxine. "You are treating the lowly men who come here to some of the finest singing in the world," Harold told Kathy.

"Jesus died for lowly sinners, I can at least sing for them," Kathy replied.

"You are so right," Harold replied, "I need to remember that too. We are having a gathering at our church today; we would like you to you come with us and sing. We will bring you home this afternoon."

Maxine spoke up, "Harold told me how good you girls are and now I can understand why he was so impressed."

"Could you detour back to our apartment before we go, so I can let my Aunt know that we will be late?" Kathy asked.

They assured her that was fine. Kathy took out her flute and played "What a Friend We Have in Jesus" while Katy sang. Kathy sang a few more songs with Gus playing the piano before leaving with Harold and Maxine. They stopped off at the apartment and told Karla where they were going. Kathy and Katy also changed to nicer dresses. Kathy grabbed an apron and a couple of oven mitts she had made after hearing they were selling stuff to raise money for the Harbor Mission.

An older black man drove the carriage and he was surprised at the pleasant greeting he got from Kathy and Katy.

They started talking to Maxine while they rode. Maxine was impressed when Kathy told her that she had made the apron, the oven mitts and the dresses for herself and Katy.

"So, what else do you do?" Maxine asked with a smile. "I have taught grade school and I like to think I am pretty good cook," Kathy replied. "I also try to be a good mother for my sister Katy but mostly we just try to help each other."

"I helped her get away from a bad man who was chasing her," Katy announced proudly.

Kathy explained how the son in law of the people she was living with had tried to assault her and Katy had got him to trip over a chair and fall. Maxine looked at cute little Katy and marveled that Katy would have the courage to face a full-grown man.

They arrived at the church early. It was a large church with a large open area in the basement. Maxine introduced them to several people who were setting up tables of stuff that people could buy. They were happy to get the apron and oven mitts that Kathy brought for sale. They were fascinated that Kathy had made them herself along with the dresses she and Katy were wearing.

"I thought maybe you had a rich husband who bought you fancy clothes," one lady joked.

"No, I have a ring from my fiancé, but we don't have enough money to get married yet. My future husband is in charge of a factory assembling furniture in St Louis, Missouri, a thousand miles from here."

Maxine was listening, "Harold must not have seen your ring, he told my son and a couple other young men that you might be here this afternoon."

"I am just a poor girl, they should be able to find a rich girl and live in a fancy house," Kathy replied.

"I think they would be better off if they could find a girl like you," Maxine responded.

Maxine, Kathy, and Katy went upstairs to the sanctuary and Kathy sat down at the piano. It was a really nice piano and Kathy played "Joyful, Joyful We Adore Thee" but didn't sing it. There were only a few people in the church and Kathy wasn't scheduled to play for another half hour. Kathy started playing some songs for Katy to sing that she had written including "I Love You Jesus but You Made Me Cry". Kathy used her flute for "Battle Hymn of the Republic" with Katy singing most of the song to the amazement of the small audience. Kathy would switch back to the piano and sing the chorus. Kathy also added a verse:

For the widows and orphans who are sadly left behind
We ask you God for mercy and for neighbors to be
kind.

The church was starting to fill up. After that song, Kathy announced they were just practicing. "Does anybody have a favorite song they would like me to sing?" Kathy asked. "Rock of Ages" was requested, and Kathy played and sang all three verses from memory.

After singing the song, Kathy talked about how it brought back memories of being attacked and nearly killed. "I had been strangled and every breath I took hurt, and I couldn't swallow. Part of me wanted to give up and go home to Jesus and join my mother and father and my baby brother up in Heaven. My little sister Katy and her friend Jade, an adorable little black girl were by my side praying for me all day and finally my breathing started getting better. Their prayers were answered, and I lived. It was several weeks later when the Lord gave me back my voice. My boyfriend says he still has nightmares of finding me lying face down with my eyes closed apparently in death, blood coming out of my mouth and a knife in my back. If he were here, he could entertain you with his fiddle, but he is in St Louis, a thousand miles from here." Kathy then sang the song she had written about the attack.

Kathy also sang a song about Heaven, a rewrite of one she had done back in Williamsburg:

> **I dreamed I was in Heaven to spend all eternity.**
> **There were multitudes of people as far as I could see.**
> **But Hallelujah, Hallelujah Heaven has a place for me.**
> **My sins were all forgiven when Christ died at Calvary.**
> **There was no pain in Heaven, there was nothing to annoy.**
> **We were all like happy children full of love and full of joy.**
> **We need to follow Jesus and ask him to forgive of our sin.**
> **His death paid for our admission so God would let us in.**
> **I dreamt I was in Heaven as happy as anyone could be.**
> **Because Hallelujah, Hallelujah Christ made a place for me.**

The Pastor, Timothy Johnson was a tall, dignified man who had sat quietly in the audience listening to Kathy and Katy perform. He had talked briefly with Kathy and said he remembered meeting her parents. He got up and spoke to the Congregation which was now about five times the size of the little church in Springdale.

"Welcome to our fund raiser for the Harbor Mission Church. We were expecting a small choir here today, but they had to cancel due to illness. Fortunately, one of our members was at our Harbor Mission Church when these young ladies came in to sing. I have been told they have been volunteering to sing there almost every day at noon for the last month. I am so glad they are here and so far, what Kathy called a practice has already given us some great songs and a lot to think about."

Kathy opened with "Come Thou Fount of every blessing". Kathy then announced that since Easter was almost here, she wanted to sing an Easter hymn. Kathy sang "Jesus Christ Is Risen Today" and followed it with "Joyful, Joyful We Adore Thee". Kathy played her flute and Katy sang "What a Friend We Have in Jesus" which she had sang earlier at the Mission church. Kathy sang "Amazing Grace" with her usual passion.

At the close, the Pastor spoke briefly. "We have been blessed and we know that men coming to the Harbor Mission Church will also be blessed by their music. Lord, we ask you to keep these young ladies safe and bless their lives. I think it would be appropriate to give these two girls a round of applause."

Kathy was surrounded by people after singing. They included several good-looking young men and a couple of ladies who had showed up. They were all students at Harvard and one of the men was Harold's son Mitchell. Katy had her own admirers who could not imagine a cute little girl like her singing so perfectly. They all returned to the large room where they had laid out items for sale. Tables were also set up for a lunch on the other side of the room. Kathy wound up sitting with the two female students and the young men on the other side of the table.

Adam, one of the young men was planning to go into the ministry. Kathy and he got into a discussion about predestination each quoting Scripture to back up their statements. Finally, Adam asked Pastor Johnson for his opinion.

"I am not going to declare a winner; I was impressed at how knowledgeable both of you are about the Scriptures. He then asked Kathy if she would explain how she had gotten so knowledgeable about the Scriptures. Kathy talked about how her father and mother would study a chapter of Scripture with her almost every night. "If I studied Scripture, my father would let me go to the Boston Public Library where I could read Shakespeare and other secular books.

Mitchell teased her by quoting from a play in Shakespeare and Kathy replied with several of the lines that followed. Mitchell was impressed but Kathy joked, "that is about all of Shakespeare I remember. Right now, I am trying to support myself and my sister Katy by sewing aprons and mittens and selling them to a general store. So far, I have been able sell enough to feed us and pay the rent."

"Did you ever try selling to that big department store downtown," Mitchell asked, "one of the managers attends our church, he is sitting behind you."

Kathy looked and saw the man that had acted improperly to her at the department store. "I did go there, that man is an evil lecher, I would not have come to this church, if I had known he would be here," Kathy replied, shocking Mitchell and the others including Pastor Johnson. Kathy then told what had happened.

Arnold had come in and joined his wife after the concert was over. He did not recognize Kathy when he came over to the table wondering why they were looking at him. "What's up?" he asked walking up to Pastor Johnson.

"I just heard some very disappointing information about how you treat people where you work."

Arnold spotted Kathy and realized the source. "I can't believe they let riffraff like you into our church," he said scornfully to her. "So, have you sold any of your junk yet?" he asked. He then turned to Pastor Johnson: "Are you going to take the word of this teenage vagabond over someone like me who has been a long-time member of this church?"

"Yes, I am going to take her word, Miss Kathy White is our honored guest and I thank her for her wonderful concert here today. Miss White is one of the most talented young people I have ever met, and she comes from wonderful parents."

"As for you Mr. Arnold, someone else had cautioned me that you have behaved improperly toward women, and you just confirmed it yourself. I feel that Spiritually you are not part of this church," Pastor Johnson remonstrated. "Please leave Miss White alone and return to your wife." Arnold did that quickly and ushered his wife and their children out of the building.

The five students led by Mitchell did a little cheer; "Yeah Kathy." Kathy should have felt victorious, but she really wanted a shoulder to cry on. Why did men with evil intentions keep targeting her? she wondered.

Katy came running over to her followed by Maxine. "I think every mother in the church including me would like to take Katy home, but she seems pretty attached to you," Maxine teased.

"Katy is a precious gift I inherited from my mother, we have been through some tough times together and made it with God's help," Kathy replied. Kathy hugged Katy and then they both had to wipe away tears.

Kathy had enjoyed the company of the students from Harvard and wished she could meet up with them again. Mitchell joined them on the ride back to her apartment and Kathy found him very nice and easy to talk to. Everyone but Arnold had been nice to her at the church, but Kathy did not want to go back there for fear of meeting Arnold again.

Kathy had trouble sleeping that night. Despite Arnold, she liked being back in Boston. Mitchell was a good-looking young man and he had ruefully commented when he saw her ring; "Nice ring, lucky man. I admit I am jealous." St Louis and Bobby were far away. That magical month last June when she had first come to the bathhouse and fallen in love was beginning to seem more like a wonderful dream than a memory. Even Sally had admitted that despite being so fun, the bathhouse was hard to justify for the time and effort it required for minimal financial gain.

Kathy had avoided Margaret in order to avoid Gerald and Bruce. She wondered if it would be different if Gerald wasn't there. Maxine's comment about mothers wanting to take home Katy was meant to be flattery for Katy but would Katy be better off if she was adopted by Maxine or Martha? Her Aunt Karla was getting frail and was becoming dependent on Kathy. Why did life have to be so complicated. She needed to pray and ask God for wisdom.

CHAPTER 37

An Awful Letter

Kathy hadn't gotten a reply from, Bobby or Martha since returning to Boston. Then just after Kathy sang at the Presbyterian Church, a horrible letter arrived from Bobby.

Bobby said in the letter that their engagement was over. He told her that he had found out she had badly beaten Gerald after he caught her stealing money from the store before leaving for Boston. He also said there were rumors she was unfaithful and was pregnant when she left. My family never wants to see you again. He said he had moved on and found a new girlfriend who doesn't have a brat of a little sister. It didn't sound like Bobby and the accusations were lies.

Still, it was postmarked from St Louis and had a St Louis return address. Kathy sat there and cried. She could send a letter trying to refute the lies, but she already had sent him a letter about Gerald assaulting her. It also hurt that he called Katy a brat. Katy read the letter and cried with her. Her Aunt Karla felt bad for her but admitted she was glad they were back in Boston.

Kathy waited a week before sending Bobby a letter in a package. "Dear Mr. Bobby Thompson: I received your letter saying that our engagement is over. I am sad that Katy and I will never see you or your family again because of Gerald's lies. I am angry about false accusations that I attacked Gerald and stole money from the store. The truth is that Katy bravely helped me fight off an attempted assault by Gerald in the school classroom. He was chasing me when Katy pushed a chair in front of him and he crashed to the floor. He told us he would kill us as we ran out. I am not expecting; I am still a virgin. We left on the train the next morning. Gerald stole money from the store to pay for gambling losses. I have never stolen anything. Clothing sales are going well, and I am confident I can support myself and Katy here in Boston. The ring you gave me is enclosed along with the nasty letter you sent me. Goodbye, we will not meet again in this life. Sincerely Kathy White."

Kathy also sent Bobby a poem she wrote with the letter:

> **I dried my tears today.**
> **I wiped them all away.**
> **To wed I will not plan.**
> **We will not meet again.**
> **The dream I had is gone,**
> **but I will still carry on.**
> **Jesus is still my friend,**
> **with me to the end.**
> **I will pray to God above.**
> **Find me a man to love.**
> **So, I wish you all the best.**
> **My heart will take a rest.**

Kathy tried to make the letter unemotional and tried not to show Katy and Karla how hurt she was. She was unsure of the address on the envelope and sent it to Bobby in care of Richard Murdoch. At night when they were sleeping her tears would flow into her pillow as she prayed to God asking why this had happened. Kathy pushed herself even harder to get more items for sale. With her engagement to Bobby over, it was up to her to support herself and Katy.

Kathy tried to be a good mother to Katy and take care of her aunt as well. She made bread by the dim light of a candle in the evening and got up early to make some of it into cinnamon rolls and then have it baked in time for breakfast.

She also used rolls and bread as a partial payment for Gina, her next-door neighbor. Gina would come over with her baby and her little girl. Aunt Karla would take care of the baby and Katy would play with the little girl. Gina would then help Kathy cut out fabric for dresses from patterns Kathy had created. Kathy taught Gina how to use the sewing machine and Gina did a lot of sewing too.

Gina was a sweet person, and her children were so cute with dark hair and dark eyes and usually smiling. Even though Kathy was younger, Gina was grateful for all the things that Kathy was teaching her. Gina's English was limited, and Kathy helped her with her English and helped her read better. They formed a strong bond that helped them get through busy days. Gina did not expect much for helping Kathy and was grateful for help with her children. Kathy made a pretty dress for her and a matching one for her daughter and she was ecstatic. Kathy figured out an approximate value for Gina's time and gave her some money too.

The husband-and-wife team that ran the general store didn't offer a better deal, but they were always happy to see her. They finally approached Kathy about her coming to the store on Fridays to measure women and make custom made dresses for them. Kathy was already exhausted but decided to give it a try. Five people showed up the first Friday and two of them ordered two dresses with different colors. Gina's sister-in-law, a sixteen-year-old girl was added to their little dress factory to increase production. Katy helped too and Kathy home schooled her.

Kathy pleased Karla by going to her church on Sundays. They had no piano, and the pastor led the singing of the few songs they did. Most of the congregation were elderly and were very friendly to Kathy and Katy. Kathy had tried to blend her voice in with the other singers. One Sunday the pastor asked if she would sing for them. Kathy did "Amazing Grace" and then played her flute and Katy sang "What a Friend We Have in Jesus." After that, the Pastor insisted that Kathy lead the singing every Sunday. The Congregation thought Kathy was great and Katy was so special.

Kathy had worried how Karla would do if she moved to St Louis to marry Bobby and left Karla alone. Karla then surprised Kathy by saying that her widowed sister-in-law had asked Karla to move in with her. Kathy encouraged Karla to make the move even though she now planned to permanently remain in Boston. Kathy was pleased by how much money she was now making but money was still tight, and she needed to buy more material.

It was a week after she sent the letter and engagement ring to Bobby when she got a letter from Clarence in Springdale. She dreaded to open it expecting a request for payment for the money Gerald apparently had claimed she had stolen. Instead, it was a check from Clarence for the money she had paid back in Springdale for the grocery shipment. It was so strange because there was also a nice letter from Martha saying how much everyone missed her. "Clarence and I are so sad you and Katy are gone and the children at school keep asking about you. Margaret and her children are still here but we ran Gerald out of town putting him on a train to St Louis. We are so sorry about what happened here while we were gone."

The money from Clarence helped her restock her dwindling supply of material for making clothes. Kathy thought she would have to sell her flute and the bracelet Bobby had given her to pay for more material. Kathy was also pleased that they still liked her in Springdale and Gerald had been run out of town. Why did Bobby have such a different story about what happened? She told herself not to get her hopes up that Bobby would change his mind. Katy told her they should pray about it, and they did.

When Kathy was young, she had wanted to travel but now she felt a part of her identity was being left behind with each move she made. Katy would not be returning to her friends Jade, Janice, James, and Alex. Neither would there be all the adults that loved Katy like Martha, Sally, Clarence, and Julia. Kathy realized that the little town of Springdale was now emotionally her hometown too but unless Bobby changed his mind, she would never return. Katy found herself humming a line from "Old Folks at Home" one of Steven Foster's songs 'All up and down the whole creation sadly I roam'.

Gerald would have been pleased to know how much hurt his fake letter to Kathy had caused her. He had limped into the store a couple of times in the week after Martha returned. He had found Kathy's Boston address pinned to the wall near the checkout counter and pocketed it. Bobby got the small package from Kathy with the ring inside and now it was his turn to be devastated. Bobby had heard that Gerald had been run out of town and given a train ticket to St Louis. After the initial shock of Kathy's letter wore off, he reached the conclusion that Gerald had sent the nasty letter to Kathy. Her final words in her letter totally demoralized Bobby; "Goodbye, we will not meet again in this life." It sounded so final and almost prophetic. The poem bothered him too – what if she did find someone else? He did not eat that night and he hardly slept. Bobby was frustrated that Kathy had not realized that the letter was fake. He decided he was guilty too. He had not replied to her earlier letter. Worse, he had misplaced her address when she sent him the letter about returning to Boston along with the newspaper clipping.

After some frantic digging in the frigid room on the roof, he finally found the envelope she had sent him earlier. Her return address matched her earlier return address. The nasty letter Kathy had received made him want to double check everything. He prayed that they would still to be married in the spring. Bobby took time off work the next morning and walked a mile and a half to a post office and mailed the ring back to Kathy with a letter telling her; "The nasty letter must have been written by Gerald. I love you; I trust you. I can't wait to marry you and Katy is the sweetest little girl I know."

At first Kathy thought the package she got back the following week had been returned but she saw that Bobby had sent it. She said a silent prayer before opening it. She read his short letter, put her ring back on and then cried tears of joy.

Kathy sent a letter back to Bobby telling him "I am thrilled that we are still engaged. I love you so much and I cried so many tears thinking that I would never see you or your family again." She also included the poem she had written about dreaming about him.

Last night I was dreaming that I was holding and kissing you.
It was almost like Heaven; all my dreams were coming true.
But then I turned and did awaken.
I felt so alone, and I felt forsaken.
Oh, darling I want to be with you, but time keeps flying by.
I can't seem find an answer no matter how hard I try.
I make money to feed my body, but my heart is starved for love.
I keep praying for some answers, oh help me Lord above.

A couple weeks later she got a reply from Bobby; "I feel the same frustration about living so far apart and not getting married. I am planning to drill a well and have an enclosed place to wash up and take a bath at the factory site."

Bobby's reply certainly made the living at the factory a lot more inviting if there was water on site. Kathy also got a letter from Sally that "everyone including Margaret wants you and Katy to come back."

It was nice to hear that even Margaret would welcome Katy and her back. It was sad when Karla moved out. Kathy still had Katy and Gina was a good friend, but she still missed the people of Springdale.

CHAPTER 38

Leaving Boston

Having Katy with her gave her comfort when she walked to the store and to the Harbor Mission Church. Even though Katy wasn't much protection, walking alone tended to attract more interest from men than when she had Katy with her. Kathy now carried a small dagger in a leather sheath in her coat pocket and vowed to use it if attacked. Boston was pretty safe during the middle of the day when she went out, but she still was a little nervous.

Kathy spent more time coaching Gina on how to sew, make patterns and take measurements for dresses. Gina then surprised Kathy by introducing an older relative who was an experienced seamstress and was interested in helping Gina take over the business if Kathy left. Kathy had been praying for guidance and felt a lot of her prayers had been answered. Kathy was making good money from her clothing sales and could support herself and Katy in Boston. She also felt she was making good use of her talents to serve God at the Harbor Mission Church and the church she attended with Karla.

Kathy had felt she had no choice but to leave Boston the first time, and no choice but to return. Other than that horrible incident at the department store, she liked living in Boston. Kathy found herself struggling over the decision of how long to stay in Boston before returning to Springdale.

Finally, Kathy decided it was time for Katy and her to leave Boston and return to Springdale.

Karla anticipated Kathy's departure and was sad that once that happened, she would probably never see either Kathy or Katy again. Kathy felt bad about leaving Karla too. Karla had been there for Katy and her when they needed a place to stay and had tried her best to help them. Life had not been easy for Karla; she had lost her husband shortly after she was married when he was killed in a hunting accident. Karla had made a meager living working as a clerk for a shipping company and now lived off the savings she had managed to set aside.

Kathy felt bad about having to tell the church where she sang on Sunday and the Harbor Mission Church that she was leaving. Poor Gus had to wipe away tears when he heard Katy and Kathy were leaving. Gus had been like a loving grandfather to Katy and Kathy.

Unfortunately, the cost of train travel was not cheap compared to the money Kathy could make selling clothes. Kathy had arrived in Springdale nearly broke after paying for her ticket and Katy's to get out there. Their return tickets to Boston plus buying another sewing machine had pulled her savings down again. Now she was buying tickets back to Springdale. Still, she was much better off financially than she was a year ago.

She knew that if she stayed in Boston, she could expand her business and survive very well on her own. She could have easily supported Katy too. She could have been a successful young businesswoman. She could have, but her heart overruled her mind. She wanted to sing with Bobby and curl up in his arms at night. Marrying Bobby would also keep her connection to Clarence, Martha, Sally, Julia, Jade and all the other people she loved in Springdale.

The first day of June in 1911, Kathy and Katy were packed up, and on a train heading back to Williamsburg, Illinois. Kathy had been almost glad to leave Boston the first time despite her fears for their future, but now, leaving Gus and the men at the Harbor Mission Church had been hard. Gina was excited about taking over the sewing business from Kathy, but it was hard saying goodbye for both of them.

Kathy partially dozed on her seat more from emotional fatigue than being physically tired. She couldn't bring the things she loved about Boston to Springdale. Then, all the adults and children that she loved in Springdale would be left behind in a few more weeks when she married Bobby and moved in with him at the factory in St Louis. She thought of Katy; she probably would have to be left behind in Springdale at least for the summer.

Kathy was wide awake by the time the train got to Grand Central Station in New York. They sat behind a couple with three small children when she boarded again and wound up with one of their little girls next to her. Kathy had brought some children's books to bring back with her and started reading stories to the little girl who was about four. She had a cute face with big brown eyes. At first, the little girl was shy but soon she was giggling and smiling. The girl got a little sleepy and Kathy got out her flute and played the lullaby song and then sang it softly. The little girl fell asleep in Kathy's lap and the train car got much quieter as a lot of adults fell asleep too. Katy was sitting with one of their older daughters across the aisle from Kathy. Kathy stayed awake and looked out the train window and watched the countryside pass by. After a two hour nap the little girl woke up and now it was Kathy's turn to feel sleepy. Kathy had brought cookies with her and shared them with the little girl and the couple up ahead and their children. The mother was so grateful.

Kathy told them about how people had been nice to her and Katy, and now, it was her turn. She told them she was returning to marry the son of the mother who had befriended her. Kathy started playing her flute and singing again. The people got off somewhere in Ohio, and they rode the rest of the way sitting by themselves.

CHAPTER 39

A Well Done

Bobby had regretted not returning home for Easter. He missed his family. Even though it would not have brought him any closer to Kathy, talking to his family would have helped. Clyde's church had an early morning service and sometimes Bobby would go there first and then go over to the black church. Bobby sometimes played his fiddle and sang in the morning service at the church Clyde attended.

Bobby made no secret of the fact that he was already engaged which disappointed a few young ladies quite a bit. One of them was very pretty and very nice but she didn't have either the intellect or the musical ability that Kathy had. Still, If she had met Bobby before he met Kathy, she might have won him over.

Sunday afternoons Bobby would ride his bike around both for exercise and for curiosity. Electricity was starting to make its way from downtown St Louis toward the edge of the city. Bobby really wanted to either rent or buy a place with electricity and water. So far nothing was available near the factory. Clyde's brother-in-law would let Clyde know where electricity was going in, and Clyde would pass that the information on to Bobby.

One Sunday in April was rather warm, and Bobby was hot and sweaty when he returned to the factory late in the afternoon. He only had a little water he could spare to wet a rag and wipe himself down. Bobby wondered how much it cost to drill a well next to the factory. He had told Kathy he would get a well installed at the factory but hadn't done anything yet. With a well, living at the factory might even be okay during the summer months.

Bobby found a shady spot on the roof and reread the last letter from Kathy. It sounded like she was doing well which was good. Though sometimes it bothered him that Kathy was so self-sufficient that she didn't need a husband to take care of her. Maybe she could survive without him, but he couldn't imagine a future without her.

It had been a great opportunity for him to run the furniture factory in St Louis, and Martha had been so impressed with Kathy's teaching ability back in Springdale. Kathy and he would be separated for the winter and get married in the spring. That was the unwritten plan until Gerald had come. There was nothing that happened that really prevented them from still getting married this spring, but Gerald had caused Kathy to return to Boston. Would he leave his job and move to Boston to be with her? That was a decision he didn't want to make. Bobby sensed correctly that leaving Boston again was not an easy choice for Kathy either.

Bobby got a well drilled next to the factory and a windmill installed to pump fresh water. He even added a shed with a sink and a tub to wash up in after a hot day. Murdoch had split the cost of drilling the well and the windmill. Bobby had used his own money to build the shed and put the tub and wash basin in. The men teased him about it but were soon asking if they could use it to rinse off before they went home. Both the well and the wash shed could be accessed from the building. They were not accessible from the outside if a gate were locked. Alma would heat up some water for the men but lock the door and treat herself to a quick rinse first. She would towel off and get dressed quickly so the next person could go in. Bobby would wait until everyone was gone before heating some more water and taking a bath.

Hanson came by to pick up completed dressers about noon one day and was treated to a good lunch. He listened to the men banter back and forth and saw the wash shed Bobby had put in. Hanson had brought a letter with him for Bobby from Kathy and Bobby read it while they were eating. Suddenly Bobby jumped up and shouted "**YES**. My girlfriend is coming back from Boston to marry me, and she said she is willing to live here at the factory."

"How is it going out there?" Murdoch asked one day him when Hanson came back with another load of furniture.

"It's like one big happy family and they still keep pushing out furniture like crazy. That black lady Bobby has cooking feeds them a great lunch and now they are washing up before they go home. That is just about the happiest work crew I have ever seen. Bobby is pretty happy too; he just got a letter from his girlfriend that she is ready to move back from Boston to marry him and live with him at the factory."

"My wife is going to be so excited; she has been waiting for a year for the two of them to get married," Murdoch replied. "I agree, Bobby and his crew are doing a great job. I had a furniture salesman come in from New England and he could not believe we were selling furniture that cheap. He told me that he had nicer furniture to offer but at more than double the price. Sounds like I will be heading for a wedding, and Bobby is going to need some time off."

CHAPTER 40

Return to Springdale

Andy, the school wagon driver came alone to pick up Kathy and Katy at the railroad station. She felt a little disappointed that he was the only one there. School had recessed for the summer, but he took her there and she was happily surprised that most of the students and many of the parents were there to greet her. She felt such joy at seeing them and hugging Jade, Janice, Sally, Martha, and most of her former students. She wanted to be with Bobby, but she loved the people in the little town of Springdale so much.

Finally, she sat down at the piano, and she played and sang "Joyful, Joyful We Adore Thee". They then celebrated with cake and cookies that Julia brought over. Julia and her hugged. Then Clarence gave her a hug, and he held her as she could no longer hold back the tears. Finally, Kathy was able to speak and told everyone how much she loved them and was so happy to be back. Sally had brought her baby girl, a little cutey with a few wisps of blond hair who was so precious.

Kathy had her choice of the upstairs or the bathhouse and decided on the bathhouse. They had taken Kathy's partition down and the bunks were back like they used to be. Margaret greeted her warmly at the house and Elizabeth came crawling over to her. Kathy picked up Elizabeth who snuggled into her arms. Bruce was both taller and thinner and was very polite at supper.

They ate outside at the patio table, and it was hard to believe it was almost exactly a year since they first came. It seemed like yesterday at one moment and long ago another. Kathy had not slept well on the train. She was emotionally exhausted. She tried to stay awake but took Martha's suggestion to get some sleep and went to bed early.

Kathy woke up early the next morning, but the sun was already shining. Kathy got the stove going and heated enough water on the stove to wash herself. They had left most of her summer clothes behind in their hurried departure in the winter. She found her bathing suit and tried it on. It was really tight both top and bottom. She took it off and put on comfortable loose-fitting dress. She walked around the garden seeing fewer plants than the previous year. It needed watering and weeding.

Martha was now in the kitchen and Kathy started helping her. They worked together like they had almost five months ago. Margaret joined them, and they had breakfast after waking up a sleepy Katy and Bruce. Clarence was already at the table drinking coffee. "It's so good to have you back, I just wish we could keep you longer" Clarence told her.

"I wish I could stay here after I marry Bobby," Kathy replied. "Even though I have spent most of my life in Boston, this town feels like home now. It does sound like Bobby has made the factory site more livable, but I will miss the people here."

"The whole town missed you," Clarence replied.

Kathy was silent for a moment contemplating the fact her talent made her a blessing to people but made them sad when she moved on. She decided that was better than people being glad when you left.

The wedding came up after they had all sat down to eat breakfast. Martha wanted it on a Sunday after church two and half weeks away. Sally and Martha had it mostly planned out and had been waiting for Kathy to return. "I hope the sewing machine still works because Sally, Katy and Janice are all going to need new dresses," Martha commented. "You probably will need to make dresses for Patty and Bonnie. Everyone keeps asking me when you and Bobby are going to get married and now it is happening so soon."

"My thoughts too," Kathy replied. "It's going to be hard to get ready after waiting for so long. Fortunately the sewing machine does work but I am going to need to get material for the dresses."

The wedding seemed to be coming up too soon. She would have to leave Springdale again after just getting back. Marriage also meant getting

304

pregnant and that was okay. She just wished that wouldn't be quite so soon. Sally's darling little baby girl had looked up at her with the sweetest little face imaginable. How could you not want a little baby like that?

Kathy had taken another look at her finances and realized she was doing okay. She could afford to pay for tickets for her older sister and her family to come to her wedding. She knew Murdoches were coming so where to put everyone would be a problem. She talked it over with Martha. Martha told Kathy to invite her sister's family, and "we will find room for them."

Kathy sent a letter to her sister Christine with the money for the train fare. They had two girls ages 4 and 6 and Kathy also asked her sister to send measurements for the girls and herself so she could make dresses for the wedding for them. Kathy wanted them to be part of the wedding. Kathy used up a lot of her remaining money in sending them train fare. Living in St Louis would have its drawbacks, but they could live cheaply at the factory or the "castle" as Bobby sometimes referred to it. Kathy planned to continue making clothing when she got there.

After breakfast, Bruce was given permission to come into the women's bath area to help water plants in the garden. Bruce worked hard at it while Kathy and Katy worked at pulling weeds. After a couple hours all three were ready for a break and Julia had cookies and cold milk ready for them. Bruce said "thank you" to Julia when she brought out the cookies. Bruce was taller and had lost the chubby look that Kathy remembered. Kathy complimented Bruce on all the plants he had watered, and he smiled back at her. They worked until lunch and decided it was too hot to continue.

Clarence had hired Ned during the winter to do some carpenter work when William had cut hours, because of slower dresser sales. Ned had reduced the size of the living room by adding another small bedroom. Martha showed it to Kathy and said it was for Katy. "She can stay here until you and Bobby have a place for her. To be honest, Clarence and I would love to be her parents until she grows up. Margaret loves the idea of having her here too."

"I hate to leave Katy behind, but I think she will be better off here than coming with Bobby and me," Kathy told Martha. "I love Bobby so much but leaving here again is going to be really hard for me."

They brought Katy in and both Martha and Margaret told her how much they loved her. "We now have a bedroom for you, and we would like you to stay with us this summer."

"Katy, I love you so much, but you have all your friends here and there will no children for you to play with in St Louis, and Jade will be so lonesome if you leave again," Kathy told her.

Katy cried and so did Kathy. Finally, Katy said, "okay."

The next day Kathy had a welcome surprise. Alphonso, the traveling fabric salesman showed up just as they were finishing lunch. Kathy was able to purchase the material she needed to get dresses ready for her wedding. The purchase left her almost broke, but she was so happy she could get started working on the dresses. Despite the heat, she continued working but had to jump in the pool a few times to cool off. She had forgotten how hot it could get in the summer. She had added more material to her bathing suit so she could wear it again.

Sally came over with her children. They had to keep boys and girls separated since most of the bathing suits were too tight to wear, especially Sally's.. Sally teased Kathy, "Bobby can't take you to St Louis until you make us some new bathing suits."

"I will leave the sewing machine here and you can make your own," Kathy joked.

"By the time I would figure out how to work it, I will need another maternity dress," Sally responded.

Kathy got a piece of paper and started writing down measurements for new bathing suits and dresses. Margaret and Martha were there trading off Elizabeth and Lily with Janice and Sally. Kathy and Katy got to hold them too. They had to be especially alert with Elizabeth who would crawl toward the water if she weren't being held. Kathy wasn't getting any sewing done. The sun and the water were making her sleepy. Kathy started to completely relax for the first time in weeks.

Kathy got a letter back from her sister a week later saying she was going to take advantage of Kathy's generosity, because she was so anxious to see them, but it would just be her and her girls coming. She had enclosed measurements for herself and her girls who were so excited about coming.

Kathy was now sewing almost non-stop. They had a crib for Elizabeth when Margaret was taking care of the bathhouse, but it was only open to the public on Fridays and Saturdays. Margaret was super nice to both Kathy and Katy. Bruce was much nicer too. Kathy was willing to help with other work, but Martha and Margaret assured her that they would take care of food preparation and running the bathhouse while she concentrated on sewing dresses for the wedding. Kathy redid Sally's bathing suit and made one for Margaret

As the days got closer to the wedding Kathy tried not to panic about all the dresses she needed to complete. She had to regretfully tell several ladies at the church that she didn't have the time or material to make dresses for them too. People at the church were sorry she wouldn't be staying both because of her musical ability and her sewing ability.

Kathy enjoyed the luxury of jumping into the pool whenever she got too hot. Kathy was hoping the weather would cool off for her wedding.

Velma came in one afternoon and proudly showed off her new baby boy to Martha and Kathy. Martha got to hold the baby commenting on how beautiful he was. They went in and showed him to Clarence who prayed a blessing on Velma, her baby and Steve. Velma said that Steve and she were now attending church in Williamsburg. "Steve still feels ashamed to show his face in Springdale after what he did, or we would attend church here."

They sat in the patio and had rolls and coffee. Velma talked about her life. "Steve and I really have a good marriage now and I have reconciled with my family. My mother cried when I came home, she said she felt so bad that I had not come back. My father told me he was sorry for the way he treated me. The boy who got me pregnant is dead. He tried to attack another girl and her father shot and killed him. Steve said he should have suffered the same fate, but he is grateful to be alive. My sister is grown up and married and has a beautiful little girl. I had so much fun playing with her. I am so happy with my little boy, but I hope to someday have a little girl too. I am so grateful that you forced me to come here in order for Steve to stay out of jail. It helped me confront my past and enjoy life again. God has blessed our marriage and given me a sweet baby boy."

CHAPTER 41

Final Wedding Plans

Kathy's sister Christine and her two girls came in on the train Thursday afternoon before the wedding. Their reunion was more emotional than Kathy had expected. Kathy and Katy had ridden into Williamsburg with Andy to pick them up. It had been six years since they had seen each other. Christine looked like an older and somewhat larger version of Kathy. Katy was only a baby back then and Christine said she now looked just like Kathy did when she was younger. She introduced her two daughters, Carla and Calley who looked like they could be Katy's younger sisters rather than her nieces. Christine and her daughters liked to sing too. Kathy played her flute accompanying Christine and the three girls as they sang as they rode back to Springdale.

They all got milk and cookies in the patio and were introduced to Martha, Julia, and Margaret. Kathy and Katy then took Christine and her two girls into the women's bathhouse which was empty. They all undressed and jumped in the pool without hesitation. "This is so great," Christine enthused, "you never wrote about this."

"I was afraid you would think it was scandalous," Kathy replied.

"We aren't always so proper either when it gets really hot," Christine responded. "We don't have any neighbors close by so on really hot days, I fill an old wash tub outside in a secluded area that they can jump into, and we can splash each other. Christine listened to the happy squeals of her daughters playing with Katy. "It is not as nice as this, my girls and I are not going to want to leave here. I really wanted you and Katy to come live with us but there just isn't any room. I am so glad Martha invited you to live here and her son Bobby sounds like a perfect match for you."

Everyone finally came out of the water and toweled off. Kathy was able to check the fit of the dresses for Carla and Calley and they fit fine. It was hard to tell who was more excited, the girls or their mother. Then Kathy showed Christine the dress she had made for her to be a bridesmaid. It was a beautiful lavender colored dress that matched one Kathy had made for Sally. It fit fine and Christine was ecstatic. They went out in the patio and showed them off to Martha and Margaret.

Kathy had invited Margaret to be a bridesmaid, but she declined. Margaret then said; "I was responsible for Gerald coming here for the sake of me and my children. I realize what a nightmare Gerald caused for you and Katy."

"You were more of a victim than I was," Kathy had replied.

Kathy and Christine talked about Katy and the decision they had made to have Katy stay back when Kathy moved to St Louis with Bobby. "We basically will have a one room place to live in St Louis," Kathy explained. "She has so many friends here and Martha and Clarence love her so much."

"She is so lovable, and my girls are so happy being with her, but we are already too crowded in our little house," Christine replied. "I think my girls will be jealous of Katy being able to stay here with so much happening here."

"I want to stay here too but I love Bobby too much not to follow him to his job in St Louis."

Supper was wonderful and Christine started telling stories about living on the farm that had them all laughing. The excitement of the trip plus playing in the cold water had gotten Carla and Calley sleepy. Calley was next to Martha who put her arm around her and Calley cuddled up to Martha and was almost asleep. Elizabeth was sleeping in Clarence's lap and Carla was almost sleeping up against her mother. Kathy played her flute and Katy sang the lullaby song and everybody was ready for bed.

Martha carried a now sleeping Calley and Christine carried Carla into the bathhouse putting them into a lower bunk facing each other. "If they don't kick each other, they will be okay," Christine joked. She took a lower bunk opposite her girls. Kathy and Katy took the two upper bunks.

Prayers were said quietly with both Christine and Kathy expressing how grateful they were that they had gotten together.

"Kathy's sister is so fun, and her two little girls are so precious," Martha remarked to Clarence before they turned in.

"There have been some problems, but the Lord has blessed us since you brought Kathy and Katy home," Clarence remarked.

Sally came over the next morning with her children. The boys went over to the boy's bathhouse after introductions were made out in the patio. Janice joined Katy and the girls in the pool while Martha, Sally, Christine, and Kathy talked out at the patio. Christine smiled with pleasure when she got to hold Sally's baby. Margaret joined them and Kathy held baby Elizabeth.

After they retreated to the bathhouse. Martha donated an old dress and Kathy made it into a bathing suit for Christine. Kathy made Carla and Calley a pair of underpants out of a blue material that they could swim in. They became somewhat transparent when wet, and Kathy said she could try to modify them.

Sally thought they were fine. "My boys aren't going to care." Christine agreed that they were okay. With everyone wearing something reasonably appropriate the boys were allowed to come over. Bruce was there too and had finally been accepted by Alex and James. Before they could go in the water, the children were asked to pick peas and beans which they accomplished fairly quickly.

After they finished picking peas and beans, all the children jumped in the water. Christine sat on the edge of the pool and watched the commotion out in the water. "I don't think my girls have ever had this much fun," she told Kathy. Janice was playing with little Calley making sure she was safe. Jade had come over too and joined the rest of the children playing a game of keep away. The commotion was finally interrupted by Martha telling them it was lunch time. Kathy had her bathing suit on, but it was dry except for her feet.

Kathy helped Julia and Martha serve before sitting down next to Christine. "You people are spoiling us really bad. It is so fun, and the food here is so good," Christine told her.

Alex, James, and Bruce were sent back to the boy's pool after lunch.

June had come over after lunch with her little girl and her little boy. As soon as June got his clothes off, June's little boy Nate ran for the water where Janice grabbed him. Christine remarked on how cute he was, and she hoped her next child was a boy.

"Remember how cute Bobby was when he was little." Sally remarked to Margaret.

"He was so sweet, and we had so much fun with him, and Kathy is so lucky," Margaret replied. "Now she gets to hug and kiss him. I wish I could have married someone like Bobby."

Kathy listened to them and did feel lucky, but she felt sorry for Margaret. "I promise to take good care of him and give him lots of hugs and kisses," Kathy told them.

"I am pretty certain that Bobby will give you a lot of hugs and kisses too." Sally replied to Kathy.

Christine joined her girls who had come over to where Janice was playing with June's little boy Nate in the water "So, do you want a little brother?" Christine asked her girls. Both girls smiled and said yes. Christine was holding June's little girl. "Are you sure you don't want a little girl? This one is awfully cute." They were a little uncertain but thought it would be more fun to have a little brother.

Kathy hadn't thought about a ring bearer but decided June's little boy Nate would be fine. Kathy mentioned it to June who loved the idea.

Christine handed the little girl back to June and sat down on the edge of the pool next to Kathy. Kathy was silent for a moment before speaking. Today was so nice that it is making it hard for me to leave Springdale. "Leaving Boston, a second time, wasn't an easy choice either. I was making as much money selling the clothes I made as most men make so I am marrying for love not money. A couple of bad things happened here, but I love this place and now that I am back. It is going to be hard to leave again."

"I guess I married for love too because we have not had much money," Christine replied. "My husband and I met in met in Boston while he was staying with his uncle when he was attended college. We went to his home in Kansas so he could help his father and younger brother take care of their farm. Today has been one of the nicest days for me and my girls that I can remember so I can understand why you hate to leave. It is so fun to be together. I am hopeful my husband, and I can add on to our farmhouse so you can visit us and have a nice place to stay in the future."

"I think when I join Bobby in St Louis, we can make enough money together so we can buy a house and you can visit us."

Margaret overheard them and said, "you and your sister are welcome to meet up back here too."

"Thank you so much Margaret, I really appreciate that," Kathy responded.

"Sounds like a wonderful offer, "Christine said, "I know my girls and I would love to come back here."

Kathy got her flute and started playing "This is My Father's World". Christine and most of the girls started singing the song. Kathy then played the lullaby song with Janice leading the singing. Toddlers and babies fell asleep. Christine dried off Calley with a towel and then wrapped it around her. Calley then cuddled up between Christine and Kathy.

Kathy then played "Savior Like a Shepherd Lead us" with Christine singing it.". Kathy played "Away in the Manger" and Katy led the singing on that song. Kathy looked around and almost everyone was sleeping or half asleep. Martha had come in unobserved and listened before she sat down next to Kathy. "I just walked in on one of the sweetest most peaceful sights I have ever seen." Martha told her. "I feel like I am marrying off my daughter to my son; I love you both so much." They gave each other a long hug

"I love Bobby and I am so happy we are finally getting married," Kathy replied, "but I also I feel like I have returned to the home I love and now I have to leave again. Everyone here is so precious to me."

"Thank you so much for letting us come here," Christine told Martha, "my girls and I just love it here."

"Nothing makes me happier than sweet little girls like Carla and Calley, so I am so glad you came," Martha replied. "I would love to have you and Kathy come back here to reunite your families."

"That would really be nice, we have gone far too long without getting together," Christine replied. "I wanted so bad to return to Boston for our father's funeral and then our mother's funeral, but it was just too expensive. I love Kathy and Katy, but I think it was so much better for them that they came here than my farm plus we didn't have a handsome young man for Kathy to fall in love with."

"Bringing Kathy home was the best thing I ever did for my son. My family and the town are all so glad Kathy and Katy came here too," Martha replied.

"The Murdoches are coming in tonight at the same time Bobby does," Martha told Christine. "They have two little girls about the same age as your children and a beautiful baby boy. Mary, their mother is like me and loves children. She has been waiting for this wedding for the last year and so has the whole town. This will probably be the social event of the year."

"I know it will be for me and my girls," Christine responded.

Martha looked at little Calley who had fallen asleep between Christine and Kathy, and remarked, "your girls are so precious."

Sally handed a sleeping baby Lily to Christine again who smiled with delight. "Sunday morning, she becomes Kathy 's niece and your two little sweethearts become my brother's nieces," Sally told Christine with a smile. "I guess then we will be sort of related."

Kathy felt such a sense of contentment that her marriage to Bobby would give her family connections to so many children and people she loved. Kathy loved the idea of coming back here and reuniting with her sister Christine's family along with Bobby's family.

Kathy decided to sing her Latin song. When she finished, Christine commented, "I don't know what she sang but it sounded awfully nice."

"The first time she sang that in Church some people thought the rapture had come," Sally joked.

Kathy took her flute and played "This is My Father's World" while Katy, Jade and Janice sang it. Kathy played it again and Carla joined in. Kathy then sang she song she wrote:

**The love of friends flows from above.
It shows to me that our God is love.
The love of friends is my secret treasure.
It fills my heart with so much pleasure.
I do not seek riches or search for gold.
For love is warm and money is cold.
So, thank you God for friends to love.
It gives me a glimpse of Heaven above.**

Martha now holding June's baby girl said, "I can't imagine anything nicer than listening to music while being surrounded by friends and sweet little children."

Kathy agreed this would be a day she would treasure in her mind for a long time. Kathy looked at Katy playing with Jade and Janice. Kathy hated to be separated from Katy, but Katy had so many friends here. She would be happy here without her.

June left with her two children and Martha went to help with supper. Martha suggested that Kathy take a nap. Kathy wasn't sure she needed a nap but fell asleep fairly quickly after laying down. She had a short nap, but it helped her be ready for the evening.

CHAPTER 42

Reunion

They were waiting in the patio area when the wagon pulled in with Bobby and the Murdoches. Bobby jumped off the wagon and ran over to Kathy. She was even more beautiful than he had remembered. They stepped out of view and hugged and kissed for a long time. Kathy wiped the tears off her face. It seemed like they had waited forever to see each other again.

Kathy managed to regain her composure and introduced her sister and nieces to Bobby and the Murdoches. Bobby greeted Christine and the girls with a big smile before running over to his family.

Sally and Mary were so excited to see each other's babies. "Maybe we can marry them off in eighteen years," Mary enthused.

"Wouldn't that be fun," Sally replied. She also joked about finding more boys for the girls. "I need one for Janice and look at all the cute girl Alex and James get to choose from."

All the girls headed for the bathhouse, took their dresses off a jumped in. The women followed but left their dresses on. Christine te Kathy, "Bobby looks really cute, are you excited about your honeyn with him."

"That's not a proper question to ask a proper Bostonian," answered. "But since I am no longer a proper Bostonian, the answe⸍

Kathy waited for Mary's girls to come out of the water. A⸍ dried off, Kathy had them try on their dresses. Bonnie's dress w too big and Kathy went back to her sewing machine and altere⸍ was glad it was too big rather than too small because she didr more material that matched. Kathy also had made swimsuits for Mary and her girls.

Christine, Sally, and Mary watched the girls play. "I don't know how I am going to drag my girls away from here, they are so happy," Christine commented.

"Mine too," Mary replied, "they have been so excited about coming back here; they could hardly sleep. I just love it here too. I am hoping we can get Kathy and Bobby to sing together tonight, they are so wonderful to listen to."

Kathy joined them and Mary asked her how she was going to get all the girls in the wedding. "I am going to have James escort in Janice and Patty. Then Alex is going to escort in Katy and Carla, Then Calley and Bonnie will be the flower girls and June's little boy will be the ring bearer."

"The children are going too be way to cute," Sally joked, "they are going to steal all the attention from you and Bobby."

"They probably will, but maybe mothers will want to buy dresses for their daughters from me when I set up shop in St Louis," Kathy replied. Kathy watched as little Bonnie played with little Calley. They were already 'nds after only an hour together. All the girls were cute. Unfortunately, of the cute little girls couldn't stay here and neither could she.

rgaret helped Martha serve supper with help from Janice and e. Bobby and Kathy sat together.

as a year ago when we first ate supper and I sat across from you not keep my eyes off of you," Bobby told Kathy. "I decided you irl for me then and in two more days I finally get my rail order

I am old enough now and I have been fattened up for the replied with a smile.

ily been a year, but it seems like I have been waiting forever,"

his fiddle and started playing a fast tempo song and even to ressed on how good Bobby was. The girls were all jiggling twi hey started doing the dance where the girls were getting until all the girls were giddy.

Kathy played her flute with Bobby and Katy switching off on "Battle Hymn of the Republic". Kathy added her own verse to the song. They then played "This is My Father's World" with the children doing the singing.

Bobby and Kathy did their love song. William and Sally left with their children while it was still daylight after saying goodbye.

After they left, Kathy played her flute and Christine sang the lullaby song with a lovely voice.

"Tonight, was wonderful" Mary said before she and Richard helped their sleepy daughters upstairs.

A sleepy Katy made it back to her bunk on her own. Christine carried Calley and led Carla. Margaret carried Elizabeth and led Bruce.

Bobby and Kathy hugged and kissed a long time before Kathy reluctantly pulled herself away. Kathy walked inside the bathhouse and locked the door behind her. She was so ready to be married. She was locking herself in as much as she was locking anyone out.

Christine came over to talk to her. "Bobby is quite the prize," Christine told her. "You both are so talented."

"Thank you, you have a beautiful voice too," Kathy replied. "Bobby and I haven't been together since Christmas, but I realized again tonight how much I love him. I am also so excited about getting together with everyone."

Kathy woke up early Saturday morning and went into the kitchen. She made an extra-large batch of pancake batter and cut up bacon to be fried. Martha joined her, expressing surprise that she was up working. "Well, I am the reason for all the food being needed so I feel I should help prepare it," Kathy replied.

"Yesterday was so fun and the next few days should be wonderful too," Martha replied. Christine joined them and helped set the table on the patio. Margaret came out carrying a sleepy Elizabeth and Christine got to hold her.

"I love it here," Christine commented, "so many cute children and babies." Calley and Bonnie both showed up next and gave each other a hug having become instant friends the day before.

Thankfully, the weather had cooled off, but they decided to hold the wedding rehearsal in the morning. They were still getting organized when they realized that Christine was playing the piano and was very good. They had Christine play for the song "This is My Father's World", and had the children sing it. Christine also played for "Joyful, Joyful We Adore Thee" and Kathy and Bobby sang it. Everyone was impressed with Christine's piano playing. Kathy was happy because she could sing while standing with Bobby while Christine played the piano.

After lunch they headed to the pool after deciding to keep the boys and girls separate.

"I wish I could take Katy back with me to Kansas, but we just don't have enough space. Everyone here tells me how much they love her so I know she will be well cared for," Christine added.

"My problem too," Kathy responded, "initially we will just have a small room on the roof of a factory. Maybe by next fall we can afford to buy a house, but this little village has become Katy's home."

"Marrying Bobby will be one of the happiest days of my life but leaving Katy and this little village will make me very sad," Kathy told Christine.

"We cried the last time you left," Sally told Kathy, "but at least we get to keep Katy this time." Kathy yawned, she was worn out from the excitement of getting ready for her wedding but also the stress of knowing she would soon be saying goodbye to so many people and she loved. They suggested she take a nap. Kathy lay down on a blanket on the grass and fell asleep.

Bobby had spent the afternoon with Richard, William and Ned discussing possible changes to the dressers and some other furniture ideas. He came back just before supper. Everyone was dressed except Kathy who was still sleeping in her bathing suit. Kathy woke up with a kiss on the lips from Bobby to the cheers of Sally, Christine, and Mary who had led him into the bath area.

Bobby got in a few more smooches before Sally announced: "Okay, she's awake, that's all you get for now."

"But I was just getting started," Bobby replied.

"Maybe you can get some more kisses after we eat supper," Sally suggested.

"Okay, I will have her for dessert," Bobby teased.

Supper was delicious but Kathy couldn't even remember what she ate. Everyone was in a good mood and all the girls were all in a giddy giggly euphoria. Bobby started playing some fast music on his fiddle and the girls started dancing to the music even getting Alex and James to join in. Sally and William danced to a slower tune and Richard and Mary did too. Christine was holding Mary's little boy and Martha had Sally's little girl. Kathy sang some of the songs she knew. They finished the evening by singing their love song. Kathy and Bobby shared a long hug and goodnight kiss.

They were both glad that next time they would not have to walk away from each other.

CHAPTER 43

Wedding Day

Kathy joined Martha in the kitchen the next morning and helped her make breakfast. She told Martha, "it seems like only yesterday and forever since I had told you that I was in love with Bobby."

"A year ago, it was too soon but it has been a long wait for everybody. Bobby fell in love with you the first day. By that night Clarence and I were hoping you would be our daughter-in-law," Martha replied and gave her a hug.

Clarence came out to the patio and Kathy brought him a cup of coffee. "The weather looks good for your wedding. You had some rough times last year, but things have turned out well for you. Martha and I are so happy for you and Bobby. We love you and Bobby so much and wish you and Bobby could stay here. At least this time we get to keep Katy."

"I hate leaving Katy and the rest of you, but I guess when the Bible talks about a man leaving his father to marry it applies to the wife too," Kathy replied.

"Bobby tells me I will have plenty to do when we return to St Louis," "Richard is going to invest some more money on the factory building to add another room on the roof where I can start a small clothing factory. Two of the men working for Bobby have gotten married earlier this Spring. They are hoping I will hire their wives to make clothing."

Charles had married Helen and Clyde had married Sapphire.

The small church was packed. Everyone remembered what a great wedding William and Sally had and had high expectations for Bobby and Kathy. They were not disappointed. Bobby went up front and stood with

Clarence but then opened the service with a fast tune on his fiddle that had the crowd buzzing. Christine then started playing the piano.

William and Sally walked in first. James then walked in escorting Janice and Patty. Then Alex walked in escorting Katy and Carla. The girls all looked so pretty in their white dresses. Then Calley and Bonnie came in as the flower girls followed by June's little boy bearing the ring. The children looked so precious. Kathy walked toward the front as Christine continued to play the piano. Kathy stopped, turned around and received the flowers from Calley and Bonnie. Then as she stood there, Bobby sang a song he had written:

My God in Heaven has set aside a wonderful girl for me.
Being with you is the only place I ever want to be.
Your beauty shines for everyone to see.
and your love is a precious gift to me.

The children then joined together to sing "This Is My Father's World". Kathy then sang a song she had written:

The love of friends flows from above.
It shows to me that our God is love.
The love of friends is my secret treasure.
It fills my heart with so much pleasure.
I do not seek riches or search for gold.
For love is warm and money is cold.
So, thank you God for friends to love.
It gives me a glimpse of Heaven above.

Bobby and Kathy then joined together singing "Amazing Grace" as Christine played the piano.

Clarence gave a short sermon telling them to "continue to rely on God's faithfulness as you have done in the past. Continue to serve the Lord with the talent that God has given you. We wish we could continue to have your musical ministry here, but we know that others need to hear God's message through music too." Clarence completed the wedding ceremony and pronounced them man and wife. They kissed and turned to face the congregation.

Then they sang "Joyful, Joyful We Adore Thee" with Christine playing the piano as they walked down the aisle.

They stood in the reception line, and everyone congratulated them and wished they could stay in Springdale. Tables for the wedding party had been set up outside. Other guests had brought blankets and sat on the grass.

Bobby retrieved his fiddle and started playing again.

Bobby played "What a Friend We Have in Jesus" and Kathy sang it. They continued to sing together, and their audience settled in on their blankets to eat lunch and listen.

William had created some additional plates for serving a lunch of roast pork sandwiches by cutting a log into thin round flat plates.

One lady told Martha "it was such a beautiful wedding, but I could almost cry thinking about them going to St Louis."

"I already have cried," Martha replied.

Bobby and Kathy entertained the wedding guests for a long time until almost all of them had gone home. Bobby then sang a song he had written.

> **A hound dog howls at the moon outside on a moonlit night.**
> **The pain in my heart makes me howl inside for you each night.**
> **So, I play my fiddle to get me through another sleepless night.**
> **I keep waiting for us to finally have our honeymoon night.**
> **I'll keep playing my fiddle until I can hold you tight all night.**

Kathy smiled. "You can quit playing darling, the time has come."

They then slipped away. A double bed had been moved into the men's bathhouse for their honeymoon. Bobby carried Kathy through the door before locking it behind them. He could finally claim his rail order bride!

Life ahead would not be perfect, but the Lord had used Martha to bring each of them to someone they would treasure for the rest of their life.

ABOUT THE AUTHOR

Alton Knutson spent most of his early childhood on a couple of farms in rural Minnesota that didn't have electricity or indoor plumbing. He was in first grade when his folks moved to Minneapolis, Mn. His education includes a Bachelor of Science degree in Business Administration from the University of Minnesota in 1966. He also took Reserve Officers Training and was commissioned as a 2nd Lieutenant in the Signal Corps. He served two years active duty in the Signal Corps including one year in Saigon during the Vietnam War. He then started a civilian career as an accountant. He received a Master's degree in Business Administration from Keller Graduate School in Chicago in 1991. He also graduated from the US Army Command and General Staff College in 1984 while serving as an officer in the Army Reserve He eventually retired as a Lieutenant Colonel. Alton has been married for 38 years and lives with his wife out in the country, a short distance west of Minneapolis. His favorite activities are traveling and downhill skiing.